What Readers are Saying about Linda Joyce's Books

"Linda Joyce's writing will transport you to the deep south where life is just a bit slower and women are a unique mixture of strength and gentleness". – *Jo Ann Reinhold, Jo's World of Books*

"Linda's books are rich with emotion, featuring captivating characters and enchanting settings that will capture your heart. Her eloquent writing style immerses you in a deeply emotional journey." – *Tessa, Poised Pen Productions*

"As a Southern girl with a deep love for New Orleans, I consider Ms. Joyce my go-to author. Her captivating writing style hooks you from the very first page, immersing you in a world filled with the perfect blend of heat, steam, and romance." – *Author CJ Bennet*

"Linda Joyce's books are always at the top of my reading list. I look forward to her next releases, knowing each will be another page turner. I also find they are welcomed gifts to friends." ~ *Roberta B.*

"Being from the South, I recognize and appreciate the sense of place that Linda creates. It feels authentic and inviting - the place is another character!" ~ *Madelyn G.*

"I have read many of Linda's books and have enjoyed them immensely!" ~ *Shirley C.*

"Crafty and talented writer! Linda creates a place in the reader's mind." ~ *Kat S.*

"Read a lot of your books and loved all of them." ~ *Sharon R.*

"I've read many of your (Linda's) books that are incredible. No one can write New Orleans books better. The books are so descriptive that you feel like you are there. Just an incredible author." ~ *Lori J*

Books by Linda Joyce

Bayou Born - A RONE Award Finalist
First Honorable Mention—Contemporary Romance Novel from OWFI

Bayou Bound - A RONE Award Finalist
1st Place —Past Presidents' Romance Award by Southeastern Writers Association

Bayou Beckons - A RONE AWARD Finalist
Received Best of Women's Fiction by Authors on the Air

Bayou Brides
Nola and Rex's love story.

Fleur De Lis Brides
Wedding stories of Branna, Biloxi, and Camilla

Christmas Bells
 set in Savannah, Georgia

Her Heart's Desire - A RONE AWARD Finalist
1st Place—Past Presidents' Romance Award by Southeastern Writers Association

Behind the Mask
Mardi Gras, Mystery, and Love

Holiday Hearts
of Junction, Georgia

Anthologies

Love Around the Table: an anthology of short stories, including *Layers of Love* by Linda Joyce, to benefit the Ronald McDonald House.

Love in the Lowcountry Volume 2: A Winter Holiday Collection—an anthology of short stories, including "A Sunrise Christmas" by Linda Joyce

Love & Grace: Romance for the soul, a gift from the heart. Linda's story is "Christmas Bells." This anthology, a collection of sweet and inspirational novellas, has an uplifting love story for everyone. Each story relates to dyslexia in some way, and the full proceeds from all the stories benefit GRACEPOINT – A School for Dyslexia.

Love in the Lowcountry: A Vacation Collection. Linda's short story, "Analysis of Love" is in this anthology.

Coming in 2025

Love in the Lowcountry: Volume 1 - A Vacation Collection. Linda's short story, "Analysis of Love" will be in this anthology.

The launch of a new cozy mystery series: *Marcèline's Mysteries*
    Marcèline's Mysteries: Murder and Messages
    Marcèline's Mysteries: Murder and Menus
    Marcèline's Mysteries: Murder and Music

Unspoken Words

Linda Joyce

Author: Linda Joyce, linda-joyce.com
Editor: Cheryl Walz
Cover Art by Suzanna Chriscoe, Elefontbooks.com
Original Photo for Cover by Alex Demyan, louisianaphotos.com
Formatting by Suzanna Chriscoe, Elefontbooks.com

Published by: Word Works Press, LLC
P.O. Box 801726
Acworth, GA 30101

Contact Information: read@wordworkspress.com
Publishing History
Published in 2025
Print (Ingram Spark) ISBN-979-8-9911288-2-7
Digital ISBN-978-0-9965811-9-6
Library of Congress Control Number: 2024911980
Published in the United States of America

Contents

Chapter 1 1

Chapter 2 7

Chapter 3 - Suzanne 19

Chapter 4 - Maggie 29

Chapter 5 35

Chapter 6 - Maggie 47

Chapter 7 59

Chapter 8 – Maggie & Suzanne 73

Chapter 9 85

Chapter 10 95

Chapter 11 – Maggie 103

Chapter 12 109

Chapter 13 - Suzanne 121

Chapter 14 – Maggie 131

Chapter 15 - Suzanne 141

Chapter 16 151

Chapter 17 - Suzanne 161

Chapter 18 – Maggie 171

Chapter 19 183

Chapter 20 195

Chapter 21 - Maggie 205

Chapter 22 - Suzanne 217

Chapter 23 – Suzanne 227

Chapter 24 235

Chapter 25..243

Chapter 26...251

Chapter 27 - Suzanne 259

Chapter 28 267

Chapter 29 – Jane, Maggie, Suzanne.................................275

Chapter 30 279

Chapter 31 - Suzanne...285

Chapter 32 293

Chapter 33 303

Epilogue...307

Acknowledgements...303

About the Author..307

Dedication

To my amazing grandmothers, Blanche Guidry Brannan, Junita Brannan, and Hiyaku Fukuhara.

Your lives enriched mine in ways I'm still discovering.

Chapter 1

Another night of little sleep. Karmic payback, I'm certain.

I shuffled to the kitchen, eyes half-open, and slowly poured coffee into a mug. Thoughts had churned in my head all night. How could I have believed escaping to Boston could break the far-reaching cords of family and friends? During my college years, I thought I possessed power to forge a new future—one different from my mother's.

But I was wrong.

"Crap."

Coffee overflowed, ran to the edge of the countertop, staining my white sweater. I grabbed a dish towel and blotted and recalled the days when the same sweater smelled of baby sweetness, but also puke and pee and occasionally poop. Much had happened since then. Days of my greatest joy... my greatest fears.

My mind strayed to my Louisiana family, my old friends, and all the suffering and sorrow and secrets, my gut hopped on a roller coaster like the Zephyr that used to be at Pontchartrain Beach. Wooden. Shaky. With five stomach-plunging drops.

I tried to shove away my thoughts, but my brain played tug-of-war with my memories. My heart hemorrhaged.

I always caved to fear.

The truth I denied in my waking hours refused to be silenced. It shattered my nighttime dreams. Guilt plowed a field in my brain, permanently changing my landscape. I tried yoga. I tried meditation. I even tried Xanax. If I weren't afraid of becoming an alcoholic like my father, I would drink.

A lot.

"Momma." Sonny Boy entered the kitchen skating in socks on the wooden floor. I ignored his whine.

"Good job with the jeans and sweatshirt." My smile was genuine for the love of my heart.

"When can I meet Grandpops?" My gregarious boy sat, plopped his elbows on the table opposite me, lifted his chin, and stared at me down his nose, that same frowning, impatient expression tired professors had given me in college. I squelched a laugh at his seriousness.

"Soon." I leaned across the table and ruffled his dark hair. "Very soon, you'll meet your southern family."

He fiddled with the napkin holder. Thankfully, it was something he couldn't dismantle.

"Will they be like Pops and Beth?"

"Sort of." Love for my adopted northern family resided alongside my long-standing ache. I still needed my southern family the way a bread pudding needs bourbon sauce. Fifteen years. Snowy winters. No grits with eggs. Fifteen years of denying and trying to trick fate. Fate tricked me. The apple didn't fall far from the tree.

And when the doctor had said, "Cancer. Again." I collapsed.

Grabbing a bowl, milk, and cereal, I delivered breakfast to my son.

"Blueberries," he demanded.

My narrowed eyes and crinkled forehead pulled the magic words from him.

"May I *please* have some blueberries?"

I complied, wanting to prolong my joy and avoid the pain waiting for me.

When he'd scarfed down the last spoonful, he looked up, his clown-grin begging for more, the little glutton. "Go play outside. Hoops maybe? Grab a ball. I have a few phone calls to make. When I'm done, we will play a game. Practice up."

"Okay, Momma." The only time he ever sounded southern was when he called me Momma. Other times he dropped his r's, his speech matching those of the kids in his Boston preschool. I had failed in my responsibility to raise a southern boy. Another strike against me.

Sonny Boy shrugged on a jacket and pulled on his sneakers, then hugged me tight before running outside into the May sunlight.

I poured another cup of coffee and picked at the button on the cushion in the booth tucked inside the bay window. It overlooked the brick driveway. From my perch, I could keep an eye on my son *and* speak with his father.

"Contacts." I searched my cell phone for Mark's number. We hadn't had a direct conversation in several years. At his insistence.

I pressed the button. Made the call. Ringing started.

"Don't answer. Don't answer. Don't. Answer."

But I knew the man was a creature of habit. On Sunday afternoons, he often took off on his motorcycle exploring the single-lane roads through the bayous. Over the *whoosh* of the wind and the *roar* of the engine, he'd never hear the phone ring.

I hoped.

"Hello?" Mark's voice rang through the speaker along with the faint sound of a lumbering diesel truck in the background.

A lump in my chest spread, choking my throat. "M-Mark, it's Jane. If this isn't a good time—"

"Good as any. On a break from my ride. How ya doin'? I overheard Maggie talking to your dad. Says you might be heading this way. Why?"

The man was direct. His charm and impish grin—the same one his son flashed at me whenever he tried to get his way—softened his frankness face-to-face but didn't translate well over the phone.

"That's what I want to talk with you about. My trip. I have some news for you."

"Don't like the sound of that."

"I want to wait and talk about it in person, but I don't want to cause a problem for Maggie. Could we manage a private chat?"

"She's pregnant."

"Pregnant?" My mouth dried as though packed with dental gauze after a root canal. I swallowed hard. If Maggie had a child of her own, then what?

"I can't promise anything, Jane. Depends on how Maggie's doin' when you come. Why don't you tell me what's bothering you? I can hear it in your voice. If you're calling—the problem is serious."

A dart to the heart. "No," I hedged. "Not over the phone. I need to see you."

"Look"—his impatience shamed me—"you know how Maggie feels about you. I don't want anything to hurt her."

His words stung. His anything was really a *someone*. I jerked on the reins of my defensiveness. "I don't want to hurt Maggie."

"Jane, *I'm* trying real hard not to hurt Maggie. Things are…difficult. But we both know our history. Yours and mine. Mine and Maggie's. Just tell me what you want me to know. You'll feel better. Do I need to play twenty questions to pull it out of you?"

"Wait. Back up. What is going on with you and Maggie? She's pregnant? Congrats. I know you both want a baby." I could fake genuine happiness over the phone but never get away with it in person. Not with Mark.

"Wanted."

"You don't *want* a child now?"

"I don't choose to discuss my current *wants* with my ex-wife, Jane. What's on your mind?"

Drumming my fingers, I wondered where to begin. My brain whirred. Mark didn't want children with Maggie? Mark had hurt her? *Maggie pregnant*? O.M.G.

"Look, either you want to talk or you don't. I'm not inclined to be alone with you when you come. I'll only see you because of Maggie and Suzanne. Our chapters ended long ago."

He was wrong but didn't know it. "Where are you, Mark?" I wanted to picture him in my mind's eye. My sensitivity provided me with the gift to hone in on people—sometimes. It was the next best thing to being there with him, despite the risks to me.

"Stopped for a drink in Lacombe. Headed over to the island. Come on, Jane, spit it out, or I gotta go."

An image of Mark appeared in my mind. Me, sitting on his bike. Him, standing a few feet away, pacing, talking on his cell. Not many people traveling the two-lane road on Sunday afternoon. I wanted to touch him, to have him fold me into his arms, tell me everything would be okay, in that big-brother way he used to do when we were in grade school.

"I hope it will be good news for you." I glanced outside in time to catch my son making a basket. He yelled, "Two points!" and danced around. His joy created mine.

"Got to ride, Jane. Can't waste any more time."

He was right. Couldn't waste any more time. "Wait! Mark…you have a son."

"This you being psychic again? Maggie hasn't had a sonogram."

"Mark." I clawed for calmness. "You. Have. A. Son. He's almost five years old. I'm bringing him home to meet you. Our son."

"A boy?" The shock in Mark's voice reverberated through me. A stun gun would've surprised him less.

"*We* have a boy?"

Before I could answer, Mark shouted, "A boy. A goddamned boy. I'm a frickin' father? For real? A father?" The irony of his deep belly laugh soothed my raw nerves only a tiny bit.

I had hoped for divine intervention. I had hoped for dissolution of my guilt. I had hoped for a positive reaction. And in a single heartbeat, I believed hope existed as his euphoria soared.

But the picture of him in my mind's eye began to fade. "Mark!" I tried to hang on to him.

"No shit." Mark's credulous tone felt like a lifesaving buoy. "This changes everything. I have to see you. Have to see him."

"Listen," I begged, but I could tell he wasn't.

"Hey, man! It's a boy." Mark's shout mixed with the sound of a passing truck in the background. Brakes screeched. The buoy's rope slipped from my hands.

Outside my window, Sonny Boy fell. Slammed his chin.

"No!" I screamed.

My hand flew to my chest. The phone went dead.

I raced out the door.

My mind blanked.
Then snapped to red.
Red.
Blood.
Sonny Boy's and Mark's.

Chapter 2

I spotted the only remaining seat on the plane and dropped into it. The chatter in my brain refused to quiet. *Mark's been dead a month. Dead a month. Dead. A. Month.*

"Fasten your seat belts," the flight attendant instructed.

I pulled on the strap to make it secure. It was the only security I had in my life, and it would only last for a few hours.

Lacing my fingers together in my lap, I pressed my fingertips into the bony tops of my hands and fought against a roiling unease that could've lifted the plane. Beyond the window, Boston's horizon gave way to blue sky and white clouds. Memories of another sky flipped through my mind. The ones where I sat on a dock, looked up, wondered about my future. The vastness of sky and time spread before me. I had been happy and hopeful and *home*.

More memories floated. New Orleans. Suzanne. Maggie. Mark. My dad. My mom, before she died. I cherished my family of choice. Would they forgive me for not letting them know Sonny Boy?

I needed a break from the backpack of Gs I toted—gloom, grief, guilt. The plane's monotone rumble hypnotized my tired brain, and I drifted into sleep.

"We'll be landing soon." The lady beside me gave my arm gentle shake.

"Thank you." I moved my seat to the upright position. My brain fog began to clear. The Gs began to chatter again.

Grief coiled around my heart like a snake. The closer we got to the ground, the tighter it constricted. When the plane bumped down, grief sank its fangs deep and sharp into my heart. Guilt—like the flow of venom—pumped through me.

"Welcome to Louis Armstrong New Orleans International Airport. The temperature is a balmy eighty degrees with eighty percent humidity," a voice broadcasted over speakers.

"Cab," I muttered to contain the Gs, then headed to double doors open to the outside world.

If I had any hope of a future, it rested here in New Orleans. Sonny Boy's future hinged on me merging my two lives—past and present. It was bad enough I had robbed him of his father. It would crush me if my cowardice caused the rest of my family to reject him. Beth and Mr. Finley in Boston were caring for him while I was away. His bruises had cleared and stitches came out of his chin, but leaving him was harder than swimming upriver in a storm.

A taxi pulled to the curb. I climbed in.

"Where to?"

"Greenwood Cemetery."

The cabbie zipped around on surface streets, dodging potholes. Businesses with familiar names flashed by. Houses of brick and cast-iron lace. Houses painted yellow, blue, green, and pink. Houses with white columns stretching to hold up second-floor porches. Their cheeriness did not mitigate my gloom.

"Would you turn the air up more?" I asked.

"Not from around here, yeah?" His *yeah* wasn't a question at all.

"Born and raised, yeah?" I might have been gone a long time and lost my accent, but no one would rob me of my birthright. "Please, take the long way around. I want to go by Gambino's Bakery on Elysian Fields." Their sweets had tattooed memories on my taste buds.

"Ain't there no more," the driver said. "Storm took them away. They got another place, though. Want to go there?"

"Drive past the ruins. After that, to Greenwood Cemetery, please."

Katrina had destroyed my city in August of 2005. Afterward, she huffed away like a diva without a backward glance. Her coming and going from the city I loved had proved more dramatic than my own.

I paid the cabbie for the wild ride and then stood on the sidewalk in front of the entrance to the mausoleum. My hands shook when I slipped the strap of my purse over my shoulder. My knees wobbled, but I remained upright. My heart thudded like a bass drum in a second line parade. Thudding so hard it cut off my breath. Paralyzed, I stood in the merciless Louisiana sun. Humidity clung to my skin like olive oil on a sweet potato before roasting in the oven. My reflection in the mausoleum's glass doors showed a tidy dress, tidy shoes, tidy hair.

Outside, calmness.

Inside, untidy screams.

I swallowed back a ball of fear, took a first unsteady step, then another. Plodding, I entered the building and nodded to the guard at the reception desk.

"Need help finding a loved one?" He scrutinized me as though he recognized me.

"No, thank you."

"Sign in here." He rose and pointed to an open guest book.

I wrote Jane and started to write *Maucele* beside it to prove I had every right to be there but changed my mind and scribbled *Landry* instead.

My father had told me where to find Mark. I searched for the correct aisle. My leather flats *shruffed* against the hard marble floors. Mausoleums reminded me of morgues I'd seen on TV, not burial grounds. A collection of people who were dead—they couldn't hear if I made noise. But I continued on my tiptoes just in case.

Finding the correct hallway, I let go of a raggedy breath and claimed a seat in the middle of a long, cold granite bench, then extracted a week-old envelope from my purse.

Did the words inside hold the truth of what Mark wanted?

Clutching the official message, I fought against the impulse to wad up the paper and throw it at him, the same way I'd thrown heated words the last time before we parted. Then, he'd been alive. Able to fight back. I wanted him to fight now.

Anguish spewed like liquid from a shaken can of Nehi soda. "NOoooo! NOoooo! NOoooo! Dammit, Mark."

"Miss Landry, are you okay?" The guard's voice echoed down the wing of the mausoleum along with the sound of footsteps beating a path in my direction. "Ma'am?"

"I apologize. Grief hit me."

"Excuse me? Who hit you?" He frowned as though I were a naughty child.

"Never mind. I'll be quiet." My inner pain fought for further release, but my outer calm took control.

His eyebrows became a unibrow. "I'm going to have to ask you to leave if you are unable to contain yourself."

"It won't happen again." I waved apologetically.

His toe-to-head scan told me he was trying to decide if he had a dangerous mental case and needed backup. A moment passed before he nodded and left.

The Gs began their chatter again. I itched to crawl out of my skin. I locked my sights on a spot of colored light. Overhead, an ornate crystal chandelier threw slanted rainbows across pale walls, suggesting tranquility for all who rested there. Tranquility had abandoned me over five years ago. Any illusion of it I clung to fled after my father's phone call confirming Mark's death.

"*Tut. Tut. Silly girl,*" the Gs taunted in my head. "*No rest for the wicked.*"

Staring at the neatly carved letters of a headstone hanging on the wall, I still couldn't wrap my head, let alone my heart, around the fact that beyond that polished marker lay the body of a man who vowed *never* to step foot in a New Orleans cemetery—unless, of course, he was dead. "*Humph.*" I snorted at the irony.

I gripped the letter tighter. My palms sweated despite the air-conditioning. My short hair fluttered in the chilled air. My cotton dress seeped cold from the stone-slab bench. Shivering produced no warmth. But I didn't deserve any comfort.

"No. No. No." I forced out the words. Rising, I paced the long aisle. "Mark, what do I do?"

I stopped pacing after the fourth trip.

Staring at Mark's name on a marble plaque was like hammering the last nail in a coffin. I wanted him to rise from the dead. Possible, yeah? After all, this was New Orleans.

But Mark was gone. And in my mind's eye, I'd seen it all.

The entire accident. The flowing of hot. Wet. Blood.

The mental images and emotional lashing of that day were shuttered away while I tended to my son's injuries. The memory of Mark's death returned with a *bam* when the letter arrived detailing the value of his life. I read it. A freight train of pain hit me the same way a semi had struck Mark.

I sank back onto the icy bench and stared at the engraved marble plaque. Mark Maucele. The date of his birth. The date of his death. And the words, *Good things come in threes.*

He remained an eternal optimist—always the counterpoint to my pessimism.

Chimes sounded from the front of the building. The pealing bells reminded me of visions of the gates of Heaven—where Mark resided.

Clack-Clack. Clack-Clack.

The unmistakable sound of high heels tapping against polished stone. The tapping grew louder and floated closer. The staccato beat stopped a few feet away. Peep-toe shoes came into peripheral view. I blinked and sucked in a long, slow breath. I recognized my childhood friend's trademark bubblegum-pink painted toes. Maggie Patterson. No, now, Maggie Maucele. Mark's widow. Words jammed my throat like a tugboat slamming a barge on the Mississippi River.

"I knew I'd find you here," Maggie whispered as though not to interrupt the slumber of those laid to rest. Releasing my breath released the sting in my lungs along with my hopes of visiting Mark unnoticed.

"I'm so tickled you've come that I won't stay mad at you." Maggie crossed in front of me, appearing to glide rather than walk, and sat to my right on the bench. She hadn't aged since high school. Porcelain skin. Delicate features. Toned dancer's body.

My nerves jumped on the Zephyr again and took a roller-coaster ride.

She faced Mark's headstone. Her eyes never lifted to the plaque. She crossed one knee over the other and twisted her wedding band around on her slender finger, then made the sign of the cross. Long auburn hair framed red-rimmed brown eyes peering at me from a face filled with eagerness.

Maggie's hug undid me.

"Ohhh." I cleared my throat to blanket my surprise. "I'm sorry about Mark." I was sincere, but my condolences didn't change the fact I'd grown into a record-holding coward. That affliction had punctuated my life...since before Momma passed away when I was eighteen.

"Shh. It's okay. We'll have plenty of time to talk about it all." With one arm fastened tightly around my shoulder, Maggie reached into her purse and pulled out a man's handkerchief—white with MM embroidered in army green in one corner. My breath stopped. My brain stopped. Time stopped.

I panted twice to kick-start me back to life.

I had given that handkerchief to Mark when he completed his Army basic training and dreamed of him using it in a second line parade.

Maggie dabbed her eyes. Nostalgia dabbed at me.

Life used to be simple. Adulthood had dulled the world with duty and drowned me in responsibility. If I could just be eighteen again, I'd make different decisions.

"For the record"—Maggie's breath reached my ear—"I *am* still mad at you, but so glad you're here. I didn't see a car with Massachusetts tags in the parking lot. Did you rent one?" Maggie squeezed my shoulders tighter. For someone who carried such an ethereal energy, her grasp was devilishly firm. I squirmed in the face of her gleeful anticipation.

"I caught a cab from the airport." I didn't own a car.

"Well, you can drive my car while you're here. I'll drive Mark's truck." Maggie's decisiveness suggested everything was settled. If I had any doubt, her nod stamped "cancelled" on it.

"But—" I couldn't admit I wouldn't need it. I had planned to slip in and out of New Orleans unnoticed. But being with Maggie made the pain of Mark's death ease up a tiny bit. Gave me a glimmer of hope as my secrets pressed harder on my mind and deeper into my gut.

Not wanting Maggie to see the letter, I scrunched paper and tucked it back in my purse. There was time to deal with those facts later. I wanted to scoop up crumbs of comfort that being with my old friend offered. I needed the sweetness of long-ago good times.

Beside me, Maggie bowed her head and folded her hands together in prayer, resting them on her crossed knee. Out of respect for Maggie's deep religious beliefs, I pressed my palms together and closed my eyes, too.

Dear Heavenly Father…

My earthly father had urged me to return home for Mark's funeral, even offered to pay for a plane ticket, which I could afford on my editor's salary, but I couldn't face Maggie and Suzanne without Mark for support. And now, all I hoped to avoid on this trip slammed into me. Here Maggie sat as if we'd seen each other only yesterday rather than seven years ago at Suzanne and Grant's wedding.

After a few moments, I opened my eyes. Opportunity had opened a door for me. I had to make things right. Had to beg for forgiveness. Had to tell Maggie about the letter, too.

Sucking in air to steel myself, I tried linking pieces of my courage together. I squeezed Maggie's hand. "How—"

Maggie silenced me with a wave of her finger.

"One…" Maggie counted.

Puzzled, I looked around. Through the big windows, a few wispy white clouds dotted a blue sky. No signs of thunder. No lightning.

As if by design, chimes filled the halls of the mausoleum.

"Two…"

A soft squeak from the scuff of leather grew closer.

"Three…" Maggie's grin widened like a child having successfully performed a new magic trick. She pointed toward the opening at the end of the hallway.

"Jaaaneeeeey!" Suzanne Maucele Saulnier sashayed from around the corner dressed in a blue and white seersucker dress. Tanned. Tall. Tailored. Shoulder-length blonde hair, perfectly highlighted, as though she'd been plucked from a fashion spread in *Garden and Gun* magazine. Her high-pitched squeal bounced against the walls. She scurried to the spot where Maggie and I sat. I smiled—my first in weeks—picturing Mark's frowning face and his palms pressed over his ears. He hated girly screams. His sister, Suzanne, had been famous for them.

"Maggie told me she knew you'd come, but didn't say that she 'knew-knew.' You know how she gets." Suzanne grabbed me by the shoulders, pulled me to my feet, and cinched her arms around me. "But we both know not to doubt our Maggie."

"Can't breathe." I fought to draw a breath. She released her grip. I staggered back a step, my legs bumping against the bench. Suzanne hadn't lost her high-school cheerleader's exuberance.

"I am sorry I was not here for Mark's funeral," I said. "I hope you liked the flowers I sent. I can't imagine how hard it was—is."

Suzanne turned toward Maggie. I did as well, and without stopping a beat of my rambling I said, "I can't believe you're a widow."

Maggie blinked and nodded.

I caught Suzanne's judging gaze. "And now you are an only child. I am so sorry I wasn't here."

Suzanne drew back. "Who is this Yankee-sounding woman parading around like our old friend Jane? Tight ass. Tight speech. Tight proper ways." Suzanne got nose to nose with me. "You did not become un-southern residing up north. Girlfriend, I expect to hear *y'all* before the next hour is over." With a flick of her finger against my chest, she pushed me to the bench. Maggie sat, too. Wide-eyed, I nodded. Mark's little sister had changed. I was not acquainted with this Suzanne.

"So what were the two of you doing?" Suzanne parked on the end of the bench next to me, sandwiching me between her and Maggie like a prisoner with a security detail.

"Praying," Maggie snipped. "You might try it sometime."

"Praying for Mark is a waste of time. We all know he was a saint." Suzanne's gaze lifted upward. "And Maggie, don't look at *me* in that tone of voice."

"I took a moment of silence." I had started to pray… Fact was, I gave up on God when Momma died. But it looked like I needed to renew His acquaintance. The indisputable data proved I needed my friends way more than they needed me, and His assistance might come in handy now.

"Mark wouldn't want all this maudlin crap. You know how he hated cemeteries. He'd want us to celebrate. Gather a second line band, wave our hankies, and parade through the Quarter. You know, Mark always blamed himself for… I hate to say 'our break-up,' but that fits."

"Mark *would* want us to celebrate." Maggie's eyes flickered, and I recognized Catholic good-girl guilt.

"I'm feelin' the need for a beer. Cold. Longneck bottle. It's not every day this woman gets to gossip with her two oldest, bestest friends." Suzanne chuckled.

Dizziness pulled me under. Emotionally drunk, I blinked, searching for my focus. I checked my watch. I could manage one drink.

Fate had brought us together again. That had to be a positive sign, yeah?

"I don't know about a beer because I haven't eaten." They didn't know it would be my first real meal in days. My traitorous stomach rumbled loudly. "I'd love to have a po'boy at Brunnings."

"Oh, darlin', that'd be nice, but PK, it closed." Suzanne's tone was that of an old book being snapped shut.

"PK?"

"Everything with her is either BK or PK. I don't mean Burger King or Preacher's Kid. It's *before Katrina* or *post Katrina*." Maggie sighed and stood. "Let's go."

"I hear a brew calling my name." Suzanne moonwalked out to the hallway. Her performance would make Michael Jackson proud. Her fingers motioned "follow me."

I grabbed my purse and trailed after Suzanne in Pied-Piper mode. Maggie brought up the rear.

The door chimed as we left the building. Pulling sunglasses from my purse, I dropped the letter. Bending to scoop it up, Maggie got there at the same time as me, and we bumped heads.

"My goodness, you're hardheaded." Maggie rubbed the injured spot.

I snatched the paper from Maggie's grasp and quickly leaned in and kissed her cheek. "Sorry. As for hardheaded, you don't know the half of it."

"Let's go," Suzanne yelled. "Eddie's."

"Coming." I tried to sound upbeat. Surely, I was allowed a moment of pleasure in the company of my old friends—before telling the truth and going straight to hell.

I took two quick steps to catch up with Suzanne, but before going farther, a hand on my arm stopped me.

"Jane, would you ride with me?" Maggie's Daisy-Mae smile didn't hide her Eleanor-Roosevelt determination. She hooked her arm through mine and guided me toward a car. "Jane's going with me," she called to Suzanne.

Riding alone with Maggie? My guilt raced like an airboat zipping across a bayou. If I didn't confess soon, I'd explode. The devil would deliver me to his lair in pieces.

But Maggie needed me to comfort her? Like old times? A role I'd played over and over when we still believed drinking strawberry soda at Saturday night parties made us "smashing."

I quelled the rising urge to blurt out my truth about Mark. Somehow, I had to stuff my Gs and concentrate on Maggie's needs. That was more important now.

And *I* needed her, too. She held my future in her heart, but she didn't know it yet.

Opening the front passenger door of Maggie's sedan, I decided to return to the mausoleum later and share with Mark all the details of our son, just in case being dead didn't come with omniscient powers.

The seat belt snugged me into place, and a scent drifted to my nose. Lavender, Maggie's scent, mixed with a clean-smelling touch of spice, undeniably Mark's. Could life turn any more surreal? I was home for the first time in years because of Mark, who had been the very reason I'd stayed away…

"It's been years since you left, Jane. You haven't changed. Serious as always. Intense. You know, I still see your daddy regularly. Such a sweet man. He always tells me how you're doing. It hurts that you cut me out of your life when I married Mark."

Maggie's words knifed my chest. What determined the best time for a confession the size and likes of mine? Maybe Catholicism offered advantages, as Maggie had said. Dark booth, confession, absolution. That's what I wanted from her—painless absolution.

"You're awful silent over there. I knew you'd come. Didn't know exactly when. But that *knowing* feeling hit me, so I asked the security guard to keep a lookout. Gave him a photo your dad sent me. And Jane, I wanted you to ride with me to tell me *why* you came now."

Maggie's directness slapped me. Could I say I needed proof my father had remained sober for the last nine months? Could I say I needed a mother for my son? Could I say that cancer hadn't skipped a generation?

Words stuck in my throat. I couldn't say my diagnosis is fatal. I hadn't quite accepted reality yet. "Well, ah–" I rambled and then clutched the seat to steady myself against Maggie's mad-dash driving.

"How long are you going to stay? Will we ever see you again? What can I do to make you stay? What could possibly be so important in Salem or Boston? We're here. Your daddy's here." Maggie's voice rushed and steadily rose. "Jesus-Mary-and-Joseph, your Momma's buried here. *I'm* the one who puts flowers on her grave."

I couldn't process the words she threw at me.

"And another thing," Maggie continued, "I don't want Suzanne hurt. When you and Mark went away after high school, she wandered around like a lost child abandoned. Then Mark came back, but *you* didn't." Maggie's tone hardened. "She loves you like a sister. Still misses you." Maggie shook her head. "She's reading all sorts of new-age, self-help crap, but…so far, no cure."

Surprise hit me harder than Maggie's tone.

Suzanne had felt abandoned?

I was well acquainted with abandonment. Abandoned when my mother died. Abandoned when my father drank himself into a stupor. Abandoned when Mark joined the Army, then again when our marriage failed... I had inflicted that kind of pain?

Assumptions made an ass of me. I had always assumed when Mark returned home Suzanne would take his side. Mark got our friends in the divorce. It never dawned on me that Suzanne would *want* the same relationship we'd had since childhood.

I clutched the door handle. My head pounded with the erratic beat of a thousand out-of-sync drums. I slipped deeper into numbness.

Somehow, I had to come clean to Maggie and Suzanne.

Would they come to my aid?

Would Maggie be my savior?

Chapter 3 - Suzanne

Suzanne pulled the dark blue BMW 650i, a gift from her husband, to the curb in the shadow of a building. Not surprising she'd made it to Eddie's Place before the others. The city made Maggie skittish. Jane had been gone so long she probably couldn't explain the difference between uptown, downtown, or midtown anymore. Of course, little looked the same since Katrina.

Now that she had hooked Jane into joining them for a drink, would Jane's love of the city reel her in and land her back in New Orleans? Would it lure her old friend to put in a permanent change of address at the post office?

She needed Jane to move home. She'd never been needy. Not like Maggie. Ever.

She needed a big dose of friendship now. After all, if her suspicions were correct, her secret would be showing soon. She shifted and shivered and swallowed.

Placing her Fendi sunglasses in their leather case, Suzanne dropped them in her Prada purse. Sunglasses weren't a fashion statement, but an essential for proper self-care. That had climbed to the top of her must-do list. Eating right. Exercising. Hydrating. Things she couldn't pay someone else to do for her.

She exited the car, then pulled on the heavy front door, and entered Eddie's. The place had changed little over the years—dimly lit, wavy glass windows, dark-stained wooden bar. The only color in the room came from bottles of bourbon, tequila, and liquors like Amaretto, Midori, and Curacao. She liked the light shining through the glass shelves. The out-of-place antique mirror was comfortingly familiar. From outside, Eddie's Place could be mistaken for a dive, but it was not unpopular with the locals.

The bar was unlike French Quarter addresses. It sat nestled across Esplanade Avenue in the Faubourg Marigny on Frenchmen. A quiet street during the day. A hot destination for music at night. Post Katrina, Eddie turned his place into a gastropub, hiring a chef de cuisine, but booze remained his cash cow. Friday and Saturday night, he charged a cover at the door when bands played and still racked up *ka-ching*. She appreciated his business savvy.

Pausing, she inhaled a signature scent of home. Aroma of roast beef for po'boys floated in the air so thick that breathing in was like eating. She loved that about Eddie's.

"Hey, Missy. Where do you want us to sit? Uncle Eddie around?" Suzanne called to the woman polishing the bar.

"Pick your place. I'll get the boss man."

Suzanne scanned the front room. Old city. Old times. Memories floated to her. Voices of the past whispered. This had been their hangout—hers, Maggie's, and Jane's—whenever their parents allowed them free rein in the city. A time before they'd been launched headfirst into life's adult disappointments.

Maybe they could begin again. Push restart.

Suzanne's vision adjusted to the dimly lit room. She leaned against the bar. Sounds of a determined stride drew her attention. "Hey, Uncle Eddie!"

"How's my favorite niece?" Eddie pushed on the swinging doors separating the bar from the kitchen. In his late fifties, Eddie's swagger deterred drunks—usually, those that imbibed too much removed themselves before Eddie helped them through the door.

"Holding up okay." Barely was more like it, but this was one time when the truth was overrated.

Tossing a dish towel on the wooden bar, he came around to her. "You're sure you're doing good? You look a little thin." He took her hand and spun her around. Eddie had always made time for her, unlike her father, though he wasn't a blood uncle, but a distant cousin on her father's side.

"I'm not." She let him wrap her in a hug. It was as though they were both hugging Mark.

"You alone?" Eddie stepped back and lifted one eyebrow.

"As in, no husband, or what?" She looked heavenward, trying to look annoyed.

"As in, I'll give you what you want on the house—*if* you're by yourself. Last time you wandered through, you brought a busload with you. Good for business, but can't be giving out *lagniappe* all the time. Come sit at the bar and talk to me."

"Thanks, but two friends will arrive any minute. Listen, don't get weird on me. Give me a nonalcoholic beer and pour it into a glass. Quick, before they get here. I don't want them to see the bottle."

He snorted. "Suz, ya want what?"

"Non-alcoholic-beer-in-a-glass."

"You sick or something?"

"Unhealthy enough to drink alcohol-free. On a health kick." It wasn't a ruse, but in a city known for overindulgences, it sounded like one.

"Fine." Eddie sighed. "I aim to please."

"Fine," she shot back. "Maggie and Jane will appreciate that."

"Jane's in town?"

"Would I lie?" Suzanne pulled out a chair at a round table in the corner. The wooden legs scraped across the floor and drowned out the blues playing softly from the speakers mounted around the room. "It's the strangest thing. I should know better than to doubt Maggie. She called and told me we'd find Jane visiting Mark. I thought it was widow's grief talking. She's not doing so great... Anyway, sure enough. We found Jane at the mausoleum. Talked her into coming here. Jane says she's hungry."

When the front door opened, Suzanne turned. Maggie and Jane stood side by side, squinting into the dimness.

Eddie placed a filled glass on the bar. Suzanne silently mouthed, "Thank you." The alcohol-free beverage in a glass wouldn't raise suspicions.

"And that Maggie, she's always been spooky that way." Eddie's loud reply made it obvious he was aware of the two women standing inside the threshold. "Not a voodoo thing with her. I'd pay attention if she ever told me something would happen."

"If I ever receive a message for you, Eddie, you'd best heed it." Maggie marched toward the table with Jane following. "But I'll bet you have a *knowing* about me."

Eddie closed his eyes and touched his index finger to the middle of his forehead. "Wild Turkey 101 and Coke." He opened his eyes and grinned.

Suzanne caught Jane's faint frown. It vanished as quickly as it formed.

"Good to see you, Janey. Been a long time." Eddie bellowed with friendliness.

"You look well, Eddie. I'll take an Abita draft, please."

Jane sounded so formal, so detached. Was this who she'd become?

"I never forget favorites of my ladies." Eddie pointed. "Maggie wants red beans and rice. Jane a shrimp po'boy with sweet potato fries, and Suzanne—"

"I'll take a salad, please."

"Salad?"

"You didn't misunderstand, and you said you aim to please." She counted on him remembering their earlier conversation.

Eddie scowled before disappearing into the kitchen.

A minute later, the waitress set drinks in the middle of the table along with a stack of napkins.

"Now a toast to old times." Jane hoisted her beer mug. Maggie raised her highball glass.

Suzanne paused. "It's been an hour, Jane. Stop with all the stiff-upper-lip politeness. It's *us*. Just us." Suzanne touched her glass to each of theirs, the *clink* reminding her of happier times. "To good friends. May we never be parted again." Somehow, they had to rebuild their tattered friendship better than the levees had been built.

After they sipped, Jane's voice rose just above a whisper. "I'm happy to be here. You are very kind. I've missed this place. I feel like I've died and gone to Heaven."

Suzanne's gut twisted. Maggie jumped up and ran to the ladies' room. Wailing filtered into the bar before the bathroom door slammed shut. Taking a napkin, Suzanne patted the corners of her mouth and then folded her hands in her lap. She and Maggie had put on a good face to meet Jane, but now the mask had slipped.

"What have I done?" Jane rose, looking toward the restroom.

Suzanne reached for her. "Let her be. She'll pull it together in a few. Sit."

Jane glanced pensively over her shoulder but returned to her seat.

"This is all just bullshit." Suzanne took a slow sip of her near-beer for courage. "I'm mad as hell at you right now, and not because of your gaffe. We needed you. We—Maggie and I—need you. My brother is dead." She couldn't control the rise in her voice. "Where have you been? You might have divorced him, but did you have to divorce me, too?" Her heart wept. Bottled grief gushed like someone had hit a water main.

Jane's eyes rounded to the size of inner tubes. Her shoulders rounded as she sat back.

Suzanne recalled her therapist admonishing her about thinking there was a shortcut to the grief process. The woman couldn't explain exactly when the pain would subside, but spouted psychobabble woo-woo. It helped nothing.

On the heels of Mark's funeral, Suzanne hated life's unexpected turn —making it harder to deal with losing her brother, comforting Maggie, and confessing the situation to her husband. That's why she needed Jane. The old Jane had been her sister, not this tight-lipped, proper preppy.

"Damn it! You took an oath to be our friend." Suzanne's fury exploded as the music in the bar ceased. "We exchanged spit and blood in that stupid childhood ritual making us blood sisters. I took all of that seriously." Her body trembled like she was caught in San Francisco during an earthquake. Her eyes misted. She ignored the dampness on her face, leaned over, nearly nose to nose with Jane. But the truth lodged in her throat. Eddie might have to give her the Heimlich before she could cough it up.

"Suzanne, I'm sorry."

Yelling had been wrong. Jane shut down, the same way someone turned off a flashlight, extinguishing the beam.

"I'm sorry," Jane whispered. There was an honest desperation in her voice.

Suzanne clung to a shred of hope—if Jane moved home, the city would pump lifeblood back into her again. Then Jane could help keep her afloat on the emotional river taking her away from the man she loved so much. Lowering her voice, she said, "Don't make my childhood memories a fraud."

"Stop it, Suzanne," Maggie drawled as she approached the table.

Surprised, Suzanne glanced up. A smile plastered Maggie's face. No sign of tears, just redder-rimmed eyes. Had Maggie taken a sedative to bring about this calm? Was she mixing drugs and alcohol?

Oh, no. Lordy, please not that.

"We've managed with phone calls, emails, and a few short visits. We've only been invited to Boston twice—more than ten years ago when Jane was in grad school. She came home when you and Grant married. How many years ago was that?" Maggie looked up, her index finger pivoted on her chin—a Kewpie-doll impression. "Seven. She didn't come home when Mark and I married. No worries. We'll get by like we always have since high school—without Jane."

"No." Suzanne shook her head. "It's always been the three of us—no matter the distance."

"Ah, ladies? Food is ready." The waitress stood beside the table with a tray.

"We scared Eddie?" Suzanne asked.

"He's made himself scarce upstairs in the office. Said only to bother him if one of you reaches for a knife." The woman placed food in the middle of the table. "I'll give y'all another round of drinks if you promise to keep it down."

"I'll take a glass of water." Jane's shoulders slumped.

Suzanne scrutinized Jane hard. A slight purplish cast rimmed her eyes. She was tired. Weary even. Too thin. Nothing like the raring-to-go leader from their childhood.

Maggie sat, picked up her glass, tipped the bottom up, and finished the last drop. "Me, too. This time, no ice."

Missy paused, nodding at Suzanne. "And you?"

"Water with lemon for me. One beer's enough. I'm now the designated driver."

The waitress hoofed it back to the bar. Only the break of billiard balls from the back room and the hum of the air conditioner invaded the quiet.

Suzanne swirled her glass, the last third of her drink funneling like a tornado in a science experiment. Her mind swirled the same way. To navigate what lay ahead, she needed Jane. "I apologize for the outburst. If I've learned anything since Mark's death from the books I've been reading, it's that I have to ask for what I want. Otherwise, I get whatever life wants to dish out. I've had my fill of that."

Maggie leaned close to Jane. "She's been devouring self-help books for the last four weeks. She even went to see a *shrink* about grief." She flipped her long auburn hair over her shoulder.

"You need to read this stuff as much as me," Suzanne encouraged.

"No. I don't. That's what I have church for."

"Well, you're both one-up on me. I have never gotten a grip on Momma dying. Now Mark." Jane's voice barely rose above the quiet in the room. "If I can't get a grip on death after all these years, how am I ever going to help..."

"Us?" Maggie snapped. "Like you used to do? Queen Belle. You had all the answers. At least you did before you ran out on us. Turned your back on us...*and* Mark. I'm telling you, Suzanne, we'll get along without her."

"How long are you staying, Jane?" Suzanne refused to consider whether or not Maggie's rant held a shred of truth. If Jane left again, that could completely sever their friendship. She might not see her again...until someone else died. They had to keep talking. "I'm sure your daddy is glad to see you."

The waitress delivered the next round of drinks and departed as quickly as she came.

Maggie grabbed her drink, chugged it down, slapped the glass on the table. "Suzanne, don't you see? Cab. From. The. Airport. No luggage. She's not seen her daddy. In fact, I know, he doesn't even know she's in town."

Perplexed, Suzanne peered at Jane. Was this Maggie's intuition or astute observation? Would Jane have snuck in and out of town without a word to any of them? Would she honestly leave without seeing her father? "Well?"

Waiting for an answer, she searched the woman in front of her for signs of her old friend. Jane's clothes were nice enough, but not designer labels. She'd been a shoe whore in high school, back when her father treated her like a princess. Now, her shoes were nondescript flats. Her nails were naked. Her brown hair, once always shiny, long and flowing, was bobbed. Not the fancy northeasterner with a degree from an Ivy League college and deep pockets as her father had hinted. Who had Jane become?

Maggie hiccupped. "Need a nap. I should gooo."

"You can't drive in your condition." Suzanne sighed. "You're slurring your words."

Maggie's eyes glazed. "I have no condition. I tried hard for months to get pregnant. *Made* Mark wear boxers. Took my temperature every day. Did a headstand after making love. I even took fertility drugs. Started having double vision. *None of it worked.*" She hiccupped again.

Jane's mouth formed a small "o." She shook her head. "Maggie, I'm so sorry." She touched Maggie's arm, but Maggie jerked away. Jane retreated, folding her hands in her lap.

"I *wanted* Mark's baby," Maggie wailed.

"I'm sorry." Jane's voice wavered. She was fighting tears.

"I can't ever have children." Maggie jumped up and ran for the ladies' room.

"Oh shit." Suzanne's elbows bumped hard against the tabletop. She rested her forehead in her hands. Maggie's fragility scared the crap out of her. She was like a delicate porcelain figurine bouncing in the back of a pickup at a monster truck rally. Would Maggie try something desperate? Desperate enough to shatter them both into a thousand pieces?

"Suzanne?" Jane asked.

Suzanne barely heard her. "Yeah?" They'd shown Jane the underbelly of their reality. Too much. Too soon. No reason for Jane to stay now. She wouldn't want to play in this sandbox of drama.

"Things are a mess here, aren't they?"

"Only organized chaos. We are not known for being unemotional. But you run along back up north. I'm sure your life is perfect there. Maggie and I will manage."

"My life is *far* from perfect *up* there."

Maggie returned to the table and yanked her purse from the back of the chair. "I have to walk. I'm going to the river." She headed out the door.

Would Maggie do something crazy now? "Save the food." Suzanne called to the waitress as chair legs scratched against the floor. "We'll be back to pick it up later." She grabbed for Jane's hand. "Let's go. For all I know, Maggie may jump."

With a pace one step from a trot, she tried to catch up with Maggie, but when she reached the corner, the traffic light halted her progress. For someone in heels, Maggie sure hoofed it fast. Suzanne crossed the street against the light, dodging passing cars, with Jane in tow. Maggie remained in sight.

"I thought she was pregnant." Jane paced her words with the rhythm of their jog. "She can't have children?"

"This is all news to me. She and Mark fixed up a nursery. Mark wanted kids. Maggie would do anything for Mark. I'm worn out worrying over her."

"What am I going to do now?" Jane spoke softly, but clearly to herself.

What could Jane do for Maggie? What *would* Jane do? Suzanne's problems were accumulating like algae in bloom, and she could no longer handle Maggie's, too.

Maggie sometimes had the ability see things about other people, knowing intimate details of their lives, and when she pointed out things to Suzanne, they made perfect sense. Yet, for some reason known only to Maggie's God, she had no insight into issues in her own life. She was made to fumble around, a blind woman seeing the world only for other people. Her special gift didn't come with a special warranty.

Suzanne followed Maggie on Esplanade Avenue to St. Peters, then to the Mississippi River. And what about Jane? How could she not need this city? The Old Man—the great Mississippi River before them—ruled New Orleans, the Big Easy. No matter whatever anyone else called it, she'd always called it home.

Ahead, Maggie climbed the levee. The sun shined bright and hot. A warm wind blew off the water, making the humidity tolerable. Suzanne wanted to wipe perspiration from her brow, but that would smear her makeup.

Nearby a musical trio performed for pedestrians. The bass, guitar, and trumpet played melodic notes as three connected barges lazily drifted on the river. Three was Mark's lucky number. He used to joke how he liked having a stepmother. That gave him three parents, which meant more presents at Christmas and birthday time. He had three beautiful girls in his life—his sister, Maggie, and Jane. And he'd said he'd cheated death three times: a football injury, the Army, and a prior motorcycle accident.

The three Belles back together again had to be a sign from Mark.

But how the hell would she break the news that in about eight months there could be a fourth Belle? News about a baby would crush Maggie. Yet she'd hate the alternative more.

How could she make Jane understand about how much she was needed?

In New Orleans.

And just how badly would Grant respond to the news about someone new calling him daddy?

Chapter 4 - Maggie

Maggie tried to outrun her pain. She started up the levee in a trot and broke into a run. Her fingers tangled in her perspiration-soaked hair. She pulled it away from her neck. Her heels sank into the grass like tent stakes. She stopped. Pulled her feet free. Yanked the shoes up. Flung them hard. They sank like ballast. Her life was sinking, sinking, sinking.

Those shoes had been Mark's favorites. He'd loved her legs in those heels. Darn him.

She made it to the top of the levee. Pain slammed her heart. Opening her arms wide like a singer on stage, she released a low sorrowful moan. Ran it like a musical scale. Louder. Higher. Peaking at a screeching yowl.

Completely out of breath, she crumbled to the grass on her hands and knees. The ends of her hair touched the ground, creating a veil over her face. Giving voice to the pain hadn't changed a thing.

She had survived Mark's teenaged rejection. She had survived Mark's marriage to Jane. She had survived Mark's funeral. But how could she survive life without Mark, unless Jane came home to stay?

"Mark! You promised to never leave me. You promised for better or worse. *This* is the worst. Where are you?" She pounded the ground with her fist, pounding on the devil's door. Would striking a bargain bring Mark back? Why had Heaven forsaken her? Had to be because of her lie—a sin as heinous as Eve offering Adam a bite of the forbidden apple.

Tears blinded. She battled full-throttled pain.

When Mark died, she cried ladylike. At the funeral, everyone had tip-toed around her as though she might break. Whispered behind her back. Their fears— readable in their darting gazes, palpable in their auras—made her more afraid.

Mark was gone. So Jane had to stay.

Jane's nurturing ways created a safety zone. She desperately needed her to give that to her again. Besides, Jane knew what it was like to be married to the most marvelous man in the world. Ironic that of all the things in their past, that one fact would keep them connected forever.

"Hey, is she all right?" a male voice hollered.

"She will be. She just buried her husband," Jane called back over the screeching of seagulls.

"Yeah, well, if you need help, I'll call 911."

Maggie withdrew into a yoga child's pose and cried harder, her soul shriveling up from wanting. Wanting to understand. Wanting to die. Wanting Mark. Wanting a baby.

Her breath grew shallow as though it only skimmed the surface of living.

A hand touched the back of her neck, another her waist, pulling her onto her side. Maggie's hair covered her face as she rested her head on Jane's thigh.

"Shh. It'll be okay. I'm here for you." Maggie felt Jane's gentle strokes on her arm.

A bump shook her when Suzanne plopped down in the grass beside Jane, and she began stroking Maggie's hair.

After several minutes, Maggie's ragged breaths slowed to short hiccups. She breathed in deeply, exhaled slowly, her heart thudded like a tugboat chugging, chugging, chugging on the river.

She'd acted a fool at Eddie's, but for all the world, she couldn't help it. Nothing in life had prepared her for losing the only man she'd ever loved.

Confiding in Suzanne wasn't an option. After all, Mark was her only sibling, and their bond was tighter than Gorilla Glue.

"We're here for you." Jane's tone was low and even. "We'll take care of you." She continued her feathery touch on Maggie's arm.

Maggie whimpered. She loved Jane, but those feelings butted up against darkness inside her. The therapist she'd seen years ago had been useless. Her deep-seated angst about Mark and Jane had remained. And now, though she wanted Jane near, needed the comfort she offered, the weakness that produced such an all-encompassing need frightened her more.

"I...I don't know what I'll do without you," Maggie whispered and grabbed Jane's hand.

"I'm here," Jane whispered back.

Since Mark's death, every time Maggie thought of him, her thoughts slipped to Jane, too. Their history remained braided together.

A warm breeze blew across the river. Humidity continued to climb like someone had turned the dial in the steam room too high. Maggie's labored breathing evened. The pounding of her heart lessened. Now she wanted sleep.

"Maggie," Suzanne whispered. "Honey, how about we go? Let's get out of this heat."

"In a minute," Maggie whispered.

"We're browning like beignets in hot grease," Suzanne groaned.

"We're here for you, Maggie." Jane reassured.

Maggie nodded. Jane was the "for-worse" baggage Mark had brought to their marriage. At times, Maggie's insecurities had bubbled up and overflowed, causing her to babble and accuse Mark of terrible things, like not loving her as much as he had loved Jane.

But now Jane was the key to salvation from darkness since Mark's death had taken the sun. And he died without ever answering a question plaguing her still. That weekend he spent away, was it a weekend in Boston with Jane? He came home and proposed to her—not the exact day, but soon after—yet he had refused to say where he'd disappeared to. She'd loved him too much to lose him, so she never pressed.

Now Jane was the one person who could navigate her through the river of grief. After dealing with her mother's death, Jane possessed a secret nautical chart to avoid dangerous spots. The irony of it—Maggie's deceased husband's ex-wife was her only lifesaving hope.

Eyes closed, she sank into the comfort of all Jane's soothing.

"I can't handle her by myself. She needs you. I need you," Suzanne pleaded. "When are you leaving?"

Breathing evenly, Maggie wanted her friends to think she was asleep. Fear knotted in her chest. Seconds ticked by as she waited for Jane's reply.

"Tonight. My plane leaves at nine."

"Will it be another handful of years before we see you again?"

Maggie held her breath waiting for the answer. When none came, Suzanne said, "You have to stay. It's Friday. At least stay through the weekend."

"I *wish* I could."

"Damn it," Suzanne hissed. "I'm calling in my marker. When your mother died, I was there for you. I helped pick out a dress for her. Your father, I don't mean to speak ill of the man, found comfort in a bottle and left you, which at the time meant me, to help you handle all the arrangements. You owe me." Suzanne's voice was razor sharp. "When my brother died, you didn't come to the funeral. Now you have to stay. I won't take no for an answer."

Maggie let out a half breath and then moved her hair to look up at her friends.

Suzanne stood and snatched Jane's purse. "No ticket, no ID, no getting on a plane."

"I have responsibilities in Salem." Jane's hands trembled against Maggie's arm.

"Jane, can't you give us a weekend?" Maggie pushed to sitting. "After *all* we've meant to each other?"

A blast from the calliope on a riverboat punctuated her plea. A seagull let out a soulful cry. Music drifted from the trio playing at the top of the levee. The trumpeter made his instrument sing a hauntingly sad song, as if radiating the sadness from her heart for everyone to hear.

"I need to go home." Maggie stood. "Jane, you must come and stay with me. Just for tonight."

Jane sighed and stood, her face a battlefield of emotions. "We'll see. I need to make a few calls."

Maggie, needing solidarity, offered her hand to Suzanne.

"Maybe is all I'm saying." Jane's furrowed brow offered little hope.

"Are you sure that's a good idea, Maggie?" Suzanne asked anxiously. "I mean, after everything you've been through today?" Suzanne turned to Jane. "Maggie's been staying with Grant and me since Mark died. She hasn't been back to her house or to the camp at the lake."

"Maggie, are you up to this?" Jane asked.

"Y'all, we go to the camp," Maggie insisted.

"The camp?" Suzanne asked. "No. Stay with me tonight. Lord knows I have room." Suzanne crossed her arms over her chest and cocked her head to one side.

"Jane, did you know that Suzanne lives in one of those mansions in the Garden District? Grant bought her one for a wedding present." Maggie forced a half smile and began the first step up the levee.

"I heard rumors."

"It's grand, but we're going to the camp." Maggie's decision sparked a seed of strength in her, the first in weeks. Suzanne's plan to bring them all together at Eddie's Place hadn't turned out so well. Maybe if they went back to their island, they could find their way back to each other again.

Then and there, she and Suzanne would figure a way to make Jane come home for good.

Chapter 5

I stood around the corner from Eddie's Place to make a quick phone call while Suzanne and Maggie disappeared inside to collect our food. Grant would arrive any minute with a change of clothes and toiletries for an overnight at the camp.

First, I checked departing flights. I could extend my stay for one night—but only if Beth's schedule permitted her to handle things at home. I pulled up her number and my stomach grumbled loudly at the aroma from the bar and grill. Hunger had to wait.

"Hi, Beth. Something's come up." I shifted my weight from one foot to the other. "Could you take care of Sonny Boy overnight? I hate that this is last minute... I'll be home tomorrow. Yes, I promise.... Oh, a gig in the Hamptons. Two weeks. Congrats! Listen, don't feed Sonny Boy any extra treats, even if he begs. May I speak with him for a minute?"

A truck rumbled to a stop, brakes screeching not ten feet away.

"Beth? Say again. He won't stop barking? Well, okay. Fork over a treat, but be judicious with them tonight. Tell him I love him. Kiss him for me. Call me if you need anything. I'll be home tomorrow."

I stared at the phone. A fluttering in my chest made it hard to take a deep breath. I'd never spent a night away from Sonny Boy. Was this his first big step to a new independence? The little guy didn't want to talk with his momma. That sliced deep.

Suddenly, someone from behind squeezed my shoulder. I jumped and bobbled my phone.

Grant Saulnier grabbed it before it hit the ground. "Hey there. Didn't mean to scare you." He moved with ease in his navy-blue Italian silk suit. Still had a disarming grin. He handed back my cell. "I can't believe it's you. Welcome home."

He opened his arms. I stepped into his embrace. "You've made my wife so happy. And making her happy makes me happy." His gray eyes sparkled silver, matching the distinguished graying of his temples. He hugged me like he meant it. A genuine gesture from a genuine gentleman.

I rested my head on his chest. It had been a long time since I'd felt the sturdy comfort of a man's arms. My last real hug had come from Mark.

"I see you found *my* husband."

I released Grant and turned. "No, I randomly hug men whenever I stand on a street corner." Thankfully, Suzanne chuckled. Maybe the old me wasn't buried so deep she couldn't be found.

Grant took the bags laden with food from Maggie and Suzanne, then planted a kiss on his wife's cheek before heading toward her car.

"What's the word?" Maggie eyes lit with hope.

"I'll leave tomorrow."

Maggie clapped.

"Well, Maggie," Suzanne said. "Don't get too excited. You and I are only a one-night stand."

I guess I wasn't totally off Suzanne's shit list.

"How did you manage to land such a fine catch?" I nodded toward Grant. "Handsome, smart, and *willing* to put up with you, yeah?"

She ignored me.

Standing in the afternoon shadows cast by a building, I was startled to see how much Suzanne resembled Mark with her toned athletic body, wavy hair the color of golden wheat, and dimples. When she smiled, she showed perfectly straight, white teeth. A few light freckles dotted her nose and cheeks. Her hazel eyes changed with her moods.

In Suzanne, I caught a glimpse of the boy I once loved and the man I'd married. Mark had attracted glances from women of all ages with his linebacker-strong body, but most didn't see his generous heart. Falling in love with him had been so sweet, the giddy romantic ecstasy of being young and head over heels. I'd never found that again. Never looked for that again. Never could even hope for that again.

Mark had taken my heart.

"Everything but me is in the car." Grant pulled Suzanne in for a toe-curling kiss.

"Thank you for your hospitality." Maggie turned away from the couple's public display of affection. "I'm ready to start out on my own. Well, with Jane and Suzanne with me. It's time for me to go home."

Grant released his wife. "Loved having you." He squeezed Maggie's shoulder and planted a peck on her cheek.

She flashed a bashful smile. Maggie exuded a beauty most artists loved to paint. Her long auburn hair, slightly tousled, hung halfway down her back. Big brown doe eyes could drown any man. The sun had pinked her nose and cheeks. She was a study in vulnerability.

Turning my attention to Grant and Suzanne who stood holding hands, I noticed what a handsome couple they made, but more importantly, how perfectly they fit together. Belonged to one another. It had never fully been that way between Mark and me, though we had loved each other desperately.

"So, Jane," Grant said. "I overheard you on the phone. You have a friend taking care of your dog? I thought you were a cat person."

"Pardon?"

"Sonny Boy barking?"

My worlds collided. My stomach dropped like a stone to the sidewalk and rolled toward the levee. How much had he overheard?

"She probably got a dog because she needs protection. I hear there's a lot of crime in Boston," Maggie said.

I could have hugged her. Instead, I bobbled my head, a truly noncommittal response. My secret had to remain secret until the perfect time.

"She doesn't live in Boston. She lives in Salem, as in those witch trials." Suzanne's impatience showed in her eye roll.

Maggie shrugged. "It's all the same to me."

"No, that's like saying Mandeville is part of New Orleans."

Maggie shrugged again.

"Well, let's go, girls," Suzanne ordered. "We'll talk about dogs and cats and everything else at camp. Eddie will watch out for Maggie's car, though, if it was stolen, that would be the perfect opportunity to replace it. Lord knows you can afford a new one."

Grant pecked a kiss on Suzanne's cheek while Maggie and I piled into Suzanne's car. A new nervous flutter sparked to life in my gut. I scooted into the middle of the backseat and buckled up, fighting the urge to unbuckle my guilt.

The Gs began to chatter.

The letter in my purse was hot enough to catch fire.

I swallowed back the rising need to blurt out my secret. I needed a day with my old friends. Tomorrow I would tell the truth.

As the car left the curb, Maggie said, "Jane, tell us about your dog. You used to be terrified of them. How did you get over that? It's a 'he,' right? What breed? How old?"

Her words stole my breath the way a riptide carries a swimmer out to sea. "Oh..." I breathed in deeply, then exhaled. "He's close to five."

Maggie turned in her seat, her eyes wide with disbelief.

"He's busy all the time. Do you still have a cat, Suzanne?"

"No, she died, *before* I married Grant."

With Suzanne's glare chastising me in the rearview mirror, I glanced out the window to avoid further eye contact. "Mind if I eat while you drive? I'm starving."

I searched through the bag and found the container with my po'boy. Suzanne stopped for a red light. Beside us, a radio from a car blasted New Orleans funk, the bass so deep it rattled the windows. When the signal light changed, I carefully kept my eyes glued for street signs and landmarks, those anchors of my old life.

The po'boy shop in the shotgun house.

The seafood joint famous for crab-filled okra poppers.

The corner where Schwegmann's used to sit, back when everybody went there to *make groceries*—outside of New Orleans, people called it grocery shopping.

I was taking a taxi through time.

While I rode, my lonesomeness spread through all cells in my body. These were the streets of my childhood, but so changed. Could I still call myself her daughter? I loved my city. Television coverage during the aftermath of the storm had riveted me. A TV news anchor's so-called New Orleans expert hadn't recognized Xavier College sitting in brown water, but I had.

Back then, I shoved my grief for the city's loss into a black hole in my heart to make friends with the grief of losing my mother. Afterward, I embraced *laissez les bon temps rouler*. Totally living in denial mode. If I dared to examine the backpack of Gs, a catastrophic flood of another sort could wash my life away.

Now I intended to battle, though, in the end, New Orleans would be my final resting place.

Suzanne drove along Elysian Fields to Gentilly Boulevard in the afternoon traffic before crossing under the interstate to the old Chef Mentuer Highway, the way we had traveled as teenagers. Back then, with a set of keys and a driver's license, we'd wound around on the two-lane blacktop in my restored metallic blue convertible—a present from my grandmother—with the radio cranked so high that on a cloudy day it tore holes in the sky to make way for sunshine.

Now, a song of silence surrounded us.

Crossing the bridge to the no-name island in East New Orleans, my heart soared at seeing the narrow strip of land separating Lake Pontchartrain and Lake St. Catherine. But nothing had remained the same. My eyes misted.

The number of properties for sale—shocking. I stroked my throat to help me swallow.

Growing up, land rarely changed hands. Unlike the city with its paved streets, the island had crushed white oyster-shell alleys inching into the lakes and creating canals. Fishing boats at every dock.

Now the rebuilding brought new structures on steel beams. So different from the quaint wooden camps of my childhood. The rising tide lapped against bare-wood pilings, skeletal remains of old docks jutting upward from the water's surface. Pelicans perched waiting to pluck dinner from brackish waters. Even five years after the disaster, one house still displayed the National Guard's spray-painted code as shown on television after the storm.

I looked away. My appetite vanished. I dropped the remainder of my po'boy into the container.

"Jane, are you okay?" Suzanne called out.

I nodded, trying to hold the shattered pieces of my heart together.

"Oh honey," Maggie said, turning sideways in the seat to look at me. "I know it looks different, as Suz says, PK. But most people are back. Wait until you see our place. Mark..." Maggie sniffed. She turned back and looked out the window. The glass captured Maggie's reflection. She pinched the bridge of her nose, as if doing so would somehow stem the flow of her tears.

"Crying is good. In just a minute, I'll join you, but if I start now—and believe me I cry at the drop of a pot these days—we'll never make it the next mile to Mark's," Suzanne said.

I wiped away my tears when the car turned right off the blacktop onto a narrow alleyway.

Tall green weeds outlined a gray concrete slab, the remains of the bar and grill that used to sit on the corner, the building ripped away by Cat-5 hurricane winds. A new structure stood a few lots over.

Suzanne's tires rolled over oyster shells, and I recalled the familiar *crunch*, which triggered an old memory of the volunteer fire station—the one my great-grandfather helped build and where we, as kids, held Saturday night parties drinking Nehi strawberry soda. Now, no sign of the building existed. Vegetation grew wild, reclaiming the land.

I covered my chest with my hands to keep the broken pieces of my heart from spilling out.

Suzanne stopped the car. A large camp on steel beams rose more than twelve feet. Numbers marked one side of one piling like a giant ruler, a gauge for floodwaters. The camp sat alone on the alleyway. BK, the Mauceles had counted the Potiers, Thibedouxs, and Guidrys as neighbors.

"Pull forward. Onto the cement. Under the house." Maggie excitedly instructed Suzanne, then leaned around to look at me. "Come see what my husband built!"

When the car had barely come to a stop, Maggie opened the door and hopped out. "Look!" She pointed to a downstairs enclosure. "There's storage, stairs, and an elevator."

Maggie's joyful innocence tugged at me. I couldn't remember a time when I felt as innocent as Maggie looked now.

When I exited the air-conditioned car, humidity melded to me. My slip stuck to my dampened skin. I breathed in the scent of the canal's brackish water. It was the unmistakable smell of the island. For a moment, all anxiety fled.

I was truly home.

Suzanne pulled the bags from the car. "Hey, come grab these groceries."

Ding.

Maggie darted to the back of the car. "That's the elevator," she cried. "Mark put this in so when his grandmother visited, he wouldn't have to drag her wheelchair up the steps."

With food and an overnight bag, I boarded the elevator with my friends. A light overhead flickered on as the doors closed.

"I have stainless everything in the kitchen. The quietest dishwasher. We have one huge bathroom with a big walk-in shower. Jets in the wall. There are three bedrooms, but mostly everyone sleeps on the porch. It's glass and screened and air-conditioned, too." Maggie beamed.

"Oh, God. How did we sleep on the porch in the summertime without any AC?" The thought was unimaginable to me after spending so many years up north.

"A big fan blew away bugs. Mosquito coils in the corners kept those nasty bloodsuckers at bay…most of the time." Suzanne smiled at me. If she regretted that the camp had been deeded to her brother rather than becoming a shared asset when their grandfather died, she never let on. Maybe it mattered little. After all, her husband could build her the finest camp this side of Texas. But…it wouldn't be quite the same thing.

The doors opened into a foyer leading to the living room. The dining room and kitchen were visible. It reminded me of beach houses I'd visited on Cape Cod with robin's-egg blue walls and sand-colored wooden floors. Glossy white kitchen cabinets gave it a fresh homey vibe. A large black cast-iron *fleur de lis*, the symbol of New Orleans, hung over the fireplace. A telescope pointed toward Fort Pike and the fast-moving waters of the Rigolets.

This was the house Mark built.

That realization struck me like a barge hitting a sunken ship. Next came the fact that my son would never know his father. What had I done? I forced myself to breathe.

"Make yourselves at home. I'm going to mix up a pitcher of strawberry daiquiris. No more Nehi for us." Maggie giggled on the way to the kitchen.

"This looks nothing like the old place. But I enjoy these finer comforts." I plopped on the couch, working hard to appear…normal.

"As if you were ever a Jane who wanted to live with Tarzan in a tree." Suzanne sat in one of two matching sleek, white leather chairs. They looked European and expensive.

"Grant and I gave them these as a wedding gift." Suzanne ran her hand over the leather.

I lifted an eyebrow.

"What? I had to know I'd be comfortable whenever I came for a visit. What better way than by giving them what I want to sit in."

"Here we are, girls. Strawberry daiquiri delight, courtesy of *moi*."

They clinked glasses.

"To us. We're finally back together again, and our secret is still safe," Maggie said.

I closed my eyes, remembering that long-ago day…

"Thanks for bringing the chairs for us." I nodded to Mark and his friend, Byron. They'd dragged chairs from the storage shed beneath the camp over to the long wooden dock.

"Just one last thing," Suzanne piped in. "We'd like some soda pop."

"Anything else, Your Highness?" Mark was sulking. He'd lost a pirogue race and was forced to do Suzanne's bidding for the day.

After Mark and Byron left, Maggie flopped down on a chair. "I can't believe my momma won't let me wear a bikini!" She reclined and slid down the straps of her one-piece. "I don't want tan marks on my shoulders."

Behind her, the sun continued upward, a hot yellow blaze in a cloudless blue sky. Suzanne and I stretched out next to her.

"Well, technically, my dear, you aren't a teenager yet." I tried to sound adultlike.

Kids from school in Slidell and others on the island had been invited to Maggie's teen party. Anticipation created a special buzz of excitement. I could hardly wait for that evening. Momma had bought me a new sundress and finally given me permission to wear heels. Just no dang stilettos.

"That's right," Suzanne chimed in. "Your momma said when you turned thirteen you could wear a bikini. Though we're having your party tonight, you're still a child until Wednesday. But, as you know, Jane and I are already teenagers."

"Shush, y'all. Mark's coming back. What's he going to think? I'll die if he doesn't ask me to dance tonight. After all, I am the birthday girl."

"If you girls are set"—cranky Mark handed out bottles of soda without making eye contact—"we're goin' to help Jane's daddy move the fire truck out of the station."

"Thanks, Mark. Thanks, Byron. We'll start decorating at noon. Will you come help?" I asked. "Momma found an old mirrored disco ball at the flea market. I'll need help putting it up."

"Yeah, sure." Mark rolled his eyes before leaving with Byron.

Maggie pulled sunglasses down the bridge of her nose and watched Mark and Byron saunter away.

"Oh. My. God!" Suzanne cried after the boys were out of earshot. "I know that look. You like my brother!"

Maggie pushed up her sunglasses, hiding her eyes.

"Mark's a little old for you, don't you think?" I sat up, pulling my sunglasses halfway down my nose, and watched Mark take his last steps down the alleyway before disappearing inside the firehouse. Was there more to him than just being Suzanne's big brother? "Mark's fifteen, right, Suz?"

"As my daddy says, fifteen and frickin' overrun with hormones. I overheard Daddy having one of those *talks* with Mark. About keeping his pants zipped until he was at least eighteen. Daddy asked Mark how he'd feel if some guy got me pregnant at fifteen or sixteen. Mark got pretty pissed."

"I don't believe Mark's like that. He's always polite around me." Maggie stretched her body long and pointed her toes. "He'll never grow up to be like Crazy Claude."

"Speaking of *that* man," Suzanne said, "Momma saw Mrs. Dupuis at the grocery store in town last night. The woman had on sunglasses, but Momma could tell she had a black eye. She tried to avoid Momma, but you know her. Anyway, Momma said, Mrs. Dupuis put her hand in front of her mouth when she spoke. Momma thinks Crazy Claude has gone too far… and knocked out some of his wife's *teeth*. Momma again told Mrs. Dupuis about the women's shelter. Momma says if the men on the island don't have a come-to-Jesus meeting with Mr. Dupuis, she's calling the police."

Maggie and I sat up and stared at Suzanne.

"What? I'm just saying…"

"He beats her? I thought she just fell a lot. That's what she told my parents," I argued.

"Of course, he beats her," Maggie said. "You're way too much of a princess. You've led a sheltered life. You've never even been spanked, let alone taken a beating."

"What?" Her words shocked me.

"Have you *ever* been hit? Spanked? Beaten?" Maggie asked.

"Of course not!" An uneasiness slithered down my spine. "You?" I stared at her, scared to know the truth.

"Well," Suzanne said. "My daddy used to take off his belt, hand it to me, and send me to my room, or least he did, back before he divorced us. I'd hyperventilate waiting for him to use the belt, like he did on Mark. Instead, Daddy talked to me and made me agree not to do whatever I'd done wrong again. I held that belt a lot, but never got hit with it."

"That's not so bad." Maggie's hushed tone had Suzanne and me leaning in closer. "My last stepdaddy, Guy, never laid a hand on Momma. Instead, he'd beat one of us. She'd stand there and beg him to stop…crying…yelling at him to not hit us girls in the face."

Shock landed hard. My gut contracted. My throat contracted. My heart contracted. "Oh, Maggie, I didn't know." I reached for her hand, but she pulled away.

"No pity. My new stepdaddy moved us here from Baton Rouge. That's when I met y'all. He's okay. Yells a lot, but doesn't beat us."

"I thought he was your birth father," Suzanne said.

"No. My real daddy, he died on a construction job. My momma gets Social Security money for each of us kids." Then Maggie whispered, "I think that's why Guy married Momma."

"Money?" I asked.

"But of course, darling." Maggie flashed a thousand-watt movie-star smile.

I swallowed hard. Maggie's homelife terrified me. I'd never been exposed to those sorts of things. Never knew anyone who beat a child. Never understood divorce. It was as foreign to me as eating chocolate-covered grasshoppers.

But my parents had taught me to always stand up for myself.

I'll always help Maggie do the same...

"Jane?" Suzanne called. "Are you slipping out on us?"

"Oh, sorry. Got up early for my flight this morning."

Maggie drained the bottom of her tall glass. "One daiquiri down. Who wants another?"

"How about if we slow the booze and eat something?" Suzanne asked.

"Slow what booze? You haven't touched your drink. You've been sipping on water." Maggie pointed to the drink on the side table. The red slush had melted. Condensation dripped down the side of the tall glass.

"I'd like to sink my teeth into more homegrown nourishment from Eddie's," I said. "My mouth is watering over jambalaya. My stomach's eating my backbone."

"All right. Suzanne, you set the table. I'll heat things up. Jane, you make us drinks."

"Got any strawberry Nehi soda?" I asked. "Haven't had one of those since our end-of-the-year high school party...too many years ago."

"In the fridge downstairs. Suzanne, will you show Jane?" Maggie rose and headed for the kitchen.

"Come with me." Suzanne sauntered to the elevator. "I'd take the stairs, but I've had my exercise for the day chasing a crazy woman across the street, up a levee and back down."

"I heard that. Your brother may be dead, darlin', but I'm still your sister-in-law. Show a little respect," Maggie hollered.

"Yeah, Suz, have a little respect for us sisters-in-law," I whispered and elbowed her in the side.

Suzanne and I rode down one floor. The doors opened. We stepped out into a room that protected the stairs and the elevator from outdoor elements. In the far corner, a freezer and refrigerator stood side by side.

"My brother knew how to throw a good party. Always had food and drink on hand." Suzanne opened the door to the fridge and hoisted out a six-pack of strawberry soda, popped a screw top on one bottle, and handed it to me. Next, she opened one for herself.

"Cheers." I clinked my longneck bottle with hers.

After she took a sip, I fixed her with a stare. No intuitive message whispered to me, so I went with my gut. "Suz, if I ask you a question, will you tell me the God's honest truth?"

"Of course."

I kept my eyes locked on hers. "No alcohol. Your very maternal manner with Maggie—I mean, *you* were stroking her hair. You've never been… outwardly demonstrative…even the night we all almost got shot. Are you pregnant and does Grant know?"

She nearly spit her soda on me. "What!" Red spots freckled the concrete floor. "You've got to be kidding. We're a power couple. I'm not ruining that by having a kid." Suzanne frowned and scrunched her nose.

I allowed silence to settle between us.

My intuition shouted, "*Liar!*"

Without a doubt, I wasn't the only one keeping secrets.

Chapter 6 - Maggie

"What took you so long?" Maggie asked when her friends reappeared, happy to be in their company again. Jane's arrival had momentarily pushed away deep grief, though Maggie feared maybe too much. She'd have to ask Father Timothy at Our Lady about the appropriateness of a widow feeling happy so soon after her husband died.

"Suzanne, pull the plates out." Maggie pointed at Jane. "Grab that pitcher of water and those glasses for the table."

Maggie dished food onto platters, ladled up three cups of seafood gumbo, then pulled hot French bread from the oven. The aromas made her stomach rumble.

Suzanne was right, she needed food. Comfort food would fill her belly and nurture her tortured heart. As a dancer, she'd been a disciplined eater. Unlike some of her biological sisters who had medicated the pain of their haunting childhood with food or fentanyl or foo-foo dust.

Satisfied that everything they needed was on the table, she passed the food. Her friends filled their plates with Cajun delicacies. She didn't often eat such carb-laden meals, though she'd kept to one tradition—red beans and rice on Mondays. Mark's grandmother handed down the cherished recipe using beef stock in the place of water as her secret ingredient. The gift of the recipe proved Maggie belonged in the Maucele family.

"Hmm," Jane murmured. "This is so good."

Maggie made the sign of the cross and made a silent plea for support. She wasn't as genius as Jane or as savvy as Suzanne, but calling on angels couldn't hurt her mission. "Jane, were you not going to call us?"

"Honestly?"

"Oh, wait right there. I'm invoking the Belle pledge." Suzanne's terseness puzzled Maggie. Had something happened when her friends went on their soda run?

"Perfect idea." Maggie straightened in her chair. "Only total honesty when the pledge is invoked."

"Help one another. The truth will set us free. Amen." They recited the three-part pledge in unison.

"We were such dorks." Jane laughed. "Louisa May Alcott, a Bible verse, and a big *Amen*. What were we thinking?"

"Nonetheless. We're still Belles. As Ms. Alcott wrote, *Help one another, is part of the religion of sisterhood*. I take the oath we made at thirteen very seriously. Religiously. It can't be undone." Suzanne leaned back in her chair, crossed her arms over her chest. Jane's heretical comment was nearly fighting words.

"Exactly how would we *undone* it?" Jane chuckled. "Remember, you were the reluctant Belle. Maggie and I had to coax you into making our secret pact."

"That's the beauty of it," Maggie said. "There is no way. We agreed to be friends forever. We need to start acting like it." She lowered her voice and leaned in. "And we must keep the secret."

"We should've written down all the rules, then we could pass this on to our children." Jane stared wide-eyed at Suzanne.

"That's not funny," Maggie blurted. Her eyes misted. She blinked stinging tears away.

Jane, nor Suzanne, had no way of knowing that the same day she buried Mark, her dream of having a child died. Her lithe body, after years of dance training, could never carry a child. No diet or drugs could cure the ache of never holding a baby of her own in her arms. That hurt as much as losing Mark. The humiliation of explaining why she had a fully decorated nursery at their home in Slidell, ready for a baby who would never come, kept her from returning there.

"I'm sorry, Maggie. I did not mean to upset you," Jane said.

"Just for tonight'—Suzanne sighed—"let's take a break from death. I loved my sainted brother. He gave me two fabulous sisters-in-law. But we're alone together for the first time in years. So, let's get back to the pledge."

Maggie let Suzanne take control. It was two against one. Surely they could convince Jane to move home.

"Now, answer the question, Jane," Suzanne prompted. "Total honesty."

Jane scooped up another bite of gumbo and ate. After placing her spoon on the saucer, she folded her hands in her lap. "I was not going to call. I did not want to see you or visit with my dad on *this* trip. But since we are not talking about death or grief or Mark, my explanation will wait for another time. However"—she drew in a breath and blew it out—"I'm glad you showed up. Honest truth."

"Are you coming back soon?" Maggie whispered.

"Soon, but not sure of an exact date."

"What if we come visit you?" Suzanne offered.

Jane's face blanked for a second. It was as though she were a machine, and someone had powered her off. She licked her lips, batted her vacant eyes a few times, and smiled sugar sweet.

Maggie held her breath. Jane's flickering expression might not be obvious to others, but those who truly knew her, knew Jane could transform from demure belle to a female warrior with mother-wolf protectiveness. The first time she'd seen Jane turn expressionless then sweet was the day after her thirteenth birthday party...

"Have you ever seen a gator up close around here?" Maggie whispered, worried her idea of skinny-dipping at the abandoned boatshed wasn't so great after all. She hunched her shoulders tightly and hugged her towel closer to her body. Taking a few quick steps, she caught up to her friends.

"Stop giggling, Jane, or we'll get caught," Suzanne growled like a drill sergeant.

"It's two o'clock in the morning. There's no one out but gators," Jane shot back.

Suzanne led the way, flashlight in hand. The star-filled sky's ambient light reflected off the crushed oyster-shell path crunching under their sneakers as they walked.

"Gators don't like us any more than we like them," Jane said.

"Subject change. Wasn't it a wonderful night? Mark asked me to dance three times." Maggie pirouetted and bumped into Suzanne.

"Twinkle Toes, my brother was just being nice. Don't get any ideas. It's just too rude to think of him kissin' you."

Maggie giggled. "Too late."

"What?" Jane asked.

"Mark kissed me on the cheek before he left and wished me happy birthday!"

"Shhh!" Suzanne snapped.

They continued their trek in silence to the boatshed. It was the place where island kids gathered to swim and dive from the rooftop, though they'd been threatened by parents with severe punishments if they didn't stay away. The man who owned the property caused folks to cast a wary eye. He didn't live on the island. Rarely visited. But rumors flew about him using the shed as a way to run stolen boats up from Florida. And his canal, dredged deeper than others, was the ideal spot for diving and swimming. It wasn't the first time Maggie had joined Jane and Suzanne in ignoring the no-trespassing sign.

They arrived at the boathouse. A woman's voice called out from the next canal over.

"I'll kill you, Claude Dupuis, if you ever put a hand on me again." A small boat motor engine started up but then died. A floodlight popped on. Thankfully, the reeds on the other side of the canal created a hedge and protected Maggie and her friends from anyone's line of vision.

"It's just the Dupuis and their Saturday night entertainment," Suzanne whispered. "Last one in the water has to kiss Byron at the next dance."

Jane threw off her t-shirt, adjusted her bathing suit, and dove, a dive so perfect she made no more than the sound of a fish jumping in the lake.

Maggie slipped off the dock. Once in the water, she shivered. Sinking deeper into the water, she breathed through her nose, sending bubbles rising, then scrunched her toes inside her sneakers and shot to the water's surface. The night air caressed her. She shivered again. Pushing her wet hair back from her face, she winced. Sneakers with a bathing suit weren't fashionable, but she'd never venture into fishy waters without them. She shuddered at the thought of her feet meeting gunk on the bottom of the canal.

Suzanne tossed in life preservers. Then she, too, lowered herself into the water.

"I'm having second thoughts about skinny-dipping," Maggie whispered.

"Oh, no. You *wanted* to get bucky," Jane teased.

"That's why we came out here tonight. A thrilling adventure for your birthday," Suzanne chimed in. "We're just tagging along as witnesses for the unveiling of your tatas."

On the next canal, the floodlight flicked off, then on again. Suzanne put her finger to her lips, motioning for quiet. The rule on the island: Trespassers were shot, questioned later.

Maggie froze at the faint sound of water splashing. Each little splash became part of a rhythm. Someone paddled a boat.

Floating to the end of the canal, she waved for Jane and Suzanne to follow. The reeds would camouflage them.

"Alligator?" Maggie whispered. Her chin began to tremble. She pressed her elbows to her side and tried to remain perfectly still.

"What if it's a boat thief?" Jane floated next to Maggie.

She flinched. Were rumors about the boatshed owner true? A boat thief was like an Old West cattle thief, if caught, people didn't leave witnesses.

Suzanne floated beside her. She led them through a small break in the reeds. Nearby, a johnboat under the power of a paddle came out of the darkness.

Something swished by Maggie's leg. She clamped her hand over her mouth to squelch a scream.

"That you, Claude?" Mrs. Dupuis hollered. "You think you want more. Come on. I'll give you more."

When Mrs. Dupuis limped away from the water's edge of her dock, the floodlight became a spotlight. Maggie gasped. Blood oozed on the side of Mrs. Dupuis's face. The woman hoisted a shotgun to her shoulder.

Panicked, Maggie waved her hands to warn her friends and almost slipped out of her life preserver.

"Go," Suzanne commanded in a harsh whisper.

Jane moved just as a boat motor started up about thirty yards away.

An explosion ripped the quiet.

"You crazy bitch. You shot me!" Mr. Dupuis shouted.

"Get out of here. Don't come back, or I'll shoot you dead. You won't ever lay a hand on me again. Not ever."

Another exploding shot rattled the night.

A boat motor engine died.

Maggie froze. She'd been raised in violence. Yet exposure to it still shocked her every time.

Jane and Suzanne moved, creating a wake in the canal. Maggie followed them. She fought against the current. They headed for the boathouse. Suzanne and Jane rose from the water and pulled their t-shirts on. Suzanne reached down and hoisted Maggie up onto the dock, grabbing the life preservers and shoving them in the boathouse through an open window.

Maggie shivered. She prayed she wouldn't pee herself.

"They're gonna wake up Momma with their yelling and gunshots. She's gonna find us missing." Suzanne groaned. "The summer's just started. I'll be grounded for a month if Momma finds we're gone."

They ran up the alley to the road and down the next alley to the Maucele camp. Leaving wet sneakers at the bottom of the stairs, they climbed, knowing which step to bypass to avoid tale-telling squeaks.

"I left my towel," Maggie wailed. It was evidence of their late-night venture.

"Don't worry. It'll still be there," Jane reassured. "And if anyone finds it, we don't claim it. I'll buy you a new one."

"But I just got it got for my birthday."

"Shh," Suzanne said.

Maggie raced off to the bathroom.

After changing out of wet clothes and drying off, Maggie helped Suzanne grab sodas and a bag of chips. They tiptoed to the bedroom. A few minutes later, she sat with Suzanne and Jane on the floor between two of five single beds on the sleeping porch. Moonlight filtered through the windows and lit the room with a soft white glow.

"I think she actually shot him. Should we tell someone?" Jane's brow furrowed. That worried Maggie.

"You really think she hit him?" Maggie asked.

"He certainly bellowed loud enough," Suzanne added.

"Well, he deserves it. I saw Mrs. Dupuis. He'd bloodied the side of her face. She might need stitches. Maybe we *should* tell someone." Maggie pondered the consequences. Would someone blame her for not helping Mrs. Dupuis? It was the Christian thing to do. Would retribution for the sin of secrecy rain down on her? She barely knew the woman. Mrs. Dupris hid her gaze and looked away whenever she encountered her, unwilling to acknowledge their mutual membership in a group with a common denominator—abuse. Not all the ugliness and the scars it left were visible to the naked eye.

Panic rose in Maggie's chest. No one ever needed to know just how damaged she was inside.

"We need to wake up your momma and tell her." Jane grew more serious. "Mrs. Dupuis needs our help."

Loud pops echoed in succession in the night air. Then another and another.

Maggie trembled. Jane and Suzanne crawled on their bellies across the floor. Rising up to their knees, they peeped out the window. After a few moments of silence, Maggie joined them, fighting the urge to run out of the room, out of the house, run far away.

Moonlight danced on the water. Everything else was still. No more floodlight from the Dupuis place.

"Everything okay in here?" Suzanne's mother burst through the door. Mark followed behind her.

"Fine, Momma."

"Get into bed. Get some sleep. I'm going to check on the problem." She left the room as quickly as she came.

"Whatcha been up to?" Mark asked. He leaned in the doorway, head cocked, staring with one eye closed.

Maggie looked at Suzanne, then at Jane, whose face flickered blank. She blinked, licked her lips, and a sugary sweet smile appeared. "Why, Mark," Jane cooed. "We were sitting here planning how to do an underwear raid on you."

"Then why is your hair wet?"

When no one answered, Mark left the room.

"Can we push these beds together?" Maggie asked.

"It might be best—if we want to sleep tonight." Jane began sliding one bed closer to another.

Maggie barely closed her eyes. She tried to sleep, but with every little sound she looked around. The few winks she managed were punctuated with images of blood. Explosions of gunfire.

First light lit the horizon before she finally slept.

Later, the smell of frying bacon lured Maggie from bed. Dressed for a lazy summer day, she descended on the kitchen with her friends. When Suzanne stopped suddenly, Jane ran into her, and Maggie ran into Jane.

"Good morning, ladies." Deputy Griffin sat at the kitchen table and lifted a coffee mug in salute.

"Mrs. Maucele's been filling me in about the gunshots last night. You girls know anything about it?"

"Oh, no," Jane quickly responded.

"We did hear something. But it could have been a boat motor backfiring," Suzanne offered. She crossed the room and poured orange juice in three glasses and set them on the table. Maggie picked one up and sipped, hoping it would stop her hands from shaking.

"I'll bet it came from those Dupuis. Why, I can hear them at my house when they get into it, and we're a canal farther away." Jane pulled out a chair next to the deputy and sat.

Either Jane was crazy or incredibly brave.

"Is that so?"

Jane nodded. "We woke up when the red lights were flashing over there. Must have been three a.m. Couldn't tell what was going on."

Maggie's heart pounded. She swallowed. She feared she'd swallow her tongue if she lied to a policeman. Jane had told a bold-faced lie. Maybe they needed to tell the officials what they had seen. Maybe then Mr. Dupuis wouldn't beat on his wife. Maybe it would save the woman's life.

Maggie couldn't blurt the truth about what they saw. Not that she ever wished dying on anyone, but if one of the Dupuis had to die, an evil man like Mr. Dupuis wouldn't be missed. For once in her life, she could help someone else. Like Jane always helped her.

Maggie's trembling lessened.

"Jesse, have you checked with the Dupuis?" Suzanne's mother filled her cup with coffee, then raised the pot, offering the deputy more.

"No, thanks. As for the Dupuis, Missus is in the hospital. Concussion. Beaten pretty badly. And a gunshot wound. We haven't found Mister yet."

Jane batted her lashes, licked her lips. A sugary sweet smile appeared. "Deputy Griffin, she's gonna be all right?"

"Yeah. Funny thing. Some guy called 911 from the corner phone booth by the bar. Wouldn't give his name. Said he heard a shotgun and yelling. We're looking for Mr. Dupuis now." The deputy began to rise from his seat.

Jane retained her focus on the man. "If Mrs. Dupuis shot her husband and he died, could she go to jail for murder?"

Deputy Griffin stared hard at Jane, then narrowed his eyes at Maggie and Suzanne. Maggie held her breath. Cast her eyes down to check if her heart was beating out of her chest.

"Just teenager talk." Suzanne's mother flicked her wrist dismissing Jane's question.

"Oh, yes. She could be tried for murder." Deputy Griffin tipped his hat and left.

Silence settled over the breakfast table. Maggie could hardly swallow. Mr. Dupuis must have shot his wife before they arrived last night. Clearly, he'd beaten her. When she shot him, did she kill him?

She gasped. Had she witnessed a murder?

If she told what she saw and Mr. Dupuis was dead, she might have to testify at the poor woman's trial. She couldn't do that. That would be a betrayal.

"Make up your beds," Suzanne's mother called as Maggie, Suzanne, and Jane left the table after finishing breakfast in silence.

Maggie hung her head and followed Jane. Where did Jane get her nerve? Her guts? She looked trouble in the eye and never blinked.

Entering the sleeping porch, Maggie bumped into Jane. Suzanne stood over the bed where Maggie had slept. Neatly folded on the pillow was Maggie's abandoned towel.

"Don't say a word. Let's make up the rest of the room, then get over to Fort Pike. I have an idea," Jane ordered.

They rode their bikes to the old fort and parked. Gathering with her friends beneath the shade of an ancient oak and away from tourists, Maggie squirmed. She wanted to run away. Wanted to wipe Mrs. Dupuis's bloodied face from her mind. Wanted to scream with rage.

By the rocks on the side of the fort, folks fished. Seagulls hovered, hoping for a meal. Maggie shivered at the haunting cries of the birds. The breeze died. She pulled her long hair behind her head and knotted it at her neck.

"We need to make a pact. Right here and now. Help one another. Silence is power." Jane's somberness lit new fear in Maggie.

"But the truth will set you free," Maggie protested.

"Amen," Suzanne whispered.

"That's our pledge. 'Help one another. Truth forever. Amen.' We'll always be honest with each other. We'll look out for one another. We'll be friends forever." Jane pulled out a pocketknife. Maggie recognized it as Mark's. Had she stolen it from him?

With a quick stab, Jane pricked her middle finger on her left hand, then handed the knife to Maggie as a small dot of blood pooled on the end of her finger.

She hesitated.

"No. I'm not doing this. Crazy town. We don't know anything." Suzanne backed away.

"I hope Mr. Dupuis doesn't die, but if he does, as my granny says, 'good riddance.' He *beats* his wife. No adult does anything about it. Our silence will help Mrs. Dupuis. Maybe a gator got him. Maybe no one will ever find him. Unlike Mrs. Dupuis, we have each other. And we *have* to do this for her." Jane could've been giving a sermon.

Convinced of the plan, Maggie followed Jane's lead. A red spot appeared at the end of her finger. She handed the knife to Suzanne.

"Are you in or out?" Jane demanded. "We've been friends forever. But if you're not in this with us…"

Suzanne cast a side-to-side glance. "I'm in. This is not the sort of thing a proper southern belle does." Suzanne, too, pricked her finger.

"And you're proper, like never," Jane insisted. "But if you want to start now, we're 'the Belles' and we'll always be strong and true and faithful friends."

They put their pricked fingers together and rubbed. Small dots of blood turned into a smear.

"There," Jane beamed. "We're blood sisters. And just like the song from that old Bing Crosby Christmas movie with the sisters—the one Momma makes us watch every year—no one will ever come between us."

Maggie nodded. Fear skittered down her spine…

"Maggie?" Jane's voice broke through the memory reel playing in Maggie's head. "You drifted away, yeah? You okay?"

"Just remembering." The past had caught up with the present.

"About our pact?" Suzanne asked. "And that awful night."

"How did you know?"

"A guess."

"As far as I know, they never found Mr. Dupuis," Jane said.

"And Mrs. Dupuis was never prosecuted for…anything."

"She moved away." Suzanne stabbed at a slice of French bread with her fork. "Like someone else we know."

"Are we going to Salem to visit Jane?" Maggie looked from one friend to the other.

"Nooo." Jane said. "I'll try to get some time off and come back. I've been talking with my dad more. I'm ready to see him. No need for you to come to Salem. I'll come back. Honest truth."

Maggie pinned Jane with a glare. Something was off. She stared harder, but no clear *knowing* popped into her head or whispered in her ear.

Yet Jane was hiding something.

Her *knowing* told her that much.

Chapter 7

The next morning, a weak sun formed a hazy outline in the cloud-covered sky. I climbed into Suzanne's car and figured the imagery was a metaphor for my brain. Accounted for, like the sun in the sky was, but fuzzy. Still, I recognized a new vibration thrumming in my chest. Happiness? Hopefulness? Maybe.

"Did you have to pick a flight so damn early?" Suzanne complained, putting the car in reverse. I ignored her grumpiness. She had never been a morning person. Somewhere around ten she came alive, bounced like Tigger and drummed until midnight like the Energizer Bunny. Silently, I chuckled. Sonny Boy would understand the analogy.

Turning in my seat, I waved at Maggie standing in the downstairs doorway. She wildly waved back. A breeze fluttered her robe. She exuded a youthful vibrancy I envied, and I blew her a kiss.

The three of us had melded into old comfortable habits—almost. Our friendship still wobbled on uncertain ground. Leaving now was like plucking out a piece of my heart. My only solace was that I was leaving it with them. And I'd be back.

I turned to face Suzanne. "My schedule isn't too flexible. I have to get back. Beth has to leave town at noon. I can't leave Sonny Boy alone."

Suzanne reached the blacktop and gunned the car's engine, making it fishtail. Something she had loved doing in my old convertible.

"How big is that dog? I mean, I've got a friend whose little dog is litterbox trained. If she can't get home, the dog uses the box, just like a cat."

"He's not that little." At almost five, Sonny Boy would understand the humor of Suzanne's comment.

"How long have you had him?"

"Almost five years."

"Does he fly, or will you drive him down? Because if you drive, I could fly up and drive down with you."

"That won't work. No one would be here with Maggie."

"There is that. I could bring her along."

I hoped my silence was noncommittal. I had to make introductions in the best possible way. In New Orleans.

We drove past our old playground at Fort Pike, heading toward the interstate. Staring out the window, I felt more than saw the memories of my childhood. Suzanne occasionally mumbled, harrumphed, and sighed. I waited for her to speak again, to raise the questions on her mind, but she remained unusually quiet. My unease began to toss about like turbulences toss a plane—one I hadn't boarded yet.

"I'm sorry about Mark." I hoped this time she'd accept my condolences. "I know how close the two of you were. News of the accident must have been a shock. Unlike when my mother died—she'd been sick for over a year."

"Thanks for understanding. While suddenness of his passing is fresh, I doubt my pain is any less than yours was when you lost your momma. You took a strange turn after she died…and I feel like that's when I lost you."

"I guess I did." Looking back on the years, I had only begun to understand the depth of my grief, a tricky emotional maze.

"And I've felt like I needed to take the backseat to Maggie around Mark's passing. After all, she's the widow." Suzanne blew the horn when a car merged too closely into her lane.

I folded and unfolded my hands in my lap. Did I really want to dig deeper into these old wounds? "Yes, but you were Mark's sister far longer than Maggie or I were ever married to him."

"I never understood why you and he couldn't make it work." Suzanne glanced in her mirrors before changing lanes to move away from the elderly woman in an old, boat-size Cadillac. "I know you loved him. I think you still do, which is why you came back. Not for me. Not for Maggie."

Her tone was nearly void of emotion but pricked me all the same. "Suzanne, please don't think that way."

"I loved it when we were sisters-in-law. And it's not that I don't love Maggie. She's great. Always makes a big ordeal out of every family holiday. Playing the hostess with the mostess. She's loved Mark—"

"Since he kissed her on the cheek at her thirteenth birthday party." I smiled at the memory.

"Yeah." Suzanne nodded. "But I think he sealed the deal for her when she discovered he'd followed us to the boathouse to make sure we were safe and retrieved the evidence—her towel. Remember? He became her white knight."

"And for a while, he was mine, too." A deep longing awakened within me. "Certainly there was no one kinder. No one more loyal. I don't think I've ever looked at another man and thought he looked more handsome than Mark."

"Yet, *you* divorced him."

Suzanne's words hit like a breath-stealing sucker punch. I gulped air before answering. "No. I *gave* him his freedom." It didn't matter if Suzanne or anyone understood. I *had* done the right thing. War changed Mark. He needed New Orleans. Needed the security of home, especially after fighting in Afghanistan. Needed grits with eggs for breakfast, seafood gumbo, his Mardi Gras krewe, and a traditional family.

More than he needed me.

It wasn't a matter of love, but survival for him.

"Interesting idea. Maybe someday I'll understand." She turned on the radio, and smooth jazz flowed from the speakers.

I could take a hint, but doubts made me want to defend my decisions more. Maybe someday I'd convince her.

How did I explain that losing my mother to cancer, then my dad to a bottle, set me adrift? The pain and the shame—I didn't know how to deal with those overwhelming emotions. A discussion for another time, another place.

Shifting the conversation, I asked, "Is something going on with you and Grant? You acted so weird when I asked you if you were pregnant."

Suzanne tapped her fingers on the steering wheel. Her mouth flattened into a thin line. Changing lanes again, she appeared to concentrate on maneuvering through the growing Saturday morning traffic. I let silence settle between us.

"I can't possibly be pregnant."

"Okay," I said slowly. "*Can't* and *possibly* don't usually go well together. Do you want to get pregnant? Is there a medical issue?"

"It's called a prenup. I signed it before I married Grant. He has two teenaged children with that shrew of an ex-wife, Kelli, *with an i*." Suzanne readjusted her grip on the steering wheel, her knuckles whitened. "He's older. And especially since he's nearing fifty..."

"Grant doesn't want children with you?" I gawked at Suzanne.

"Not any. Not with anyone. Oh, he's a good father, which requires me to perform as the perfect stepmother. PTA meetings, parent-teacher conferences, soccer games, and ballet lessons. I coordinate with his chauffeur to haul those kids around. Meanwhile, Kelli takes full advantage of it."

"I see." I tried to take it all in. I couldn't imagine Suzanne trading motherhood for marriage.

"So what would Grant do, hypothetically speaking, if you were to tell him you're pregnant?"

Suzanne snorted. "Mr. Board of Directors, hot metrosexual male, would have his attorney call me, tell me I'd violated clause 141.b of the contract, finally he'd ask if I would mind terribly packing my bags and leaving."

"No. Not Grant."

Suzanne glanced at me, then changed lanes again. "Honestly, I don't know what he'd do. But it doesn't matter. *If* I were to get pregnant, I probably wouldn't tell him. I'd just take care of things myself."

Her words stole my breath. Implanted an ugly bleak image. Stunned, I blinked. I glanced out the window to wipe away the mental image lingering in my mind. Had we changed so much in the years since high school? Had we made decisions we wanted to turn away from now?

"Suzanne." I hesitated. My heart raced. "Is there anything *I* can do to help?" I couldn't believe her read on Grant. They had built an enviable life. Surely, she was mistaken. But she lived with him day in and day out. Who was I to doubt her words?

She pulled to the curb at the airport. "Get your tuckus back here as quickly as you can. Before Maggie and I screw up our lives royally."

I threw my arms around her neck and hugged her before getting out of the car. Little did she know how much I needed her and Maggie. That was coming soon.

The uneventful plane ride landed me back at Logan International Airport. From there, I hopped a train. Had it only been twenty-four hours since I left home? The clatter and sway of the ride lulled me. I struggled to stay awake. So tired. It was as though someone pulled the plug on my energy, drained it like water flowing out of a bathtub.

I exited the MBTA in Salem and caught a cab. Pulling out my wallet, I watched the letter I'd hidden from Maggie fall out of my purse. I tucked it back inside determined not to think of its consequence until I'd had more sleep. But sooner or later, I had to deal with it…and all the ramifications it brought.

When the cab pulled to the curb on River Street, I stumbled out, zombie-like. No longer could I survive on two or three hours of sleep. Youth had fully left me behind. Last night, every time I started to doze, Maggie or Suzanne would wake me excited about a memory of something we did back in junior high or high school. Sleep deprived, I would've agreed to almost anything if they'd let me close my eyes for more than a half hour.

"Good morning!" I jumped when the voice sounded behind me, and I caught myself from falling.

"Could you wait a minute?" Beth asked the cabbie. "I need a ride to the station. Let me get her inside, and I'll be right out."

We stepped into the front hall of Mr. Finley's tidy house. Beth had coffee waiting on the hall table.

"You are a godsend." I wrapped my hands around the cup of steaming liquid, and the aroma of coffee lifted me. I only took a sip in hopes of crashing into my bed soon.

"I figured you probably hadn't had much sleep, and from the looks of you, I was right. Wish I could stay and chat—dying to hear about your trip—but got to go. Call me later. Sonny Boy's still asleep in your bed. See you in two weeks."

"Bye." I realized I spoke to a closed door. Beth was already gone.

Gazing about at the place I'd called home for a number of years, my good memories lifted my tired spirit. Staying in Boston after college had been out of the question. It was one thing to work there, but my salary didn't stretch far enough to rent a house on my own. When I searched out a roommate, before Sonny Boy was born, I found Beth. Then she found the historic home on River Street. I appreciated the quaintness and historic charm of Salem, Massachusetts. Far less big-city-lights than Boston.

We lived downstairs. Mr. Finley, the owner and a dear friend, lived upstairs. Over time, we had become a family. Now, I was about to change all of that. I had spoken in uncertain terms about returning home to live. Beth and Mr. Finley both agreed, under the circumstances, it would be best. It saddened me to know I might never see them again. But New Orleans was only a plane ride away.

Shuffling down the hall, I went to peek in on my son. When Sonny Boy was born, Beth, a singer who worked nights, had watched him during the day. Now that he was in school, she picked him up at three p.m., and the two of them entertained each other until I arrived after work. Sonny Boy, thanks to Mr. Finley, called Beth "Sister."

Four years had rocketed past, turning the calendar like an old-fashioned slide show. With Beth and me working with him, Sonny Boy learned to count and identify all his colors almost as soon as he could talk. Mr. Finley took to my son from the time he started to walk and called him Sonny Boy instead of using his name, Christopher Marcus Landry. Sonny Boy called Mr. Finley, "Pops."

Tiptoeing toward my bed, I couldn't wait a minute more to see my angel. Such a physical sleeper, he lay slanted across the bed, his eyes closed, his little mouth open. He looked dead to the world.

Bad choice of words.

He looked restful, peaceful. I itched to run my fingers through his dark brown hair, but I needed sleep. Waking him now would ignite a superhero on steroids for hours—unless Mr. Finley would take him to the park for bit so I could nap.

I peeled off my jacket, then the rest of my clothes, and pulled on an oversized t-shirt. It took me back to the night Suzanne, Maggie, and I witnessed the murder. After Maggie's story of abuse and knowing Mr. Dupuis beat his wife as regular as the mail was delivered had fueled a fierce protectiveness that I'd never known before.

Back then, guilt riddled my conscience over my privileged life. We weren't wealthy like the people living in the Garden District, but I had nice things from Nordstrom. My parents remained together while Suzanne's parents divorced. Maggie had several stepfathers in a row and wore hand-me-downs from her two older sisters. The only new clothing Maggie's mother ever bought her was underwear.

On that long-ago summer night, all the nuances of my life coalesced in the moment of that final gunshot. I couldn't save Mrs. Dupuis, but I could darn well protect my friends. Would at any cost. After all, I'd kept kids from teasing Maggie about her clothes when she moved to the island—created a community closet between the three of us. I tutored Mark in English. I even maneuvered a prom date for Suzanne.

Then life ripped control from me and planted cancer in my mother, eventually whisking her away. Afterward, I drifted away from the Belles. Away from my island. Away from my city.

I desperately needed them now. I had to come clean. About my son. About the money...and about my illness. Time was not on my side.

Moving my sleeping son to one side of the bed, I carefully climbed in. If luck smiled on me, I'd manage sixty winks before he woke demanding blueberry pancakes with toasted pecans. My little man had developed a truly defined palate.

I closed my eyes.

"Momma. Momma. Momma. Wake up." Little hands rubbed at my shoulder. Groggy, I swatted them away. If I pretended to be asleep, maybe Christopher would quiet down. Truth was, bone tired was like being drugged. My body could've been made of lead and my eyes welded together. I resisted rising.

"You're home."

"Christopher Marcus Landry, come snuggle with your momma. Is the house on fire?" I asked, my eyes closed.

"No, Momma, it's not. The smoke alarms are *shhh*." The *shhh* was something I taught him as a toddler.

"Then be a good boy, lie here, and let Momma sleep."

"But Momma, I'm hungry."

I rolled onto my side and pulled covers over my head.

He patted my hidden shoulder. "I'll make breakfast for you." The bed moved when my son climbed down. His little feet pattered out of the room. A cabinet opened in the kitchen. The refrigerator door opened and closed. A loud clatter of metal brought me straight up out of bed.

Turning the corner from the hall into the kitchen, I stopped in the doorway. My son sat on the floor with a box of pancake mix, a carton of half and half, and a bowl. He twirled his hand back and forth like a mixer, making mush of the ingredients.

I started to scold him, but he smiled ear to ear, looking so darn cute.

"Momma, I'm making pancakes."

"Yes, darlin' boy, you are." He tickled my funny bone. There would be no more sleep. What I needed to survive the morning—coffee.

After cleaning Sonny Boy up, I sat him at the table, poured him juice, and finished making breakfast.

"Did you have a good time with Beth?" I flipped slices of ham and pancakes sizzling on the griddle.

"Yep. And Momma, Pops read a book to me at bedtime last night. It was about a family. About what everyone does in a family. Pops said you went to visit your family. Who are they? Are we a family?"

"Of course we are." I turned the pancakes, worried about where the topic would lead us.

"Beth and Pops, too?"

"Yes, darlin' boy, them, too."

"But, Momma?" He climbed down from his chair and came to me, his mouth open slightly, his big eyes searching my face. "Where's my daddy?"

My knees weakened. My hand went to my stomach. Shame made the cells in my body shrivel like heat on shrink-wrap. It would be hard enough to explain to Maggie about Mark's son, but how did I begin to explain to my baby that his father was dead? I had robbed my boy of his father. And no way to make it up to him.

"Momma?"

Getting a grip, I plopped pancakes on the plate. "Here, how about you eat?" My hands trembled, but I managed to set the food on the table. "We'll talk about family later. Okay?"

"Promise?"

I kissed the top of his head, then squatted until we were eye to eye. "Yes, I promise."

Sitting across the table from Sonny Boy, I picked at my food. He rose and knelt on the bench seat, then spooned a big chunk of syrup-laden pancake into his mouth, dripping syrup on his shirt. He chomped like a cow chewing cud. I was a breath away from scolding him but stopped and beamed a dimpled smile. My heart melted the way butter liquefies when heated. His twinkling eyes and shiny disposition were the sunshine of my life. I didn't deserve to be his momma.

When exactly had I become a wimp? I used to fix problems in other people's lives. But when it came to my own, I buried my head in the sand, denial my favorite state.

The Gs chattered, "*Coward. Coward. Coward.*"

The phone rang, and I welcomed a break from my damning thoughts. "Hello?"

"Good morning, Jane," my father said.

"Good morning." I purposely didn't use any term of endearment with Sonny Boy close.

"I don't know if I'm more hurt or disappointed. You were here and didn't call me? I heard from Maggie."

Maggie's tattling? "I can't talk right now, sir. Please don't be disappointed. I'm sorry. I'm working on a plan to return. And I'm going to bring the one I promised you could meet."

"My grandson is in the room, I take it."

"Yes, sir. Being a clown with pancakes."

"I can't wait to see that sight. I'm glad you finally trusted me enough to tell me about him. And Jane...I've been sober for nine months now." His hope-charged baritone voice conveyed commitment and conviction. But could I truly trust that?

"I'll keep my promise. You'll meet soon enough. I need to arrange some details."

"I love you, Jane. We've lost a lot of time, but I've always loved you."

Choked by emotion, I barely eked out, "I love you, too."

I put the phone back on its stand and smiled big at my son, hoping he wouldn't see my tears. I had to take action. He deserved the most secure childhood I could provide, including a grandfather, an aunt, and a step-mother... Despite my past desire to keep him all to myself, fate's sardonic sense of humor was a sharp knife.

Monday arrived too soon. I hopped a train to work. It was a welcome relief to the weekend when my brain had freewheeled on a hamster wheel. I was due an Olympic Gold for speed and cycles per second. I guess the Gs were good for something.

I found a seat, put my earbuds in, and considered the two plans I'd determined to be the best way to break the 'Sonny Boy' news to Maggie and Suzanne.

Plan A: Take him home to meet them. Let them fall in love with him. They wouldn't be able to resist my boy. After that, go with the flow and find the right time to tell them the details of his parentage—then fall on the *mea culpa* sword.

Plan B: Present them with a timeline, segue into the important dates—when Suzanne and Grant got married, when Mark came to visit me, when Maggie got engaged. When Sonny Boy was born. But that plan was a last resort. My bad behavior and bad choices could color their opinion about my son. I couldn't allow that to happen. B would be utilized only if A failed.

I waved at Kara after she boarded the train. Often we chatted during our trek to the city, but we had agreed ear buds meant silence. She took a seat next to me, squeezed my hand, and put her ear buds in, too.

Before I could take action on my plan, I needed a green light from my boss. She allowed others to telecommute from home—she couldn't discriminate against me. If I worked remotely and stayed with Suzanne until I could find a place of my own, my routine could continue. The same daily schedule would be good for my son. Give him stability and a sense of security. Plus, Sonny Boy might be a good influence on Grant—in case Suzanne was pregnant.

And in New Orleans, I'd have the support I needed to face the white coats and stethoscopes.

Devastating. That's how the doctor's news hit me. I thought I had beat the odds by having a hysterectomy after Christopher was born. It hadn't kept the Big C monster away.

My Boston doctor urged me to take serious action immediately. Not to delay. That gave me the best chance of Passing Go and Collecting Two-Hundred Dollars—maybe. He confessed it wouldn't be an easy journey. He didn't like the odds. This cancer was a Goliath.

My mother died from Big C complications. It didn't take a medical genius to make a Sherlock-Holmes deduction. The doctor made what I was facing sound like a quest to find the sword in the stone, but in the end, the chances of success would be…remote. I respected his education, his experience, and bet his medical malpractice insurance required him to paint an accurate picture for patients. I'd been down this path with my mother. Had my own waltz with it once. Treatment was paint by numbers. And I didn't want to paint anymore.

Truthfully, thinking about my fate was like looking into a crystal ball and seeing only a vast expanse of black. I wanted to live and love. I wanted to run to the end of the earth, open my arms and jump. I wanted to experience the adrenaline rush of the mile markers in Christopher's life.

I didn't want drips or drugs or draining of my energy.

My internal clock was ticking, ticking, ticking.

And before the alarm blared, I had to secure a future for my son. He would not go through what I went through with Momma—years of hoping, praying, battling, only to have the cure kill her.

I wanted to be me—everyday momma—with him, for him, for as long as possible.

I did not want him to stand behind the fence and watch me climb on the cancer carousel. I did not want him to pray to God to take me to rid me of pain. I did not want him to be a long-suffering bystander.

I wanted to go out with dignity. I wanted to spare him the torture I'd endured. For that, he would need his Auntie Suzanne. His stepmother Maggie. His grandfather Landry. I intended to give Christopher a loving southern family.

It wasn't lost on me that I'd deprived him of that very thing.

How would my father handle the news of my sickness? Momma's death had hit him hard. He tried hiding his drinking problem. However, at night, he had smelled like a booze bottle, and I hated him for it. Six years ago, he came to visit me in Boston. He wanted a pub crawl—to experience the "Cheers" he'd seen on TV. We never made it beyond the first establishment. I hailed a cab to get us home. I couldn't suffer the humiliation of my father crawling like an animal on his hands and knees.

I needed him sober now. Could I count on him once he heard my news? Or would history crawl again?

Exiting the train, I pulled my blazer closed and buttoned it. In the last weeks, spring weather had turned cool overnight. A sharp contrast to the sticky humidity of New Orleans. I rehearsed my speech to my boss as I walked, the one I'd practiced at home in the mirror.

Squaring my shoulders, slightly lifting my chin, I allowed confidence to settle over me.

I turned the corner. My boss appeared up ahead.

"Nora, wait up. I need a minute of your time." I sprinted to catch up with her on the way into the building.

"Now is as good as any, what's on your mind, Landry?"

"I have a proposition for you." I tried not to show I was out of breath. "Since you allow Justin, Abbey, and Margaret to work from home, and that's been a success, I'd like to do the same. I need to be back in Louisiana. I would like to work remotely. I'll incur any extra costs."

"No."

Her quick response dazed me. "But, why?"

"Well, since it's my company, because I said so should be enough, however, that's not the reason."

"Not the reason?"

"You're too valuable. Abbey is taking vacation in a month. Justin barely gets his work done. I'm thinking of pulling him back in. Margaret—"

"Wait. All the data is fine, but doesn't answer my question."

"I told you, you're too valuable. Since you're pressing and I see you're upset, I'll be announcing your job change. You'll be running things while I'm in France. You're the new operational manager. It comes with a nice raise."

At any other time, her offer would've had me cartwheeling down the hall. But my days of hiking my career up another rung on the corporate ladder were over. I had to work remotely. Had to. "I have family business in need of attention. I must be there in order to get it handled."

"Fine."

"Fine, what?" My intuitiveness failed me.

"Starting next week, take two weeks of vacation. Then come back. I'll see you in the planning meeting at nine."

I stopped at my office. Nora continued down the hall. The clack of her heels against the marble floor echoed, leaving me with an anxious echo in my heart.

Two weeks? Not enough time. Forgiveness wouldn't come from father and friends so quickly. And I had to consider a treatment plan…

Two weeks.

Two weeks.

Two weeks.

I had to find a way to make it work.

Or as the saying goes, die trying.

Chapter 8 – Maggie & Suzanne

"**I**'m only doing this because I love you, Suz." *And because I need Jane.*

Maggie zipped up her energy more. Tourists swarmed Canal Street. Rarely did she venture into crowds unless music was involved. Today was an exception.

"And I love you back." Suz's I'm-being-patient-with-you smile didn't make her feel better. "We need the city to give us inspiration. No better way than being a tourist."

Maggie had agreed to lunch on a riverboat cruise with the hope of seeing the city with fresh eyes, to gather inspiration, and to hatch a plan to entice Jane—who was arriving in twenty-four hours with her little dog, Sonny Boy—to stay. At least if she had it her way.

Drawing a long, slow deep breath, she drew in the auras of what made New Orleans wonderful. Fun. Food. Festivals. Every street dripped with history, BK *and* PK.

But crowds bombarded her with fractured messages. The larger the crowd, the more messages splashed against her like splatter art made at the fair. Information flooded her senses until she was dizzy. It had taken years for her to learn to protect herself from sensory overload. Still, there was no guarantee against slimy energy slipping past her barriers.

She and Suzanne headed for the riverboat landing. A man approached them. A Mr. Moneybags in his crispy white shirt, artsy red tie, diamond cuff links, and Cartier sunglasses. A sport coat, hooked on his finger over his shoulder, dangled behind his back. When they were within a few steps of him, he smiled. Either his genes gave him perfect, straight white teeth *or* he'd paid a cosmetic dentist a lot of money. He was sex on legs.

His eyes locked on Suz. Lust radiated off him. Maggie flinched at the intensity.

"Men are predictable. Doesn't matter the packaging." Maggie huffed. Construction worker. Bus driver. Businessman. Underneath, mostly they were all the same. Primal and lustful. But Mark had been different.

Suzanne continued her pace. The only recognition she gave the guy was a slight lift of her chin. Her Versace sunglasses hid her eyes. She always drew attention. Today was just more of the same with her in black straight-leg jeans, white deep v-neck shell, and a soft pink Chanel blazer. Shoes to match. Suz had studied fashion design after high school and excelled.

Maggie *humphed*. "An incorrigible flirt is what you are."

"You had your ways of making Mark happy. Keeping him interested. I have mine with Grant. I adore my husband. I make sure he adores only me. Knowing that other men find me attractive keeps me on my toes."

A *knowing* whispered in Maggie's ears. *Compensation for father rejection.*

Now wasn't the time or place to broach *that*. She hadn't considered the damage Suzanne's father had done by abandoning his kids. They always seemed well-adjusted, but who wouldn't be compared to *her*. Maggie hadn't seen the senior Mr. Maucele since her and Mark's wedding—and even then, his attendance was a surprise.

"Do you ever get tired of men staring?" she asked.

Suzanne's snort was part giggle. "You're the beautiful one. Flowing auburn hair. Impish smile. Flashing eyes. And that porcelain skin. You're angelic and witchy, too, like Glinda, the Good Witch of the South. People gravitate to you."

"They don't see me. Subconsciously, they feel my energy, think I'm a safe harbor and can make their life better."

"There—that's witchy." Suz's stride never missed a step.

A passing streetcar screeched to a stop. Maggie shuddered at the metal-on-metal grinding. "That sound hurts my heart."

Suz stopped, pulled off her sunglasses, placing her hand on Maggie's shoulder. "I'm sorry. I know this is hard for you, but how do we take that ugly sound and turn it around—make it a positive for Jane? That screech is one of the sounds of this city."

Suz had a point. The streetcar screech was as iconic to New Orleans as light saber sounds were to Star Wars.

"But why are we walking? Why not take the streetcar?"

"When was the last time you experienced Canal? The shops. The people. The tourists. The pulse."

Maggie followed Suzanne when she started walking again. She looked around and up at a tall hotel on the other side of the street. As her eyes scanned each floor, she caught snippets of whispers. The more she lifted her gaze, the louder the whispers. Whispers about music, money, sex, and booze.

She looked beyond the roofline to the sky. Focused there. The noise evaporated. "I stick to the heart of the Quarter or Magazine Street. If you don't want to ride the streetcar, we could take a bus around the city."

Suzanne stopped. "Bus?"

"Too unglamorous for you?"

"Not the point. *Jane* won't ride a bus."

"She might. No one would expect *you* to climb aboard. You have your trophy-wife image down to a science."

Suzanne shrugged one shoulder. "Don't judge. I dress for success."

Maggie sighed, afraid to hear that explanation. "What kind of success? We're hiking in heels. Does Jane even own any?"

"Well, Glinda, Good Witch of the South, you forgot your magic wand. Without it, we walk. This is New Orleans PK. It's changed. A lot."

Maggie nudged Suzanne with her elbow. "I hate it when you call me cutesy nicknames."

"I know. That's why I do it. You're so easy to tease." Suzanne chuckled and opened her arms. "See what our city has to offer." She pointed to the palm trees in the neutral ground lining Canal Street. At night each lit with magical white lights. "And hear the languages. Standing on a street corner is like being at the UN. Sniff and your nose is stimulated by aromas."

"You mean the stinky garbage smell that comes with the heat of June?" Maggie crinkled her nose.

"More like the smell of baking French bread, frying beignets, and daiquiri shops. Let's go. Think about the city from Jane's perspective."

Keeping a steady pace, Maggie and Suzanne skirted a group of people clustered near a corner preacher standing on a milk crate. He waved a Bible, hurled threats about sin and eternal damnation. Maggie's ears tuned in to the scuffing of leather soles against concrete. She turned around and bumped into Mr. Money. Suz grabbed her arm and pulled her aside. Was he following them?

"Excuse me, ladies. I'm looking for a good place to eat. Could either of you point me in the right direction?"

Suzanne slid her sunglasses halfway down her nose and raised an eyebrow. Maggie's stomach soured when Mr. Money lifted his sunglasses, too. His gaze rested on Suz's cleavage.

"Why, honey"—Suzanne tossed her golden hair—"this is New Orleans." Her voice was throaty and sexy. "There's not a bad place in this city to eat."

Mr. Money sidled next to Suzanne. Maggie watched his aura heat up. It was as red as his fancy silk tie. She took two steps away to escape the uncomfortable energy.

The man reached for Suz's shoulder. She flipped him *the* look, then continued down the street, leaving Maggie rushing to catch up. Her heart thumped double time, and not because of the short jog.

"See what I mean? You attract men like ants to pralines at a picnic."

"No matter. There's only one man for me."

"And does that *man* have any suggestions about a job for Jane? Will his connections get her an interview at the college? Or a job at the bank?"

"He says he's working on something. He'll tell me once he's sure."

Maggie's thoughts swirled. Jane was a leader. Sharp critical thinker. Kind. And now, oh-so proper. She'd lost some of her *joie de vivre*. There wasn't a magazine company good enough for her talent and credentials in New Orleans. What were they going to do?

Pressure built in Maggie's chest. The more she searched for an answer, the more the pressure grew. If she didn't find an answer, she just might pop.

Crossing Convention Center Boulevard, they made their way to the riverboat landing. A calliope sounded on the next boat over. Music always soothed her, notes appearing on a page in her mind. A welcome distraction. Maggie's unease settled a bit. She blew out a deep breath.

"I don't want to count on Grant for this." Clearly, Suzanne had been thinking about Jane's situation, too. "He doesn't know Jane like we do. We'll come up with a plan. What does she need? What do most people need? A house, a job, and a family. That's the American Dream."

"But Jane has always been different. She's principled. Savior of lost souls." Maggie looped her arm through Suzanne's.

"She. Needs. Us." Suzanne's voice hitched with recognition. "As much as we need her." That wisdom Maggie understood to be true.

"Problem is, she doesn't know how to accept help from anyone."

"A blessing and a curse." Maggie nodded.

After boarding the riverboat, she sat across a table from Suzanne. The big boat's red paddle wheel churned. Tourists gathered around, posing for pictures with paddles dipping and scooping the muddy Mississippi River. Few knew that big diesel engines did the work—the paddles were just for show.

Maggie mused. Like the paddle wheel, life went round and round and round. Each scoop an experience shaping the character and heart of a soul. What shaping experiences had changed Jane?

Suzanne scanned the mostly out-of-towners in the dining room filled to half capacity. Sensitive about Maggie's discomfort with crowds, she selected an inside table away from the mist and roar of the paddle wheel, away from the throng of sneaker-wearing, oversized-bag carrying, and loud-flower-Hawaiian-print shirts wearing tourists. A table with a window view of the city they both loved. Sitting, she said a silent prayer that Maggie's good mood would continue, and they wouldn't have a meltdown until the boat had docked again.

"Hello, ladies." A waitress appeared beside their table. "May I take your orders?"

"Unsweetened tea and shrimp salad." Suzanne removed her sunglasses and placed them on the table. "White balsamic vinaigrette on the side."

"The same, please." Maggie relinquished her menu to the young woman.

"Have *you* thought of any ideas to keep Jane here?" Suzanne tapped Maggie's hand after the waitress departed. "Your ideas are usually not uninspiring."

Maggie sighed. "Actually, I've avoided thinking about it. It makes my heart ache. If she doesn't stay… I can't go there. But I'm not ready to forgive her for everything. I know, I know, I said I did, but…thinking about the situation makes me jumpy, like being barefoot on hot cement. With each new hop, you think you've landed in a comfortable place, but after a second, you know you're not."

"I'm puzzled." Suzanne steepled her fingers together. Glancing around, she made sure no one was close enough to overhear their conversation. "You take such stock in your religion. Isn't it better to forgive?"

"It's your religion, too," Maggie pointed out.

"I'm Catholic by birth—inescapable in my family—and then commu-nion. Haven't been to any church since you and Mark married. But Maggie, there's no doubt in you. You live your faith comfortably. Me, I question everything. Don't trust anything."

"Wrong. You trust Grant."

Taken aback by Maggie's words, until recently, she would've agreed. Now she wasn't so sure. What *would* he do if her suspicions about a pregnancy were confirmed? She couldn't think about that right now. "So this grudge you carry must be heavy, like an anchor for a cargo ship. Jane's been gone for years."

"And now she's back. I'm just supposed to...do what?"

Suzanne lifted one shoulder, next the other, for a long shrug. She hadn't planned this lunch to fight. They'd agreed, after Jane's phone call about her return trip, to turn her two-week vacation into a permanent relocation.

"You could forgive, and not forget."

Maggie played a key role in their cause. After all, Jane had elected herself Maggie's protector when they were growing up. Suzanne hated to admit it, at times jealousy ate at her over that relationship. But she never doubted Jane's loyalty. Even now, she believed Jane would come through.

Time had changed each of them. Fate brought them together again. Mark was dead. Maggie needed help. And Suzanne needed Jane to stand by her as she faced an uncertain future.

"I have forgiven her. It's just that not forgetting is like a loose tooth. It's irritating."

Suzanne sighed. *Then pull the damn thing and get on with it.*

Maggie cast her glance down and lined up her flatware with the edge of the white linen-clad table, perfecting the tablescape. It had to torment her—her love and hate of Jane.

The waitress stopped at their table and slid shrimp salads in front of them. "Enjoy." The woman smiled, placing a bottle with vinaigrette on the table.

Maggie poured dressing over her salad. Suz caught a whiff and fanned her hand near her nose.

"Oh, God." She drew back from the plate.

"What's wrong?" Maggie asked.

"The smell. Awful."

Maggie sniffed. "It's fine. Are you okay?"

"My stomach's going round and round. More than that paddle wheel." She shoved her plate aside.

Maggie took a scoop of Suzanne's salad and tasted it. "Nothing wrong. Are you coming down with something?"

"Of course not." Her stomach turned over again. "Must be excitement over Jane's upcoming visit. Meeting her little dog." She pushed the plate farther to Maggie's side of the table.

Maggie pushed it back. "You need to eat."

"Not that." Nausea welled.

"Flag the waitress and order something else."

"In a minute." Suzanne sipped tea and nibbled on a cracker. "Back to Jane." Suzanne had to invoke mind over matter. If she didn't think she was sick, she wouldn't be.

Maggie moved the offending salad to the far corner of the table and took a bite of her own. "I can't remember why, but I'm sure there's a logical reason Jane was afraid of dogs. Seems like a lot of devotion to bring the animal with her." She continued eating. "We could dognap and hide the puppy to keep her here."

"A dog bit her when she was young."

"Really? But now she has a dog. Strange."

"Not everything in life is logical. Take those *knowings* you have for example." Suzanne raised her eyebrows at Maggie.

"Last night, I had one about *you*. But I've been too preoccupied with other things to think about it."

"What? Don't make me make you. Tell me." Suzanne placed her napkin over the plate of shrimp salad hoping to finally convince her mind, and then her stomach, she was fine.

Maggie sipped her tea. Suzanne waited impatiently.

"I was sleeping and heard the giggle of a little boy. It came from the room down the hall at your house. Only, as I became more conscious of the dream, I wasn't dreaming."

"I'm confused." Suzanne scrunched her nose.

"I heard you talking to a little boy. Not your child, though that came next—"

"Maggie, please. Straight talk."

"I know you're going to have a little boy in your future that's somehow related to you. He'll be a big part of your life. But, he's not your child. And this isn't Grant's son."

Suzanne shook her head. How was that even possible? Her only brother was dead. Was a long-lost cousin going to appear?

"Wait. Rewind. What did you mean, 'not your child, though that came next'? What are you saying?"

"I don't decipher information. I just pass on messages I receive." Maggie scooped up a bite of salad and chewed. Satisfaction settled on her face. A definite change from her earlier mood. Then she winked conspiratorially. "There's going to be a baby in your life."

"No. No. No." Suzanne shook her head. "For a million reasons. No."

Maggie's smile drooped. "A baby is a gift."

"You're sounding Catholic and serious and emphatic, like Jane." Suzanne broke a saltine cracker and popped half into her mouth. Nausea. Irritation. Fear. She needed a drink.

"Just be forewarned."

"Maggie," Suzanne threatened. "What?"

"Well, I was in the dream, too. Jane and I were helping you with the baby. Those kinds of *knowings* are...risky. The truth is buried within the message. I don't ever receive clear signals whenever I'm involved."

"You're saying there's a little boy in my future along with a baby?"

Maggie shrugged. "Maybe?"

The waitress arrived to clear their plates. "You didn't like the salad?"

"Not hungry." Suzanne tapped her glass. "But I'll take more tea." The woman refilled her glass and presented a dessert menu. Maggie took a quick perusal with an I'll-have-some-if-you-will look.

"I don't dare eat sweets," Suzanne told her. "But you have something."

"Thank you, but no." Maggie handed the menu back to the waitress.

"Sure I can't tempt you with bread pudding? Bourbon sauce. Toasted pecans."

Maggie licked her lips. She was salivating over the suggestion, but she shook her head.

"Can we move on now?" Suzanne pulled a small notepad from her purse. "I've made a list of Jane's competencies, besides being a magazine editor. Take a look at the list. What would you think about her running our new spa? Making her a business partner?"

"I can't imagine she would enjoy working *for* us."

"She wouldn't. It would be an *equal* partnership."

"Suzanne, just where do you think she's going to get money to invest in the business? You know Jane, she's got pride, probably more than all the encyclopedic knowledge in that brain of hers. She won't take charity, so we can't just give her the money."

"We offer her a job—one she's qualified to do. Work out the rest of the details later."

"No. 'That dog won't hunt,' as Mark would say. You know how she was raised. Her father's voice will be ringing in her ears. 'Neither a lender or a borrower be' was one of the tenets of life he instilled in her, and in me."

"Too bad he didn't have a rule about drinking," Suzanne muttered, casting her gaze at the river.

"I heard that. Mr. Landry is dear to me. A father, more than any of mine. His *drinking* is an illness." Maggie briefly squinted, her mouth tightened. "Besides, he's not drinking anymore."

"Hmm, does Jane know he gave you away at your wedding? To the same man he gave her away to? There's irony in there somewhere. Lost on me."

"Is that a threat of some sort? It's not like it was a secret. She was invited to the wedding. Anyway, I will agree Jane would make a great business partner. She's got brains for keeping the books, running things, and doing all the duties that keeps a business going—securing business licenses, paying taxes, advertising. She'd be much better than I am at that."

"We're in agreement. Jane's our new business partner. Now we just have to appear broken and helpless without her support. She'll feel compelled to take the job. She's good at rescuing. I'll even bet the dog is a rescue mutt."

The riverboat groaned, the sound of large engines vibrating as the boat prepared to dock. Suzanne rose from her chair and slid her sunglasses on her face. Maggie followed.

They stepped out into the warming afternoon, moist with humidity. Suzanne gripped the metal handrail. Her stomach sloshed.

"Suzanne? You're pale." Maggie took her hand. "We need a cab. You don't look good."

"I'm fine."

"I don't know..."

"I'm fine." She descended on the gangplank to disembark from the riverboat.

I'm fine. I'm fine. I'm fine. Mind over matter.

Once on land, Suzanne's stomach settled. Maybe she just needed solid ground under her.

"Suz, about Jane. I've missed her. If I take Mark out of the equation, there would be no lingering problems."

Suzanne draped her arm over Maggie's shoulder. "Why is it with us women, where there's a problem, a man's involved?" Mr. Dupuis's face appeared in her mind. She could taste the tinny flavor of fear she'd felt at thirteen when the police questioned her several times after the shooting. She'd withstood the intimidation but not without crossing her legs and silently praying not to pee her pants. After that, she vowed never to show fear to a man, any man. Women had to stick together. That's why the sisterhood was so important. Together with Maggie and Jane, she could conquer anything.

The vow she'd made had served her well, kept her from falling for just any guy. In high school. In college. In business. Until Grant.

When she fell, it was off a cliff so high, she'd never landed.

The exhilaration of loving him, sharing a life, made all the little day-to-day problems disappear. Grant made the moon rise and the sun set every day of her life. But now? If her suspicions were confirmed?

Yes, a man was the root of her problem.

Maggie stopped at the corner as the streetcar approached. "If you're sure you're feeling up to it, let's go to the spa and inspect the developments. If things continue on schedule, it won't be a stretch to tell Jane we need her. We'll open on schedule."

"Even if it's going great, a little white lie wouldn't hurt to play on Jane's sympathy."

"Yes, but"—Maggie shook her head—"it's always better to tell the truth. If you're honest up front, then you won't look like a fool—because you always get caught telling stories. It's a when situation because we *all* get caught in the end."

Chapter 9

I couldn't smile any wider. My heart raced with joy like a runner racing to the top of a mountain to claim victory. "Thank you, Tom, for the ride to the airport."

"Gave this old man something to do." He smiled and kept his eyes straight ahead on the road.

"Momma, I'm gonna fly on one of those?" Sonny Boy's eyes widened and rounded and he pointed to a plane taking flight, lifting higher into blue sky.

"Yes, little man, you are."

"You're going to mind your mother, right?" Tom Finley asked, turning the car into the entrance of Logan Airport.

"Yes, sir." Sonny Boy snapped his hand beside his forehead in salute.

"Thank you, Tom, for all of your help." I gazed at my son in the backseat beside me. All mothers thought their children were wonderful. But did other mother's children keep them in stitches? My little guy was growing up fast and funny. Would Maggie and Suzanne find him amusing? Would my father love him unconditionally?

Uncertainty tried gnawing my gut, but happiness shoved it away. Now that I'd reconnected with my friends, I selfishly wanted everything to be as it was when we were kids. Solid. Safe. Sincere. I needed them.

Tom pulled the car to a stop by the curb. I reached across and unbuckled Sonny Boy from his car seat. Tom came around, opened the door on the passenger side, and Sonny Boy flung out his arms to be picked up.

"I want my backpack," Sonny Boy said the moment his feet touched down. He tap-danced on the sidewalk. I ignored him while gathering our things from inside the car.

"I want my backpack! I want my backpack!"

Tom opened the latch to the car's trunk, pulled out a blue pack, and held it up as though holding a smelly fish. "I wonder who this belongs to?"

"Me! Sonny Boy."

"This is yours?"

"Yeah."

"Yes, sir," I corrected. My son needed solid southern manners. I had no one to blame but myself for his lacking. With help from Maggie and Suzanne and my father, maybe Sonny Boy would grow up polite as well as funny.

"Yes, sir." Sonny Boy hung his head as if truly repentant. "It's mine." He didn't fool me for a minute with his sad puppy-dog eyes. "May I have it?"

"Let me help you put it on." Tom's arthritic fingers held the pack's straps apart. Sonny Boy looked up at him, grinning. "Thank you very much," he shouted over the noise of plane engines, then slid his arm in place and pulled the backpack on properly.

I kissed Tom's cheek. "We'll see you soon."

"I have a birthday in three weeks!" Sonny Boy's the-world-is-my-oyster smile spread wide across his face.

These little moments I savored most, tucking them away in my heart, hoping to carry them with me forever. And ever. And ever.

"You do. I'll see you then." Tom waved goodbye.

Sonny Boy ran to him, his arms grasping the older man's legs. "I miss you, Pops."

"I'll miss you, too."

I hoisted a heavy tote bag onto my shoulder. "Let's go have an adventure. Take my hand." I grasped Sonny Boy's hand and grabbed the car seat.

"This is your first plane ride. You are going to have so much fun when we get to New Orleans." I used the native pronunciation— Nyou Ahhlyns. My accent hadn't totally disappeared. I'd camouflaged it. Learned to do it in college after my southern speak pegged me as an outsider. By the time I finished school, I could've broadcasted the evening news sounding like a Connecticut Yankee. Now it felt good to let go of the practiced way of speaking and slip into my drawl.

"Why are we going to Nyou Ahhlyns? Tell me again."

I laughed and ruffled his hair. My northern-born boy could grow up with southern sensibilities. But that would take more than two weeks. "Well, remember how Mr. Finley read you that book about family?"

"Yeah. I like it when Pops reads to me."

"Yes, ma'am," I corrected. "You and I have family there."

Sonny Boy scowled. "How come? I thought our family was in Salem. Pops says our family lives in Salem's Mc...Intyre."

"Historic McIntyre District. That's true, but that's not where Momma grew up. I'm taking you to see all the places I love in the city where I was born. Your grandfather is there. So are your aunties. Let's get on the plane."

"Okay."

I loved how he lived in the present. I needed to take a page from his book. Now was all I had.

Suzanne paced the hallway at the airport. Hip-hop played on someone's phone and competed with the piped-in airport music.

Someone needs to give that kid a headset. Give everyone a rest from that racket.

"The flight from Atlanta was delayed." Maggie returned from checking on incoming flights. "A storm grounded planes until the weather passed."

"But they're in the air now?" Suzanne asked.

"Yes."

"I need a drink, Maggie. I can't believe she's coming. Even if for only two weeks. And she's bringing... I can't wait to see this dog. I mean, Sonny Boy?"

"It's not yet noon, and you want a drink? I made a new rule when I woke up this morning. No drinking until after five p.m. How about food instead?"

"Good rule. I don't want a lush for a sister-in-law."

Maggie turned her wedding band on her finger as if to confirm her connection to the Maucele family. Earlier, on their way inside the airport, a group of obviously out-of-town businessmen had run into each other as they passed. Maggie's elegant, flowing sundress drew appreciative stares. She'd blushed as pink as her bubblegum-pink colored toenails.

"Are you flirting?" Suzanne had demanded.

Horror had spread across Maggie's face. "How could you say such a thing? I'm a grieving widow."

It didn't take much to get a rise out of Maggie. Suzanne sighed. She doubted Maggie would ever even consider another man in her life. She would always be Maggie Maucele, though Mark wouldn't want that for her.

"I hate that you think I'm a lush. Mark introduced me to Wild Turkey 101 and Coke. The only time I've *ever* had more than one was at Eddie's with you and Jane. Maybe I'll join you on your health kick and stop drinking altogether. Remember, I'm still Mrs. Maucele."

"Of course, you are." She patted Maggie's arm. "And we'll both be non-alcoholic now. Whatever I order, I bless it a cocktail with vodka."

"You're the most irreverent person I know."

Suzanne linked her arm through Maggie's. They continued through the main concourse in search of a restaurant, dodging travelers arriving in New Orleans. "Aww, thanks. It's an old Maucele family tradition. And you're one, so this story is part of your history, too. My dad told Mark and me the Great Depression story about when our grandfather was a boy.

"During Lent, Great-granddaddy welcomed the parish priest into the house. Supper—roasted duck—on the table. The priest started to leave, but Great-granddaddy wouldn't let him go—the priest might not eat that night if he didn't share their food. He asked the priest to say grace. Great-grandmother nearly passed out—her serving red meat on a Friday during Lent."

Maggie rolled her eyes. "Your father ever kiss the Blarney Stone?"

"The priest bowed his head. Asked the Lord to bless the fish."

"Wait, you said it was duck." Maggie scrunched her nose as if she smelled a foul fowl.

"There's a moral to this Maucele story."

Maggie frowned. "What?"

"You can do anything…if you bless it first."

Maggie slapped at Suzanne's shoulder. "You lie. That can't be true. No priest would ever do that."

"And yet, he did. That's exactly what our dad told us."

"Why are we still friends? Exaggeration is one thing. Lying is something entirely different. And about a priest."

Suzanne ignored Maggie's judgy words and walked into a restaurant. "Two, please."

If any of us knows about lying, Maggie certainly does.

The hostess showed them to a table. Sounds of Satchmo's horn played in the background.

"Mark told outrageous stories." Maggie jerked open the menu. "Teased me all the time."

Suzanne gently pushed Maggie's menu down. "Honey, they're just family stories. Part of Daddy's ways. Even if he wasn't much of a daddy."

"I had hoped I might give him a reason to change."

"Change?" Suzanne prompted Maggie to continue, but she looked away.

Did Maggie think to somehow redeem the elder Mr. Maucele? The one who never saw his son play high school football. The one who never watched his daughter cheer. The one who hadn't attended her wedding.

When the waitress returned, Maggie ordered a po'boy fully dressed and sweet tea. Suzanne asked for a salad with grilled chicken. "And add a strawberry daiquiri, minus the alcohol part. I've given alcohol up for Lent."

"Sure thing." The waitress left the table chuckling.

Maggie glared. "You know good and well Lent is over."

"But it sounded good. And she laughed."

After their food arrived, they ate. Suzanne broke the silence. "I think I want bread pudding or pecan pie for dessert."

"Since when did you hatch a sweet tooth?"

Suzanne changed the subject. "Maggie, why haven't you been back to your house in Slidell? You haven't been since the day Mark died."

Maggie lowered her chin, casting a glance to the diners at the next table. "Their bread pudding looks good." She turned and tried to catch the server's eye. "Let's get you that dessert."

"You can't put me off forever. I have keys to your house, remember, in case of an emergency?"

"I don't want to go there. I don't *have* to go there. I have, thanks to you and Jane, good memories at the camp. I'm able to sleep there."

"But *why* don't you want to go back to your house in Slidell? Would you like Jane and me to help you deal with Mark's clothes and other stuff?"

Suzanne hated it when Maggie's eyes pooled with tears. "No. Mark's only been gone for a little while. Maybe that's enough time for you to throw out your memories of him, but not me. You had lots of boyfriends before Grant. Jane, well, don't know about her love life after Mark. My heart belonged to only one boy. Only one man. Mark Christopher Maucele."

Maggie rose and walked out.

Suzanne's heart lurched over the pain she'd caused one of her dearest friends. Maggie had managed to hold on to her innocent delight of life despite childhood abuse. She'd grown into a fine woman.

"Suzanne, open mouth, insert foot," she muttered and flagged the waitress to remove her plate.

Maggie returned a few minutes later. Fresh lipstick. A smile so sweet that Scarlett O'Hara would hate her. "Let's go get the third member of our group." She slid a ten-dollar tip under the plate for the waitress.

Suzanne paid the bill. She'd been wrong to push Maggie. She missed Mark desperately, too. What about Jane? Did she miss Mark, too?

"Sonny Boy, I am so proud of you. You were a perfect little gentleman on the plane." I helped my son with his backpack when we arrived at the luggage carousel. "Now, let's sit you over there. You're in charge of the car seat. Don't let anyone take it. And sit so you can see me all the time. Understand?"

The boy nodded, sat on the bench holding tight to the top part of the car seat, and glanced from side to side as if making sure no car-seat thieves lurked. His seriousness let me know he understood this was a time to listen and obey instructions.

I walked ten feet to the carousel. Most of the other passengers had gathered their luggage and gone. I purposely waited until the place was empty so I could keep one eye on Sonny Boy at all times.

"Jane!" Two voices called out. Suzanne and Maggie headed my way. They looked ready for Derby Day in Kentucky. Summer dresses. White high heels. Suzanne wore diamonds: ring, earrings, and bracelet.

My childhood friends were socialites?

I imagined Maggie in her wide-brimmed hat with a pink satin ribbon taking tea at Oak Alley. If ever there were a true Southern belle, Maggie fit the bill.

Side by side with my beautiful friends, I would be Plain Jane with watery blue eyes and short brown hair.

At least I had hair again.

"Jane!" Maggie and Suzanne cried in unison. They scurried to me and wrapped me in a group hug. A few passersby clapped at our reunion. All the while, I had one eye trained on my boy.

"Let me look at you." Maggie held my hand and made me twirl.

"I've only been gone a week."

"But we both know life changes at the drop of a pin." She said it matter-of-factly, as though she hadn't been a victim of it.

"Where's the critter?" Suzanne looked around.

I sighed an it's-time-for-a-reckoning sigh. "Don't be too mad at me. I am aware I have lots of explaining to do. But"—I paused when they eyed me curiously—"just remember, *I* never said Sonny Boy was a dog."

Maggie gasped. "A cat can't bark."

I shrugged and turtled my neck, trying to pull my head inside my body. "He's more like a short, two-legged human-boy child."

At that moment, Sonny Boy ran to me. He wrapped his short arms around my legs. Then he reached for Maggie and Suzanne. "Momma? This our family now?"

Maggie and Suzanne both looked down. Disbelief flashed on their faces. Wide round eyes. Dragging dropped jaws. Not a good socialite look.

"Oh.My.God." cried Maggie. "A little boy." To my ears, Maggie sounded as though she spoke of a rare animal at the zoo.

"Oh sister"—Suzanne wagged her finger in my face—"you're in deep sh—doo-doo." Her eyes flared with sharp accusation.

My courage withered.

"That's potty mouth, lady." Sonny Boy lifted his chin, scowled at Suzanne, and then grabbed for my hand.

Was he seeking protection or trying to protect me?

Either way, my heart tugged with love.

"He's adorable. He's handsome. He's the spitting image of you." As Maggie spoke, I waited for the important question: "Who is his daddy?"

However, she didn't ask, though Suzanne's eyes flashed that question, along with a list of others.

"Sonny Boy"—I knelt in front of him—"This is our family. Not all of them, but most of them." I wiggled my eyebrows, hoping my friends would catch the hint to be mindful of what they say in the boy's presence.

With a slight nod of recognition, Suzanne and Maggie crouched at eye level with Sonny Boy. "We absolutely are your family," Suzanne said.

"Do you know my grandfather Landry? I'm gonna call him, G-Pop. Momma told me on the plane that my G-Pop was her daddy. That he lives here in Nyou Ahhlyns."

"May I have a hug?" Maggie whispered as if Sonny Boy might be an apparition that could evaporate into thin air.

I watched my son launch himself into Maggie's arms. A weird sensation washed over me. This was the moment I'd always feared. Maggie meeting Christopher Marcus Maucele.

And her being a better mother than me.

She put one hand on the floor behind her to keep herself from toppling over. She stood, picking Sonny Boy up and holding him tight to her body. "I'm your Auntie Maggie. Welcome home. I'm so happy to meet you." Her soft whispers were like a lullaby. Sheer pleasure settled on her face. It was as if she were a small child finding her long-lost teddy bear.

I drew in a steadying breath. My lie of omission could destroy my friendship with Maggie. Several deep breaths more didn't calm my racing pulse.

"Hand him over," Suzanne commanded. "I'm Miss Suzanne. I promise to watch my potty mouth, little mister." She tousled Sonny Boy's hair, then set him on the floor, and reached for his hand. "My car's waiting. I see you have your own special seat. I think I hear a juice box calling your name."

My nerves jumped to high alert. My pulse popped like sparklers on a dark night. I worried about speaking the truth about Sonny Boy's father. I worried about the letter still tucked away in my purse and how it affected Maggie. I worried Suzanne might be denying her pregnancy.

I worried, worried, worried.

But in the moment, I couldn't do anything about those things. This moment was all I had. My precious son was meeting two of the most important people in his life, and that provided a heartbeat of peace and a sliver of hope.

"Coming, Jane?" Maggie called. The three were leaving without me.

Suzanne neared the exit door with Sonny Boy in tow. Maggie took the boy's other hand. I grabbed our two suitcases and the car seat and hustled after the two women charming my son to pieces.

Please, God, let this be the start of a new chance for us. Don't let my past ruin the future for my boy.

Chapter 10

My cowardice kicked into overdrive during the ride toward the city. *Tell them. Tell them. Tell them the truth.* The Gs chatter rose in my mind the way the water rose in New Orleans during Katrina. Was I going to drown? I swallowed past the lump in my throat.

What was truth? Real facts, of course. Fact one—I threw logic into Boston Harbor after peeing on a stick, the same time I received news about Maggie and Mark's engagement. Fact two—I couldn't think my way out of all I'd acted my way into. Fact three—I loved Maggie and Suzanne and my father.

And the old saying was true. We always hurt the ones we love most.

From the front seat, Suzanne and Maggie teased and entertained Sonny Boy. They shared all they loved about New Orleans. I felt as though I was outside the bubble that surrounded them.

Weariness set in. I had to look ahead. Sonny Boy's future sat like a crown on top of my to-do list.

"Have you ever ridden a streetcar?" Suzanne asked Sonny Boy.

He tugged my hand. "Momma? Have I?"

"Not yet, but that'll be part of our adventure here. The streetcars are famous. Before buses, that's all people had." I slipped my fingers through his hair, moving long strands off his forehead and away from his deep blue eyes.

Suzanne turned the car off St. Charles Avenue onto Third Street, shaded by trees blocking the hot noon sun. Construction trucks lined one side of the narrow road. A Greek Revival was undergoing extensive renovations.

"First thing we do today is get this boy some sunglasses." Maggie's mothering instincts showed. "Next, we take the streetcar to Audubon Park, go to the zoo. For dinner, we'll catch a riverboat cruise. Tomorrow, the aquarium, maybe a swamp boat tour. And we can't forget a carriage ride."

"Slow down, Maggie," I laughed. "He's only four. We will be here for two weeks."

"I'm gonna be five!"

"When's your birthday?" Maggie asked.

He looked up expectantly. I whispered, "It's okay. You can tell them."

"June," he shouted.

"What day?"

"The seventeenth," I offered. "I think the first thing this package of energy needs is lunch, then a haircut. Maggie, would it be too much if we went to your salon after lunch? I doubt he'll take a n-a-p." The effort it would require to get him to rest would zap my dwindling energy.

"She could cut his hair on the pool patio," Suzanne suggested. "Save us the trip."

"A pool?" Sonny Boy's eyes widened as if he'd seen chocolate chips raining from the sky. "I can swim. I don't want a n-a-p. Momma, I know what that spells."

"I see I need to have a talk with Pops about taking away my secret weapons. Maggie, I'd really like my boy to have a whole hair salon experience. At home, I cut his hair." Were my ulterior motives transparent? I wanted to see her place of business, and Sonny Boy needed a bonding experience with Maggie.

"Shades and a shave it is."

"I'm too young to shave, Auntie Maggie. Pops said so." Sonny Boy crossed his arms over his chest and bobbed his head. "He goes to a barber."

Maggie turned from the front seat. "He's just too cute."

"Shhh, he'll hear you. He's already impossible enough." I grinned. Deep love reverberated through my body for my little guy.

"Who's Pops?" Suzanne asked.

"Ahh…Tom Finley." I realized I wanted to choose my words carefully. I didn't want to reveal something that might detonate my friends' simmering nerves. Suzanne, in particular, put on a mask, but she couldn't wait to get me alone—a person of interest to a crime. This one I committed. "He owns the house on River Street where we live. He lives upstairs. My friend Beth, and I share the downstairs. The area has old, historic houses. Some date back to the seventeen hundreds. Northern style with gables and steep roofs."

Sonny Boy kicked his feet against the backseat. I stilled his legs.

"Pops and Beth are my family up there. Momma says you're my family here."

Suzanne and Maggie glanced at each other. Suzanne smiled, facing the road again. For once, I wished I could read minds.

Maggie giggled. "Sonny Boy, you're adorable."

"Let's unload. Have lunch. After that, we storm the salon," Suzanne said. "Not Slidell. Maggie owns a second shop on Magazine. And news flash. We're opening a salon and day spa at a boutique hotel in the French Quarter. She's now a glamour entrepreneur."

"That's great." The surprising news sparked my concerns. Would she have time to be a mother to Sonny Boy? A new spa required a sizable investment. Was she financially successful? Had Mark provided for her?

Knowing those answers could lessen my struggle about approaching Maggie about money. The notice from Mark's life insurance company naming me the beneficiary still hung in limbo—with me feeling as though I were hanging in purgatory. One-hundred thousand dollars. A whole pile of money. Enough to sock away a sizable amount into an education fund for Sonny Boy and take care of his needs. Like a new bicycle.

Or a car when he turned sixteen.

My eyes misted. I would never see that milestone in his life.

But what if Maggie needed money? How did I delicately handle the subject? I was Mark's ex-wife. If he had not provided for his widow, I could not accept all the money. Had Mark forgotten to change the beneficiary?

Suzanne pulled to an iron gate and it slid to the left, providing access to a brick driveway on the side of the house. She nosed the car close to the garage entrance. The door rolled up.

Awed by the grandeur, I murmured, "Suzanne, you have a mansion. Maggie didn't exaggerate."

Maggie pointed to the house. "Documents indicate the house was designed by Gallier, maybe 1910. Five bedrooms, five and a half baths. In-ground pool. One of the biggest lots in the Garden District. And we could walk to my salon from here. Suzanne's a lucky girl. No way would Mark and I... will I ever afford such a palace."

Maggie wasn't jealous. Old-world ostentatiousness wasn't her thing. She was cozy and contemporary. It showed in the way she redecorated the camp. Suzanne, on the other hand, had always loved antiques. Her sprawling home intimidated me.

"Grant's away on business," Suzanne explained. "We have the house to ourselves."

"I had hoped Sonny Boy would meet him." I tried to conceal my disappointment as we climbed out of the car.

"We'll introduce his male competition to him when he returns," Suzanne teased.

Maggie beamed. "I looked at houses with Grant. He insisted on surprising his bride. I tried to talk him out of it, but at least with my help, Suz got something closer to her liking than if he'd picked it out all by himself."

Suzanne patted Maggie's shoulder. "You did good." Then together they pulled my luggage from the trunk.

"Suzanne, you've become a grand-house belle rather than a plain ol' boatshed one."

Suzanne laughed. "A pool-house girl. There's a small cabana in the back."

"Maybe just us girls can take a midnight swim?" Maggie suggested. "Get bucky for old times' sake?"

I gave her my you've-got-to-be-kidding eye roll. "We never got bucky. *You* talked about it. And that night ended badly."

"I wonder if they ever found old Claude." Suzanne locked the door.

"We'll talk about that *later*." Maggie's sharpness surprised me.

"Momma." Sonny tugged my hand. "What's bucky?"

"It's when—" Maggie started.

I covered my son's ears, then squatted in front of him. Moving my hands away, I whispered, "It's like when you streak around the house after your bath."

Sonny Boy twisted his mouth from one side to the other. "You and Auntie Maggie and Miss Suzanne are gonna do *that*?"

"No." We all spoke at the same time.

Suzanne ushered us into her palace.

"I'm taking this little guy for a tour of the pool." Maggie took Sonny Boy's hand, leading him outdoors.

"He can swim," I hollered, peeling off my blazer. Suzanne pointed to hooks in the rear entryway, and I hung up my coat. Against the backdrop of a grand setting, my yellow and white striped, cotton seersucker dress with tiny embroidered pineapples, purchased on sale at Brooks, suggested I was *haute couture* like my friends. But Suzanne paid as much for a scarf as I spent on groceries each month. Unlike her, any spare dollar I had was deposited into Sonny Boy's education fund.

"Let's make lunch." Suzanne crossed the large u-shaped kitchen. White cabinets. White marble countertops. A hammered copper farm sink.

I washed my hands while Suzanne pulled bread from a plastic bin inside the fridge. She warmed the bread in a toaster oven and then spread peanut butter and jelly on two slices as though she did it every day.

"He does eat PB and J, right?"

"Of course."

"I know you're not feeding him dog food. Later when we're alone, *sistah*, you got some 'splaining to do. In the meantime, grab salad fixin's from the fridge."

Thoughts jumbled in my head. I still hadn't formed an eloquent string of words to express the truth. My reckoning moment edged closer. The only thing I could do was account for my behavior chronologically, starting with my divorce from Mark, my visit from Mark, and march up to present day. Truth. Facts—with the emotional backstory thrown in. Then I would throw myself on their mercy. That was the best plan I could conjure in my brain.

Much easier thought than done.

I tossed salads for three. Suzanne poured sweet tea into tall frosted, sugar-rimmed glasses. Through the window over the sink, I observed Maggie with my boy. She held his hand as they walked around the pool, the two deep in a private conversation. She laughed and waved her hand at something Sonny Boy had said.

My son was a ladies' man.

My moment of joy clouded over. Would he prefer Maggie to me? As much as that prick of my heart dripped blood, I needed the two of them to be close. Maggie had a tender nature. Would be the best candidate for Sonny Boy's mother. The news that she wasn't able to have children had to be a near-deadly blow for her. In a twisted fate kind of way, she and Maggie could help each other.

I chewed my bottom lip. When did I explain to Maggie that Sonny Boy was Mark's son?

Lunch lost its appeal. Tiredness settled over me. I swayed, then steadied myself.

"Jane? You okay?" Suzanne carried the salad plates to the table.

"Fine." I lied. If I sat down, my face might end up in my plate. If I were to lie down, I'd be asleep in seconds.

"Fine? You don't look well." Suzanne wrapped an arm around my shoulders and squeezed. "You're not superwoman. You are not untiring." Suzanne shook her finger at me. "As a stepmother of two, I know what I speak of."

Sliding a smile into place, I tried for perky. "You jazzed up the salads with pecans and dried cranberries. Yum."

"I could take Maggie and Sonny Boy for his haircut while you nap. I don't know how you do it. We have a cook, housekeeper, part-time tutor, and a driver to help."

Help? That was an army. But Suzanne and Grant could afford it.

"Thank you, but I couldn't miss his first salon haircut. Besides, he can be a handful. He's minding his manners right now."

Suzanne stepped closer to the window. "Maggie has him all to herself. I want my spoil-time with him, too. Sometimes, mommies just get in the way." She winked.

Whoosh. Pain came. I had no idea a single sentence could rip my chest apart. I swallowed hard, trying to keep my tone neutral. "Would tomorrow afternoon work for you? I'd like to visit my dad."

I moved beside her, into the sunlight slanting through the window. Its radiating heat warmed my face. If only it were liquid. I could soak in it and that could cure me. That kind of radiation I'd opt for in a hurry. "We're going to the cemetery to tend to my mother's grave. I need some time with my dad before he meets his grandson. Could you take Sonny Boy to the zoo? Or head to the aquarium, where it's air-conditioned. That would help me out."

Beyond the window, Maggie knelt beside the pool, ran her fingers through the water, and flicked droplets at Sonny Boy.

"Maggie puts flowers on your mother's grave on Mother's Day. When was the last time you were there?"

There was no accusation in Suzanne's voice.

"A while. But don't worry. My dad tells me how wonderful Maggie is. All she does, including their dinners together. She is thoughtful that way."

"She envied you." There was a weight to Suzanne's words. "Your parents, were better to her than her own."

"I am grateful to her for looking after my dad all these years. I think his inability to convince Maggie's mother to let her live with us sooner made him try harder with her. Her mother only cared about the Social Security check sent every month. But she did pay for Maggie's one passion—dancing."

"If I recall correctly, you had something to do with that. After high school, Maggie tried and tried but wasn't accepted at the local dance company. That scholarship to a private Catholic college never materialized. Enrolling in cosmetology school may have been the best thing that happened—if I were to next-day-quarterback her life. And you know Maggie and her Hail Marys. Catholic school might have made her more…devout."

"Obsessed. That's the word you're looking for. She's been devout since the day I met her. And that's part of her charm." Maggie's neediness was the glue between us…before we became blood sisters.

"She's a natural with Sonny Boy." Suzanne pointed to the pair. Sonny Boy chased Maggie, who shuffled in heels, allowing him to catch her.

"Not to have children… What a big blow for her. More than it would've been to me. I hadn't planned on him." I held my breath. I'd revealed too much. That tidbit of info would tickle Suzanne's sleuthing. I waved at Maggie and Sonny Boy, motioning them inside for lunch.

Suzanne's eyebrow lifted. "Hadn't planned? Interesting. I signed papers for Grant, agreeing we'd never have any. My choice was Grant."

"Signed papers? Contracts get renegotiated all the time. The question is when did you decide you didn't want motherhood? You swore when your father remarried that you'd have four kids *and* stay married forever."

"The old saying, 'that was then, this is now,' ring a bell?"

"Doesn't answer my question."

"Momma!" Sonny Boy burst into the room, tugging Maggie behind him.

"Yes, little man?"

"Auntie Maggie said I can go swimming if I sit real still for my haircut. And she said I could visit her at her house. She has a room full of little boy stuff. Like trains. Like Thomas!"

Maggie's face was lit like a New Orleans sky on New Year's Eve at midnight. My gut cinched. My muscles contracted.

"We'll see," I said. It was too much, too soon for me.

But when would be the right time?

Chapter 11 – Maggie

Maggie let go of a deep sigh. What an afternoon of adventure. Sonny Boy's haircut. Swimming in Suzanne's pool. Shrimp boil for dinner. It had taken all of that to finally drain the endless energy from the sleeping angel who hadn't moved since she put him to bed five minutes ago. How did Jane manage alone?

Closing the plantation shutters to darken the bedroom, Maggie crossed back to Sonny Boy. His blue eyes had closed the minute his head hit the pillow, and it wasn't yet eight o'clock. Affection warmed her heart. She had fallen in love with him with the fierceness of a mother bear protecting her cub.

She and Suz could *not* fail to make Jane stay.

Otherwise, this angel would head back north taking her heart with him. That would kill her.

A ray of light from the hallway slanted across the guest room floor. A ripple of energy approached her. She didn't turn in the direction of the sensation. "Go away. Not now." Whatever spirit wanted her attention would have to wait.

Lightly, she stroked the cheek of the little boy in the bed. "You're precious." She touched his chest. Her fingers subtly rose and fell with each small breath. A miracle of life.

Her mind flashed to Mark—his breathless body, rigid in a casket, all dressed up and heaven bound. Did he stand at the pearly gates in that suit? Or did a soul shroud itself in something flowing and gossamer when it crossed over? She shuddered, recalling her fingers against Mark's chest when she touched him for the very last time. He could've been a mannequin made up to look like the man she loved. Lifeless. Cold. Dead.

But now she had a gift. Sonny Boy was a special little guy. Love curled around her heart. Who wouldn't love him? Jane's son.

Her heart had tumbled when he wrapped his little arms around her leg in a hug and asked if she was his family now. How darling was that? Sonny Boy constricted her grief and made an opening for… laughter, love, life.

Brushing the fringes of his freshly cut hair, Maggie thought how Mark would've loved this child. Not only because Sonny Boy belonged to Jane, but because the little boy found humor in everything. She chuckled and sighed. Why had God refused her continued pleas for a child? She'd been born to be a mother. Her childhood had shown her all the things not to do. She had love to offer a child. And thanks to Mr. and Mrs. Landry's support, she'd learned love always found a way to help a child thrive.

Unable to leave the room, Maggie fought the need to scoop Sonny Boy into her arms and hug him tightly. Rock him. Instead, she pulled a side chair close to the bed and rested her fingers on top of his hand.

She'd never have a blessing like him. But why? Had angels posted a sign-up list on a cosmic bulletin board somewhere and not told her? She never made a bargain to never have children with the man she loved. The exact opposite had been her prayer for years.

Mark *and* a family—the kind of family they both dreamed about. A father and mother who loved each other. A complete family unit. It's what she and Mark had both craved. Circumstances couldn't be more unfair.

Losing Mark gave her a deeper understanding of what Jane went through when her mother died. Life ripped the rug out beneath her…and she had been so young. Yet, Jane went on with her life. Maybe all this time she'd been hating Jane's desertion, Jane had been trying her best to survive. Just as Maggie was doing now.

She rose, kissed her finger, and pressed it to the little boy's cheek. She paused at the sensation of being watched. Behind her, she was certain Jane spied from the doorway. When Maggie turned, no one was there. Jane might have wanted to slip away unnoticed, but Maggie had sensed the change of energy in the room.

Conflict rattled a warning the way a rattlesnake did. Her emotions about Jane swirled like a merry-go-round propelled by jet engines. Could she and Jane get through the pain of the past? Was Sonny Boy the glue to mend their relationship?

Maggie moved to the door and took a last look at the sleeping child. Would he grow up to be brave like his momma? Jane had been her super-woman. Jane confronted her mother and stepfather. Afterward, the abuse stopped. Her mother barely looked at her. Her stepfather left the room when she entered. Thirteen-year-old Jane had saved her life.

Made breathing in and out possible.

After that, each time Maggie went to church, she lit a candle for Jane.

But God knew her heart.

She couldn't lie to Him about the braiding of love and hate.

At Suzanne and Grant's wedding, she'd wondered when Jane and Mark would announce an addition to their family. Instead, a month later, they announced their divorce. Mark returned to New Orleans. Jane remained in Boston. As much as Maggie loved Mark, the loss of Jane in her life hurt. It was as though part of her heart never fully beat again.

Since then, she and Jane had exchanged brief phone calls, emails, an occasional text, but never once did Jane let on that she had a child. Did her father know? What happened between the perfect father and lifesaving daughter? Neither had ever said. They closed ranks. Because she wasn't blood kin, she stood on the outside looking in.

"Little man, I'm going to pry open your momma's secrets," Maggie whispered. "I promise to use kid gloves. Who is your daddy? Is he helping financially? But I know firsthand, sometimes fathers aren't worth the pain of having them in your life. Your momma took care of me when I desperately needed it. Now, I'm going to take care of the two of you."

Maggie left the door ajar and headed down the hall carrying the child monitor speaker, just in case the little guy woke up. She would give Jane a break. The poor woman looked as bedraggled as Raggedy Ann in a storm.

She neared the family room with its view of the pool and underwater lights changing from red to blue to green to yellow. The surface of the water danced with ripples from the fountain. Jane and Suzanne sat on a couch facing the window.

Maggie slowed when she overheard Suzanne's question.

"I know what a traditionalist you are, Jane. Did you get a wild hair up your ass and name the child Sonny Boy? Or does the name have a connection to the father?"

Curiosity pulled Maggie closer. She tiptoed into the room.

Jane raised her glass. "Promise me you won't be disappointed when I tell you the mundane answer? I can tell it's been burning the back of your throat all day."

Jane sounded sassy, but her aura exuded sadness. She sipped her cocktail and shoved her hand through her short hair.

Maggie waited. Her breath hitched in her chest.

Jane kicked off her shoes and then collapsed onto her side on the couch.

Suzanne collapsed on the other side.

Maggie pushed out a breath. Tension pushed her into the room. She had to see Jane's face for the "father revelation."

"He's asleep." She pulled an oversized pillow from beneath the coffee table, placed it on the floor in front of the couch, and plopped down.

"Drink, Maggie?" Suzanne rose. "We're one ahead of you."

"Tonic and a twist. No alcohol. Someone has to be sober if that little boy wakes up."

"My God." Jane's tone was accusatory. "Listen to you. You've known him for less than twelve hours, and you're already declaring me an unfit mother."

"Did not."

"Maggie, your tone rings like church bells on Sunday morning. If written, it would be twenty-two font, bolded *and* italicized. I'll have you know, I can count on one hand how many drinks I've had since he was born. And all three times have been here in New Orleans. With the two of you."

"Hush, now," Suzanne interrupted.

Maggie caught her threatening glare. She was expected to make nice.

She turned and rested her chin on the couch near Jane. Curiosity had a choke hold. The boy was the spitting image of his mother. But he wasn't born through immaculate conception. Probably not through in vitro either.

She lifted her gaze to meet Jane's all the while feeling Suzanne's stare burning a hole in her back. "What is Sonny Boy's christened name?"

Jane chuckled. "Christened name? I never got around to that."

"The child hasn't been baptized?" Maggie drew back. Gulped. That had to be fixed ASAP.

"You're. Avoiding. The. Question," Suzanne said.

"Old friends. You know me too well."

Maggie's pulse skittered like a water skier bouncing on waves of a wake.

Jane waved her hand. "It's not a secret. Sonny Boy is the nickname Mr. Finley gave him. His name is Chris, like the song by Kenny Loggins—my momma's favorite about the boy and his bear—the story by A. A. Milne. Remember?"

Maggie's vision blurred. She blinked. It was as though she looked through shadows and into Jane's unveiled soul. Maggie's heart thumped. Irregularly. Pounded hard like a bass drum without a beat.

A *knowing* struck her.

Jane lied.

Chapter 12

I drifted awake. Pelting thoughts tapped louder and louder. Squinting against the fullness of morning, I blinked several times. Forced my eyes open. The room that came into focus was luxurious. Pale blue walls, high ceilings with glossy white crown molding, and floral with stripes on silk drapes. This had to be the dream part. I closed my eyes. Opened. Nope. This was real.

Where was I?

Duh. Suzanne's house.

Now I recalled.

Here, I was safe for a few more minutes. I snuggled into the covers to float off to sleep again, the only sound in my ears was the whisper of my breath.

"Knock-knock. Knock-knock."

"Oh," I groaned. My darling son needed a volume button. "Who's there?"

"Momma." Sonny Boy opened the door and burst through, a tsunami of energy. Bare feet smacked on the wooden floor until they hit the thick sculpted carpet. He grabbed the bedcovers, used them like a climbing rope.

I held on for counterbalance to keep him from falling. He hoisted himself next to me in the tall, four-poster bed.

"Momma, guess what."

Already dressed in denim shorts and a New Orleans t-shirt, Sonny Boy looked ready for the day. His new clipped haircut reminded me of when Mark came home from basic training with a military-issue buzz cut.

"Inside voice, please." I stretched my arms over my head trying to push away lingering brain fog. What a lightweight I'd become. In my past, a time or two, I drank a guy under the table. That was before my father needed AA meetings. I quit drinking after that. Oh, I tried it once—after Sonny Boy was born—three glasses of Pinot Noir—my pity party before the hysterectomy that was supposed to prevent cancer's arrival date, or at the very least, slow it for years. "Old, tired, sick," my body had screamed.

"Momma, guess," Sonny Boy insisted, pressing his nose to mine and crossing his eyes.

"A clown has come to wake me up?" I giggled, grabbed him, and pulled him down beside me, our heads resting next to each other on the pillow. "I give. What?"

"They have cool stuff here."

Panic pinged. Had he broken some priceless antique? I hadn't considered Suzanne's museum-like designer house wasn't childproof.

"Like what?" To my ears, my voice rose two octaves.

"Like *pain perdu*. I ate it. It didn't sound good, but it tastes like the French toast you make. I ate warm berries with it. Blueberries, strawberries, and raspberries. And...Miss Suzanne told me about lan...lani..."

"*Lagniappe*," I said. Suzanne had started my boy's New Orleans education.

"Yeah. They have that here."

"Kiss me." I pointed to my cheek. "Your kisses are my *lagniappe*, my something extra special." He kissed my check. I kissed his nose.

"Do I have a Cajun bone in my body?"

"What?"

"Latisha said she don't think I have a Cajun bone in my body. What bone is that? Where?"

I tickled his ribs. The grammar lesson would wait for another time. "I'm looking for your Cajun bone."

Sonny Boy squealed. Squirming, he twisted and giggled. His laughter was joy. No matter how difficult a day, a smile and laughter from my son cured everything. A dog was man's best friend? Maybe. But a little boy was certainly this woman's joy. Even when said boy pretended to be a barking dog. "Is it here? Or here? Or here?" I tickled his neck, his belly, and when he kicked, I grabbed his foot and tickled there.

"Who's Latisha?" I continued the tickle attack.

"My housekeeper." Suzanne stood in the door. "And part-time cook."

"Good morning." I was pleasant but resented the interruption. These moments with my son were precious, priceless, sacred. They caused time to stand still.

Sonny Boy sat up. I twisted around and sat cross-legged on the bed. Suzanne lounged with her shoulder against the doorjamb and her arms folded. Skinny jeans accentuated her long legs, and the combination of jeans and white t-shirt made me think of her skipping rocks down by the river. Evidently, Maggie had gotten ahold of her toes last night. They shined bubblegum pink.

"She's from Terrebonne parish. She made breakfast. She and I decided not to wake you. Sonny Boy was hungry. Oh, and Maggie left early. I think she's rejoining the world. She's off to run errands. A first since…"

I reached and poked a spot on my son's side. "There's your Cajun bone. You're a Landry. Don't ever forget it. Now, go brush your teeth and I'll inspect when you're done."

Sonny Boy slid down from the bed. The second his feet hit the floor, he fisted his hands and scampered from the room like he intended to leap and fly—the bathroom was only two doors down the hall.

"He hasn't broken anything, has he?" I asked. "I'll pay for it."

Suzanne chuckled. "I put away the priceless items—I was expecting a dog. I'm more worried about him falling in the pool than him breaking anything."

"He can swim."

"You said that yesterday. Really?"

"Threw him into a canal. Said, 'Happy birthday, boy. Swim or be gator bait.'" I mimicked a man from our past.

"My dad." Suzanne crossed the room. Moving the curtains aside, she opened the shutters. Sunlight poured in. She sat in the wingback chair near the window, curling her feet under her.

"Actually, he took floating lessons after he learned to walk," I explained. "However, I don't want him around the pool unsupervised. But should he fall in, he can swim from the deep to the shallow end. He's tough, my little man." I gathered the robe from the foot of the bed and pulled it on.

"Athletic. Hmm. Not a trait from you. You hate to break a sweat. Does he get his natural athletic ability from his daddy?"

I jerked my attention to Suzanne. Had I revealed something last night in my drunkenness?

She stared me down. I flopped backward on the bed to break eye contact.

For weeks, I'd racked my brain for the perfect words to explain. The script could've come from a D-List movie: "By the way, Sonny Boy is Christopher Marcus Landry. Your nephew. Your brother's son."

For years, the need to protect my life and to keep my son close proved to be a stronger need than telling the truth. After all, my world shifted like the Titanic sinking when my mother died. Shifted again when Mark and I divorced. Shifted when I learned the depth of my father's drinking problem. I shifted. Shut down. Sonny Boy gave me life.

"From your silence, I hit a nerve." Suzanne cocked an eyebrow.

"You're just fishing."

"You fell asleep last night before Maggie and I could start our interrogation. We know *where* he was born. *When.* You gave us his first name, though Maggie doesn't believe you. Who brought the male DNA to the party? Are you involved with the dude?"

My feet hit the floor, and I met Suzanne's glare. "I am here for only two weeks. Can the grilling start, oh, maybe tomorrow? I'm meeting my dad"—I reached for my watch on the gilded antique chest next to the bed—"in less than two hours."

"You have thirteen days and counting down."

I hated the threat in Suzanne's singsongy reply.

"I promise to tell you. But it's a two-way street. You never answered my question about motherhood. If I have to sing, then you do, too."

"Go have lunch. Tell Charles, 'hello.' I'll take Sonny Boy to the zoo." Suzanne rose and started for the door. "Where's lunch? In case I need to contact you."

"Court of Two Sisters."

"You better get going. Cab?"

"I'll use the streetcar and foot power. Like old times."

Sonny Boy appeared in the doorway. "Momma, check my teeth." He crossed the threshold into the bedroom. "Where ya going?"

"I've got to get dressed, darlin' boy. Miss Suzanne will check your teeth to be sure you did a good job. Let me have some privacy. I'll see you before I go."

"Where?"

"I'm meeting someone for lunch."

"Who? Where? Whatcha gonna have for lunch? What am I having for lunch?"

Clasping my hands to my chest, I couldn't hide a grin. "You're spending the afternoon with Miss Suzanne. This evening, you tell me and I'll tell you. We'll share about today's journeys."

"But where am I going with her?"

"It's a surprise." Suzanne looked radiant when she smiled wide.

I whistled at her. "Put your mommy skills to work and take this urchin from my room." I pointed toward the door.

Suzanne put her hand on Sonny Boy's shoulder and attempted to herd him away. He slipped out of her grasp and ran to me. I knelt down and opened my arms.

"Momma, I love you." He laid his head on my shoulder and hugged me tight.

"I love you, too," I whispered. A mist blurred my vision. "Go have fun. I'll see you at dinner tonight."

As quickly as he came to me, he ran back to Suzanne, and grasped her hand. "I'm ready for adventure."

But was I?

Later that afternoon, I pressed down on the crown of a wide-brimmed straw hat and secured it on my head. It protected my face from the sun. I linked arms with my father, and we strolled through the oldest section of the

Greenwood Cemetery in a familiar comfortable silence. His graying temples gave him distinguished look. A look of a man who was once again whole.

I was thankful for the slight breeze and a break in the humidity. Summer had not officially sashayed according to the calendar, yet it always blazed sooner in the South than it did in Salem. Silly of me to have forgotten.

We walked in the direction of the family plot. "Thank you again for lunch, Dad. I haven't eaten at The Sisters since the last time I was there with you."

His strong, steady hand patted mine. "I love you. I'm sorry I failed you. Failed us both. But we can go forward from here."

His sobriety gave me back the father I used to know. I wanted to trust.

"I…I don't…know where to begin," I said. "There's so much to talk about." Should I reveal my diagnosis? I paused a heartbeat to consider.

No. Not now. I had too much to accomplish before I introduced that monster.

We picked our way through the gravel and oyster-shell pathway between the crypts in the hush of the afternoon. No one else mingled nearby.

"Jane, say what you need to say. Ask what you need to ask. I'll answer any question. I've changed. I want to meet my grandson. To have him in my life."

His voice rang with sincerity. I even heard regret. A magic salve for my wound…but still hesitation lingered.

We wandered past a tall crypt with a large winged angel looking down. Maybe that was the sign I needed to bridge the past—angels watching over us.

"Dad, looking at you now, it's hard to imagine I ever saw you falling down drunk. I wish I could wipe that old image from my mind. Wish it were a figment of my imagination."

He winced. The pain on his face planted a stab in my chest.

The corners of his mouth drooped. "Fair enough. I wish I had the power to wipe away pain from the past."

The silver at his temples gave him a distinguished appearance. He'd aged since Suzanne's wedding. Time had rushed past. I had regrets, too. Too much time without family and old friends. Too much time without the anchors of my city to ground me. Too much time without a clear conscience.

Dad stopped and drew me into a hug.

The back-up bell of a truck beeped in the distance.

A kid yelled at another.

My dad hugged me and nothing else mattered. Not the sun or the sounds of others. I was sixteen again and life was grand.

Only I wasn't sixteen. I was thirty-two, and it was time for me to have an adult relationship with my dad.

"There are many proud moments in my life." He released me from the last squeeze. "When I married your mother. When you were born. When you and Mark got married. But then your mother was sick for so long—nothing I did saved her. She died…"

I let him talk.

We walked a few steps more before he continued. "She rallied when you and Mark got engaged. I begged God for her recovery. But"—he shrugged—"your mother declined when you left for your honeymoon. She made me promise not to tell you the truth of her condition until you'd started at Emerson. She didn't want you waiting at home for her to die. She wanted you to live your life."

My mother's lie of omission. My father sworn to secrecy—a dying woman's last wish. My heart wept for them. For me. I wanted my momma with me now. To tell me what to do. To tell me it would work out all right. To tell me Sonny Boy would be fine without me.

"How like her. Superwoman. An example I can never live up to."

"Oh. You're wrong, Jane. She'd be so proud. She wanted happiness for you."

I hugged his arm. "My son makes me happy." Thinking of Sonny Boy made me giggle. His life lived in high gear.

"I can't *wait* to meet my grandson." The nudge was evident in my father's voice.

"You will. I needed this father-daughter time with you. Selfish on my part."

"I'm sorry about the past." He sighed. "About my drinking, embarrassing you when I came to visit. I'm ashamed and deeply regret the pain I caused you. And I'm equally serious about staying sober. I want a relationship with you and my grandson. We're family."

I considered the feelings behind his words. My shoulders loosened and my heart opened a bit. A slice, much more than a sliver, of hope bloomed in my chest.

We continued until we found the large crypt with roses carved into the stone. That was our marker to turn right and head down the road. I hadn't been to the cemetery in many years, but the location of graves hadn't changed, many of them standing for more than one-hundred years. A quickening breeze fluttered the brim of my hat. It was as though Momma welcomed me.

"Dad, I'm sorry, too. We are family. But some of this is going to take time. I wish I could magically erase the past away."

"Have you no good memories that you carry with you?" His deep sigh squeezed my heart. I had to let go and let some slack into the rope that wrapped me in the past.

"One of the happiest moments of my life was having Momma at my wedding." I tried to sound cheery. "I know the marriage didn't work out, probably doomed from the beginning. We rushed into it." A breeze fluttered the skirt of my sundress. It was as though Momma was tickled to hear her name from my lips. We continued our walk to Momma's grave.

A memory of my wedding fluttered into my mind. Her crying as Daddy walked me down the aisle. Her tears of joy triggered mine. I had tried so hard not to smear my glamour-shot makeup.

My wedding to Mark would be the only one I'd ever have, but my dad didn't need to know that yet. I'm guessing, from Heaven, Momma already knew.

We stopped in front of the raised plot trimmed with black and white granite. The tall headstone shined free of green mold, unlike so many other grave sites where family members never came to visit. Wilted pink roses lay on top of the grave—Maggie's doing, I was sure. She always brought pink roses to Momma and continued that tribute after she died.

She'd been a more faithful daughter than I.

"Dad, when I think of Momma"—he put his arm around me and I laid my head against his chest—"I remember her laughter. Her smile. I remember her at my wedding…"

The orchestra started to play. Mark and I took the floor for our first dance as husband and wife. I bent down to grasp the wrist loop from the train of my dress and lifted it with a Cinderella flourish. My gown was stunning. Crystals and seed pearls dotted the bodice. An off-the-shoulder white dress. My parents had spared no expense for the June wedding. Not for the dress. Not for the cake. Not for the reception.

"Shall we?" Mark's lazy grin set my heart thrumming, hummingbird wings couldn't flap faster.

He twirled me past my mother. Her eyes glistened with tears. Her hands went to her heart. She blew us a kiss. A hundred and fifty guests looked on. The swooning expressions on my bridesmaids, Maggie and Suzanne, filled me with happiness. The mischievous glances of Mark's groomsmen, Byron and Parker, made me wonder what surprise they'd plotted.

In City Park's Pavilion, I glided in Mark's arms, floating on the lilting notes from the orchestra's violins. I memorized every moment as my mother smiled and held court with family and neighbors and friends.

The last rays of sunlight flickered to dusk, and the room blazed with tiny white lights. Scents from swags of pink roses and stargazer lilies filled the room. The energy was lively, lovely, and so romantic.

"You're beautiful, Jane." Mark looked deep into my eyes.

"I love you, Mark." I squeezed his hand and then brushed a lock of hair from his forehead.

I loved him beyond reason. We'd been friends forever. He was male-model handsome. Football-player strong. And Cupid's arrow had struck us just before he left for college in Baton Rouge and I began my junior year of high school.

I certainly believed absence made the heart leap with love.

A long-distance relationship heightened my anticipation of seeing him—it was always a very long two-hour commute.

When I started my senior year, we ventured into the "what if" game, talking about a future when making out got too intense. Intensity that heightened with each passing month. But our pact was no sex until I reached eighteen. That didn't stop heavy breathing, fondling, exploring. That heated up many date nights.

My strategy for keeping my promise—never remove my panties.

Mark was a saint, loving me enough to wait.

Now music carried us around the dance floor in a fairy-tale setting. When the orchestra stopped playing, he pulled me into his arms. I kissed him hard. I wanted the sensations of his mouth against mine, his body pressed against mine, his love merging with mine to sink deep into the cells of my body, so I would never forget…never ever forget.

The entire room of guests burst into applause.

My father claimed me for the next dance. His smile didn't disguise his pain. Last night, I'd overheard him comforting Momma. "We'll manage. I'll be strong. She'll go to college. I won't allow her to give up."

While my father twirled me, his movements still and stilted, I shut my heart and my mind to his pain and shifted my thoughts to Mark.

His proposal had swept me away. A moonlit night on his boat after the Christmas bayou boat parade. Sparkling cider and two crystal flutes. A platter of strawberries with whipped cream. Handmade chocolates. And a blanket on the deck.

We sat on thick cushions facing each other. A sip of sparkling, a bite of berry, and chocolate covering my lips. He licked it away. My heart stuttered. My insides heated, a contraction in the core of my most feminine part.

"Jane, I can't breathe without you." His warm hand cupped the side of my face. "Marry me, yeah?" It wasn't a question.

I searched his face. We'd never talked "wedding" before. Only to agree it had to wait until after I finished college.

"I figured it all out. After you graduate high school in June, we get married. Move to Boston for your Emerson scholarship. It's what your momma wants."

Cancer was taking her cell by cell. Chemo and radiation failed. He, too, realized Momma's life was counted in weeks to months, not years.

"But what about you? Football. LSU."

"As long as you're with me, that's all that matters. College doesn't suit me. I'm gonna get a job and figure out what I want to do. I can do that anywhere. This scholarship is a must-do for you." His sexy dimples showed.

How could I do anything but agree? He loved me. I never doubted that, though girls, including Maggie, had tried to wheedle their way into his heart. I didn't blame them. Mark Christopher Maucele was one of God's perfect creations.

"And your momma will see her princess in a wedding dress on her wedding day."

His words had won me over…

A rumble of thunder brought me back to the present. Overhead, the sky had darkened. A gusty breeze tried to flip my hat from my head. Sunlight played hide-and-seek through the building clouds. As the oncoming summer storm strengthened, so did my grief. "I'll bring flowers before I leave and put them on Momma's grave." I wiped a tear away. "Daddy, the past is over. All we have is now. I forgive you. I want us to be a happy family again."

He smiled and tugged my hand. We headed back. Back to his car. Back to Suzanne's house. Back to unfinished business I needed to settle with my friends.

"I worried about you and Mark marrying so young," my dad said. "But I understood you and Mark did it to give your momma the greatest joy—seeing you walk down the aisle."

"I remember Momma smiling." And Mark's smile, too.

My dad opened the car door for me. I climbed in and closed the door. He raced around and slid into the driver's seat. Rain began pelting the car.

"Mark was the most selfless guy. He fulfilled his promise to Momma. He and I had plans to see the world…but the military changed him."

"But Mark lives on, in your son. I can't wait to see him."

Chapter 13 - Suzanne

The afternoon started dazzling bright. Suzanne bubbled over with excitement. Sonny Boy charged at full rocket speed. Together, they munched on popcorn, wandered the trails, and watched monkeys swing, bears sleep, and giraffes reaching high to nibble on leaves. Sonny Boy talked nonstop about family: monkey mommas and their babies, momma bears and their cubs, and giraffe mommas with long necks pulling at leaves for their young.

And so it went as they visited each exhibit. Showing off Audubon Park Zoo proved more educational than she imagined.

The untiring tyke strutted, spoke to the animals as though they were longtime friends, and made up stories about their lives. Maybe the little mischief-maker was indeed a comedian-in-training. The more she laughed, the more outrageous his stories grew.

At the elephant exhibit, a show had already started, and the zookeeper introduced an Asian elephant. The man spoke about habits of the males. When the show ended, the zookeeper pointed to a gate where stairs climbed to a landing. The man announced anyone wanting a ride needed to line up with a ticket.

Sonny Boy jumped from the bleachers before she could catch him and zigzagged through the crowd. Panic pulsed through her. She lost sight of the short little guy in the sea of adults. Pushing past people, she barked like a momma sea lion calling to her pup, "Sonny Boy. Sonny Boy."

"Miss Suzanne, I'm in line."

She raced to him, crouching to check him over. Jane would never forgive her if the child had been hurt. Cupping his ears first, she ran her hands from his shoulders to his fingers, inspecting him. She turned him around and checked him head to toe. To onlookers, she probably appeared as a helicopter parent.

"Are you going to ride with me?" Big hopeful blue eyes looked up at her.

"It's only for kids." Suzanne glued on a smile and tried to catch a calming breath. "Here's your ticket. I'll take pictures."

"I get to ride a daddy elephant. I can't wait to tell Momma."

He rode the pachyderm a lap around a worn track with two other children. All three squealed as though in competition to see which one could hit the highest note. Afterward, Suzanne stood in line with him so he could ride a second time.

Had she ever seen a child enjoy himself so much? Certainly not her stepchildren, they kept their noses glued to some sort of device.

Later over ice cream, most of which smeared Sonny Boy's cheeks, she sat at a picnic table with him. He cocked his head to the side and twisted his mouth as though trying to figure something out.

"Whatcha thinkin'?" she asked.

"Do you remember my daddy?"

His question floored her. "Y-your daddy?"

"Momma says you knew him. Before he went away."

She frantically searched her mind for a clue. The boy looked just like his mother, especially her eyes, the shape of her face, her infectious grin—back when she smiled. Jane hadn't been home since her wedding to Grant. How could she possibly know the boy's father?

"What do *you* know about your daddy?" She wiped a dribble of ice cream from his mouth, trying to dispel a niggling sensation rising in her gut. One that hinted there wasn't a happily-ever-after story.

Sonny Boy scrunched his nose as if that helped his brain think better. "Momma said he was a great soldier. He fought in a war. And I should be proud of him."

Of their friends from high school, several from their graduating class had joined the military. Some fought in the army. Had someone from home ended up in Boston with Jane? She hadn't heard any rumors at their high school reunions. Did the man even know he was a father? That would be cruel of Jane. Who could it be?

"Oh. God." She clamped a hand over her mouth.

Sonny Boy frowned. "You're not supposed to say that unless you're praying."

"Sorry. I'm praying." She had to be wrong. Had to be incorrect. "Why don't we wait and talk about this with your momma? Maybe she can jog my memory about your daddy." Even to her, the words sounded warbled and forced, but it must have satisfied the boy.

He perked up and smiled. "I have lots to tell Momma today."

Sonny Boy, victim to the heat and humidity, had fallen asleep on the short drive home. She hoped he didn't wake with a stomachache after she'd fed him nearly all the junk he wanted—anything to sway the subject away from his daddy.

Carrying the boy to bed was like carrying a forty-pound bag of potatoes. Score one for her—she managed not to wake him.

With the baby monitor in hand, she rushed upstairs to her office and rifled through her old journals, locating the specific one she sought.

The proof wasn't conclusive, but...damning.

She swallowed. Staggered downstairs to wait for Jane's arrival.

Suzanne peered out the window. Dark gray clouds, thick like batting, blanketed the city. The house across the street appeared as a bleary watercolor painting through the rain-streaked window. Streetlights flickered. Thunder rumbled. Lightning cracked and flashed bright and slashed jagged in the sky. White-hot and angry.

Matching Suzanne's mood.

With each new rumble of thunder, she pictured her hands in karate class—a split second of impact could have an adversary writhing in pain. Thankfully, yoga and meditation kept her from harming humans.

But she might be willing to make *an exception* for Jane.

Which she would never do because hurting Jane meant hurting Sonny Boy. She wouldn't hurt an innocent.

It took only one afternoon for her to fall in love with the little boy, and she was most certainly *Auntie* Suzanne.

Outside, a car pulled to the curb. Charles Landry held an umbrella for Jane, which helped little in the deluge. He walked her to the front door. The father-daughter resemblances were obvious in their faces and their movements, too. His smile showed his father's love.

The sound of a key turning in the lock vibrated in Suzanne's head like a simmering gong. She fought for calm. When Jane opened the door, a bolt of lightning struck nearby. Jane gasped and bumped against the front door, which rattled the stained glass window.

"Thanks, Dad. Sonny Boy and I will see you tomorrow morning. St. Louis Cathedral at eleven. Remember, nothing big or overdone. Just let him get to know you. Time together is what's needed."

As Jane passed the open parlor door, clearly on the way to her bedroom, Suzanne didn't call out to her. Instead, she watched Charles return to his car. He practically skipped. Climbed in and drove away.

But then, why shouldn't he be happy? He knew about his grandson.

Jane had only lied to her friends.

Suzanne poured two fingers of crème sherry into two highball glasses and carried them down the hall. Her bare feet made no sound on the polished wooden floor. The truth she'd discovered today was five years and nine months past due. She didn't need Jane to tell her. All she had to do was tell Jane…then watch the reaction flow.

Today, truth would pour down and the lies would end, just like the rain.

She stood in the doorway and watched Jane rubbing her short hair with a towel. Her dress hung on a hanger on the doorknob, the bottom of the dress crinkling into wrinkles on the floor. Suzanne tapped a glass against the door.

"Hey there. You startled me." Jane whipped the towel around her hair.

Not as much as you shocked the hell out of me.

"Hey, yourself." Suzanne contemplated throwing the drink in Jane's face—Maggie's melodramatic style. Maybe she'd knock back the sherry and brain Jane with the glass instead. More her style. Or used to be.

She offered a glass to Jane. Outside, thunder rumbled like a bass drum, rattling the windows. Another bolt of lightning struck nearby.

Jane flinched as she took the glass. "Thanks."

Suzanne stared at her. Their families had been friends for generations, had camps on the island across a canal. One of her earliest childhood memories included Jane. Them holding hands on their first day of kindergarten and walking through the front door. During their teenage years, they'd shared books and jewelry and clothes. Never boyfriends, though.

She hated it when Jane fell in love with Mark. Jane didn't drift away, instead, Mark became a fourth in most everything they did. And now, Jane's secret made it hard to breathe. It was as though an elephant wrapped its trunk around her chest, squeezing the air from her lungs.

"How was the zoo? Did it make you want to have one of your own? Child, that is, not zoo." Jane smiled and sat on the bed.

The woman before her—did she know her at all? The honor student. Debate team captain. Twirler. The girl who made her swear to never tell about the night crazy Claude Dupuis got shot. The girl who stopped Maggie's abuse. Jane was the glue that had held the Belles together.

But the Jane she knew wouldn't have let Mark go to his grave without knowing he had a son.

Anger burned bright and hot as the last lightning strike.

"Suzanne, are you okay? Something the matter?" Jane's concern sounded genuine, but con artists were good at that.

"I'm trying to decide if I really know you."

A blank look slipped over Jane's face. "What do you mean?"

"In my mind, I've killed you a hundred times in the last hour." Suzanne ground out the words, her hand curling into a fist. She set her glass on the side table. "Since when did you start lying to me? To Maggie? And for God's sake to Mark! We took an oath to always protect each other. To always be friends. How in the world—"

"Momma?" A weak plea sounded on the baby monitor Suzanne carried with her. A door down the hall opened and slammed. Sonny Boy bolted through the bedroom door, his tear-stained face scrunched in pain. Jane crouched as Sonny Boy launched himself into her arms.

Jane scooped him up and laid him on the bed, then scooted next to him. "Shush. I'm here. What's the matter?"

Sonny Boy whimpered and pulled on the quilt, then buried himself beneath it, snuggling up to his mother.

Tenderness embossed Suzanne's heart. This was *her* nephew. Her brother's only child. Her protective instincts spread as quick as gossip on the internet. She released a guttural groan. Something had frightened her nephew. Her sharp voice? That thought cut her deep.

She crossed the room to peek at him. Jane motioned for her to climb up on the bed and join them. She took the invitation, sitting on the edge beside him.

"Sonny Boy," Jane cooed. "Is it the storm, darlin' boy?"

A head beneath the covers nodded.

"That mean old storm won't hurt you. Miss Suzanne and I will protect you," Jane whispered.

Suzanne rubbed the spot on the quilt that looked like a shoulder might be beneath it. Her heart surged. She'd do anything to protect this child. Love wrapped around her heart. If she could have one wish granted—this child would grow up knowing all of his family. "Why don't you tell your momma about all the animals we saw at the zoo today?" she whispered.

Small fingers clutched the top edge of the quilt and lowered the cover to reveal blue eyes. "Had a good time." His voice was small.

"Little mister, tell Momma all about it."

Another rumble of thunder sent Sonny Boy back under the covers, but the rain no longer pounded the roof. She waited with Jane for Sonny Boy to say something more.

"He loves animals." Jane braced herself on her elbow.

"We had so much fun."

But he caused a moment or two of terror.

Carefully, Jane lifted the edge of the quilt. Beneath it, Sonny Boy's rhythmic breathing told them he'd fallen asleep.

"I'm sure he's out now." Jane rose from the bed. She crooked a finger, motioning for them to leave the room.

Suzanne resisted. She wanted to be close to him. Sonny Boy had brought new love and laughter into her life.

"In the family room," Jane whispered. "I want to hear why you want to kill me." Jane tiptoed from the room.

Suzanne rose, tucked pillows on either side of the boy to protect him from rolling off the bed, and followed Jane's lead, tiptoeing to the door. She turned at the door for one more look at her nephew. Maybe he'd have Mark's shoulders? Maybe his football-receiver hands? Maybe he'd like karate, like her.

But no doubt about it. Being both a Landry and a Maucele, that boy had *only* Cajun bones.

Suzanne reached the family room. Jane had already taken a seat in the wingback chair, looking like a queen on a throne. Back stiff. Hands folded in her lap. Eyes cast downward. As though she waited on terrible news.

Suzanne's heart softened. A mother would do anything to protect her young, which might explain Jane's well-buried secret.

But not tell her and Maggie? Why keep it from Mark?

She swallowed past seesawing emotions. Heat flushed through her body like a fast-rising tide as she tried to find the right words. Words to make Jane confess. Words to make Jane stay.

"Suzanne, you look pale. Let's sit you down." Jane rushed to her side, grasped her elbow, and directed her to the couch.

She clung to her friend's arm. Nausea clung to her. She pulled Jane to sit on the couch beside her. Closing her eyes, she took slow deep breaths, counting to seven on inhale, then seven on exhale. After three times, nausea slowly released its grip. She released her grip on Jane.

Had the junk food made her sick?

"I don't know what I've done, but can we talk about it, rather than fight?" Jane asked.

"A sip of water, please."

Jane rushed to fulfill the request.

"Thanks." Suzanne sipped, then motioned for Jane to sit again. "My truth. I've been keeping journals since I turned thirteen. My entire life is captured between those pages. My first teenaged party, the shooting, braces, and missing my dad.

"I wrote about the uncertainty I felt when you and Mark got married, though I loved being a bridesmaid. About my fear when Mark went to war. The relief of his return. The ache and anger when the two of you got divorced. My pangs of jealousy about being a third wheel when Mark started dating Maggie."

Beside her, Jane listened.

"Sonny Boy and I talked about family at the zoo." She patted Jane's hand. "He asked me about his daddy."

Jane's eyes grew wide, then she scrunched them closed. "Go on."

"He said his daddy was a soldier who went to war. That you told him I knew him. I can't tell you the emotions that caused me. When we came home, I put him down for a nap. I rummaged through my journals. Found one from about six years ago. It covered the dates of when Mark went on a trip. I'm guessing he went to Boston to visit you." She paused. If she'd hoped for a gushing confession, she'd missed the mark. Jane remained statute-still. Her trembling hands were the only clue that she was real.

"I did the timeline. Mark's visit. Mark's return. Mark asking Maggie to marry him. You not coming to their wedding." She paused again, hoping for a denial. Once she uttered the words she had to speak, once the information was out, there would be no turning back. No un-ringing the bell. This wasn't like catch-and-release fishing.

"And then I figured in Sonny Boy's birthday. You were pregnant, weren't you? That's why you didn't come back for the wedding," Suzanne barely got the words out. The pain of knowing tightened the band around her heart. She hated forcing Jane's hand, but they had to deal with the past before they could handle the future.

Jane hung her head.

"And, Sonny Boy's name isn't Chris, is it? It's Christopher. And not as in Christopher Robin, but as in Mark Christopher Maucele."

Tears trickled down Jane's face and dropped off her chin.

"How much of it did I get right? What is Sonny Boy's full name?" Suzanne closed the space between her and Jane. She hugged her.

"Oh, Suz." Jane let go of an anguished cry. "I swear, I swear, I swear. I always intended to tell you. To tell Mark. I never intended to keep my darlin' boy a secret. I always wanted him to know his father, you, and his family."

"What happened?"

"It's so complicated. Oh, God, it's complicated." Jane hid her face in her hands.

"I guess we're both in the praying mood," Suzanne said dryly. "I've got all night. And we'll talk about this for days, weeks, even months, because I think it might take that long for me to forgive you. When are you going to tell Maggie?"

Jane's arms hung limp. Resignation etched her face. Sadness oozed from her.

"If you don't tell her before you return to Boston, then I promise you, I will. The ostrich-strategy has come to an end."

"I didn't purposefully bury my head in the sand. I don't know *how* to tell her. You're Mark's sister, but Mark was Maggie's hero. The sun, moon, stars were hung by Mark Maucele. I think Maggie always loved him more than either of us."

Suzanne held her, uncertain what to say.

After a few minutes, she leaned away and wiped the tears from Jane's face. "Maggie's coming for dinner. Think about telling her about *my* nephew then."

The doorbell rang.

Jane jumped up and ran toward the bedroom.

Suzanne let her go and made her way to the door. "Hey, Maggie. You look lovely. How's your day? We have lots to talk about."

Maggie smiled. "The nicest greeting you've ever given me. Is something wrong?"

Suzanne stepped aside, opening the door wider. "There's a whole new world for us to discover now."

Chapter 14 – Maggie

*E*arlier in the day…

"Why did I tell Suz I'd come for dinner tonight?" Maggie opened the pantry door, reached to the bottom shelf, and wrapped her hand firmly around the neck of a bottle.

"Here's to you, Mark." She waved the bottle of an expensive limited edition bourbon. "Let's get drunk. No? Why not?"

Good-girl Catholic.

The words reverberated in her ears as though someone had spoken them aloud. She turned them over in her mind. "No. But I've got a desire to wash away the stink of my life."

Opening an upper kitchen cabinet, she grabbed a cut-crystal highball tumbler, a wedding present from Jane's father. "I think Jane helped me truly find my meaning of faith. Before her, I had prayed and prayed to be removed from this earth."

Maggie stepped toward the sleeping porch and turned the radio on low. Through the window, the darkened sky made it look more like evening than afternoon. Typical summer in the south. "I wasn't suicidal," she continued, hoping Mark could hear. "But I just couldn't see a reason to live…Momma and a revolving door of stepfathers. Me, left to care for the younger ones. And now, not a one of them speaks to me. Not even a condolence card or a flower at your funeral."

Pausing, she listened for some response. None came. Could Mark hear her?

"I'm told Heaven runs on its own kind of time. Like a dream, time has no beginning or end. That's difficult for me to grasp when so many times in my life I wanted to stop time, or in the case of you dying, rewind it."

Setting the glass on the side table next to an overstuffed chair, she broke the seal on the bottle and poured two-fingers of bourbon into the glass. The bottle *thunked* against the wooden tabletop. She lifted the tumbler. Swirled the bourbon. The deep amber liquid shimmied down the sides. Fascinated, she watched. "I read sweeter wines are more viscous, therefore, the tears flow slower down the sides of a glass. I don't get the reference to 'legs,' but tears makes sense. Bourbon isn't wine, but to me, alcohol is alcohol, the way sin is sin. By comparison, am I sweet because my tears for you came slow? You always liked my legs."

She placed the crystal glass beside the bottle. "This could make a nice little still-life painting. But it would need an open raw oyster and a bottle of hot sauce in the picture in order to sell in this part of the country."

Tucking herself into the overstuffed chair, she checked the time. Then, from her pocket, she pulled an amber bottle with ten remaining anxiety pills and set the pill bottle beside the bourbon. "I'll need the entire bottle of bourbon to help me get all these pills down."

Crack!

She hunched in the chair. Lightning struck nearby, searing the earth with a bolt of white-hot light. The stormy display rivaled a Fourth of July fireworks show. Deep rolling thunder sounded like timpani drums, rattling the glass in the windows and rattling her conscience. Looking out over the Rigolets' fast-moving currents and south toward Lake St. Catherine, Maggie wondered if the punctuated *booms* were a message from Heaven about lying and loving and hate.

Straightening, she eyed the glass of bourbon. Such a pretty color in an elegant glass.

Full of false promises.

Just like the pills.

How did someone ever get back to living when half of them was gone?

The ache of missing Mark whipped up at unexpected moments, like a swift-moving summer storm. However, maybe it was true. When one door closed, another opened. Maybe Sonny Boy would be the new guy in her life. A soft smile spread across her lips. He'd captured her heart immediately.

Jane's son.

A pang of jealousy pinged in her chest. Had Sonny Boy enjoyed his zoo outing with Suzanne? When would she get her turn at playing auntie? Was Jane playing favorites?

"*Beeeep. Beeeep. Beeeep.*" A weather warning interrupted the classical playlist on the local radio station. The news reported fifty mile-an-hour wind gusts.

Maggie drummed her fingers on the arm of the chair. Hope and worry buffeted her the way the storm buffeted the boats tied up at the dock. Another loud crack split the quiet. Maggie jumped. Her breath caught. Muscles tensed from the shock. Thunder followed. Her nerves quaked from fright.

Letting go of her breath, she settled back into the chair. "Okay. Okay. This Catholic girl will go to confession." She needed to atone for the moments when she'd hated Jane. God wouldn't ignore even a second of that emotional poison.

"I swear, I *don't* hate her. At least. not anymore," she whispered. Maybe angels would hear her plea and intervene on her behalf?

She needed Jane to stay. Needed the comfort of knowing that, along with Suzanne, the three of them would always stay friends. Their childhood oath had to withstand any test through time. She craved the security their friendship provided, then and now.

"We've been sisters for years." She hugged her knees. "Though over the last seven or so, communications came like quarterly newsletters with dates and times of events and weather. Not much personal content. How could Jane have neglected to tell us she gave birth to a son?"

She waited, not really expecting an answer, but still hoped for a comforting *knowing* from the other side as her human brain screamed, "A lie of omission."

"A son, Mark. Jane has a son," she whispered. If she could grow the love she held for them, then jealousy and envy—deadly sins she'd carried in her heart for years—would be pushed out.

She'd loved Jane wholeheartedly. At twelve, when she moved to Slidell and started school midyear, she never dreamt she'd have friends, let alone close ones who would embrace rather than shun her once they discovered the truth about the chaos of her homelife.

Jane sought her out the very first day and invited her to sit with her at lunch. When they made their way to the lunchroom, Maggie followed Jane's lead into the noisy auditorium.

"Is that all you've got to eat?" Jane leaned over and peered into the crumpled brown paper bag.

Ashamed, Maggie pulled out a sloppy peanut butter and jelly sandwich wrapped in crinkled waxed paper.

"Let's share." Jane took half of Maggie's sandwich and handed over half of her homemade chicken-salad sandwich. Dazed, Maggie stared. No one had ever done that. At her house, her siblings always grabbed for more food, never gave anything back.

"I've got chips and an apple. I'll get a knife, and we'll split it."

Gripped by the surprise of kindness, Maggie mutely nodded.

Jane returned and sliced the apple evenly. "Momma's a great cook," she said between chips. "She always makes my lunch. I don't like what they serve on the lunch line." She scrunched her nose, then smiled. "Hey, could you come over after school sometime and help us make cookies? We take them to the women's shelter. Momma is big on helping others. That's what we do."

Jane chatted. Maggie listened while they ate. A roar of voices surrounded them.

Halfway through lunch, a girl arrived and stood beside the table. "Sorry, I'm late. Band practice ran over."

"Hey, girl, this is Maggie. Maggie, this is Suzanne, my sorta-sister."

Suzanne eyed her. "Hey."

Maggie flashed a smile, hoping to disarm the guarded energy swirling around Jane's friend. At least Suzanne didn't give her a stink eye.

Maggie learned the two had been friends since before preschool. That kind of bond remained rock-solid strong. To hear them tell it, growing up they had an umbilical cord stretching across the canal between their families' camps. She also learned their mommas *and* grandmommas had been friends. A new concept for her since she didn't have any close friends and barely spoke to her own relatives. Her two older sisters stayed away from home as much as possible—for good reason. Her younger siblings were too young to understand. Back then, her only thought had been that if she submitted, then she could protect the babies from abuse.

Now her best childhood memories were shared with Jane and Suzanne. She chuckled remembering that fateful day on the bus a few weeks after meeting them. And where was Byron Guidry now? That day on the bus ride home, he sealed the friendship between her and Suzanne after he'd teased about his intention to kiss her once they got off the bus. He puckered his lips, showed the tip of his tongue, motioning as though licking. Terrified, Maggie slunk down in her seat. Suzanne, sitting several seats ahead, turned around and belted out for all to hear, "Byron Guidry, I'll beat you with a cane pole if you try to contaminate *my* friend with your sloppy spit." Byron had laughed but kept his distance after that.

Days turned into weeks. School ended. Summer arrived. As the heat and humidity climbed, friendship knitted her closer to The Two, which was how she'd thought of Jane and Suzanne. She spent time with them on the island swimming and racing in pirogues in the canals. Those were some of her most cherished memories.

And those Saturday night dances... she fanned herself. So much fun!

Until *that* night.

Had it not been for Jane, she would've fallen apart. Nothing prepared her for watching a man get shot. Claude Dupuis—the secret they'd never told anyone.

The day after the shooting, Suzanne's and Jane's mothers had insisted she join them, along with Suzanne and Jane, to visit Mrs. Dupuis in the hospital. The woman's battered face, bandaged eye, a red slash down her right cheek, and a wrapped gunshot wound on her upper arm were visible.

Maggie shivered.

Even then, she'd known the hospital gown covered other telltale marks of abuse. Seeing Mrs. Dupuis helpless in bed struck Maggie hard. She understood pity through the eyes of others. From that moment on, she had to choose wisely. She never wanted a man in her life like her dead father, abusive stepfathers, or Mrs. Dupuis's husband.

The past might be the past, but strands of it grew like vines into the future… The rootstock was still the same, and as such, two became three, who became the Belles—they would always stick together. She counted on it.

While the love and support of her friends boosted her feelings of safety, old lies still haunted her like glowing white chalk marks on a blackboard.

Maggie rose from the chair and stretched. Her body ached. She hadn't exercised or danced, all activities of her usual routine, since Mark died. Shaking out her hands, she tried to shake off the melancholy of old memories. "I know it's not my place to judge, but I believe Claude Dupuis deserved to die."

She argued her case as she stretched but still feared God's wrath for lying about what she saw. The police had questioned her a second and a third time, and she'd faithfully kept to the story Jane told her to tell. She'd made a conscious choice to lie and then prayed for forgiveness every night to save Mrs. Dupuis from jail for defending herself.

"And Mr. Dupuis's body was never found, so *maybe* he isn't dead," Maggie whispered. A sliver of hope had remained all these years. After Downward Facing Dog, she stood and looked heaven bound, hoping absolution would rain down on her.

Outside, the sky lightened. The wind settled. Rain no longer poured. Maggie straightened and checked her watch. If she wanted to arrive on time, given rush-hour traffic, she needed to leave for Suz's in a few minutes. Trying to ground her energy more, she took a deep breath and let it go. The Belles were all together again, plus one. Sonny Boy. Who was his father? Where was his father? Did he help Jane in raising the boy, or was he an absentee father? Did he pay child support? Or was he dead, like her own?

Thunder rumbled in the distance as if on extended long play. The table lamp flashed off, then on. Maggie blinked. If only her emotions would stop flashing back and forth.

"Jane has a son." She wanted to stop jealousy from rubbing old wounds.

From their first meeting, until the day Jane married Mark, she'd shared every major life event with her friend. First day of junior high. First day of high school. Learning to drive. First dates. Trials and initiations that led them to adulthood. And through it all, the hardest moment had been surviving Mark and Jane's wedding day.

Maggie sipped the bourbon. It went down smooth.

The bottle of pills stared at her. "Not today."

She flicked the bottle, knocking it on its side, picked up her purse, and located her keys. A vibration of uncertainty tingled in her fingers.

Maggie covered her stomach with her hand. The push-me/pull-me tug-of-war made her physically ill.

Had Jane ever discovered her secret feelings for Mark?

Just as her *knowing* had foretold, after Mark and Jane divorced, Mark turned to her. She became Mrs. Mark Maucele. After she married him, the island Jane and Suzanne loved so much became her home, too.

The irony was she was the only one of the three to live there now.

It was the only place in the world she wanted to be.

With keys in hand, Maggie slipped on her shoes. "Help me, Mark. I need Jane's strength and guidance and support now that you're gone. And I'm sorry I disappointed you."

Wishful thinking, dutiful praying, and following all the rules hadn't gifted her with what she wanted most—Mark and a loving family of their own.

In the background, the radio played a piano concerto. If Mark answered her plea, his whispers were mixed with the music and she couldn't hear it.

A *knowing* popped into her mind. *Help Jane!*

"How?" she whispered. "What do I do? Does she need money? Help raising her son? Tell me *how* to help Jane."

After going over finances with an accountant, she had a better fix on her situation. Mark had left her a hefty sum as his life insurance beneficiary. Financially, she was in good shape. Maybe she could start a college fund for Sonny Boy. Maybe teach the boy to fish and crab and swim. Maybe, when he was older and she just old, she would deed the camp to him.

Mark might like that.

But how did she approach Jane about all of this? The woman's pride was as thick and dense as a brick wall. She was good at helping others but never at accepting it.

When the worst of the storm had played out, Maggie locked the door and ran down the stairs. Her first day back in the real working world had been exhausting. After balancing books for her hair salons, paying overdue bills, and ordering supplies, her dinner with the family would be the perfect ending to a trying day.

She turned onto Highway 90 and passed a truck carrying pilings. It turned onto Touche Road. Pilings could mean only one thing—building construction. A dock in the making? A house rising above the ground? Had someone bought the old Dupuis place?

Her mind flashed to the night of the shooting. She cringed and shook away the memory.

Maggie jumped on I-10 to bypass one-way city streets. She exited near the Superdome onto Claiborne and headed for the Garden District.

She couldn't wait to see Sonny Boy again. Maggie smiled. The nickname suited the little tyke. Chris didn't fit. Jane had said she named him that, but Maggie had only heard her call the child "Sonny Boy" or "Little Man." That didn't mean his name was Chris any more than Sonny Boy was. No, Jane's Momma had loved the name Christopher—that had to be it. Just like Mark's middle name. It was yet another thing they had in common.

Pulling up to Suzanne's house, she parked and made her way to the front door. Suzanne greeted her with a let's-get-Bourbon-Street-crazy smile, but her aura read sadness.

Over what?

Maggie stepped into the foyer and slipped off her shoes before hugging Suz. "What's wrong?" she whispered.

"It's been a long day. Jane is changing…I think. And Sonny Boy, at last check, had buried himself in Jane's bed. The storm got loud and frightened him."

Maggie nodded. Something about Suzanne's words didn't ring true. *Knowings* made it hard to trust what people said. Sometimes people lied to her, but she'd learned more often they lied to themselves. Discerning between the two took work.

Inside the house, a door banged open, and the sound of running feet drifted closer.

"Ta-da," Sonny Boy cried. He ran and hugged Maggie's legs. "I missed you."

She scooped him up, hugged him, then planted a big *swack* on his cheek. "Hey, Sonny Boy. Tell me about your day."

When she put him down, he took her hand and Suzanne's, guiding them into the family room. They sat on the couch while he sat across from them on an ottoman. He smiled wide as his feet swung up and back.

"Aunt Suz." He looked up at Suzanne. "Mom says I can call you that. Is it okay if I do?"

"Sure."

"Aunt Maggie, Aunt Suz took me to the zoo. I saw lots of animals. I even saw a bear. I think I'll call him Pooh, since…" A mischievous grin lit the little boy's face, like he was holding tight to a secret and about to pop.

"Pooh, who?" Maggie teased him. She knelt beside him and tickled his side.

"Hey! That's where my Cajun bone is. Momma said so." He looked resolute. "I need to tell Latisha, I am so Cajun."

"Of course you are, you're a Landry. So you're at least part Cajun."

Suzanne coughed as if to clear her throat. A prickling sensation climbed up Maggie's back. When she looked at Suzanne, Suzanne looked away, as though mesmerized by something beyond the window.

"So, who's this Pooh?" Maggie turned her attention back to Sonny Boy.

"He was a real bear, just like in the zoo. Only, in the story Momma read, he was in a book. He lived in the woods with his friends." Sonny Boy smiled as if proud of himself, then crossed his arms. "Pooh was a bear with a friend named Christopher Robin…but I'm just Christopher."

"For some reason I thought you preferred to be called 'Sonny Boy'."

"I did. Except…today at the zoo, a man said he liked my soldier's haircut. Asked me if my daddy had one. I told him, 'I donno, but my daddy was a soldier.' "

Suzanne began coughing hard. Maggie patted her on the back.

"Water," Suzanne eked out.

Maggie ran for the kitchen. Grabbed a glass from the cabinet and filled it halfway. When she made it back to the living room, Sonny Boy stood on the couch next to Suzanne. He patted her head, then hugged her. "It's okay, I'm here," he cooed, sounding just like Jane. Witnessing tenderness from a little boy with her often-cynical friend, Maggie's heart oozed with love. He was so darling.

Suzanne gulped the water.

A movement from across the room caught Maggie's attention. Jane in a robe and tousled hair leaned against the doorframe, fingers together as if in prayer. Her chin rested on her fingertips. Her face glowed with love.

Love for a little boy.

A stab of pain struck Maggie. She would never know that kind of love. She would never feel that feeling. She would never experience that kind of pride. It only came from being the mother of a child.

But maybe, just maybe, she could get close? Maybe Sonny Boy was the child she'd been waiting for? A surrogate son.

Chapter 15 - Suzanne

Suzanne stood in the doorway to the dining room. Her family readied themselves for dinner. The idea of that warmed her from the top of her head to the tips of her toes. They'd been apart for years, yet a closeness still knitted around them as though they'd always been tangled together.

"Don't let it burn." Jane pointed to the kitchen, then she gathered silverware from the china cabinet's drawer.

"Never worry." Moving back to the cooktop, Suzanne stirred the sautéing onions. Old roles took over today. Jane set the table. Maggie tossed the salad. They moved as though friendship muscle memory kept them in motion, but they were still hiding behind polite smiles.

She added green peppers and garlic. The vegetables sizzled. She stirred the ingredients in the cast-iron pan.

If iron determination could keep them connected then she had enough for the three of them. She'd lost her family to divorce years ago. Lost her brother recently. She would not lose Jane. She would not lose Sonny Boy. She would not lose her family of choice.

Their relationship was a like a three-legged stool. Each leg was equally important. And their rocky relationship would undoubtedly grow rockier before reaching a leveling harmony.

"I'm hungry." Maggie grabbed a spoon and tasted from the pan. "Yum. Seasoning is perfect." She collected salad dressing bottles from the refrigerator, deposited them on the dining table, then went to the family room to be entertained by Sonny Boy.

Suzanne added shrimp, and the frying pan sizzled again. Familiar scents filled the kitchen. The aromas brought back memories. She glanced at Jane. She showed no hint of the secret she held. Since Jane hadn't confided in her about Sonny Boy, could she trust her with a secret that could potentially devastate her entire life?

Suzanne poked at a shrimp with a fork, wanting to take a jab at Jane for creating the mistrust pinging inside her.

In fairness, Jane wasn't alone. Maggie had lied, too. She never told anyone she was pregnant, nor mentioned she and Mark had set up a nursery. Grant discovered it when he'd retrieved clothes for Mark's burial. He described it as perfect for the "Best of New Orleans Interiors."

Suzanne turned off the gas burner and stirred in breadcrumbs to the shrimp mixture. Tonight's entrée was shrimp-stuffed mirlitons—or, as her daddy used to call them, ve-ge-ta-ble pears. They were ready for the oven. Sonny Boy's menu included a hot dog, mac-n-cheese, and sliced cucumbers. Where he picked up that propensity, she had no clue.

She shivered. Anticipation was like the first bite of cotton candy at the fair. She almost expected Mark to walk through the door. Her big brother with his warm brown eyes, broad shoulders, and large football-catching hands had made them feel safe. Loved them all, but in very different ways.

Suzanne gazed at her friends. They made her grief over Mark's death bearable. Beside the sadness beat an ache, and instead of Mark hanging around, mooching something to eat, making excuses to be near Jane, as he had when they were teenagers, his place at the table remained an empty, loud-echoing silence.

She wrinkled her nose and sniffed to force back tears. Her wonderfully protective, predictable southern-male brother with his definite ideas about women and marriage would never sit down to a meal with them again. She stifled a sob trying to escape from her throat.

"Oven is ready," Jane said.

"As though I didn't hear the chiming bells." Suzanne turned to prevent Jane from seeing her distress. "Always the mother of the group."

Maggie took Sonny Boy to wash his hands. He reappeared moments later in the dining room, smacking his hands together.

"I wash'em, Momma. See?"

"Jane, do you want an adult beverage with dinner?" Suzanne asked. After pulling out a tray of garlic bread, she slid a baking pan with the stuffed squash into the oven, closed the door, and set the timer. "Twenty minutes. Shall we start on our salads?

"Yay for food," Sonny Boy proclaimed.

"A beer, please," Jane called over her shoulder as she wrangled her son into a chair.

"I'll take one, too," Maggie called out.

"Me, three!" Sonny Boy cried, clapping for each word. "Me, three!"

"You, little man, be quiet," Jane scolded. "You're not old enough to drink beer. I'll let you know when that day arrives. Maybe when you're thirty. Until then, it's juice for you."

Suzanne brought a small tray from the kitchen with two bottles of beer, a cup with grape juice, and a cocktail in a tall champagne glass. She placed their drinks in front of them.

Maggie eyed her. "That's something new for you. What is it? I like the color and fizz."

"A pomegranate cocktail." Well, she hadn't lied completely. Pomegranate juice was the primary ingredient. She'd added ginger ale for bubbles instead of champagne, though she wished for something alcoholic. She needed liquid courage.

Would tonight be the night she confessed to Maggie and Jane about the reason for her health kick?

She let go of a breath. No. Tonight was for bonding. Besides, one secret a night was enough, and that honor was all Jane's. Sonny Boy made the loss of Mark more noticeable, and at the same time, offered hope. A part of her brother lived. The energy of his little son filled the room the way the aroma of country-fried chicken was comfort food. Sonny Boy, like his daddy, charmed them by just being himself.

Sitting, Suzanne motioned for Maggie to sit on her right across from Sonny Boy and Jane. "We must get you a booster seat," Suzanne told the boy.

"What do we do before we eat?" Jane slid a napkin over her lap.

"I think we have everything." Suzanne passed a basket with garlic bread to Maggie.

Sonny Boy smacked his hands together as if he'd spent every day of his life having dinner with them. "My turn to pray," he announced. Then he bowed his head, his forearms resting on the table's edge with his forehead on his fingertips.

"Bless the zoo. Bless Auntie Suzanne for taking me to the zoo. Bless this food. Amen."

"Amen" echoed around the table.

When Suzanne opened her eyes, she caught the tilt of Maggie's head. "Since when is it *Auntie* Suzanne?"

She shrugged slightly.

As the others began to eat, Suzanne soaked up Sonny Boy's exuberance. Mark would've loved being a father. Teaching his son to cast a net for blue crabs and paddle a pirogue through the canals at Lake St. Catherine. He'd teach him New Orleans traditions, like how to suck crawfish heads, deep-fry a turkey, and catch throws at carnival. And at least once, Mark would teach him the ropes of being King at the Maucele family Mardi Gras party.

"Eat." Maggie smiled and handed her the salad bowl.

Jane cut up the hot dog on Sonny Boy's plate. "What was the most fun you had at the zoo today?"

The boy furrowed his brow and pondered. It was as though he mentally replayed each moment and was trying to select the best. "Ah…I think…the elephant ride! It was a daddy elephant."

"Really?" Maggie chimed in.

"Ah-huh."

"Yes, ma'am," Jane corrected. "You have to show others your manners."

"Okay, but Momma?" Sonny Boy looked around the table at each of them. "Why do daddies make everyone sad?"

Stunned, Suzanne coughed and reached for her drink.

Silence hung in the room.

"Who's sad?" Jane pushed salad around on her plate with her fork.

"You're sad when you talk about your daddy. You get really sad when I ask about *my* daddy. Auntie Maggie's sad about the man who died. Well, he wasn't her daddy, but a man who made her sad. And Auntie Suzanne's sad because of her brother…but is she sad about anyone else, too?" Sonny Boy turned his big searching eyes on his mother.

Suzanne clutched the napkin on her lap. She dared not look at Jane or Maggie. Dread gripped her chest. She held her breath. She'd heard children could often be highly intuitive. Did Sonny Boy have intuition he didn't yet understand?

Maggie chuckled. "Little man, you've got great perception. But, you know, sadness is a part of life. It's okay to be sad. And when you share your sadness with friends and family, then you're not alone. You also know it won't last forever. Are you sad?"

Suzanne turned to look at Sonny Boy. He pondered, his mouth twisting to one side. "Nope. I'm not sad."

Maggie clapped. "Yay! So how about we talk about going to the aquarium tomorrow? Have you ever been to one?"

"But wait, what's per . . . per—"

"Per-cep-tion," Jane repeated. "It's like making a guess about something and being right. Like when Beth asks you to pick a card, and then she tries to guess which one you picked."

"Oh." Sonny Boy looked contemplative. "Like I knew that Jimmy was sick?"

"Yes, like that."

"What was wrong with Jimmy?" Maggie asked.

"He had to go to the hospital. They gave him stuff that made him lose his hair," Sonny Boy said.

"Sonny Boy sensed something was wrong with his friend before the boy or his mother did. But he didn't know how to articulate it. He doesn't understand about cancer." Jane spoke in a quiet even tone.

Suzanne resisted moving her hands to hide her stomach. All she needed was for Sonny Boy's powers of perception to hone in on her condition and blurt it out at the table. The first store-bought pregnancy test had turned color. The second one had two lines instead of one. The third showed a plus sign. But nothing about her body felt different. Those tests had to be false positives. A trip to the doctor on Wednesday would deliver the definitive results. However, she planned to weigh all options before then, just in case the damn tests were true.

The oven timer chimed. Startled, she jumped.

"I'll be right back." Suzanne left the table. She'd never been a drinker. An occasional beer or mixed drink. But if there ever were a time when she wanted a shot of bourbon, this was it.

She pulled dinner from the oven and carried it to the table and set the baking pan in the center.

"Auntie Suzanne! I'm going to the aquarium with Auntie Maggie tomorrow. But first I get to meet my grandpops!" Sonny Boy clapped. His whole body wiggled with glee, reminding her of a dog shedding water from its coat after a romp in the lake.

"I'll want to hear all about it."

As the dinner conversation continued around her, her thoughts drifted. *Would Mark have liked being an uncle? Would Grant even consider fatherhood again?*

She had loved Grant from the moment she saw him—sweaty, tanned, and moving rigging on a shrimper. The physical attraction brought her to her knees. Well, her heart dropped to her knees. She stared. Her mouth turned desert-dry though she was drinking a beer. Somehow, she had the presence of mind to wave. He waved back. Struck dumb, she'd fallen in love with a fisherman. Later she learned Grant considered manual labor better than working out at the gym to keep his body toned since most days he sat in an air-conditioned office behind a big desk and ruled a construction empire.

She imagined the horror on his face if she told him she was pregnant. He'd never shout. Just show disappointment with an icy silence. She'd witnessed that during one of his difficult business transactions.

She sighed. With her, he'd always been straight up about not wanting kids. Made the rules of their marriage very clear. And she'd completely agreed and had given up on the idea of ever having her own family after dealing with stepchildren.

"Sor-bet. I like ice cream better," Sonny Boy said when Suzanne served up dessert.

"What flavor? We'll have that tomorrow," Suzanne asked, though her thoughts still swirled with worry about Grant.

After dinner, Maggie took Sonny Boy by the hand. "Let's get you a bath, little guy."

"I like lots of bubbles and toys. Are there toys?"

Maggie's response faded as the pair headed down the hall. They were cute together. Her smiles made life easier, lighter, but how would she ever tell Maggie—the woman who had given daily updates for the last year on her quest to conceive—that she'd chosen a husband and marriage over a child? Would ending a pregnancy be the very thing to end their friendship? Not having Maggie in her life would be like losing Mark all over again.

"Suzanne?" Jane's voice interrupted her thoughts.

"Sorry. Just thinking."

"How about I clear? Would you like another drink before I start?" Jane stood and picked up her plate.

"Thanks, but no more for me." She had to get up and move.

Jane's head tilted and motioned toward the kitchen. A prickling fear inched up Suzanne's back. Her friend clearly wanted to discuss something in private. No way would Jane finagle her way out of telling Maggie the truth. Besides, whatever she would say might give her clues about what words to use to reveal her own secret.

She hit "play" and smooth jazz flowed from hidden speakers. It calmed her trembling hands. She hated keeping a secret from Maggie and Jane, but Jane most of all. Their friendship had been glued together since they were toddlers. Jane had the answers to life's problems, and now she needed her wisdom.

They tidied the kitchen and put away the remaining food. Jane plunked two glasses with ice on the counter, poured water, then squeezed in some lemon. Squeals of joy mixed with Maggie's laughter punctuated the flowing jazz music.

"Let's go sit by the pool," Jane said. From her tone, Suzanne understood that refusing wasn't an option. She followed Jane out, her stomach somersaulting ahead.

They sat in chaise loungers side by side. The water reflected a cool blue. Lights inside the pool illuminated the water and cast a soft glow on Jane's face. Suzanne remained quiet, waiting for Jane to speak.

"Suzanne?"

Half-reclined, she held the glass of cold water with both hands, resting it on her stomach, and closed her eyes. "Yes?"

"Are you okay?"

"I couldn't be better. You're here. Maggie's here. And I have a nephew. This is the real world. Mark can't be here. Grant will be home soon. Life is perfect."

"Would you *tell* me if something was wrong?"

"There's nothing to tell."

"Does one lie deserve another? Is that what this is about? I didn't actually lie. I just didn't tell the truth."

Suzanne took a deep breath and quietly exhaled. "You're going to split hairs over semantics? I have a nephew. It took him nine months to get here. He's going to turn five shortly. And to be clear, *you* never told me about him. I guessed."

"Fair enough. Now I'm guessing. I saw you when Sonny Boy spoke about his friend being ill. A very confusing thing for him. He kept telling me Jimmy had a ball inside of him that shouldn't be there. I thought the kid had swallowed something. His mother took him to the doctor. They discovered a tumor inside a kidney."

"Wow. Sonny Boy knew that?"

"I saw your movements when we were talking about that…and the look on your face. You're hiding something. I know about hiding things. And you have to know, if you need me, I'm here for you. If you're sick, I'll be here for you."

Suzanne sat up, surprised to see a glistening stain on Jane's cheek.

"I watched my momma die. Mark's gone. I will fight with you and for you. You can't die on me, too!"

"What exactly do you think I'm hiding?" She hesitated. Was this confession time? Setting the drink aside, she faced Jane and reached for her hands, needing support as much as wanting to offer Jane comfort.

"Do you have cancer?" Jane whispered.

"Oh God! No!" Suzanne's stomach tightened. There was something worse than being pregnant, and it took Jane to make her see it.

"Then what's wrong?"

"Hey, there!" Maggie called out. "Y'all disappeared on us."

Suzanne turned to see her nephew running straight for her, his arms open wide with no shred of doubt she would catch him. Would Grant do the same for her?

Chapter 16

*I*blinked, then closed my eyes again. No hint of day filtered between the slats in the shutters. Quiet was a welcome blanket before sunshine flipped a switch, snapping on the day. Bone-tired, I pulled the covers over my shoulders and moved my feet. They connected with a bump near the foot of the bed. I rose up and noticed a lump wrapped in a blue blanket. It looked like a turtle hiding in its shell.

"Sonny Boy," I whispered. "Come here."

The bump moved.

"Just follow my voice to a warm cozy place."

With his eyes shut, my son crawled toward me. I threw back the bedding. He snuggled close, and I covered him.

"Sleep. You have a busy day of exciting adventures." My chest hurt. My heart was about to pop from loving him so much.

He must have snuck in during the early morning hours and tried not to wake me, knowing I'd carry him back to his bed and tuck him beside his old teddy bear. It had taken work to get him to sleep in his own bed all night in Salem. But a strange house with a huge bed in a big room could scare even a tough guy. I smiled, resisting the urge to run my fingers over his hair. Gone were the short locks. His military buzz cut brought out a number of subtle changes in him.

Like last night.

I had stared when his eyes lit with excitement as he shared about different animals at the zoo. Something about the way the corners of his smile lifted made me think of Mark. And even for a pint-sized boy, he understood he had a captive audience. He played it to the hilt, flirting before he even knew the word.

It left me with a longing for Mark. My childhood friend and then my teenaged boyfriend. Our relationship had blossomed into us becoming lovers. Not long after that, I walked down the aisle, and we exchanged "I do's." However, life spun us three-sixty degrees and back to being just friends. He had remained an important part of my life even if he wasn't the last man I'd kissed. But he *was* the last man I'd been intimate with in a biblical way. Was it shameful of me to hold so tight to the memory of the feel of his lips, his hands, his skin against mine?

Would he have any advice about how to break the news about Sonny Boy to Maggie?

Soon the first rays of light peeked around the bedroom shutters. I rolled, careful not to wake Sonny Boy. Night began to slink away, but it didn't drag my anxiety with it. I'd fallen asleep searching for the perfect way to tell Maggie the truth. My thoughts came quick, lots of false starts as I practiced but no follow-through. Needless qualifying words crashed together like a twenty-car pileup on I-10 on a foggy morning.

Actually, the words were simple to speak: I love you. I need you to be Sonny Boy's mother. Mark was his father.

The "after words" worried me. The emotional fallout. Exhausted, I had fallen asleep turning different scenarios around in my head. None of them included her running to me, wrapping her arms around me, and telling me she forgave me. Beyond what Maggie might *say*, what would the news do to her?

After much rumination, one thought distinguished itself from the rest—I was moving home. Whenever my end time came, New Orleans would be my resting place, just like my mother's. Until then, this is where

I wanted to be. I needed time to rebuild trust. I couldn't further risk my son's future. Some of my buried relatives had been riverboat gamblers, but they didn't pass that risk-taking DNA to me. I couldn't roll the dice. Sonny Boy deserved to be encircled by loved ones.

Dang, Mark. You were always the optimistic one. Said everything would work out. What do I do?

Sonny Boy flailed an arm and rolled over again. I chuckled. He'd interrupted my conversation with his father. With a light touch, I palmed my hand over my son's shorn hair. Mark's hair had felt the same after basic training. I closed my eyes, remembering...

"Recruit Maucele reporting for duty!" A loud voiced called from the other side of the tiny Boston apartment door. When I opened it, he jerked to attention.

"Mark!" I had missed him for the last two months. "You didn't call! I wanted to meet you at the airport."

He pulled me to him, scooped me up, and kissed me hard. The kiss sent heat shooting to my toes and it pooled low and warm in my belly. I wanted that tingling deep desire to last forever.

"If you came to the airport, I couldn't do this." He carried me across the threshold, kicking the door closed, a bang as loud as a gun blast rattling the living room window. He didn't stop until he hovered me over our bed. Then he pressed his lips to mine with an urgency I'd not experienced from him before.

Love flooded my heart. Excitement made me flush. Left me burning for the man I'd married. College football player turned soldier. And he was home for a week.

Setting me on the bed, he climbed on and lay next to me. His fingers started with the top button of my flannel shirt. His gaze never left mine. He didn't hurry his actions. The heat he caused was about to burn me alive.

"*Mark.*" My urgency was real. I grabbed for the buttons on his uniform.

"Lie still, darlin'." He patted my hands away. "I'm gonna *love* every inch of you. We're gonna do it slow."

Him undressing me, kissing me, left me light-headed with desire. *Making love each and every time with him since I married him had been heaven…*

I shook my head to clear my mind of the memory. But the afterglow of lovemaking, *that* I would always feel whenever my thoughts drifted to that part of our relationship. We had chemistry. Sharing love was the one thing we'd always done right. But life beyond the bedroom challenged us in ways we never imagined before we married.

Love hadn't conquered all.

Gazing at my sleeping son, I pushed all thoughts aside to cherish the moment. Closing my eyes, I imagined, for a few minutes, peace existed on earth.

"Momma?" a small voice whispered. Then wet smacking lips kissed my forehead. "I love you, Momma."

"Hmm." I drifted between asleep and awake.

"Get up. I want to meet Grandpops."

I squinted one eye open and closed it quick. "I smell bacon frying. Who do you think is in the kitchen?"

"Don't know. I'll see." He rolled, his feet hitting the floor with a *plop*, and then he ran out of the bedroom.

"I could kill myself for all the nights I partied instead of sleeping. I should've been saving up for when I became a mother." I groaned and threw back the covers. Daily, I grew more tired more easily.

By the time I managed to stand, Sonny Boy ran back in the bedroom, his fists pumping in time with his footsteps, reminding me of an old-fashioned steam locomotive.

"Do I like as-per-ra-gus?" His pinched brow almost made me laugh.

"Asparagus?"

"That's what I said."

"I don't know. I don't think I've ever fed you that. Why?"

"Latisha is making casserole. Don't know what that is."

I giggled at my son's new learning experience. "How about we be adventurous and try it? Even if I explain it to you, you'll have no way of knowing what it's like until it's in your mouth. Now, get dressed. How about shorts and your New Orleans t-shirt?"

My pint-size boy quirked his mouth to one side and closed one eye as if in deep contemplation. "Okay." He marched like a toy soldier out of the room.

I went to the closet and found my sundress.

"You're *so* good with him. The perfect mother."

"Oh! Suzanne, you startled me. Did karate teach you the art of walking silently to scare your opponent?"

"Are *you* an opponent?"

I huffed. "No, of course not. I meant—"

"Didn't mean to scare you. I love watching the two of you together. I can't imagine I could ever be that nurturing. I've grown too selfish."

"What kind of crap is that? You'd be a fabulous mom. I see you with him."

Suzanne's face softened. Her body relaxed. "I love him."

My heart flip-flopped. "I know you do. He loves you, too. And I know you and Grant have this 'no children rule,' but Christopher Marcus could use a cousin."

Suzanne shook her head. "Not in the cards. And now we know Maggie can't have children. I guess Sonny Boy's going to be one spoiled little guy."

"But, Suzanne—"

"Look, you want him to have more kin, then get married and have more children." Suzanne held up her hand to silence any objection I might have wanted to voice. If she only knew I wished for that option, too.

"Breakfast will be ready soon. Egg casserole with asparagus and bacon. Hollandaise sauce. I'll go make sure *my* nephew is dressed." She left the room and left an ache in my heart.

After breakfast, I pulled a camera from my suitcase and tucked it into my purse before gathering my boy for a new adventure. After seeing my father yesterday and learning sobriety maintained a high priority in his daily life, my misgivings about bringing my son and his grandfather together had diminished, though not entirely disappeared. Hope floated around me. I grinned and skipped down the hall.

When I reached the family room, my heart somersaulted so hard I stumbled but managed to keep from falling. Photo albums our mother's had kept were stacked higher than my son was tall on the coffee table. He sat on a cushion on the floor, his profile in my direct line of vision. Suzanne flipped pages that captured all the memories the Landrys and Mauceles shared in glossy four-by-sixes. I paused, wanting to trust Suzanne wouldn't offer any information about my son's parentage, but a tugboat of doubt nagged as I eavesdropped. My stomach clenched.

"You and Momma and Auntie Maggie look really funny here." Sonny Boy pointed.

"I know. That was before our senior prom. We had big southern hey-ya."

"Hair?"

She laughed and rubbed the top of his head. "Yes…something teenage girls did to look glamorous and attract boys. Someday, you're going to find one you like."

"I like girls now," Sonny Boy insisted. "You, Auntie Maggie, Momma, and Beth. Latisha, too."

"Yes, but you'll take it to a whole new level someday."

He rolled his eyes and his head as though to say she was crazy.

Suzanne's laughter lilted airily like well-tuned chimes.

The clench in my stomach eased.

Suzanne might be mad about me keeping my boy a secret. However, her devotion to the little guy radiated in her voice.

"Who's that?" Sonny Boy pointed to another picture.

Suzanne lifted the picture for a better look.

"That's my brother Mark. He died about six weeks ago. He was married—"

My heart dropped. I raced into the room and spoke in a rush. "Suz, we're going to meet my dad at the cathedral. Will you join us?"

"Yeah!" Sonny Boy jumped up and clapped. "Please. Please."

"I want to take Sonny Boy on his first streetcar ride. Experience the old world." My laugh was forced. "Like when we were kids. He's going to meet Grandpops. We'll have some lunch before Maggie takes him for the afternoon. Why don't you join us?" My heart beat double time waiting for Suzanne to respond.

"Well, I haven't seen your dad in a while…if I wouldn't be intruding."

Sonny Boy pulled Suzanne's hand. "Get up. Let's go."

"All right. It will be *interesting* to see you and your grandfather together."

I didn't miss Suzanne's raised eyebrows. If looks could kill, I would be pulverized estrogen. But then, she had crossed the line, and I still could give stink eye as good as I could as a kid.

As we walked out the back door of the house, Suzanne produced a baseball cap and plunked it on Sonny Boy's head. She held his hand and walked with him a few blocks to a St. Charles streetcar stop. I tagged along behind. The idea had been to include Suzanne in my plans, not for Suzanne to commandeer the outing. A stab of jealousy pricked me. Usually, Sonny Boy and I did most things together, the two of us. Beth now and then. Mr. Finley sometimes. I would have to shift my paradigm. I would have to share him. Though I hadn't given much thought to how expanding the family circle might impact me, never considered I'd feel like an intruder when it came to my son's life.

"Don't worry about me, I'll follow behind." I pulled on sunglasses.

Blood is thicker than water.

The whisper of words tickled my ears. I stopped. "Mark?" I whispered back. No response. "If it's you doing that, then stop. Unless you've got real advice."

I sighed. I didn't hate that he was right. I hated that he wasn't there for me to argue with, before giving in and finally agreeing with him in the end. That's how almost everything between us went…except for the divorce.

The streetcar stopped.

"You take him." Suzanne stepped aside. I climbed on with Sonny Boy in tow, took a seat by the window, pulling my boy onto my lap. Suzanne paid the fare, then slid next to me.

"Sonny Boy, I spy something that begins with the letter *a*. Do you know what it is?"

"Airplane!"

Suzanne chuckled. "Yes, airplane starts with *a*. The I-Spy game is about seeing things around you. Do you see an airplane right now?"

"Sure, up in the sky." He squirmed in my lap, leaned, and pointed outside the window. His hand reached beyond the opening.

"No, sir. Hands inside. You have to obey the rules." My words came quick and sounded harsher than I intended.

"Okay." His smile turned sullen.

To keep the moment from dissolving into a pout-fest, I sat him up, bounced him on my knee until he chanted, "Giddy-up. Giddy-up."

"Humph. That's rich coming from you." Suzanne leaned close and whispered, "I think you've broken every rule of our friendship."

"Don't start. We can argue about that later. In fact, after he leaves with Maggie, *we* need to have this out," I hissed in a low breath. "I will not have you telling my son *anything* before I want him to know it. And you know exactly what I mean."

"A threat? I have every right to tell him about—"

"About what?" Sonny Boy cupped my cheeks with his hands to get my attention.

Suzanne turned and looked away.

"Auntie Suz wants to tell you about all the wonderful things at the aquarium, but she really doesn't want to spoil the surprise." I smiled my best Pollyanna grin and removed his hands.

The streetcar stopped. Suzanne stood first. She took Sonny Boy's hand and helped him off while I brought up the rear.

"Look, Sonny Boy! *B* is for balloons. And look over there. A man making animals out of balloons. Let's go see him."

Before I could make it to the first step down, Suzanne and Sonny Boy hit the pavement, making a laser line to a street performer. The balloon man made a crown and placed it on Sonny Boy's head. While Suzanne paid the man, I checked my watch. We had several blocks to walk to Jackson Square. I did not want to be late. To keep peace, I asked Suzanne and Sonny Boy to lead the way. Once again, I balanced out the group by bringing up the rear.

"How many more feet?" Sonny Boy wailed after they crossed St. Louis Street.

"Hang tough. We're almost there," Suzanne said. "Keep thinking about meeting Grandpops. You're going to love him. I think you have his ears."

Sonny Boy halted and pulled his hand from Suzanne's. He covered each of his ears with his hands. I tried not to laugh at the confusion on her face.

When she crouched down to his eye level, he frowned. "These are mine. Not his."

"Auntie Suz only meant your ears look like Grandpop's ears. Like mine." I pulled my hair back, allowing my ears to become prominently visible.

"Landry ears have a certain shape, kind of like butterfly wings. That's how we know other Landrys when we see them."

"Oh." He didn't look convinced. "Okay."

We journeyed down the uneven sidewalk—in any other town it would be blocked to pedestrian traffic until repaired.

We passed a bakery where aromas of French bread wafted when a customer left the shop, then we passed a ladies' hat shop, and a Mardi Gras mask store with a mask in the window covered in more peacock feathers than any one peacock had. Art galleries nestled beside hole-in-the-wall restaurants with the scent of gumbo spilling through their open doors. Drivers beeped their horns. The back-up beeper from a truck blared.

Sights and smells just as I remembered. Giddy, I followed behind my son and his aunt. Soon we reached the back side of Jackson Square.

"Christopher Marcus!" a man on a bench outside the cathedral shouted. "Come give your grandpops a hug."

Jerking free from Suzanne's hand, Sonny Boy ran and launched himself into my father's open arms, as if he'd known his grandfather all of his life.

I grabbed for my camera and snapped a photo. Then another. And another.

A true heart-memorizing moment.

I only hoped my father wouldn't let me down, and I wouldn't need to retouch the pictures in the future.

Chapter 17 - Suzanne

Suzanne spotted Maggie peering through the window of the restaurant in Pontalba Square and waved to catch her attention. Maggie waved back, then opened the door and headed toward our table, weaving her way through the thinning lunch crowd and dodging exiting customers. The sweet innocence of her smile lit her face with a glow.

Suzanne's breath caught.

Maybe she needed to rethink pushing Jane to confess her secret to Maggie. After all, joy hadn't painted her face this happy in months.

"Hey there! Mr. Landry. Sonny Boy." Maggie buffed his head with her hand. "Hello, ladies." She kissed the air beside Suzanne's cheek, then Jane's. She pulled over an empty chair from the next table and sat between them, hanging her Louis Vuitton purse on the back of the chair. To onlookers, they probably appeared the perfect happy family.

"You look like a perfume commercial." Suzanne grinned, then sipped her coffee. There had to be a way to help Maggie keep this newfound *joie de vivre*. A clearer picture of Jane's struggle about revealing the truth adjusted for her, like the lens on a camera.

In a dark denim jean skirt and a curve-hugging, off-the-shoulder, flowered top, Maggie could've passed for a teenager at first glance. Suzanne chuckled at her model-perfect sister-in-law. Only Maggie would dress to the nines in designer summer wear for an outing with a little boy. Her fingernails matched her famous bubblegum-pink polished toes visible in her barely-there heeled sandals. Her hair was scooped into a twist. Neat and cooler in the New Orleans humidity. Flawless makeup dared not melt.

"Dad, will you take your grandson to the restroom and clean up his face and hands?" Jane rolled her eyes at her son. "If he wears fried grouper on his cheeks, the fish at the aquarium might want to take a bite out of him."

Mr. Landry stood and beamed. "This way, *Grandson*."

"Your father grows more handsome every year," Maggie said to Jane.

Jane turned in her seat to look in the direction her father and son headed. "I guess. I never thought about it."

"I'm surprised he never remarried." Maggie tapped her mouth with her finger as though pondering the idea.

Jane gasped. "Oh God! Me with a stepmother?"

Suzanne's attention perked up. Jane's expression displayed a variety of emotions: shock, horror, and fear.

"It wouldn't be the worst thing in the world. He's lonely, you know. You've been gone since your mother passed away," Maggie said.

"Don't try a Catholic guilt trip on me. He abandoned me when Momma died. He fell into a bottle."

"In fairness, Jane"—Suzanne shook her finger at her—"your momma was sick almost a year before we graduated high school. You directed all of your efforts into making her well. Kind of pushed him out of the way. Then you rushed to the altar, left on a honeymoon, and landed in Boston. Miss Princess, you're the one who abandoned your dad…and us."

Maggie stared defiantly. "Besides, he wasn't…like *that*…all the time. I have dinner with him at least once a month, mostly so we can catch up about you. Maybe he would've stopped drinking sooner if you'd been a part of his life. Besides, *you* can't know what it's like to have your spouse die."

Jane's face reddened. "Why? Because I divorced mine so you could scoop him up?" Hurt tinged her sarcasm. She narrowed her eyes. "You think Mark's dying doesn't affect me? If you only knew!"

"Time out," Suzanne interrupted. "This is not the time or place. We'll continue our discussion after dinner in private. After Sonny Boy's asleep. Maggie, you're staying the night, yeah?"

Maggie fidgeted and squared her shoulders. "I still have a few things left at your house, so I guess I could, though I hadn't planned on it."

"Look, Maggie, I'll ask for forgiveness now." Jane grasped Maggie's hand. "And I know I'll be asking for it later as well. However, please, please keep an eye on Sonny Boy today. He has a way of getting excited and then getting away. We had an incident in Boston. He got lost in a crowd. He was beside me holding my hand one minute, then gone the next. I almost died until he was found."

"*I* won't lose your boy." She sniffed and lifted her chin.

Suzanne started to interrupt but backed away. Let her friends peck away at the issue. She would referee only if necessary. She continued to sip her sweet tea.

"I'm not suggesting you would. I'm suggesting he'll lose you. Just promise me you'll hold tight to him. I tucked a note in the pocket of his shorts with Suzanne's address and all of our cell phone numbers. Suzanne wrote her phone number inside his cap. Short of putting a tracking device or chipping him—"

"I got it. You're worried. Don't be. I'll treat him just like he's my own."

Suzanne swallowed hard, trying not to spit her drink. If Maggie only knew.

"Thank you. That's all I ask." Jane pushed her fingers through her short hair and appeared to relax a bit.

Suzanne leaned close to Jane. "Stepmothers. Think about it."

"What's that supposed to mean?" Maggie demanded. "What am I missing?" Her eyes narrowed and pinned Suzanne with a stare.

"Hey, look, our guys are returning." Suzanne avoided Maggie's gaze, but the heat of it bore into her, a habit of Maggie's from when they were kids whenever she felt left out.

Sonny Boy walked up behind Maggie and attempted to pull out her chair. "I'm ready," he said.

"Oh," Maggie giggled. "Such polite manners you have. Where did you learn that?"

"From Grandpops. He did that for Momma and Aunt Suzanne when we got here."

Maggie rose. "We'll see you in a few hours."

Sonny Boy kissed Jane on the cheek and his grandfather, too. Then he wrapped Suzanne in a big hug.

"Phone if you're going to be late," Jane called out as Maggie and Sonny Boy headed for the front door.

Suzanne placed her hand on Jane's arm. "It'll be fine. Now, and later."

"Excuse me. Just remembered something I need to tell Sonny Boy." Jane stood and scooted away. She managed to catch up with her son as he stepped outside the restaurant.

Suzanne smiled at Mr. Landry. An awkward silence stretched between them. She raised her glass to a passing waiter who refilled it. She busied herself stirring sweet tea.

"It was a long time since I've seen you, Suzanne," Mr. Landry said. The mellow richness of his smooth voice helped settle the butterflies in her stomach. "The funeral wasn't exactly when and where I'd hope to see you again. I'm so sorry for your loss of Mark."

"I see how his death impacts you, too. I'm sorry you and I drifted apart."

What apology could she give to a man who'd been like her father when she was growing up, especially after her own father disappeared from her life when she was fourteen after he married his new wife? She had intended to visit Mr. Landry, but time moved so fast, and then when Jane and Mark divorced, the distance between them grew uncomfortable. Maggie kept her informed.

"So, I take it you know all about Christopher Marcus?" Mr. Landry asked.

Suzanne stirred her tea more. His information stirred irritation in her chest. "Funny you should mention that." She set the spoon down on her plate. "Until now, I thought his name was Chris Landry. A few weeks back, Jane led me to believe Sonny Boy was a dog. It wasn't *what* she said, but failure to clear up a misunderstanding. Recently, she said Christopher Marcus needed a cousin, but I was in a snit at the time. That piece of information didn't register like it does now. I would've put two and two together sooner, if I'd known his full name. But what I don't understand is why she didn't give him the Maucele last name."

Mr. Landry's brow furrowed. "I don't know the details, and I don't want to make problems between you and Jane. I'm just happy to have my daughter *and* my grandson in my life—no matter what name he's called. And I want to give her a reason to *stay*, rather than making it so she feels the need to retreat back north."

"Sorry. I don't mean to be harsh," Suzanne said. "But Jane created this conundrum."

Mr. Landry nodded. "While I won't disagree with you, a man who lives in a glass house shouldn't throw rocks. I won't judge. I understand all the reasons she left. And maybe even why she kept silent. She has always loved you and Maggie like sisters." Mr. Landry tapped her wrist. "Can we work together to find a way to keep her here? Or are her sins insurmountable?"

Well, the man had her there. She was still holding on to a secret of her own, which wasn't so bad, except depending on her decision about it, the sin could be insurmountable for Maggie. Maybe Jane, too; she'd chosen to have a child and raise him on her own. No help at home or child support to lighten the load. In the past, Jane would've supported her no matter what, but had this Jane changed with motherhood?

"It's a complicated situation. The three of us used to be so close. Now…I'm not sure where we stand. Or if our relationship can endure." How could she uncomplicate things?

Tonight, her secret wouldn't poke its head out of the box—any of the three hidden in her bottom drawer.

However, when it came to Jane and Maggie, for her, no sin was too great. Like it or not, when they became blood sisters, they joined their DNA. She could no more cut all ties with them than she could cut off her arm. They meant that much. But the circumstances they faced were complicated.

"Mr. Landry. I'm in a place of "*and*." I feel one way, but at the same time feel another. Jane was my BFF, but she abandoned me with her acceptance to Emerson and moving so far from home. That about killed me. Then she divorced Mark. Somehow I lived. I tried to understand what was in her head—but she refused to confide in me. And now that my brother—whom everyone loved—is gone, I learn Jane forgot to mention for, oh, years, she's got a child! I'm doing the best I can right now with all this information."

She softened her voice. "I, too, want her to stay. I need my best friend back in my life."

Mr. Landry patted her hand. "I think we need a round of forgiveness."

"Hey, you two. Why so sad?" Jane's chair scratched against the polished concrete floor as she pulled it out to sit.

Suzanne smiled weakly, then said, "Just catching up."

"Jane, I'm holding you to your promise. Sonny Boy will spend Friday night with me. What time will you bring him by?" Mr. Landry asked.

"What if we drop him off after we pick up Grant from the airport?" Suzanne asked Jane. "Your dad's not far from there. Hubby's coming in around 2:30." She turned to Mr. Landry. "That way, Grant will have his first *Sonny Boy* experience. I can't wait to see the look on his face."

"Good idea." Jane nodded. "Now, Daddy, please don't give the boy a lot of sugar. No caffeine. No soda. A bath and to bed by nine p.m. Life works best for him if we keep to a schedule." Jane grinned. "And if you find yourself getting weak about the rules, remember, you'll be the one to suffer for it. He gets wound up and bounces off the walls. And he gets up with the sun."

Mr. Landry saluted his daughter. "I bought several books to read to him and a few toys. And...I take my marching orders seriously, General."

"If he's grumpy on Saturday," Jane said. "You have to take him back."

"That's not a disincentive. Well, ladies. Work calls. I'll pay the bill on my way out. It was the best lunch I've had in a long time. Thank you for your company."

Mr. Landry kissed Jane's cheek, then squeezed Suzanne's shoulders before he left.

"So, how long has he known?" Suzanne asked.

"Known?"

"That he has a grandson named Christopher Marcus. Clearly, he's known for a while."

Jane glanced down. Suzanne let silence fill the void. She wanted Jane in the hot seat.

"About a year ago," Jane answered.

"And he's known who the father is?" Suzanne tried to keep her voice even. Heat rose up the back of her neck. The muscle in her jaw tightened.

She wanted so much to make the past different, to have known about Sonny Boy before he was born and watched him grow over the years.

As often as she had repeated the words, "I have a nephew," since she discovered Jane's secret, the reality of the situation felt surreal. To end the silence, Suzanne said, "You can't *not* talk about this with me. It's the least you can do. My brother died never fulfilling all of his dreams. Yet, you held one of them in your hands and kept it a secret. Told only your father? Why?"

"I told my dad about Sonny Boy about a year ago and said if he embraced sobriety for nine straight months, I'd bring his grandson to visit. During that time, I sent him photos, drawings, and other trinkets Sonny Boy made to encourage my father along a path away from drinking. I can't make him stop. However, if wanting a relationship with his grandson is the *gold* that makes him manage his problem, I'm all for it." Jane crossed her arms over her chest.

Suzanne sighed. A heavy weight sat on her heart.

"What?" Jane demanded.

"I'll pick it apart and try to handle the information in pieces. Why did you reject Mark when he came to Boston to visit you before marrying Maggie, then manage to get pregnant? I still don't understand. Then, you never told him about the baby. He would've been happy to pay child support." Suzanne tried to keep her voice from cracking. "He wanted so bad to be a father. To give his son a way of life that he'd fought for."

Jane's face crinkled in pain. "Oh God, Suz. I know you think I'm awful. In my defense, do you know what it's like to carry around a secret when you're amazingly happy? And that secret morphs and grows into something awesome. Then a little human. And to experience life through the eyes of that child? Where life feels so complete that without that pint-sized person you'd die?

"I never intended to hurt you, or Mark, or Maggie, let alone my dad. No matter how much of a drunk he was, or still is, he's my father. And believe it or not, I want my son, Christopher Marcus Landry, to know all of his family—the connection to all his Cajun bones. Though he is the love of my life, the pain of telling everyone—news that potentially would change all of your lives—and possibly bring pain… It wasn't that I never wanted to tell you, I truly didn't know how."

"For five years?"

"What should I have done? Call Mark before he married Maggie and say, 'Hey! Dude! You're going to be a father'? That would've killed Maggie. She always needed lots of attention. I've always known she loved Mark. But Mark wasted no time in dating her after the divorce. Would Mark have married Maggie if he knew about Sonny Boy? I don't know. But I couldn't do that to Maggie when I knew Mark and I would never make it as a couple."

Suzanne shook her head. "Maybe so, but a secret for years?"

"If you're such a sage, Suzanne Maucele Saulnier, give me the words to tell Maggie tonight so I won't hurt her now. I'm open to suggestions because right now my plan is to make sure all of the guns at your house are locked up tight, get her tipsy, and then tell her. That way, I know she can't shoot me. And if you think I'm kidding, think again. Sorry about the pun, but I'm dead serious."

Jane's words were like a knife to her throat.

"Excuse me, ladies. More sweet tea?" A waiter hovered with a pitcher.

"No," Jane said. Suzanne echoed the same.

The weight on her heart grew heavier. She had no script to provide Jane. No clue how to tell Maggie. Tonight, sober or not, Maggie would receive the news. Probably take it like an exploding bomb. There was no way to cushion the words to prevent them from breaking Maggie's heart.

Was now the wisest time to share this secret? Or would this, on top of Mark's death, be the blow that pushed Maggie into an emotional hell so deep she wouldn't fight to climb out? Maggie considered Jane an icon of good decisions, voicing over and over again during the years of Jane's self-imposed exile that whenever making a tough decision, she always asked herself—what would Jane do?

Frickin' secrets! They were only bearable when shared.

The weight of her own bore down. The idea that she could love a child as much or more than Grant scared her beyond belief. The thought of living without Grant—that was life without color or food or soul.

Was it possible to feel all the same ways about the life beginning to grow inside her? Like the mother-bear protectiveness Jane bubbled around Sonny Boy? Was the glow on Jane's face and the strong tender bond with her son a magical mystery triggered with giving birth? Or was it only doled out to special women?

She could be the one passed over.

"Jane, for a couple of hours, how about we practice denial? We'll go shopping. Retail therapy. Let me take you to this sweet boutique and buy you a new outfit. We'll consider it donning clothing courage."

"Whatever." Jane rose and walked to the restaurant's front door.

Suzanne followed, recalling Mr. Landry's words. "People who live in glass houses shouldn't throw stones."

The secret she held close to her heart was growing by the minute. She needed to tell her friends about her baby before Grant arrived home.

Or should Grant be the first to know?

Chapter 18 – Maggie

"**D**id you have a good time?" Maggie's heart skipped an anxious beat. All she wanted was for Sonny Boy to be happy. She handed him a cup of vanilla ice cream with chopped pecans *and* warm caramel sauce—just as he had requested. He attacked the ice cream with the same determined conviction she'd seen Jane do when tackling a problem. And if an ice-cream gene existed, he had to have inherited it from her.

Maggie sat in a chair on the opposite side of a table from Sonny Boy in the food court at the Jax Brewery Mall, tired, but oh-so satisfied with surrogate motherhood.

"I like cones." His pout was cute, even after an afternoon hide-and-seek and catch-and-reel. She'd spent more time chasing him down than showing him the exhibits. However, she wouldn't trade that time with him for all the Louis Vuitton shoes in the world. Her heart swelled. Love melted away any lingering angst. Warmth spread through her chest. The urge to hug him tugged hard.

"I do, too, but I usually make a mess with them, and I don't want to return you to your momma covered in ice cream. We *don't* want her mad at me. I want her to let me take you for other outings." She tucked a napkin on her lap.

Sunlight lit the food court through the mall's floor-to-ceiling windows. Voices of shoppers floated up the escalator from the floors below. Using a brochure, Maggie fanned herself. Air conditioning and fresh squeezed lemonade were cooling, but it had been a hike from the aquarium to the mall. Jane had been right. The boy could dart, move, escape faster than a slippery fish.

Sonny Boy waved at a boy who appeared to be about his age. The other child smiled and waved back before his mother patted his arm, directed him to a nearby table, and made him sit.

Maggie gazed at her boy. He never met a stranger, and that added another of layer to his appealing charm. But had Jane taught him about stranger danger?

Sonny Boy lifted a spoonful of frozen ice cream and let it slide off the spoon and into his mouth. He swallowed and smiled. "Momma doesn't care if I spill."

Neat-as-a-pin Jane wouldn't mind if ice cream covered her child? "Tidy and efficient," as well as "southern strong," were words for Jane's future epitaph. If she truly didn't mind a messy child, her friend had changed in spades.

Spooning up another mouthful of ice cream, Sonny Boy flicked it into his mouth, closed his eyes, savoring it as she'd seen his mother do many times as a kid.

"When we were growing up," she told him, "your momma always made sure I had a napkin on my lap to protect from spills. She really doesn't care if you spill stuff?" She stuffed the urge to make a napkin bib to cover his shirt.

"She says, 'It'll wash' and I should enjoy each lick."

"That's a good philosophy." Jane had good mothering skills. A stab of sadness turned in Maggie's chest. She fought a downward spiral. She could never be a wise sage of a mother like Jane. "You never said what you liked best about the fish zoo." Her favorite part had been leaving with the child she'd entered with and her nerves still intact.

"Hey! It's not a *fish zoo*. It's an aquarium."

Maggie smiled. "I know. It's just what I like to call it."

"You're funny. I liked the white alligator. He's cool."

"He's an albino. That means he has no color."

Sonny Boy's forehead creased. He planted his spoon into the ice cream and twisted his mouth to one side.

"What's wrong?" Maggie asked. "Auntie" work was more challenging than she considered. Sonny Boy had to have had a perfect fun day—one wrong turn might be all it took for Jane to revoke her auntie status.

"White is a color."

Relief flooded, and Maggie chuckled. "You're so right. White is a color. However, an alligator, which should be green and isn't, means he's missing his color, so he looks white."

The worried look on Sonny Boy's face deepened. "He's missing his color?"

"That's right."

"But white was his color."

Maggie leaned across the table and buffed the top of Sonny Boy's head. "Someday, you'll study biology and genetics. You'll understand then. In the meantime, you learned a new word—albino."

"What if a person is red or brown?"

Maggie furrowed her brow. "Red or brown people?"

"Yes, ma'am." The boy smiled as though pleased with himself over his manners.

"That boy—" Sonny Boy pointed to the child he'd waved to a minute ago—"he's got red. His mother has brown. I don't know what that means."

Maggie's gaze followed from the child in her care to the woman and child seated several tables away. The little boy had no hair. Was he sick? "Sweetheart, the woman is Asian, and I'm guessing that's her son. They are neither red nor brown."

"They are. I *see* it."

Cocking her head, Maggie tried to imagine what the boy was talking about. "Can you tell me more?" she asked gently.

Sonny Boy scrunched his nose. "I don't like brown. Ask Momma. She doesn't like it either."

The woman is brown? The boy is red?

"Do you see other colors?"

"Ah-huh."

"Like with me?"

Melted ice cream dripped from his spoon onto his hand. Smears of caramel streaked the sides of his mouth. "You're"— with the spoon in his hand, he swirled the air in front of her—"kinda gray and purple. Momma taught me a lot about my colors."

An understanding began to take shape in her mind, the thoughts vibrating strong and slow in her gut. The boy's intuition might be stronger than even Jane realized. "What about your momma and Auntie Suzanne?"

"Momma has some red." He hadn't paused a second. "Auntie Suzanne is pink."

Pink? Suzanne? Nooo.

He had to be mistaken. And red on Jane? Where? Could she have an ulcer or stomach problems? A single mother raising a child alone in a big city couldn't be easy. That was stress with all capital S's.

"How about we discuss this more when we see your momma?" Asking more questions of Sonny Boy might cause him to misinterpret her intention. He shrugged and returned to attacking his melting treat. His eyes darted to the boy several times. When the boy and the woman left, Sonny Boy waved goodbye.

Had she ever been that carefree as a child? Never. And never loved by a parent like Jane. But who was his father? Maybe after a few drinks tonight, Jane would open up.

"Let's go wash our hands. You did a good job. No ice cream on your clothes." However, that wasn't true for his hands, arms, and face.

She rose and herded the boy toward the entrance of the ladies' room.

"No!" Sonny Boy cried.

"What?"

"Grandpops takes me to that one. I want to go in there." He pointed to the sign that read "Men" in blue tiles at the entrance.

"But…I can't go in there with you."

"I'm going to be five. I can go by myself." He jerked away before she could stop him.

"Sonny Boy, come here."

"Hey, honey! If you're cute, I'll be Sonny Boy for you!" A male voice hollered, then laughter from several men bounced off the tiles.

Maggie hovered at the opening to the men's room and checked her watch. She'd give him two minutes tops, and if he didn't show, she'd nab one of the food-court workers to check on her escaped ward. Taking five steps toward the opening of the ladies' room, Maggie turned and paced, retracing her steps.

A minute later, her heart raced. "I'm still waiting, Sonny Boy."

She stood in front of the water fountain in the open space between the men's and women's restrooms, trying to swallow down her panic. Who knew one little child could put her into emotional overload. Trying to keep pace with an about-to-be five-year-old was harder than she'd imagined. Whisking him away for a haircut at her salon bore no resemblance to maintaining a laser line on a tyke with no fear.

She glanced at her watch again.

Two minutes.

"Sonny Boy? Are you okay? Do you need any help?"

No answer.

"Sonny Boy! Please answer me."

Silence.

Walking closer to the opening to the men's room, she stopped before she could see inside, not wanting to embarrass anyone or herself. "Sonny Boy, where are you? You must answer me now."

"Ma'am, don't know who you are, but there's no one in here but me, and I ain't Sonny Boy."

Fear ripped through Maggie like a gator taking down prey. "Oh God! Where is he?" She ran toward the ice-cream vendor, grabbed a male food-court worker by the shirtsleeve. "My boy went into the bathroom, but he won't answer when I call. Please check on him."

The young man frowned and pulled his arm from her grasp. "Sure, lady." He entered the restroom.

"Well, is he there?" Maggie asked when the young man reappeared.

"Unless he's about sixty, no."

"I stood right here the whole time. He never came out. In fact, no one came out." Her breath grew quick and shallow. "Where is he?" Maggie cried.

The young man straightened. "I don't know, but around the corner is the other entrance to the men's room. Look around there. I'll call security. Do you have a picture of him?"

Maggie ran off before answering, holding onto a slice of hope and visions of finding Sonny Boy waiting for her. She grabbed for the wall for balance as she rounded the corner. The other entrance to the men's room opened up to another wing of shopping with escalators. A few people milled about. No child in sight.

"Sonny Boy!" Maggie hollered. "If you can hear me, yell back!" Her mouth dried. Her hands began to shake. "Pull it together, Maggie. Find Jane's boy." She urged herself onward.

A petite woman approached her and stopped. She looked up. Maggie looked down.

"You lost a kid?"

"Yes, a little boy. He's wearing jean shorts and a t-shirt with New Orleans on it. He's got medium brown short hair. Military cut. Have you seen him?"

"Nope. But I'll help you look for him."

Overwhelmed, Maggie gushed, "Thank you. His name is Sonny Boy."

"Were you on drugs when you named the kid?"

"What?"

"Who the hell names—"

"Forget it. I don't have time for this." Maggie darted into the closest shop and headed to the cashier.

"May I help you?" a young woman asked.

"I'm looking for a little boy. He came out of the men's room right there." She pointed beyond the storefront.

"I saw a little boy come out with another little boy, and an older man followed behind them."

"Another boy and older man?" Panic seized Maggie. "Which way did the boys go?"

"I don't know." The young woman tossed her hair over her shoulder as though she didn't give a flip. "They walked off that way together." She pointed toward the escalators running in the center of the mall.

Maggie ran out of the store. She stopped at the entrance to the moving staircase. One side descended while the other rose, bringing customers to the second floor.

No Sonny Boy.

Her stomach rolled. She swallowed hard.

"Ma'am," a voice behind her called. Maggie turned into a brick wall of a chest on a man in uniform. She looked up into a solemn dark face with intense dark eyes.

"You found him?" Maggie cried anxiously.

The security guard shook his head. "No ma'am. But I'm here to help. Do you carry a picture of your son?"

Opening her purse, she pulled out her phone. "He's not actually my son, he's the son of my best friend. Here, look at this. We were at the aquarium earlier."

Large hands grasped the device. "You say he's *not* your son?" The man looked at the screen, then back at her.

"His name is Chris Landry. His nickname is Sonny Boy. No. He's not my son. His mother's *my* best friend. You have to find him."

The man handed back the phone. "We'll call the police *and* the boy's mother." He sounded as though he suspected her of something. "I need your name and number. I need her name and number. In the meantime, there's a security guard on each floor looking for the boy. I'll radio a description. I'm Officer Michaels. Please follow me to the office." The large man turned to walk away.

"No," Maggie said firmly.

"Excuse me, ma'am?" The security guard turned back. "You *need* to follow me." His voice was punctuated with authority.

Maggie pulled a small black notebook from her purse. "*I'm* going to look for him. Here, the info you want." She scribbled. "Chris is the boy's name. Here's his mother's name. Her number. My info. And that of his Aunt Suzanne Saulnier. They're staying at that number."

"This boy is kin to Mr. Grant Saulnier?" The man's tone took her by surprise.

"Yes." It was only a little white lie. Anything to find Sonny Boy.

The man spoke into the small speaker clipped to his starched white collar. With his urgent tone and thorough instructions, surely they'd find the child any minute now.

Provided some perverted old man hasn't kidnapped him.

Maggie's heart sank. She shoved the thought from her mind and replaced it with a positive one—hugging the child when she found him.

"You look for him, too. I'll call the mother. My security staff will find him. Take my card. Call me if you find him. Otherwise, I'll call you when the mother arrives."

"Thank you, Officer." Maggie turned to continue her search. She started into a sports paraphernalia store, dreading the phone call the security guard would make to Jane. Maybe she should call her first. No, the best she could do was find Sonny Boy before Jane showed up.

"Hello. I'm looking for this little boy." Maggie showed a man behind the counter the picture on her phone.

"Oh. I think he took the elevator. I saw him with an older gentleman."

"You're *sure* you saw this little boy with an older gentleman? Was there a second boy with him?" Maggie prayed the man's memory would change. If anyone hurt Sonny Boy, she'd die. Just die.

"No. Just the one boy and the older man. Yeah, cute little guy. Full of questions."

"Would you know who the older guy might be?"

"Naw. Looked like a tourist. Hawaiian-print shirt, shorts, and a ball cap."

"Anything else you can remember?" She mentally implored the man to speak and provide a clue to the boy's whereabouts.

"Nope."

It was times like this when her intuition most failed her. If Suzanne had let the boy escape, she'd have a better chance at locating him. This was her error in judgment. Her sin. And she had to suffer the consequence. "But Lord, please spare him," she prayed.

"Do I need to call security for you?" the man asked.

"They're looking for him now. But could you give them a better description of the man than you just gave me?"

"Sure. I'll call them."

Maggie rushed to the next store and showed the photo again. No luck. Then she rushed to the next store. Same result. She ran to the escalator for another look, hanging over the railing to the floor below. No child milled about.

Shaking, Maggie pulled her phone out of her purse and pressed Jane's number on speed dial.

"Hello?" Jane answered. "How late are you going to be? I *told* Suzanne we had more time to shop. The one thing I can always count on, *you* never being on time for anything." Jane laughed.

Maggie collapsed on the nearest bench. Mall security hadn't called yet. "Jane…"

"Yes?"

Maggie flinched and swallowed hard. "I need you here. Right now."

"Don't you dare tell me something's wrong with my son. I entrusted him to you."

"Mall security is going to call you. Sonny Boy slipped away from me. I'm frantic looking for him, along with the security guards on each floor of the mall."

"I told you to hold tight to him. I *told* you!"

A *clunk* sounded in Maggie's ear, followed by Suzanne's muffed voice in the background, then a mournful cry.

"Maggie?" Suzanne's voice came through the phone.

"Get Jane down here as soon as you can. I've lost Sonny Boy. Oh God! Suzanne. What am I going to do?"

"You keep looking for him. I'll bring Jane now. Where exactly are you?"

"Jax Brewery mall. Second floor. We came for ice cream."

"We'll meet you in front of the ice-cream shop. I'll call you when we get there. Go *find* him. Now!"

Silence rang louder than Jane's scream had.

"Where are you, Little Man? Are you okay?" She focused on the opening where the escalator continued to bring visitors up to the second floor. Kicking off her shoes, she stood on the slatted wooden bench and hollered, "Sonny Boy! Sonny Boy! Yell if you can hear the sound of my voice!"

Store employees came to the doors of their shops and gawked.

"Hey! I'm looking for this little boy." She held up her phone. "Anyone seen him?" She hopped off the bench and ran to a store clerk and showed Sonny Boy's picture.

Each time she held a glimmer of hope, but each negative response sliced deeper. Losing a husband was hard enough, but losing a child—devastating. She wouldn't stop until Sonny Boy was safe in his mother's arms.

"Ma'am, Officer Michaels assigned me to this side of the floor. I'm looking in every store, every corner, every private restroom. I haven't found him yet."

She wanted to shout there were five other floors to cover, but instead, she thanked the security guard, then added, "Have your boss call me the minute you find my boy."

With no success on the second floor, Maggie dashed to the descending stairs and ran down. The hard steel-slated steps pressed into her feet, but that was a tiny price to pay to find Sonny Boy.

Reaching the bottom, she scanned the area. Not many folks around. Only a few coming and going from the mall entrance. Easy enough to spot a pint-sized person. "Sonny Boy!" she shouted, walking along the row of storefronts. "Sonny Boy!"

"Where is he?" Jane's voice split through the lull of the mall's noise, though Maggie hadn't spotted her yet.

"Maggie?" Suzanne called.

"Over here, by the cooking shop."

Jane and Suzanne appeared from around a wide white pillar. Jane's face was wet with tears, Suzanne's mouth set grim.

"I'm so sorry." Maggie's vision blurred. "I'm so sorry."

"Don't be sorry, look for him!" Jane wiped her face with her hands. "Sonny Boy!" Jane yelled. She turned and scanned the growing crowd. Suzanne started yelling, too.

Maggie opened her phone and pulled the security manager's card from her pocket, then punched in the number. "Ms. Landry, Sonny Boy's mother, is with me on the ground floor along with Suzanne Saulnier. Okay, we'll wait here. See you in a minute."

"We're looking for a little boy. He's four, almost five years old. He's wearing jean shorts and a t-shirt with New Orleans in gold and black on the front. Please, look for him!" Maggie called to the gawking crowd.

Officer Michaels and a female security officer came down the escalator. Jane and Suzanne ran to him.

"Ma'am." Officer Michaels pointed to Maggie. "Please come over here."

When Maggie joined him, a female security officer escorted Jane and Suzanne away from the open mall area. "Mrs. Maucele, please, no more yelling. You're alarming other shoppers. Let us do our job. We're looking at surveillance films of the exits to see if he's left the building. Why don't you come with me to the office? The police have arrived and want to ask you some questions."

"I've told you everything. I'm going to continue to look for him." Her heart pounded jackhammer hard. Jane had warned her about Sonny Boy's escape-artist abilities. Arrogantly, she'd thought she could handle a little boy. Thought she'd be a good parent. After all, she had good mothering instincts. Yet, when trusted with the most precious thing in Jane's life, she let it slip through her fingers.

Anguish pushed upward to her throat and lodged there. If something happened to the child, if he'd been harmed in any way, she'd never be able to face Jane. She'd kill herself and end up lying beside Mark in all eternity, his epitaph of "Good Things Come in Threes" to hers "Death and Destruction Times Three."

A sob stuck in Maggie's chest. She clutched her stomach. The barren place where no child would ever grow. Jane had given her a chance to share in the love of a child.

And she'd totally failed.

"You cannot escape the responsibility of tomorrow by evading it today."
Abraham Lincoln

Chapter 19

"**I**'d rather stand," I told the police officer who offered me a chair in the small windowless room. He sat in the other chair and started in with a question. I gave an answer. Question and answer. Question and answer.

"He'll be five years old the week after next.

Mrs. Maucele is a friend since sixth grade.

I'm certain she'd never do anything to hurt him."

I paced. Only answered the questions I was asked. I didn't want to confess my crimes. I didn't want to say, "Sonny Boy's father died about a month ago without meeting his son. The sad woman downstairs, who claims to be the boy's mother, is actually his stepmother—but doesn't know it. And Mrs. Saulnier is next of blood kin, his only aunt."

Anxiety slammed around the room like a racquetball. It slammed me. Knocked me so hard my knees wobbled and ripped away my breath.

Where's my son?

"Ms. Landry, we're doing our best to find him. Just a few more questions."

What if they don't find him?

My stomach lurched. My hands trembled. A metallic taste flooded my mouth. I stumbled, grabbed for a chair, sank onto the seat. I didn't dare cry. I had to hang on to a rope of hope. I had to trust that Maggie's great goodness and Suzanne's loyalty held enough positive karma to protect Sonny Boy and bring him back to all of us.

"Lord, take care of him, please," I prayed. I'd shunned church, religion, and faith when Momma passed away. But I've have done anything to believe right now.

The officer's all-business expression offered little comfort. "We're setting up the viewing." The man rose. "We want you to look at the surveillance tapes. See if you recognize anyone or your child. I'll be back to escort you there in a minute."

Dread rammed my heart. Opening my purse, I tore through it. "Where is it?"

I looked up when Suzanne entered the room. "What do you need?"

"My phone. To call my dad." I desperately wanted my father's support. Needed him to be strong for me. Needed him to…to be my dad.

I tossed my purse on the table, pulled out my stuff until I located my cell phone.

"Jane"—I looked up at Suzanne—"I swear, we'll find Sonny Boy." Fear skittered through her eyes.

"We have to." I pulled on my emotional armor. Calm and strong on the outside. Inside only mush. And I wanted my momma—she was the cookie-baking, only-offering-advice-when-asked, shopping-therapist-to-cure -boyfriend-blues, and wiper-of-tears. I needed her now.

I braced against the wall and vowed to remain strong. I needed to be the capable woman Momma had raised. And I called my father.

"Hello? Jane?"

"Daddy. Christopher Marcus is lost. I *need* you. We're at the Jax Brewery mall. Can you come?"

"Nothing will stop me."

"Thank you." Tears clouded my vision. "Thank you. Call me when you arrive so I can find you."

A security officer and a police officer returned to the cubicle as I ended the call.

"Ms. Landry. We're ready." The two men, bookends of broad shoulders and serious eyes, faced her. I shook their hands.

"Could we make a change, Officers?" I asked as an idea struck me. "Mrs. Saulnier knows more people than God in this city. She can spot a tourist at fifty paces. Let her look at the tapes. I'm going to search for my boy. Call me if you find anything." I silently dared them to challenge my decision.

Two pair of dark eyes narrowed on me. Clearly, they weren't pleased.

"Suzanne, call me, if you find anything."

I raced to the escalator, trying to take in the entire scene. Aromas of burgers, pizza, and Creole seasonings wafted to my nose. Shoppers, mostly tourists, milled about by the tables in the airy food court. Several people stood outside the window of a clock shop, their noses pressed against the glass. A woman, who could pass for Delta Burke, came out of the art gallery wearing sunglasses.

I stopped and slowly scanned the mall again, taking in every single person in sight. The only one missing—my son. Around me, time ticked on. Life continued for others. But not me. Not until I found Christopher Marcus.

Jogging down the escalator to the first floor, my momma-bear radar sharpened. I couldn't afford to miss subtle details. I studied my surroundings. "Where would Sonny Boy go?"

I scanned the names of the shops. Kites. Jewelry. T-shirts. Fudge. "Everything NOLA" caught my eye, and I headed for the shop tucked into the corner.

Maggie came toward me—tear-stained face, hair askew, and carrying her heels—like she'd come from a streetcar wreck.

"Jane. Oh God." Maggie inhaled raggedly. "I can't find him."

"We'll find him."

How in God's name could you have lost him? I warned you!

She grasped my hands. I needed her to buck up and not be needy. "Suzanne is looking at video. Security is checking the exits and outside. I'll go store to store."

"But I already did that," she wailed.

"Did you find him? No. So I'll keep looking."

Maggie hung her head. I didn't have time to take care of her. I headed to the nearest store. "I'm looking for my son. He's five years old. About this high—" I motioned to a spot below my waist.

"Security has already been here. Sorry, haven't seen him."

"Do you mind if I look around? Sonny Boy, that's my son, he likes to play hide-and-seek."

"Look all ya want. I'll make another pass, too, but I know he isn't here."

"Wait." Maggie entered the store. "Look. Here's his picture." She pushed her phone toward the clerk. "We took this one this morning at the aquarium."

"Cute kid. Sorry. Still haven't seen him."

I looked around. Bottles of hot sauce. Cooking utensils. No boy.

I went to the next store.

And the next.

The same response each time. "Not seen the boy."

Numbness submerged me. Hopelessness twirled me. Desperation still drove me. "Maggie," I turned to her. "I *really* need your help."

"Anything," Maggie whimpered.

"Let's sit over there." I led her to a small marble-topped table with two chairs outside a fudge shop and motioned for her to sit.

"You're the intuitive one, Maggie. You have that special connection. I'm asking you, begging you, do what you do. Your *knowings*. Get a message. Find Sonny Boy."

Confusion flashed on Maggie's face. "What do you think I am?"

"Use all of your woo-woo to help me find my son."

"It doesn't work like that."

My anger flared. "How do you know unless you try? Really try. Focus."

"I tried already. No message came. No picture in my brain. No whispered words in my ear."

"Try harder." I grasped her trembling hands and squeezed. Each minute my son was missing was a lifetime for me.

"It doesn't work that way." Maggie pulled her hands from mine and stood.

I reached for her arm and pulled her back to the chair. "In all my life, I've never asked you for *anything* for me." I gritted my teeth. "In fact, part of what led me home was Mark naming me as beneficiary on a one-hundred thousand dollar life insurance policy. I want the money for an education fund for *my* son." Anger jerked me along like a prisoner headed to the gallows. "But I thought of you."

I stood, the chair collapsed backward to the floor. "I couldn't take *all* that money if Mark hadn't provided for you. You're his widow. I'm just the damn ex-wife. But I loved him. I love him still." I choked on a sob. "I love my son. Mark would've loved him, too."

My vision blurred like watercolors running together. I hugged myself to prevent a complete meltdown. My breath was ragged. Onlookers cast glances, as though not certain if what they were witnessing was real or performance art. I wished it were only a scene from a play.

But no. This was my reality.

Tears streaked down Maggie's face. She came and stood beside me. "Let's go upstairs where it's quiet. We need to talk."

I swatted Maggie's hands away when she tried to hug me. "I'll try again. Maybe a *knowing* will come," Maggie said. "Too many distractions here."

"Jane?" a male voice called.

Racing to my father, I threw my arms around his neck and clung to him. "Daddy, we can't find him," I wailed. "We've looked everywhere." I buried my face in his chest and cried.

"Janey, honey. I'm so sorry. Stay here with Maggie, and I'll search." My father patted my back. A police officer showed up beside him, showing no emotion.

"But—"

"Let me talk to the police and mall security." Holding my dad was reassuring. I didn't want to let him go.

"If you could come upstairs, Ms. Landry…" the police officer said.

My father wrapped his arm around me. We took the escalator upstairs. Maggie followed. I wanted to shake her until a *knowing* spilled from her lips. I believed she could find Sonny Boy if she really wanted to.

My son was my heartbeat. Without him, I didn't need anything or anyone. Not Maggie. Not Suzanne. Not Mark's money.

We arrived at the security office. My father opened the door, and my phone rang. Suzanne stood in the doorway with her phone to her ear. She ended the call when she saw me. "I've watched all the tapes. I don't believe he's left the building. We've been searching downstairs. I think we need to go up."

I pulled away from my father. Raced to the up escalator, made the switch at each level, landing at the top floor.

"Sonny Boy," I shouted.

Behind me, a stampede of footsteps drew my attention—my father, a police officer, a security guard, Maggie, and Suzanne.

Each branched out to a different store.

I went to the men's room. "Sonny Boy."

No response.

"Guys, I'm looking for my son. Cover up, I'm coming in."

A couple of men came out as I rounded the corner. No boy. I pushed open the doors on the stalls. No Sonny Boy.

Exiting the opposite way I entered, I scanned the area. Only a few shoppers were on this level. So much time had passed. Where was my son? Where? Where? Where?

"Jane?" a woman standing outside a shop called out. "Officer, over here."

I looked in the direction of the voice. The police officer ran to her. I sprinted after him. My sandals clacked with my heart beating, "Hope. Hope. Hope."

"You must be Jane. The man said to call your name. You lookin' for a little boy?" The woman was as wide as she was tall, standing with her hands on her hips.

"Yes," the officer replied. "Do you know where the boy is?"

"This is him." Maggie shoved her phone at the woman.

"Follow me." The woman lumbered away. "The man, says he's the grand-father, found him. I just started my shift. He came in and discovered the boy. But *shhhh*."

I was a step behind the police officer and the woman, making her way through a maze of merchandise to the far corner of the store.

"*Shh*," the woman whispered again. "No need to scare him."

The small, closet-size space was dimly lit and cool. Overhead, mobiles hung from the ceiling. Floor-to-ceiling shelves displayed teddy bears dressed in t-shirts bearing logos of college and pro teams. On the floor, large stuffed animals huddled together, as if napping. My father sat on the floor next to the centerpiece of the stuffed menagerie—a teddy bear rising at nearly four feet tall. Cradled in the lap of that bear, hugging a small stuffed white alligator, my little boy slept.

"Daddy, you found him." My breath caught. " Sonny Boy," I whispered. Joy bounced inside me, *bonga, bonga, bonga.* Just like when Sonny Boy jumped on the bed—joy jumping, he called it.

I dropped to my knee. Relief flooded me. Light-headed, I drew a deep breath. "Sonny Boy." I kissed the top of his head. "Wake up, little man." I rubbed his earlobe. He swatted his hand at me.

I rubbed his cheeks, his arms, his legs.

"No," he groaned and snuggled the alligator closer.

I gently poked at his Cajun bone. "Sonny Boy. Momma's here."

He squinted through sleepy eyes. "Momma?" Then he began to whimper.

I sat and scooped my boy into my lap. Hugging him, I rocked back and forth. "I'm here. I'm here. Momma's here."

Maggie let out a choked sob. She stroked the back of Sonny Boy's head. "You're safe. You're safe."

Sonny Boy reached out his hand. Maggie leaned close. My son cupped his small fingers on the side of Maggie's face. His thumb wiped a tear—a gesture I'd done whenever he'd cried.

Maggie covered Sonny Boy's hand with her own and closed her eyes as though in prayer.

"Aunt Maggie, it's okay. Grandpops?"

I staggered to rise with Sonny Boy in my arms. I shifted his weight. He wrapped his legs around my waist, his hands around my neck, sandwiching the white stuffed animal between us.

"I'll leave you to it." The saleswoman left the room.

The police officer stepped beyond the threshold and announced in his radio the missing boy had been located. My father took Sonny Boy from my arms. The stuffed animal fell to the floor.

"Alligator…alligator, please?"

I picked it up and gave it to him. I'd buy him all the bears in the room because I believed they'd kept him safe.

"Ms. Landry, we need to talk to the boy. Does he need medical attention? We need to ensure he's unharmed."

"Were you hurt?" I rubbed his back.

"No, Momma."

"Did anyone try to take you away from Aunt Maggie? Anyone do anything to you?" I used my calmest voice so as not to frighten him.

Sonny Boy whimpered, "No, Momma. I'm sorry, Momma. I'm sorry."

"Shh. It's all right. You're safe. Grandpops is here," my father said.

"I want to get him home."

"I realize this has been traumatic, but I do need to ask some questions. If the boy doesn't need medical attention, now would be a better time."

"Christopher," the officer said. "Are you hurt?"

He shook his head.

"How did you get separated from Mrs. Maucele?"

"He means me," Maggie said.

"I got lost when I tried to talk to the boy." He looked at Maggie. "The boy with the red."

"Red?" I asked.

"Ms. Landry, I'd like to take this discussion to the office." The man raised an eyebrow at me. "It would be best."

"Yes, sir."

I followed the parade of people leaving the store. Stopping at the checkout to pay for the stuffed white alligator, I waved the woman over. "Thank you so much for helping me find my baby. I want to pay for the toy."

"That's okay." The woman smiled. "My present for him."

Her generosity touched me. "Thank you. Thank you, again."

I made my way to my family. Sonny Boy, Dad, Maggie, and Suzanne. They were surrounded by security. Onlookers had gathered. Everyone talking at once. The crowd swelled closer. A police officer cupped my father's elbow and led him toward the down escalator.

I moved away from the crowd. A loud rushing sound flooded my ears. My knees started to buckle. If I didn't sit, I would fall over.

I collapsed onto a bench. Put my head down. Two pair of sandal-clad feet with painted toes, bubblegum-pink and red, appeared.

Suzanne and Maggie squatted in front of me.

Maggie offered a bottle of water. "Sip."

"No." I feared it would come up before it got all the way down.

"Let's finish here and go home." Suzanne's tone was soothing.

With a friend supporting me on each side, I rose from the bench.

We made it to the suite of security offices and sat around a small conference table. My son sat in my father's lap, hugging the white alligator.

"How did you get lost?" a policeman asked.

"Don't know." Sonny Boy shrugged. "I went into the bathroom—the same one as the boy. I wanted to talk to him, but he ran out. After that, I didn't see Aunt Maggie."

"You didn't hear me calling for you?"

He shook his head. "A man asked if I was lost. I said, 'no,' and he walked away." Sonny Boy leaned closer to his grandfather's face. "I know where I am. I'm not lost. I'm in NOLA."

My sob, mixed with a chuckle, eked out.

"Then what happened?" my father asked.

"A man tried to take my hand. I ran to the es-cur-later and went up." Sonny Boy puckered his lips to one side. "I went to find Aunt Maggie."

"How did you wind up in the bear's lap?" I asked.

"I dunno. I got sleepy. Bear said it was okay."

A chuckle rippled through the group.

"No one touched you? No one gave you food or drink?" the officer asked.

Sonny Boy pointed. "Auntie Maggie gave me ice cream."

"Did you talk to anyone else?"

"No." Sonny Boy shook his head.

"If you're sure he's okay…" I appreciated the officer's concern, but I wanted Sonny Boy all to myself for a little while.

"I want to take my son home. Thank you." I offered my hand to the man.

And as soon as I had my son settled, some of the secrets I'd been holding tightly to had to be released. I dreaded what would come, yet after enduring nearly losing my son, nothing could be so hard.

But I was fully aware of what else I would be losing.

Later that evening, at Suzanne's front door, I hugged my father goodbye. Dinner had been a cheery time with tension served as a side dish. Sonny Boy, fresh from a bath and dressed in his pajamas, stood next to me.

My father bent down. Sonny Boy hugged him, nearly pulling him over.

"Bye, Grandpops." He waved and scurried down the hall to the family room where Maggie and Suzanne waited.

"I'll talk with you tomorrow." I kissed my father's cheek. "Thank you." Emotion lapped at me the way the lake water lapped against Pontchartrain Beach. "If you hadn't shown up… You dropped everything to help me…" I brushed away tears. "Your support means everything to me."

His mouth tightened and he shrugged. "It's hard to provide it when you live so far away."

"You're right." I nodded. "You are so right." I'd been thinking that same thought. I had an idea, but I wasn't ready to share until I worked out more details.

"Then let me help you. Let Maggie and Suzanne help you. It's time for you to move home." Hope lit his face. "That would be a wonderful gift for Father's Day."

"I get the hint. Good night, Daddy." I wanted to give him what he wanted, but would Suzanne and Maggie want me once all secrets came into the light?

I closed the door and followed the path my son had taken down the hall. Achy, tired, emotionally spent, I almost dropped to my hands and knees to crawl. The day had sucked my energy the way pumps sucked water from New Orleans to keep it from flooding.

Now it was time to tackle the truth.

The Gs chattered, "*Ha.Ha.Ha. Good luck with that.*" Trepidation fluttered in my chest. But I had faced the worst today and things worked out fabulously. Buoyed by hope, I traipsed to the family room. Then stopped.

"Ohhh…" My heart glowed. Maggie and Suzanne in plain-Jane clothes found only in the very back of their closets—cutoff denim shorts and white t-shirts—sat on the couch with Sonny Boy sandwiched between them.

They watched a movie about a boy and his pet lion. My son held each woman's hand. My best friends took turns feeding him popcorn. Why was a camera never handy at the perfect time?

Now wasn't the time to unleash a hurricane of hurt.

I'd tell them the truth soon.

"*When? When? When?*" the Gs chattered.

"Tomorrow," I whispered back. The sun would come up tomorrow, light the day, light the path for me to travel. Tomorrow would be the right day.

Right?

Chapter 20

I sat alone in the middle of the couch while Maggie and Suzanne put Sonny Boy to bed. I swirled the ice cubes in my drink. At first, the cubes clunked together. Then the more I swirled, the more the margarita in the glass grew into a tornado.

Unleashed, nothing man-made could stop it.

Earlier I'd watched a few minutes of TV. News reports of earthquakes, flooding, and tornadoes.

Houses moved off their foundations.

Cities buried by mud and water.

My foundation had been moved. I had been buried by grief, and then shame.

My mother's illness introduced anxiety into my life in a way no textbook had ever adequately described it. It ripped away any notion I clung to about safety, security, stability. I learned bad things happened to good people. Bad things happened to bad people. Bad things just happened. To anyone at any time.

Anxiety started creeping from my chest to my throat. I sipped my drink, stopping the tornado. Tornado in the glass and my tornado of emotions.

The only thing good that came from Momma's cancer—I'd married Mark.

My parents had had an enviable marriage. Their love was a verb *and* a noun. They'd set the relationship bar high. Chin-ups I could never do.

I swirled my drink again—a smaller tornado—then stopped it. It disappeared as if it had never existed. The calm after the storm.

How wrong I was to think that by marrying Mark, *I* could have what my parents had? Cancer pulled the Landry family apart. Mark's love and guiding hand had kept me from falling apart. But hard truths end up as hard lessons.

Love hadn't saved my marriage.

In fact, love is what tore it apart.

I'd thought if we loved each other enough we could endure anything. It wasn't the bad that tore us apart. It wasn't his tour in Afghanistan. It wasn't me going to school in Boston. It was everyday living.

We had needs the other didn't know how to meet.

Counseling hadn't closed that gap. The Velcro that strapped us together couldn't withstand the wash and wear of day to day.

I loved Mark enough to let him go.

It broke my heart as much as watching Momma die. Scared me. Maimed my soul.

Mark returned to New Orleans. Alone. We loved each other still. But Boston was a world away from the warm waters of Louisiana, its culture, his normal daily life, and all Mark needed from a woman.

He had found what he needed with Maggie. A bond from familiarity. Shared history. Contentment from a simple life. A cultural connection with the south.

All that, and Maggie worshipped him.

I took another sip of my drink. My brain had been on warp drive since meeting up with Maggie at the mausoleum. Choices. Choices. Choices. When and how to tell her about Sonny Boy tormented me like the ten plagues Pharaoh brought upon Egypt—his choice for failing to heed Moses's pleas. However, that was nothing compared to the hours I endured worrying about finding my son.

If that was the worst life could throw at me, I should have no fear about telling Maggie the truth, yeah?

Footsteps drew my attention. I drained the margarita.

"Maggie, I'm beginning to worry about Jane. Drinking alone again." Suzanne shook her finger at me. She and Maggie raced for the couch, plopped down next to me. They giggled like junior high schoolers.

"Then don't let me drink alone. Maggie, grab two glasses. I made a full pitcher of margaritas." I pointed to the counter.

Suzanne stiffened. "No, none for me."

"What's up with you?" I asked. "No wine with dinner. No margaritas. You don't have an ounce of fat. Grant can't possibly complain about the way you look. So, what's up?"

Suzanne rolled her eyes. "*Humph.*"

"Leave her alone. We'll drink her share." Maggie rose and started for the kitchen. "Anything I can bring you, Suz, while I'm up?"

"Lemonade. In the fridge."

"Maggie." I waved to get her attention. "Bring the pitcher back with you."

Liquid fortification might help me start talking.

And Maggie might need the anesthetization.

Suzanne turned on jazz. Trumpet, sax, and guitar. The three of us slouched on the couch, our feet resting on the long leather ottoman. I was sandwiched between them. We rocked our feet side to side to the beat of the music.

This was the moment I'd been waiting for. All I had to do was speak. Explain the connection each of them had to Sonny Boy.

"I—" Maggie spoke at the same time as me.

Maggie laughed. "You go first."

"No, you first," I insisted.

"I want you to know I love your son. I love you, too. I'm so glad you've come back into our lives. I'm very sorry about this afternoon. If I get another chance to take him anywhere again, I swear I'll put a leash on him, never let him from my sight. I'll follow him into the men's room."

My heart surged with rising hope. Maggie now understood the scary side of parenting. This was the perfect time for me to step up. Reveal the past. Tell the truth. Replace the taunting chatter of the Gs with hope, happiness, and love.

I patted Maggie's leg. "I'm glad you love him. I'm hoping that will make what I'm about to say easier to hear." Miss Margarita helped my filters drop and my bravery poke its head up.

Suzanne set her drink on the side table and turned sideways to face me. She rested her hand on my forearm and squeezed. Her support meant everything.

On the other side of me, I felt Maggie straighten. She took a big gulp of her drink.

"Go on," Maggie urged.

"I haven't been a good friend. *I'm sorry.* I care about you. I don't want anything to jeopardize our friendship. It's very important to me. Critically important for the future."

"I hear a 'but' coming." Maggie scrunched her brows and sipped her drink.

"I want you to know how deeply sorry I am. I have a confession." I reached for Maggie's hand and held it tight, hoping the physical connection would help ease the pain of the news. Hoped the connection would convey my sincerity… Or stop her from hitting me.

"Sonny Boy had a father…And you know him." I searched for some flickering recognition in her face.

"Had a father." Maggie tilted her head. "Wait, he wasn't created was he? I mean like…in vitro?" She looked aghast. "You got his father's sperm from a fertility clinic in New Orleans?" Her brows knitted together.

"Well, yes, but no." She threw a curve at me I wasn't expecting. Getting the next words out was hard. "He's buried here."

Maggie stiffened again. When she tried to pull her hand away, I held tight. "Sonny Boy is Christopher Marcus Landry."

"You named him after Mark?" She said it as though I'd said I had sex with the Pope.

"How twisted is that. You named your son after the man you divorced. Named him after *my* husband?" Her eyes grew wide and wild.

"He was my brother, Maggie." Suzanne moved to sit on the arm of the couch beside her. She put her hand on Maggie's shoulder. "I knew him longer than the both of you. You don't get to claim sole ownership over him."

"It's not the same, and you know it," Maggie snapped.

I held Maggie's stare. Her eyes flashed, then narrowed.

"It was never just Mark and me in our marriage. You were the ghost in our marriage. The 'worse' Mark brought with him." Maggie spat out the words.

"I can't say I truly understand, however, *please*, let me finish." My voice hit an octave I didn't know I had. The vise around my ribs was tighter than any corset I'd ever donned. I tried for a deep breath but could barely draw in air.

Maggie's level of denial was a tsunami. Would she hate me forever? Reject me? Reject Sonny Boy?

"For God's sake, Jane, tell me. It's not like the news is going to kill me. I mean, Mark died and I'm still here…"

Were my worries about her fragility overblown? "Maggie, Mark…Mark Christopher Maucele…is Sonny Boy's father."

Maggie sprang from the couch. Eyes wild. Hair wild. "You lie! You lie!" She pointed at me as though she could throw lightning and strike me dead.

She lunged for me. "You lie, you lie, you lie."

I pulled my knees up to protect myself from her blows. Suzanne grasped Maggie's shoulders. Pulled her away. Maggie shoved Suzanne. Her arms flailed. She tried to catch her balance.

I grabbed Suzanne to try to keep her from falling over the ottoman. Maggie grabbed my arm and bit me, pushing Suzanne into me.

Suzanne fell onto my bent knees. Maggie fell on top of Suzanne.

"Oh." Suzanne's breath hit my face. "My stomach," she groaned.

I froze. There was nowhere for me to move that wouldn't cause Suzanne more pain or possible injury.

Maggie rolled off and collapsed on the floor. Suzanne rolled to her side on the couch and clutched her stomach.

I jumped up. "Are you okay? Do we need to take you to the ER?"

She moaned. "No doctors." She curled into a fetal position. I sat on the couch beside her. Maggie sat cross-legged on the floor at her feet, panting, staring.

"It can't be. Sonny Boy can't be Mark's son." Maggie's blank expression worried me. "The one thing he wanted, a child. The one thing I couldn't give him." Her panting words rose barely above a whisper. "And all this time"—she gulped and panted—"*you* had his son?" I feared she might go into shock.

"Maggie, I'm sorry. Suzanne, are you sure I can't take you to the ER?" I didn't know which woman to focus my attention on.

"You're awful!" Maggie jumped to her feet. "I would've never believed you could be so—dishonest, disloyal, disastrous." Her body trembled. Her hands curled into fists. "*You* were my best friend. And I was jealous of you. Guilt ate at me. I did penance over it. *For years.*" She crumpled to the floor, sitting on her knees, shoulders slumped. "After I married Mark, you… haunted… our… marriage." Maggie's voice turned flat. Expressionless. Like she read from a script—no inflection, no intonation. "But I think, I hate you now. It would've been hard to learn you and he had a child, but we would've helped you. We would've loved the boy. If you had told Mark he had a son, he might not be dead."

I was not expecting those words to be flung at me. "What?" Maggie blamed me for Mark's death? I gripped Suzanne's arm for support. I expected Maggie to rant. Get loud. Maybe even throw something at me. But this?

My bones turned to jiggly Jell-O. I didn't know what to think.

"I begged Mark—Sell. That. Motorcycle. It will kill you," Maggie continued. "If he'd known he had a son, he might have been more cautious for the boy's sake." She shook her head. "You never told him. Evil. You're evil, Jane."

Shock punched me in the gut. My breath rushed out with a whistle. Was there truth in Maggie's words?

"No, Maggie." Suzanne sat up. Her tone was soothing and calm, as if speaking to a child. Her face said she still battled pain. "An accident killed Mark."

"But—"

"Be *thankful* he didn't know about Sonny Boy. He would've had the boy with him. They might both be gone."

"How can you side with Jane?" Maggie's shoulders hunched. She held her knees. Curled inward. A wounded child trying to protect herself from the cruelty of life. "Just like when we were kids, you did what Jane wanted." She lifted her head. Her eyes narrowed. "You *knew* about Sonny Boy, didn't you?" She ground out her indictment. "How long?"

Suzanne still clutched her middle and shook her head.

"She didn't find out until after the trip to the zoo," I whispered.

"And you didn't tell me? I'm your sister-in-law. Jane's been missing in action since high school. You'd keep a secret like that from *me*?" Pain clanged loud in Maggie's voice. She started to whimper. Soft sobs. Ripped my heart. Could this have gone any worse?

"I told Jane," Suzanne insisted. "She had to be the one to tell you, or I would do it."

Maggie leaned, folding her arms in front of her on the couch. She rested her forehead on the top of her hands. Her body began to shake. She mewled with pain like an injured animal.

I melted to the floor beside her and stroked her hair. "I'm so sorry, Maggie. I always intended to tell you and Mark. All my intentions backfired. I'll tell you whatever you want to know. I'm so sorry. Please forgive me."

"I don't know what to think." Maggie's words came in ragged breaths. "I'm dying inside."

"I know. I know. I know. I'm so sorry. I never wanted to hurt you."

Maggie cried. Each sob stabbed my heart. I wanted to comfort her. Wanted to pull the pain from her into me. I was strong enough to bear it. Had to be. And I deserved it.

"Momma?" Sonny Boy's small voice split the air.

I looked over to see my son toddling in my direction. He rubbed his sleepy eyes.

Suzanne jumped up as if to intercept him, then doubled over, fell on the couch, and groaned. Sonny Boy ran to her. I scooted around Maggie to grasp Suzanne's hand.

"What's wrong?" I asked.

Suzanne was holding her breath.

"The way through the pain is to breathe. Let go of the breath. Let go of the pain." I held Suzanne's hand tight. Sonny Boy stood next to the couch and patted her head.

"You okay, Auntie?" he asked.

"Yes, Christopher. I'll be fine. Go back to bed, little guy."

I scooped up my boy and carried him from the room. No need to traumatize him, too. "Back to bed, little man. It's sleepy time for you."

"I heard crying."

"I think that was Aunt Maggie." I crossed the threshold into Sonny Boy's room.

"But the phone didn't ring."

"Huh? What?" I pulled the covers back, hugged him tight, and plopped him in the middle of the bed.

"You cry after you talk on the phone."

"Oh, really?"

"Yes, Momma."

"Well, how about you go to sleep, and we'll talk about this in the morning?"

He snuggled into the covers and grabbed his white alligator. "Gator and I will go to sleep, but you stay here." He reached his hand out to me. I kissed the top of it, then stretched out on the bed beside him. He rolled over, his back to me, and placed Gator's head on the pillow next to his. I shuttered my thoughts about Maggie and Suzanne, giving Sonny Boy my full attention.

I began to hum to lull him to sleep. My son would grow up to be a good man like his dad. He would know compassion for others. His life would be shaped and molded by love.

Maggie might hate me now, but she loved Sonny Boy. She would come around. She would come around. She would come around. She *had* to come around.

It would take time, but hopefully not too much. Fingers, toes, hearts crossed.

I hummed until Sonny Boy's breathing grew soft and even. I kissed his cherub cheek, then rose, leaving the door ajar when I left. My heart thrummed with a mother's love. I knew Maggie's heart could thrum in harmony with mine.

When I returned to the family room, Suzanne remained in the same fetal position. Maggie sat next to her on the couch, her expression flickering with fear.

I knelt on the floor in front of them. "Suz, I need to take you to the doctor."

"Just sit with me."

I held Suzanne's hand and squeezed. I grabbed hold of Maggie's hand. "I'm asking for forgiveness. I was afraid. I was afraid you and Mark would take Sonny Boy away from me. Afraid the two of you would be better parents for him than me, a single mom. Afraid. Please, Maggie. I need you. I need Suzanne. Sonny Boy needs you both, too."

Maggie stared. No condemnation. But no empathy either. "We'll finish our fight later. Suz won't tell me what's wrong." She pointed at me. "Do you know what's wrong? And don't lie to me."

"I'm not sure." I wasn't going to share my suspicions. Suzanne hadn't confided in me. I couldn't confirm or deny what I was thinking. But the puddle of concern I had was now a lake.

"Maggie, there's nothing wrong." Suzanne's eyes remained closed. "I don't want an ER doc poking around me. I have a doctor's appointment in the morning. All of this can wait until then."

"We won't leave you in pain all night." I wouldn't be able to sleep.

"Grab me a blanket." Suzanne pointed to an antique steamer trunk in the corner of the room.

"What in God's name is she talking about?" Maggie was panic-stricken. "We have to get you to the doctor. Now."

"No." Suzanne was adamant.

"You could be bleeding internally," Maggie cautioned.

"And whose fault would that be?" Suzanne grabbed Maggie's arm. "Stop it. You're the religious one. I'm not going to the doctor until tomorrow. In God's name? If God is in control, then this is His will. If you want to be helpful—pray. Now leave me alone. *Both* of you, go away."

Maggie huffed out of the room.

Tonight had been rough going. More pain added to Maggie's deep well of sorrow. But were Suzanne's fears founded? Would Maggie do something drastic? If so, who could I count on to raise my son?

I turned out the light and sat in a nearby chair. "I'll be right here, Suz. I know what it's like to not ask for help. Not tell the truth. Not know the right thing to do." I placed both of my hands on my chest to steady my erratic heartbeat. "So no pressure from me. Just know I'm here for you. Right here."

Suzanne drifted off to sleep, and a little while later, I peeked in on Sonny Boy.

Maggie was on the bed and curled around him protectively. It eased my fears greatly but also produced stabs of hurt. A person could die from a thousand tiny cuts.

I choked back a sob. Covered my mouth. Fought back the pain.

My days were numbered.

Maggie's days with my son would be endless.

Eleanor Roosevelt

Chapter 21 - Maggie

Maggie woke when Sonny Boy flopped his arm onto her chest. The house was dark and quiet. Gingerly, she slid out of bed, trying not to wake him and headed to the guest room down the hall where she normally slept.

Jane would be mad if she knew I had comforted her little boy.

Crawling into bed, Maggie punched the pillow, then grabbed a second one, and plopped it beneath her head. She closed her eyes. Rather than darkness, taunting images of Mark and Jane swirled, circling around like a carousel in her head.

He kissed Jane after his first college football game.

He kissed Jane at their engagement party.

He kissed Jane at the altar.

Then he kissed Jane when….

"Stop it." She covered her eyes with her hands. She would not imagine them sharing intimate caresses. Tasting of lips. Consummating love. Producing a child.

How could she bear it?

Christopher was Mark's son.

The news shook her, shocked her. The blow was beyond startling. It was breath-stealing, like being struck by lightning and slammed to the ground.

She shouldn't hate Jane, shouldn't hate Jane, shouldn't hate, but dark emotions balled tight in her gut, sticky like hot tar and caustic like acid.

Why had Jane given the child her Landry last name? Why not Maucele? If Mark was the boy's father, then Jane robbed Sonny Boy of his father and the birthright of his name.

Hands fisted, she pounded the bed. Jane had a child that rightfully should be hers. A new tear ripped in her heart, a heart already weak and shredded.

Maggie's thoughts drifted back to the weekend Mark had rejected her seduction. Was that when he went to see Jane? She forced the old memory to the forefront, remembering every second of their time together before his getaway, an "undisclosed destination" trip. That had to be when Mark shared intimately with Jane....

Mark pulled a suitcase from the closet and opened it on his bed. "Maggie, it's only a short trip."

"I'll reschedule my hair clients and go with you." She folded his shirt and placed it on the stack with the other three. After six months together, she hated to think of a day without his smiles, his touch, his love.

"Aww, baby. We've been over this. You can't go with me."

Why? He refused to say. Only that he had to get away. For more than an overnight.

Hope tickled the back of her mind, tickled her heart. Tickled something deep and low in her belly. Was he ready to take their relationship to the ultimate step? She wanted a ring on her finger before they fully consummated their love.

Secretly, she'd been saving bridal pictures for inspiration and creating wedding lists. Sharing the joys of day-to-day dating life was simple, special, spectacular. Living with him would be heaven.

Her heart tap-danced. Delicious shivers ran up and down her spine. And if he didn't respect her as a good-girl Catholic, she'd haul him into bed now. She burned with need, had dreamt of covering her naked body in whipped cream, splashing on chocolate sauce, splaying herself on his bed, a seduction ending with them tangled together in a most biblical way.

She was hot. Horny. Wet.

But Mark was Mark.

He respected her faith and stood by her belief that sex came only after marriage—he never mentioned she wasn't a virgin. He affirmed her convictions and said to his way of thinking, she'd never consented to sexual abuse, so that hadn't violated her virgin status—his words were so important to her. She loved him for understanding.

But every day for the last six months, she sensed—never had a *knowing*, just a sense—he still longed for Jane. It caused an ache in her that rose and fell but never went away. She hated Jane for that. It was bad enough Jane had thrown Mark away, discarded him like used clothing. She worried his heart was too broken to ever commit to her.

Mark laid jeans in the bottom of the suitcase. Maggie watched his strong hands smooth them flat. She envied the jeans and remembered Suzanne's crude joke that when it came to Mark, Maggie couldn't rape the willing. Could she hope?

"Don't pout." Mark slid a finger over her bottom lip.

She crossed her arms and turned her back to him.

Mark pulled her close. A thrill shot through her. He wrapped his arms around her, locking her in an embrace, her backside pressed against him. His hardness sent a delicious thrill through her.

She *did* have an effect on him. The one she wanted.

"Maggie. Maggie. Maggie. I can't cross the line with you."

He started to put space between them. She strained back to feel more of him, reaching around to hug his butt, keeping him pressed close to her. "What line is that?"

"I don't want Father Thomas shaking his head at me *if* I show up in church." Mark's breath tickled her ear. Her insides melted.

How would she bear his leaving? He'd left when he became Jane's husband. She saw him before he shipped out to the Middle East, went to war—but then he was married to her best friend, and she couldn't tell him she was desperately in love with him. She had lit a candle every single day for his safety. Had bargained with God that if He wanted a soul, He should take hers instead.

Mark's hands roamed up her sides. His caressing touch steeled her determination. No matter where he headed, he would leave with her naked body embossed on his.

Any penance she paid would be worth the price for finding bliss in Mark's arms.

Maggie plopped the rest of Mark's clothes in the suitcase, then placed it out of the way. Facing him, she slowly unzipped her shorts. Let them fall to the floor. His eyes widened. She ran her tongue over her bottom lip. Taking a step, she kicked aside her shorts. Button by button, she peeled the blouse away, exposing skin.

Mark's eyes glazed with want. He licked his lips. His Adam's apple bobbed when he gulped.

She offered him a coy smile. Her blouse drifted off her shoulders. Fell from her arms.

Desire was readable in his half-hooded eyes, in his mouth slightly ajar, in his fingers twitching to touch her though his arms hung rigidly by his sides.

She unhook her bra from behind. Mark leaned in. He wrapped his arms around her, trapping her arms behind her back. Excitement licked her belly. He dialed her up hotter, hornier, and wetter. Her knees wobbled. She had almost reached the top of the mountain. She needed him to touch her there…and her body would rocket like a fireworks show.

"Ahh, Maggie." His breath came out ragged. "Are you sure I'm what you want?"

"Only you." She barely got the words out. Her insides heating and melting more." She turned, ran the tip of her tongue across his bottom lip. "Want me?"

"Yes." His whisper was strangled.

She wrapped her arms around Mark's neck, balanced on one foot, and then wrapped her leg around his. "Perfect." She ground herself against his hardness. Joy surged when he hardened more. His whole body tensed, pulsed with need.

She didn't need a *knowing* to understand he was on the edge of finally being her lover.

Mark groaned. "We can't do this, Maggie."

She froze. "*Can't*?" her voice squeaked.

"Oh, sugar." His laugh was shot with pain. "I'm dying here. But until I can give you what you want…I can't allow myself this pleasure."

"Want you." She whined. Gripped him tighter. Had to merge their bodies.

"Please, Maggie. Don't make me dishonor what you hold dear."

"I'll beg sweetly."

He brushed her hair back over her shoulders. Cupped her face. His eyes flickered with a montage of emotions—lust, love, desire. "Maggie, I respect your absolute faith in God. Look, I once convinced a woman to put aside her beliefs for me, and it ended badly. I won't make that mistake twice."

Hurt branded her heart. Jane. Everything *always* came back to Jane. "I know what I want." She brushed her lips over his, a sensual expression of her love and lust.

"I'll know what's next for us when I return." He scooped her and tossed her on the bed. *"Until then, let's just lie here, you wrapped in my arms…"*

The memory dissolved from her mind's eye. Maggie exhaled, remembering the feel of Mark. She ached. That night, after he'd gone on his trip, she'd prayed when she and Mark finally shared the most intimate man-woman moment, she would conceive.

Then Mark would never leave her.

Had Jane wished for the same thing?

I pulled up the covers Sonny Boy kicked off and tucked Gator next to my son. Unable to sleep, I eased away gently.

Anxiety pumped with each beat of my heart. My mind was a hurricane of thoughts. Sleep elusive.

I pulled on a robe, twisted the crystal doorknob, opening the door slightly. I had to check on Suzanne.

A light glowed at the end of the long hall, lighting the path to the family room. When I reached the room, I watched Suzanne sleep.

A buzzing started somewhere in the kitchen. Moving quickly, I had to stop it before it woke her. The muffled sound came from her jacket. It rang louder when I pulled it out. Quickly, I stepped into the garage.

"Hey, Grant. It's Jane."

"Oh? How's it going tonight? Is Suz around?"

"She's asleep."

"Anything wrong? We always talk at midnight when I'm away. We end one day and start another together." He chuckled.

I chewed my bottom lip. Should I spill my suspicions? What if they were wrong? But what if I'd guessed correctly? Would tomorrow's doctor visit confirm my guess? Or had Suzanne planned to terminate the pregnancy, hoping no one would find out? What to tell Grant?

"Jane? What's wrong?"

"It's been a day, Grant."

"Sorry, but is Suzanne okay?" His voice had panicked edges.

I decided to stick only to the facts. "We had unwelcome excitement. Maggie took Sonny Boy for an outing. The little bugger got away. Mall security called the police. Good news, we found him."

"Maggie took the dog?"

Uh-Oh.

"Grant? I'm having a hard time hearing you. Suz is tired. Already asleep. I'll have her call you tomorrow." I ended the call and leaned against the door.

Suzanne hadn't told Grant about Sonny Boy?

Maybe she had her reasons. Maybe.

Heaving a sigh, I entered the house and went to the laundry room. Suzanne stored large towels for the pool there. Stripping down to my bra and panties, I headed outside to the pool, seeking relief from the brick wall of tension building between my shoulders. Dangling my feet in the water would help me think—at least, it worked when I was a kid.

Landscape lighting lit the path to the pool. I searched and found matches in a sealed container on the table, then lit the mosquito torches. Sitting on the edge of the pool, I fluttered my feet and counted my breaths to quiet the Gs.

"I have to. I have to. I have to." I have to move back. I have to make things right. I have to prepare…for the future. As limited as it might be.

Suzanne woke to silence. A single light dimly lit the family room. Everything looked perfectly normal.

When she started to rise, her stomach clenched. She moved slowly to the kitchen for a glass of water. Through the windows, flickering torches caught her attention. Had one of her friends sought refuge there?

"Want company?" Suzanne neared the pool.

"It's your pool."

When she got closer, Jane patted a space on the stone decking next to her.

"I need padding." Suzanne grabbed a cushion from a patio chair. "Want one? It's easier on the *derrière*."

Jane coughed out a laugh. "Butt on hard concrete is tantamount to the kneeling rail at church. Thanks. I'll bear the penance."

"Suit yourself." Suzanne plopped onto the cushion beside Jane and wondered where Maggie had gone.

"Grant called."

"It must be after midnight." Suzanne looked upward and sighed. "He's probably worried. What did you tell him?" As she waited for Jane's response, a muscle tightened in her gut. Placing a hand over the spasm, she took a relaxing breath.

"You mean, did I tell him I suspect you're pregnant?"

Suzanne sighed. Maggie was the most intuitive one. If Jane sensed the situation, then the secret would be out soon. "You guessed correctly."

"I didn't tell Grant. But take it from me, keeping secrets about kids, born or unborn, isn't a good idea. Look at the mess I've made of things."

Suzanne grunted. "This is different."

"Keep telling yourself that lie. It'll work for a while."

"Why *didn't* you ever tell any of us about Christopher?"

"Fear." The word emphatically dropped from her lips.

"Couldn't be that simple, Jane."

"Fear is one of the most heinous four-letter words in English. Sums it all up, though." Jane's voice lowered to a whisper. "So, are you having an abortion?"

Suzanne gulped. "Don't know." Jane just threw the A-word out like a stripper dancing in a window of a Bourbon Street club, ripping off her pasties. Naked. Bold.

"The appointment tomorrow?" she prodded.

"I've got three pee sticks that say I'm pregnant. Not sure more technology will dispute the fact. But I'm going to the doctor to find out and learn about my options."

"Suzanne, what do you really want?"

She paused. Drew in a long slow breath. "I want it all. Want to stop worrying about whether or not Maggie will hurt herself. Want you to move home. Want my husband *and* our baby. That became crystal clear when I was doing the stomach-over-your-knees trick. 'Protect the baby' was my only instinct." Defeat rippled through her. "But I can't have it all."

"You don't know that," Jane protested.

Suzanne swatted a mosquito on her arm. A red spot appeared where there used to be a bug. Life and death at her hand. Could she possibly do that? Until tonight, the possibility of life inside her hadn't been real. She could do without a big house, sports car, and many luxury things, but to give up the love of her life? To have Grant walk away...

Her stomach flip-flopped. She quickly drew a breath and exhaled, trying to land at calm.

Grant was her everything.

"Suzanne?" Jane clasped hands with her. The squeeze was comforting. Like maybe the old-warrior-Jane was still with her. The teenager who stood up to bullies, abusive parents, and the police.

Suzanne faced her. "There's death with either choice I make. An abortion or a divorce. Mark just died... this is an impossible decision I'm facing."

"Let me put this in a different perspective." Jane grimaced. "I cheated my son out of his father. Because of fear. Fear that Mark and Maggie would take him from me. Fear that Sonny Boy might love them more. Fear that my son would reject me. It shackled me like a prisoner and slowly dragged me to the gallows."

"Mark would've never tried to take your son." How could Jane think he could be that kind of man?

"Maybe. I couldn't risk it. My mother's death—she left me. My father's drinking—he left me." Jane hid her face in her hands. "I loved Mark, I still do. And I made him leave me."

"He was hurt and angry when he returned home. I just don't understand you."

"Mark was dying in Boston. A long, slow, protracted death. He hated it there. Everything about it… except maybe the seafood. He didn't fit. After my mother, and then my father, I tried to give Mark his life back. We were too different as adults to make it work. You and Grant. Not different at all. You are the Yin and Yang of each other. Don't do it. Don't decide because of fear. Abortion takes away your options."

"What options?" Drops of hope puddled in Suzanne's heart.

"Tell Grant. Give him the opportunity to help you decide. If you terminate the pregnancy, you'll never know how he feels."

"I *do* know." After seven years of marriage, she understood her husband well. He never deviated from a plan he committed himself to. Which had included winning her heart. She respected his boundary about no more children. All laid out in an ironclad prenup. She understood it. Agreed with it. Had signed it.

"He may surprise you. If you terminate, there's no telling his honest emotions. Don't make the mistake I did. Don't let fear rule. If you love him, trust him to be honest. Only after that will you know enough to make an informed adult decision."

She squeezed Jane's hand. "You're the wisest. That's why I need you here."

Jane shook her head. "Kind of you to say so, but I've had the experiences you should seek to avoid."

Her words made sense. But fear had wiggled its way into Suzanne's thoughts. Rooted there. Tossed candy to entice her emotions to follow along. Tomorrow when the sun came up, she would be in full adulting mode. With full confirmation, then she'd make a decision. "I'll sleep on it."

Suzanne leaned closer to Jane and wrapped her arm around her shoulders.

"That would be wise." Jane chuckled.

Suzanne didn't want to think about it any longer. Not tonight. Other things pressed on her mind. "In other news," she said. "I've been thinking about how to keep you here. Either way I go—baby, no baby, husband, no husband—I need your support. What about a publishing job here? Maybe not as glamorous as the one you have, but similar."

"Are you trying to buy my silence?" Jane eyed her.

"Don't look at me in that tone of voice. Years ago, you bored like a bug into my life. I want you here. Selfish of me, I know."

"On one condition."

Only one? Jane would consider a permanent move? Hope flowed through Suzanne like the fountain flowed water into her pool. She eyed her. "You're going to blackmail me, aren't you?"

Jane's grin spread as wide as Lake Pontchartrain. "Doesn't take Maggie's gift to figure me out. *You tell Grant* you're pregnant before you make a final decision. *I'll tell you* what it will take to make me stay."

"You'll honestly consider staying?"

She nodded.

Suzanne straightened. "I hate you right now. That was too easy."

"Just remember, you love me, too."

"You'll stay if I tell Grant? Regardless of his decision?"

Jane's mouth formed a thin line. Suzanne feared she would say it was a joke.

"We can't link our futures over demands or half-truths or fear. I can promise you, I'll give moving back careful consideration. But only after you tell Grant."

She hugged Jane tight. They bobbled together, almost falling into the pool.

"Okay, okay," Jane laughed. "And by the way. Your husband still thinks Sonny Boy is a dog. I think I need to call him and tell him the truth."

"Let's video chat instead. I want to see his face when he hears that news." And maybe after tomorrow's doctor visit she should do the same. Video chat and tell Grant.

A jolt of fear raced through her. What if he flat out rejected her?

Now she understood fear as an ugly four-letter word.

She doubted she'd sleep tonight.

It could be the last night her husband ever truly loved her.

Chapter 22 - Suzanne

Suzanne opened the plantation shutters to let in dawn's first light, then lay on the chaise in her bedroom. She closed her eyes for the millionth time. The antique mantel clock in her bedroom softly chimed six times. She squirmed for a comfortable position. Across the room, her king-sized, four-poster bed loomed large and lonely without Grant, and she couldn't bring herself to slide into it.

Sleeping on the chaise made her feel a little less like she'd betrayed him.

A cool hit of air brushed her shoulders, and she pulled a thin blanket up to her chin, wiggling toes at the loss of warmth. Would she grow big and round and heavy such that she wouldn't see them again until after the baby was born?

If the baby was born…

Would Grant find her changing body repulsive?

His appreciation for her form, firmness, and fitness made her ripple with pride. He loved her flat stomach. Loved her shapely thighs and slender ankles. Even loved her feet, especially with painted toes. He loved the curve of her neck, the curve of her hips, and the curving swell of her breasts.

Yet Grant was a self-proclaimed ass man.

She chuckled, recalling catching him checking out the backsides of other women. But it was only *her* firm ass he touched. He never neglected to remind her how much he loved it.

She loved his caressing hands. Loved his kisses. Loved the melding of their bodies. Making love with him was energizing and always ended with tenderness when they cuddled.

They were as good in bed as they were out of bed. They had the perfect life.

She'd never wanted to give Grant a reason to leave her.

"What the hell are you thinking? You can't have this baby." She jerked her hands away from her belly.

She was a do-him-wrong song. Grant had always been up-front. Never wavered in his decisions. Not when he bought her three-carat diamond engagement ring. Bought the house. Bought the car. But he never flashed attitude about his wealth, never tried to buy her love. He had that from the very start.

An ache in her heart grew. A lump the size of an eighteen-pound bowling ball weighed heavy on her chest. A deep loneliness settled there. Only one person understood her deep-seated fear of abandonment. And Mark had gone off and left her.

"Mark?" she whispered. "If you can hear me, I need to talk."

She waited for a sign. That was how Maggie got her *knowings*, right?

"Mark. I need my big brother."

A slight shadow flitted beyond the plantation shutters. A hummingbird. She stared harder, but it vanished. Had it been an apparition?

A creak sounded from the wooden floor, like footsteps. A slight draft, a chill, swirled around her. Signs from her brother, or had she gone crazy? She'd heard hormones did that to women. "Pregnancy brain," they called it. But she wasn't far enough along for that. Besides, New Orleans was haunted. It made sense she'd have a modern-day ghost to go with the antique one the realtor said came with the house.

"Mark," Suzanne whispered. "You've left me with two crazy sisters-in-law. I don't want to hurt them." A soft wave of air caressed her cheek.

"What do I do? About Jane. About Maggie. About a baby? Mine, not yours. Though he's a little boy, not a baby now. You'd love Sonny Boy."

She imagined Mark crowing. He would love being a father. Spending time at his camp, teaching his son how to fish, shrimp, and crab.

"I know you'd be thrilled if I had a kid who called you 'Uncle.' But until last night, staring at a pee stick, okay, three of them, didn't make it real. Reality is sinking in. I'm scared. Daddy left me. Jane left me…once. You've left me. And Grant, I'd walk through hell for, will leave me, too." She sniffed. "When he finds out about this baby." She used the corner of the blanket to mop her tears. "I guess I'll walk through hell the rest of my life if I go through with this pregnancy."

Her cold feet warmed as though someone massaged them. She felt honest-to-goodness friction. Mark was with her. He remembered how much she loved a foot massage. Not that she believed he actually did it now but used some sort of heavenly magic.

"Jane's right. What if I terminate this pregnancy and Grant hates me? He might not want me pregnant, but making myself un-pregnant…he might find that repugnant. I can't risk losing him. Won't risk it. Better to do the A-deed than tell him. My dirty secret."

Suzanne pulled her knees close to her chest. Her perfect life was crumbling in the light of day. "Mark, please help me."

I groaned at the sudden light in my eyes. "Close the blinds." I pulled the covers over my face and rolled.

"Time to get up." Suzanne's voice came to me as though through a long tunnel.

"I just got to sleep," I moaned.

"Get your lazy carcass out of bed. Things to do. It's eight o'clock." Maggie startled me. Her voice, but Mark's words. An echo from the past.

"Where's my son?" I sat up, flipped the covers down, and scanned the room. Suzanne sat on the edge of the bed. Maggie stood at the foot of it, her arms crossed, expression stormy and impatient.

"He's having breakfast." Maggie turned up her nose at me.

"He's in the kitchen with Latisha," Suzanne said. "And she's trying to satisfy his Cajun craving for *pain perdu*."

"Something his *mother* didn't make for him." Maggie spread her sarcasm all over me.

"Enough. Truce, you two. At least until after my doctor visit. Then we'll put on boxing gloves and take this outside by the pool."

I scowled at her. "You're one to talk."

"Something's going on. Suzanne, tell me. Right now. Or I walk." Maggie straightened and lifted her chin.

"I told you last night about this checkup." Suzanne pointed a finger at Maggie. "Un-wad your panties, girl. I don't grill you about doctor visits." Then she turned to me. "Jane, would your father watch Sonny Boy at lunch? Give us girls a chance to talk?"

"Maybe. He might take the afternoon off. Hand over my cell, please." I pointed. "On the dresser."

Suzanne complied. "My appointment's at ten a.m. We'll leave here at nine thirty."

"I'll be ready." I waited for them to hustle off. Maggie continued heaping her attitude on me with a tilt of her head and the corners of her mouth pointing down.

"Go. Now." I shooed Suzanne. "Take the emotional gorilla"—I pointed at Maggie—"with you."

Maggie lunged for me.

Suzanne jumped out of the way. "I'm not getting in the middle of you two again."

Maggie straddled me on top of the covers. Rather than fight, I lay there trying to appear calm. I swear she could see my heart hitting my rib cage, about to burst.

"I've had it with you." Maggie's body heaved as though she'd run around City Park. "If you want me to forgive you for being a…lying… cheating heathen—"

"You can't even say what you feel." I pushed up to my elbows. "Tell me what you really think of me. How do you feel? For God's sake, get it out! We'll all feel better when you do."

Maggie's chest rose and fell, she puffed like a blowfish. Her nostrils flared. She snorted. Her hands curled into fists at her side.

I wished she'd hit me. Get out her pain. But I knew Maggie would never strike me. "Christ! For once, tell me how you feel without thinking about whether or not you're going to have to confess to your priest." I sat up and thumped Maggie's chest. "You keep your feelings bottled up. Little Miss Perky Sunshine with her signature bubblegum-pink everything. There's no one perkier than you, Maggie."

Suzanne strode to the door. "Take your voice down a notch, Jane. I'm going to find my nephew and occupy him." She closed the door. "Don't come out until you've hugged each other."

"I never thought you'd be a slut," Maggie spat.

"Is that the best you can do? News flash—I'm not. Now, get off me." I scooted backward until my back bumped the headboard. Bending my knees, I pulled the covers up and pulled a pillow onto my lap. Just in case Maggie did let go and try to punch me.

She collapsed on the bed and began to cry. "Mark never told me where he went one weekend. I did the math. Figured Sonny Boy's birth date. Which means Mark saw you. The two of you played man and wife. But you were *divorced*." Her face scrunched. A high-pitched screech rolled toward me. Maggie buried her face with her hands. Her shoulders began to shudder.

Filled with remorse, regret, and resignation, I wished she had hit me. "It's complicated, Maggie." I touched her shoulder. She jerked away. "We never intended to hurt you."

She scooted to the far corner of the bed. "Exactly one month after Mark returned, he asked me to marry him. But you knew all along, we were dating. I made sure you knew. Yet, you slept with Mark anyway. How could you?"

"I'm sorry. I'm sorry. Guilty as accused." The Gs chattered loudly. *Guilty. Guilty. Guilty.*

"But why?" she whimpered. "Why did you do it?"

How did I explain? Mark and I had been friends way before Maggie met him. We had history. Family connections. Love. But different needs. Different goals. Driven by different fears and hurts and emotional wounds refusing to scab over and heal.

We'd loved each other. Truly. Deeply. Madly.

But we didn't fit together in everyday life.

After that weekend with Mark, I hadn't slept with anyone. It might sound like a romance novel, but the man had ruined me for anyone else.

Facing Maggie now, I couldn't confess the rest of the truth to her.

Mark had proposed to me again. If I'd accepted, he would've never married Maggie. I would go to my grave with that tidbit. To share it would be cruel.

"Oh Maggie," I began, my voice cracking. "The easy answer is it just happened—because it did. We didn't plan it. I was a safe fling because you were the real thing. I think that's what he discovered. Mark had a big heart. He had enough love for the two of us."

"That doesn't justify what you did. You could've said no."

"Guilty as accused. I'm sorry. I will say I'm sorry every single day for the rest of my life to make this better. What happened was never meant to hurt you. *I* never meant to hurt you." I crawled toward her. She held up both hands to stop me.

"Why didn't you tell us that you were pregnant? Why didn't you tell us when Sonny Boy was born?"

"Well…" I grimaced. The words stuck in my gut. I made several starts to speak, but the thought of causing Maggie more pain kept me from uttering anything.

"Tell me!" Maggie demanded.

"When I figured out I didn't have the flu"—I took in a quick breath and blew out the stuck words—"my dad told me Mark had proposed to you. You loved Mark. I loved both of you. Mark and I couldn't make it work. I believed the two of you could. If I had announced I was pregnant…I just couldn't ruin your happiness. I was about seven months along when you and Mark married."

Maggie wiped her eyes. "I told you, I did the math."

I thought confession was supposed to be good for the soul. Inside, I was like sugar burning in an oven on broil. Wave after wave of anxiety rolled. I rocked with the waves to keep from throwing up. Maggie deserved the truth. Only afterward could we begin to heal. "I was alone. Only my friend Beth was there when Sonny Boy was born. And I knew you were trying to get pregnant. How could I pop in and say, 'Oh, by the way, Mark, here's your boy'? That would have devastated you."

Maggie pounded the bed. Flailed her feet. The bed quivered under her attack. "At any time after Sonny Boy was born, you could have told us. You waited years. Now Mark is dead." She began to cry. Her moans ripped through me.

I got off the bed and approached Maggie from behind. Wrapped my arms around her. We rocked while she sobbed. Her shoulders shook.

"I would never purposely hurt you. We're sisters. Blood sisters. Maggie—I need you. Please don't turn your back on me." Tears tracked down my face. I held Maggie and continued to rock with her.

She sniffed and shook her head.

"Please, Maggie. Please."

She pushed my arms away, breaking my contact. I stepped back.

"Why?" Maggie demanded, turning to face me. "You're going to leave. That's what you do. You leave. You left your mother. Left your father. You left me and Suzanne. Eventually, you left Mark. You left New Orleans, and I *know* how much you love this city, but you left anyway."

I left my mother? My father? What was she talking about?

"What's the point of friendship? I'll be civil to you for Suzanne's sake. But truthfully, you and I don't ever need to talk again."

She hopped off the bed.

My skin burned with tightness. Desperation beat me, as though I was being flogged. I couldn't breathe. Swaying, I grabbed for a bedpost and sank to the floor. "Maggie," I called, her rejection blinding me with tears. "I never realized...never understood..." I had been so wrapped up with my mother's dying—her forcing me to leave for school. My father literally shoved me while I cried out of the door. Mark dragged me to the car. Too ashamed to tell Maggie or Suzanne about that day.

"Maggie, I'm sorry."

She stood in the doorway. Behind me I heard her say, "I had hoped we'd remain friends. You were always the sister I wanted, more than any of my own. Growing up, I envied you so much. You were brave and smart and pretty. And Mark loved you. Now in my bubblegum-pink perky mind, I thought I could talk you into staying. That we could be family again. I love your son. Even before I knew he was Mark's. I wanted to set up a college fund with insurance money Mark left me. Lord knows, I don't need it. But Jane, you and I are done."

"Please, Maggie," I pleaded. I didn't want her to feel trapped with Sonny Boy. I didn't want her to step up out of pity. And I couldn't tell her the rest of my truth.

The bedroom door popped open. I jerked around. Sonny Boy bounced inside, bounced across the room, and climbed on the bed.

"Whatcha do'n?"

Maggie sank into a chair.

"Talking." I climbed on the bed next to my son.

"Auntie Suzanne said to get ready. Did you call Grandpops? Do I go with him today?" My boy tried to tickle me. I tried to tickled him back, but he squirmed over the side of the bed, landed on his feet, and ran to Maggie.

He pulled on her arm. "I love you, Auntie Maggie. I'm sorry I got lost yesterday. I won't do it again. Are you still mad at me?" Sonny Boy took her hand and kissed the top of it.

Maggie's bottom lip trembled. She blinked and blinked and blinked. "I'm not mad. I was never mad. I was scared." She placed her arm around him and pulled him onto her lap. "Do you ever get scared?"

His eyebrows scrunched. "I don't like to talk about being scared."

The two of them had an easy rapport. I realized that as long as I kept Sonny Boy in Maggie's path, she couldn't close her heart to him. Maybe there was hope after all. Sonny Boy's birth might be a wedge between me and her now, but my boy was the link that could bridge us back together.

"Son, here's my cell phone. Please take it to Auntie Suzanne. Ask her to call Grandpops for me. Auntie Maggie and I will be along in a few minutes."

"But, Momma, Auntie Suzanne told me to get you. She was serious. She told me so." His little fists went to his hips, just as Suzanne would do.

"We'll be just a minute longer." I held out the phone to him.

Sonny Boy scampered down from Maggie's lap. Her face softened. Her shoulders relaxed as she watched him. She reached her hand out to touch him, but he was gone in a flash, on his way to Suzanne.

"Maggie?" I tested the waters. "You love him."

She nodded, as though helpless to do otherwise.

There was no way I could patch up my relationships from Boston. I had to be here. Conviction tethered me to New Orleans. Energy flowed through me. It pulled the bowling ball from my chest, boulders of guilt rolling off my body. Everyone and everything I needed was here. "For his sake, we have to heal the pain. I need you to be in his life. An anchor, like I was in yours…in case I'm not here for him someday."

"You leaving?"

"I'll tell you a secret—"

"No!" She covered her ears with her hands. "No. More. Secrets. Truth. Truth. Truth."

I crossed the room to her. Gently, I tugged on her hands, held them in mine. "I'm going to stay."

"Secrets aren't healthy. Lies are worse." Maggie pulled back, shoving her fingers through her hair, it cascaded down around her like lace. Sadness rimmed her eyes. A smile never formed.

"I'm a horrible person. But your faith must allow for second chances. Give me one. Please."

Maggie tilted her head. Wrinkled her nose as though my plea were too much.

I needed her to cross the bridge to my side. But how?

"We have to teach Sonny Boy all the things Mark would want him to know. You're his stepmother. There's a responsibility that falls on you with that title. It's different than Suzanne as his aunt and me as his mother."

Outwardly, I needed to be calm. Not beg. Or plead. Be the anchor she needed.

"Stepmother?" Her mouth drew into a straight line. "Stepmother." This time, she said it as though she were trying it on for size. "Stepmother." A faint muscle in her cheek twitched. She squelched a grin.

Inside, my momma-bear instincts roared with triumph.

The road wouldn't be easy, but I believed we'd made a very positive turn.

Now *all* I had to do was to keep us on the path. If Maggie would follow.

"Bad news isn't wine. It doesn't improve with age."
Colin Powell

Chapter 23 – Suzanne

Suzanne carried bottles of water from the fridge in the garage to her car parked on the driveway. If blue sky and low humidity were the gauges of a good day, this one would be fantastic. Birds chirped, answering the back-up beepers from construction trucks across the street. Whiffs of roses from the garden perfumed the air. However, her mood more closely matched an approaching thunderstorm. Where would lightning strike?

Maggie climbed in back next to Sonny Boy. Jane sat up front. That she knew of, the two women hadn't spoken since she left them alone. Now the silence between them screeched like the brakes of two Mac trucks about to hit head-on.

She sighed. If she hadn't been so concerned about her own emotional overload, she would've stayed to referee. But the problem they faced belonged to them. And she wouldn't allow them to make her choose sides.

Oh, but to be a fly on the wall…

She climbed in the car. "Here." She handed over the bottles to Jane, who handed one back to Maggie.

Suzanne settled her sunglasses on her face. "Ready to roll."

"Go. Go. Go." Sonny Boy giggled.

The iron gate swung open, and Suzanne backed the BMW toward the street.

"Hey, little guy, I've got your nose." Maggie pretended to hold Sonny Boy's nose between her fingers. It was an old game father and grandfathers played with young children.

Suz studied Maggie's reflection in the rearview mirror. Something about her voice…a note of hope? Happiness? Could she now stop worrying about Maggie hurting herself?

She drove away from the construction noise. Like the old house getting rehabbed, she and her friends had some rebuilding of their own to do. Trust wouldn't come easy. Hopefully at lunch, the three of them could clear the elephants from the room and wipe the windows clean for a fresh view of the future.

Last night Maggie shocked her. Gentle doe eyes had bulged, dark and angry. Snapping and snarling. She'd swear Maggie grew long, pointed nails to scratch Jane's eyes out. In contrast to last night, she now bubbled bright, glittering in the light. Suzanne wasn't sure who enjoyed the playful banter taking place in the backseat more—Maggie or Christopher.

But last night wasn't a dream. Maggie *had* lunged. Jane *had* protected herself. Suzanne *had* stepped in to halt the attack, never thinking she'd be face down with Jane's knees in her stomach.

Beside her, Jane stared out the window. Silent and serious. There had been no good way for her to share the truth she'd hidden away in Boston. News was years late in coming. That factor in particular exponentially increased Maggie's pain.

And Jane wasn't off the hook with her either, not without some specific agreements about her nephew's future. "Sonny Boy, where are you and Grandpops going today?" Suzanne asked.

He clapped his hands. "Riverboat ride."

"Have Grandpops take lots of pictures."

Jane stared out the window still but gave a thumbs-up. Suzanne rolled her eyes. She'd missed Christopher's first four years. She wanted pictures. Videos. Something to close the gap between when he was born and now.

He looked so much like Jane, only a shred of Maucele in the boy. Still she loved him. Totally loved him. The bond happened with a hug, when he wrapped his arms around her legs and said they were family.

God, she was a sucker for the male species.

"I'm going to take you in a pirogue," Maggie said.

"Pee-what?" Sonny Boy asked.

Jane chimed in with a description of a Cajun canoe. Sonny Boy's face flashed from googly eyes to cross-eyed and back again as he faked rowing a boat. The boy was cute. Adorable. And Suzanne's, too—blood-related.

She had to be a part of his life. He needed to know Maucele family history. She wanted holiday trips with him. Summer vacations at the lake. Fishing and swimming and crabbing. Those times wouldn't be enough. She wanted to see him act in school plays, play an instrument in a marching band, band together with other boys to play football, like his daddy.

The only way for that to happen—Jane had to be here. What persuasion could she use to entice Jane to take a job offer?

"Momma, inside voice." Sonny Boy's pleas cut through Suzanne's thoughts.

"Tujague's," Jane insisted.

"No. Johnny's," Maggie countered.

Bickering again? At least, they were talking to each other.

"Sonny Boy, are you taking Gator with you?" Suzanne ignored her friends.

"Yes, ma'am. But he's staying in the car—take good care of him. Gator likes to nap in the sun."

"Suzanne, I'd like to take a drive through the city. See my grandmother's old place," Jane interrupted. "After we have lunch."

"Shush," Suzanne said to Jane.

"What?"

"I'm talking to my nephew. Sonny Boy," Suzanne said over her shoulder. "We're going to buy you a Saints t-shirt. Football is big in the Maucele household." She'd started to say, "Your daddy played college football for LSU," but she caught herself. Mentioning Mark might ignite a world war.

"You won't—" Maggie tapped Jane on the shoulder.

"Shush," Suzanne said again.

"—recognize the area." Maggie finished.

"Shush," Suzanne ordered.

"What?" Maggie leaned forward from the backseat again.

"Shush, I said."

"What's the matter with you?" Maggie's voice spiked with irritation.

"I'm having a conversation with my nephew."

"Am I Aunt Maggie's nephew, too?" Sonny Boy asked.

Silence hung in the air thick and dense and weighted with angst.

Suzanne looked at Jane—dazed confusion.

"Well…" Maggie began.

"Sonny Boy, we'll explain it to you later," Jane said.

"We'll use paper and crayons and draw our family tree." Suzanne hoped to shut down the dangerous discussion.

"I don't have any paper here. My crayons are at home," Sonny Boy said. "Momma, I put them away, remember?"

"Yes, that was a good thing. You're a good boy." Jane sounded as though she teetered on a tightrope and was about to fall.

"I'll get you art supplies this afternoon." Suzanne pulled into the mostly empty parking lot at the doctor's office.

"Yay!" Sonny Boy kicked his feet, banging against the back of the front passenger's seat. "There's Grandpops!"

They piled out of the car. Sonny Boy ran into his grandfather's open arms. Wrapped his little arms around Mr. Landry's neck. His grandfather stood and swung him up in the air.

"Wheee!" Sonny Boy squealed.

Mr. Landry set the boy on his feet and began a round of hugs. When it was her turn, Suzanne hugged the older man tightly. "It's good to see you," she whispered. "We're family. You're the grandfather, and I'm the aunt." Love tingled inside her, spreading like warm honey.

Mr. Landry released her, smiled, nodded, and then embraced Maggie.

Suzanne wondered how much he knew about Jane's confession last night.

Jane kissed her father's cheek. "We'll see you at dinner. It's my turn to cook tonight. I think we'll do a shrimp boil."

"Come on, Grandpops!" Sonny Boy tugged on his grandfather's hand.

"Hey. Little man. Give your momma a kiss." Jane squatted and tapped her cheek. Sonny Boy giggled and ran to her.

Suzanne kept her eye on Maggie, who took a step closer to Jane.

"I want a kiss goodbye, too." Maggie kneeled next to Jane.

Sonny Boy wrapped an arm around his mother's neck, and then Maggie's, too.

Thwack. Thwack. Thwack. Thwack. He alternated kissing them.

A grin tugged at the corners of Suzanne's mouth. Her nephew was a charmer.

Sonny Boy stepped away. "Gotta go!"

Busy, busy, busy boy. He scurried to the car where his grandfather waited. He waved goodbye, throwing kisses, something Jane must have taught him.

Suzanne draped an arm around Maggie and Jane. Together they watched the car drive away. They had to pull it together. Otherwise, they wouldn't be the only casualty of a crash and burn. They had Sonny Boy to consider now.

She turned toward the door to the doctor's office. What additional angst would her news produce? "This way, ladies."

A minute later, she was ushered to the inner sanctum. A petite nurse prepped her: weight, temperature, blood pressure. Then handed her a cup.

"You pee, then give me blood. Don the fashionable paper gown, and I'll suck your blood." The nurse wiggled her eyebrows.

Suzanne climbed on the examining table. The paper covering crinkled loudly in the silence of the room. She barely felt a prick. It wouldn't do for anyone to know needles made her faint. As long as it remained out of sight, she could handle it.

Dr. Davidson entered a few minutes later. "I'm surprised Grant isn't here with you." She sat on a stool next to the examining table and looked over the top of her glasses.

"He's away on business."

"You didn't tell him, did you?"

"About the appointment or about my suspicions."

"Both."

Suzanne looked away. "You're *my* doctor. Not *our* doctor. I need to know what's right side up before I involve Grant."

If I involve Grant.

When the rolling stool squeaked, Suzanne turned back to find Dr. Davidson standing beside her reading a printout.

"Yes, you're my patient. I'll honor your confidentiality. However, you and Grant perfected marital bliss. The rest of us drool and hope. Is there something I should know? Your blood pressure's up."

Suzanne shook her head and stuffed her worries fighting to rise. "Will you please do the exam, and then we'll talk about options?" She wanted to sound authoritative. Businesslike. Clinical. But the words eked out. Now that she was face-to-face with exacting science, truth ballooned up. What if she was pregnant? What if she terminated it? What would she tell Grant?

"Let's talk. The exam can wait a few minutes." Dr. Davidson cocked her head.

"No. Exam." It was all she could say, blinking against the mistiness in her eyes.

"Lie back. Count to five. Three deep breaths in and out. Relax. This is possibly a life-changing moment." Of course, the doctor would have to say that, flash it like a red neon sign.

Suzanne scooted and positioned herself. Looking up, she hated the Georgia O'Keefe print on the ceiling. The flower looked softly feminine, genteel, and sacred. Suzanne's emotions ran counter to that. Sour. Sick. Scared.

Throughout the examination, Dr. Davidson spoke in a low calm voice, one she might use on a child teetering on the edge of hysteria. The nurse never spoke other than to respond, "Yes, Doctor."

"You can get dressed. Meet me in my office."

"Wait. Tell me…something," Suzanne begged.

"In my office, I will."

Shaken, a tad unsteady on her feet, Suzanne dressed and then walked to Dr. Davidson's office to wait. She swallowed, then swallowed again. Her wingback chair faced a matching empty one. One Grant should be sitting in, sharing this with her.

She smoothed imaginary wrinkles on her dress. The turquoise and white silk was one of Grant's favorites. She wore it to feel close to him.

"Hey, there." Dr. Davidson sounded upbeat. "Sorry to keep you waiting."

Resignation settled over Suzanne. A sigh slipped out. "Just tell me. Yes or no."

Dr. Davidson sat in the wingback chair across from her. "This is girl to girl. I'm worried about you. For someone I thought would be dancing, you seem upset."

"Options. What are my options?" Suzanne managed a forced smile.

"What options do you want to discuss?"

"This your way of confirming I'm pregnant?"

"Yes. Suzanne Maucele Saulnier, you are pregnant. About seven weeks. You have three reliable home pregnancy tests. My strips say you're pregnant. The blood test will be back in a day, but I know what it's going to say."

"Oh God," Suzanne whispered. "I know the moment I conceived. I felt it. And it happened before the news of my brother's death."

"*This* isn't good news?"

"Not really."

"Why? You're young. In shape. Eat right. The pregnancy should be a breeze. You should have a healthy baby."

"I never wanted to get pregnant."

"Never?"

Suzanne remained silent. It would be a lie to say she *never* wanted children.

"Women come through my doors and pay big bucks to conceive. Some are unsuccessful. A few choose to adopt."

Another's plight had no bearing on her own. It wasn't that she had no empathy for childless couples, but she was in the fight for her life.

Her heart pounded. Fear shot helter-skelter through her, like an old-fashioned pinball game. Buzzers rang in her brain. Lights flashed behind her eyes. She'd wanted life and love—with Grant. However, the life she'd built with the only man she ever wanted had suddenly tilted.

Game over.

"Suzanne, are you okay? You wanted to discuss options. What kind of options?"

Her mouth dried. Suzanne tried to swallow. She leaned to lessen the space between her and the doctor. "I want to know about…" she whispered.

"Yes?"

She chewed her bottom lip. Blood roared in her ears. She covered them with her hands. Her stomach raced, doing roller-coaster loop-de-loops. "I want…I want…to know about termination." To her ears, her voice echoed around the room.

"Termination?" The doctor's lips moved, but Suzanne heard no sound. She blinked.

Her vision narrowed as though she looked through a small, round pipe. She tilted her head.

The doctor rose. Suzanne's eyes fluttered. A hand on the back of her head guided it toward her lap.

"Suzanne! Suzanne! Nurse! Nurse!" the doctor shouted.

Suzanne jerked upward, emerging from a weird void. The nurse ran into the room.

"Grab a blanket. Get a cuff. I want to check her blood pressure," Dr. Davidson shouted.

Around Suzanne, the world moved in slow motion. The roar in her ears returned.

A half hour later, Suzanne rested in a chair with a glass of juice and nibbled on a cracker. She couldn't make eye contact with her doctor.

"Suzanne, I'm sensing a barge-load of conflict. If you don't want me to share this news with Grant, I must honor that. However, I strongly urge you to tell him. It took two of you to make this pregnancy. Either way, the two of you should decide together. But I don't do the procedure you asked about."

"Doctor, decide together? I do not disagree."

But she did not want to kiss her husband goodbye forever.

Chapter 24

I sat in a chair against one wall in the waiting room and rubbed my bare arms, shielding them against the blasting air-conditioning. Maggie and I were the only people creating body heat in the space that resembled someone's homey living room: upholstered furniture, a fireplace, and paintings by local artists.

"Maggie, please sit over here. Let's talk. I'll go to counseling with you. I'll go to church with you. I'll...what can we do to heal?"

Maggie ignored me, taking a seat on a couch on the opposite wall.

Since our talk this morning, every time I spoke, my words set her off. She didn't snarl and lunge at me, like last night, but the jerk of her shoulder and the roll of her eyes hurt more. The truce between us was as solid as cheesecloth.

I looked around when the aroma of coffee caught my notice. I might need a cup to fight the frigidness in the room.

"How long does this take?" Maggie spoke aloud. I doubted she expected a response from me.

Twenty-five minutes later, she glared hard at the door leading to the back side of the office as though willing Suzanne to appear.

A wave from the doctor's receptionist caught my eye. I crossed to the desk.

"Mrs. Saulnier won't be much longer," a woman in scrubs said.

"Dr. Davidson must be good. I've never been in with a doctor for more than fifteen minutes."

The receptionist smiled. "Dr. Davidson makes time according to a patient's needs."

Her words set off an alarm in me. Needs? Had Suzanne made a decision and not shared it with me? "Does the doctor do terminations?"

"Terminations?"

"If my friend came in and…wanted to terminate."

"I'm not sure I follow." The receptionist's brows furrowed.

I leaned in and crooked my finger, motioning her closer to me. "*Abortion*," I whispered through clenched teeth.

The woman drew back, startled, then regained her composure. "Dr. Davidson does not perform that procedure."

"Good to know." I drew a deep breath. Half of the knot in my stomach unclenched.

"I can't discuss Mrs. Saulnier's medical condition with you."

I nodded. "I understand. I'll wait."

When I took my seat again, Maggie marched across the room and stood directly in front of me, staring down.

"I heard what you said to that nurse-person. What do you mean, *abortion*?" Maggie's eyes darted side to side, like she couldn't bear to look at me. "You and Suz are keeping a secret from me? She's pregnant? How *could* she?"

I held my hands in front of my face, half in surrender and half to protect myself in case Maggie lunged.

"Jesus. Mary. And Joseph. It's not my secret to tell. But yes, she's pregnant."

Maggie's eyes widened. Her mouth gaped. Her hand flew up to cover it. "Really pregnant?" She looked down at her own flat stomach. "No. No. No." She raced across the room, grabbed her purse, charged to the door.

"Maggie, wait." I was out of my seat and chasing her outside.

She stopped and pivoted. Held up her hands for me to halt. Her eyes radiated red-hot anger. "Don't come closer. I...I don't think I know either of you." She shook her head. "I'll catch a cab. Leave me alone."

I watched her stride down the street, my feet rooted to the sidewalk. I couldn't charge after her. She was entitled to her feelings and her privacy and her time to process. But that didn't mean I wanted to let her go. My heart oozed pain. Helpless, I choked back a sob.

Traffic zipped by. Humidity rose in equal measure as the sun rose in the sky. Around me, life carried on normally. Except the farther Maggie walked away, the harder the connection between us jerked on my heart. Would she pull it from my chest?

Returning to the office, I took a seat in front of the window. How betrayed Maggie must feel. I shouldn't have revealed anything. That was Suzanne's news to tell. But did Maggie know about the prenup and Grant's insistence on no children?

"Suzanne, now I know how you felt while you waited for me to tell Maggie my secret." I shoved my fingers in my hair. "What are we going to do? Will Maggie come around?"

I held my stomach. I couldn't reveal to Suzanne how I so wanted Sonny Boy to have a cousin. A contemporary connection to the family, someone to be there for him when I was gone and she was old. However, her decision wasn't one to be made by committee. That she might choose abortion pained me. But I would not judge.

Echoes of my father's quote ran through my mind: *People who live in glass houses shouldn't throw stones.*

I was a walking list of sins. I pretty much failed at everything...except loving my son.

And now I was faced with telling Suzanne the rest of my truth, which now needed to include how I'd revealed her secret to Maggie.

Suzanne walked to the checkout desk. "Here's my credit card for the co-pay." She slid the card across the counter.

The woman swiped it and handed it back. "Your friend in the waiting room is pretty stressed out."

"My friend?"

"Yes, the one waiting for you."

Suzanne frowned. "There should be two." She signed for the charge. Had Maggie and Jane had another fight? Tension ramped up in the muscles of her neck.

"Don't forget your prescription for prenatal vitamins. Let's set up your next appointment."

"I'll call." Suzanne pushed on the exit door and stalked into the waiting room.

Jane stood, dropping the magazine she'd been reading to the floor, and rushed forward, her eyebrows scrunched as though she were in pain. "And?" she demanded. Her fear was a palpable heartbeat.

"Where's Maggie?" Suzanne looked around.

"She left. Tell me, Suz. *I* waited. Frozen like shrimp on ice in this office."

Suzanne inhaled and blew out a breath. "Nope."

"Nope, what?" Jane demanded. "Nope, you're not pregnant. Nope, you're not going to have a baby? Nope, you're not going to terminate. What?"

"I'm not going to share without Maggie." Suzanne shook her head. "We've had too many secrets separating us. This is my news. I get to decide when, where, and with whom I'm going to share."

"Shit," Jane muttered.

Startled, Suzanne stared. That was the first profanity to slip from Jane's lips since…forever. Jane never cursed. Whatever happened had to be bad.

"Suzanne, you have to tell me." Her eyes pleaded even more than her voice.

"Begging is not becoming, Jane. You never told me about your news, which was my news because he's *my* nephew. I'll tell you what you want to know, but only when you and Maggie are with me in the same room."

"What's next?" Jane's smile barely turned up the corners of her mouth.

"We find Maggie. Where she's gone?"

"Home. I guess."

"Slidell? Or the lake? Let's ride out to Slidell." Suzanne mapped a route in her mind. "You haven't seen her house there. That's where her secret is kept. Did you say something to cause her to leave?"

"I...well..."

I could not tell Suzanne what I had done. I also did not continue to try to wheedle news from her.

Once in the car, we traveled roads I hadn't seen since before Katrina. New buildings and houses under construction. Fresh black asphalt with clean white lines. Yet every so often I spied a rusted boat on its side, like a beached whale, near the road.

The route to the old fishing village of Slidell now had a new vibe.

"Oh. The rink is gone." The old indoor roller skating rink with marred wooden floors and murals on the walls was where I had my first kiss.

Suzanne patted my hand. "PK."

The hurricane mirrored my life. Slidell had changed. I had changed. Nearly unrecognizable, both of us. Only in my case, I'd brought the destruction to my world. Poor decisions made. Made out of fear. Made out of mistrust. Though I'd tried to convince myself otherwise.

I hadn't intended to hurt Maggie. I knew she and Mark had dated, but news of their engagement felt sudden. Like Mark was punishing me somehow. And, if I were totally honest, I was a little jealous. Okay, maybe more than a little.

But I stuck to my convictions to protect my son. A baby needed its mother. Fathers could be helpful but not necessary in the early days. Look at my own. He'd checked out when I needed him, and I was a teenager then.

Why confuse a toddler with a father and stepmother who lived so far away? Not only in different states, but in different cultures, too.

If Mark had known about his son, attorneys would've been involved... because I wasn't going to subject my baby to a long-distance relationship until he was old enough to understand what a father was.

As barely familiar scenery flashed outside the window, truth flashed new insights for me. Somehow, I had harbored the idea that New Orleans caused Momma's suffering. Put me at risk for the same if I stayed. Not logical. Irrational. But when would anyone argue fear-driven decisions and cancer were logical?

"What's wrong?" Suzanne asked.

"Nothing."

"I can feel churning emotions emanating from you. The sighs suggest you're muddling your way through a swamp of problems. It might help to talk. That's what we used to do. That's what *friends* do."

"Swamp. I remember that. This is different. I'm in a foreign land now. It's like someone wiped away the past."

"That's not how it works. We're living with the past even though it's not visible to the eyes."

She was trying to pull me into a conversation I didn't want to join. "I'm commenting on the scenery."

"Jane, stop lying to me. You came back and dropped a bomb on us. Your storm has been brewing for years. What are you going to do *now*?"

The cut of her tone put me in the hot seat. "You haven't walked in my shoes. Don't lecture me. You—the pregnant one with the fabulous life and wealthy husband. You've lied for years. You, darlin', have *always* wanted children. Don't stand in judgment on me or I'll—"

Suzanne snorted. "You'll do what?"

I turned to stare out the window. What could I do? I needed her. Needed Maggie. Well, Sonny Boy needed them. And I needed him to be happy and settled before I started down my path of doctors and drugs.

"You'd do well to remember I *do* have a rich husband. I'll use all resources to ensure my nephew has a place in my life. I will battle you in court if necessary. You *stole* Mark's son from him."

Stunned, I faced her. It was as if she'd given me a one-two workover. A slap to the face and a punch in the gut. I narrowed my eyes. "Don't threaten me, Suzanne Maucele Saulnier. Or I'll— "

Suzanne slammed on the brakes, squealing rubber onto a driveway. "We are not going to fight like this. We're not going to hurt each other anymore. This" —she pointed to a house—"this is Maggie and Mark's house. We'll talk about this after we find Maggie." She shook her finger in my face. "Know this, the Dupuis secret we shared hurt as much as it bound us together. I will *not* let secrets destroy us now. If you think you're going to run and hide again, and take my nephew with you—remember, gators are large and swim slow, but quick on land. Like gators, we Cajuns, Mauceles and Saulniers, always catch our prey."

I jerked the door open and got out. I would not listen to a pregnant woman's rants. Slamming the door made me feel a sliver of justification. Beside, Suzanne's threats had no meat, just bark. No bite.

I stormed to the front door of the traditional red brick with white cast-iron trim, noting the white hurricane shutters. When I rang the doorbell, Suzanne came up behind me with her keys.

She put a hand on my arm. Her sadness had a weariness to it. "Maggie has secrets, too," she whispered.

That was hard for me to believe. Angelic Maggie was perfect in every way, yeah?

"True compassion means not only feeling another's pain but also being moved to help relieve it."
Daniel Goleman

Chapter 25

I paused when Suzanne opened the door. Trepidation halted my legs, my feet.

Suzanne pushed past me. I took one step, entering Maggie and Mark's house. Vibrations of him came to me. Mark. Mark. Mark. His home. Where he laid his head at night. Where he watched football. Where he made love to Maggie…

An essence of Maggie washed over me, too. Her love. Her devotion to Mark. Her sorrows and pain.

I slowly crossed the room to a gallery of framed photographs on the wall. A large one of Maggie held a place of honor. The picture captured Maggie's sweetness. Her face shone with hope. In the group photo, everyone flashed radiant smiles, all of them Maucele.

"They must keep a dentist happy," I mumbled, moving closer to examine the pictures.

I ran my finger over the tops of several frames. Not a speck of dust. Maggie had to have been there recently or someone came to clean.

I walked farther into the sanctuary of Maggie and Mark. The house balanced feminine and masculine tastes. An elegant crystal chandelier in the dining room. Plantation shutters covered windows. A large TV over the fireplace in the family room. Built-in shelves showed off Mark's sport trophies.

Walking through the home, I noticed polished stones of various sizes: jade, rose quartz, amethyst, and others. Had to be Maggie's woo-woo touch.

I halted and Suzanne bumped me from behind.

"This is a far cry from the girl we met in the sixth grade." Suzanne's hushed voice boasted with love and pride for Maggie. "This is the first time I've been here since she finished this house. PK. Usually, we met at the camp."

"We shouldn't be here." I looked over my shoulder at Suzanne.

We were intruders. This was their private place. Only the two of them. The outside world didn't come here—all parties were at the camp at the lake. A stirring reverence for their privacy made me want out of the house. I was a trespasser. Invader. Violator.

"It's *not* like we're breaking and entering." Suzanne moved past me and toward a hallway. "We are not entirely uninvited."

I turned into the living room. A frame grabbed my attention. A flutter of fear hit my gut. Tiny tremors traveled up to my throat. I swayed on my feet and grabbed for something to support me from falling on my face.

Maggie was Mark's wife.

A wedding photo of Maggie and Mark in an antique filigree silver frame sat on the mantel. I'd not seen any wedding photos before. Maggie as a bride. Radiant. Mark as her groom. Marital bliss.

But he'd been mine, too. I still pictured him in his tux when he waited for me at the altar.

I sank to the floor to keep from falling. A new reality settled within me. I pictured Mark and Maggie as teenagers. Maggie's puppy love for Mark. Him playing the strong silent hero with teenage angst. In this photograph, their happiness sparkled. They glowed with a magical kind of love. Maggie made him happy, gave him a joy that he never had with me. Maggie wore the look of a woman who knew her man. *A woman*, not a lovesick child.

Pain slammed my heart as it sank to the bottom of an empty cavern, too dark and deep for me to see when it hit. I was jealous of Maggie. It was me, not Maggie, who needed to stop hanging on to the past. Jealousy locked up my heart.

That was the truest reason I'd kept Sonny Boy a secret.

My truth sickened me. Gloom. Grief. Guilt. A hard ball of darkness growing for years inside me tightened.

I'd messed things up in epic proportions. I had to make amends. Had to.

"Suzanne," I shouted, urgency forcing me to the front door. "Let's go. Have to find Maggie."

"Jane, come here. Now!" Suzanne's urgent command drew me toward the hall.

I moved quickly, peeking in an office—Maggie's—dressed in purple and pink. Across the hall was Mark's office. A framed LSU flag hung on one wall.

"Jane?" Suzanne called.

"Where are you?"

"Follow my voice. You won't believe this. Oh. My. God. Jane. Jane. Jane."

The hallway made a turn. I passed the master bedroom, unable to look, and kept following Suzanne's muttering voice. Shock? Awe? Emotion spilling over in her voice like I'd never heard.

I nearly collided with her when she bolted through the double doors. Grabbing my arm, she swung me around and pulled me inside.

I froze.

A pale blue room resembled the pages of a fairy-tale book. Pale blue walls. Overhead, on a track attached to the ceiling, a hot-air balloon floated around the room. A mobile of animals dressed for an old-time big-top circus hung over the crib. And the crib—gilded in gold and silver with pale blue satin linens. Two gliding chairs, thrones for a king and queen, sat near the crib. One entire bedroom wall was lined with shelves and displayed books, empty silver frames, and a collection of stuffed animals.

Suzanne opened a shade, breaking the spell of the room. Sunlight streamed in.

I closed my mouth. "What the…?" I whispered and faced Suzanne. Her face registered shock, too.

"Grant told me she'd decorated a nursery. He discovered it when he came to get clothes for Mark for the funeral home. He never gave details. I never asked. I figured footballs, boats, and teddy bears."

At a loss for words, I nodded.

"She never said anything about it, not even a hint. I knew they were trying—hell, they'd been trying since the day they got married. I learned, when you did, that she can't have children. I didn't want to talk about it until she brought it up—so much heartache after losing Mark. But we know—she wasn't pregnant when this was done." Suzanne slowly twirled.

I crossed to a chest of drawers with a white marble top. A plaid blue and white card lay open. I picked it up and read:

My darling husband Mark,
We've waited so long, tried so hard and now God has blessed us. We're going to have a child...and I KNOW it'll be a boy. All of our prayers are answered. We're going to have a family of our own.
Your adoring and faithful wife,
Maggie

Mark's words echoed in my mind. "Maggie's pregnant."
She'd lied to him. Maggie lied. Lied.

Meanwhile, on the island...
Maggie paced the room, the phone pressed tight to her ear, and glanced out the window of the camp. A crane moving a piling at the next canal over caught her attention. Before she could ponder a new neighbor, she had to make her attorney understand her situation. "Alfred McDonald, there's got to be a way. I'm this boy's stepmother. Look something up in all those legal books you have."

"Maggie, Maggie. I know the law. I'm sorry. But you have a bigger problem. The camp isn't in your name. Mark's father is asserting his rights to it. Trying anyway. I didn't want to bother you about it until I finished researching. So far, what I've learned...won't benefit you."

"What?" Confusion popped in her mind like bubbles from soda rising to the top of a glass. "No Sonny Boy *and* no camp?" She sank into a chair. Her heart sank to her feet.

"I know you're upset. Let me finish what I've started. My secretary will call you and schedule an appointment for you to come in. We'll discuss a strategy. I'm due in court now. We'll talk later."

Mr. Attorney ended the call.

She dropped the phone into her lap and pushed her fingers through her hair. A hollowness in her core spread lower—she would be forever barren. The hollowness spread higher—she was forever childless.

Widowed. Childless. And her friends—who had they become? Jane had a child out of wedlock. Suzanne was considering an abortion?

Now the this-is-the-law discussion with her attorney plunged her life further into emptiness. It all left her feeling adrift, like a buoy carried by the tide out to sea. Alone. Inconsequential.

She had no rights.

No claim.

No power to ensure Sonny Boy remained in her life.

She couldn't demand visitation. She couldn't make Jane keep the boy in New Orleans, let alone Louisiana. She couldn't legally *make* Jane do anything.

Because she wasn't blood kin.

And now Mark's father wanted the camp?

No. No. And no.

How could Mark have done this to her? No will? Alfred had said that under Louisiana's Napoleonic Law, only blood next of kin had property rights. She'd be out of her home on her rounded butt, bounced down the stairs and down the driveway to the dock.

At least, the Slidell house was jointly in her name. Otherwise, where would she live?

Bitterness burned in the back of her throat. She and Mark had fought about having all necessary legal documents in order. She'd demanded it after telling him she was pregnant. It had been a desperate move. But an ugly urge she didn't understand pushed her.

Was that a foretelling of Mark's death? After losing the love of her life, she'd lose the home she loved most? Punishment for her lies.

"Think, Maggie, think." She paced the room. Her brain hurt trying to conjure an image. Her ears hurt from trying to capture a whisper. Her heart, well, it just split in two.

But Mark would want her to take care of his son in some way.

Maybe…Jane had the answer—a trust fund for his education.

Maggie curled her fingers into fists, rose, and stalked to the window. "Why can't I ever have a *knowing* about what the future holds for me?"

Silence answered.

Beyond the window, a large bass boat scooted across the water's surface, taking advantage of the warm day. Sunlight rippled silver against dark lake water. A breeze ruffled the reeds. A pelican glided gracefully. The feathered creature survived all weather. It took flight, climbing higher in the sky. Then it dove, breaking the water's surface, disappearing beneath.

Maggie held her breath.

She waited. Only when the bird surfaced could she breathe.

It was just the sort of sunny, lazy afternoon she loved sharing with Mark. This had been *their* home. She had to keep it. Without it, she couldn't maintain a connection with him. And his son deserved to be a true Maucele with a lifetime of memories at the camp. Sunburned nose, fishhook in the finger, and later, Saturday night dances with the old disco ball that still belonged to Jane.

Thinking about Sonny Boy's smiles, energy, antics, slowly filled her with a renewing energy. All of her life, she'd been a faithful follower. To her church. To her friends. To her husband. Where did that get her?

Widowed. Childless. And at war.

Like the pelican, it was time for her to fish for herself.

She picked up a framed photo of Mark, remembering the day it was taken. He'd sounded the boat's horn when he came into the canal after a day of fishing. Not much of his face was visible in the photo, his baseball cap and dark sunglasses. A broad smile filled his face. He held up a stringer.

"Dinner for my darlin'," he had said, completely delighted with himself.

To her, he looked like Adonis. She'd run down the steps to meet him and taken the photo on the dock.

Now she stroked his face in the photo. "I love you, Mark." Love polished her heart, smoothing the rawest edges. "You were always there for me. I won't let you down. Your son will know you. And I'll try, really try, to make things work with Jane and Suzanne."

Years ago, the death of a man had bound them together with a secret. The death of another man had reunited them now. She had to do her part to make the friendships work with Jane and Suzanne.

Their love of a little boy would bind them together forever.

And back at the house in Slidell…

"Let me read." Suzanne snatched the card from Jane's hand and read the words several times.

Maggie had to be in real pain. Understandable, given Mark's death. She missed her brother, too. Grief was a tricky thing. She had to find a way to help. Correction. She *and* Jane had to find a way. Jane had a part in all of this, too.

Maggie had lost her husband. That reality hit Suzanne in a new way. A chill chased down her spine. She couldn't lose Grant. He was the first person she thought about when she woke in the morning. The last person she talked to each and every night. There wasn't enough money in the world to buy her love, which was why she'd signed the damn prenup in the first place. Life with Grant fulfilled her. They were a team. Could handle any problem—together. And they had joy…so much joy.

A baby created a problem.

But she wasn't alone in her dilemma. Maggie suffered from a child problem. Jane, too. Irony was a teacher in the harsh light of day. The Belles with baby problems. She'd laugh if the whole mess wasn't so sad.

"Suzanne, I have to get out of here." Jane bolted.

Suzanne pulled herself out of the chair. It was her turn to be the net weaver and knit their friendship back together.

They needed each other. She'd make them see that. Even if it meant stooping to apply guilt. And if that didn't work, she'd enlist a voodoo priestess for a potion or a spell.

But even before that…she could start with Maggie's type of magic—prayer.

Chapter 26

A little while later, I sat at the bar at Eddie's, my elbow planted on the top, my hands hiding my face. Suzanne sat quiet. You would've had to poke her to know she was alive. Tab Benoit belted "Nice and Warm" from the old-fashioned jukebox. Life had taken a slide into cold-as-hell.

Suzanne and I were alone, except for Eddie in the kitchen and a couple of waitresses in the dining area wiping down ketchup and hot sauce bottles, preparing for the dinner rush. So easy to clean bottles of gunk and grime. A vinegar bath wouldn't help me. Too bad there wasn't a "people wash," like a car wash, to make my life shine.

I licked the back of my hand, salted it, licked the NaCl, knocked back another shot of tequila, sucked a lime slice so tart my mouth puckered. Squinting, I swallowed and plunked the glass on the bar top.

Suzanne swirled a straw in her ginger ale and shook her head.

"What?" I asked.

"Since when do you knock 'em back like that? You'd better slow down. I can't carry you out of here."

247

"Only my third." Where was her judgy attitude coming from? It was shocking to learn Maggie had lied. Not a little white lie, but a big one. And to Mark. The evidence was in writing. "One more, Eddie." I slapped the bar.

"Eat something first. I don't let drunks hang out in here." Eddie swiped the bottle from the bar and placed it on the shelf completely out of my reach. "Red beans and rice coming up."

Some bartender he was. I turned the stink eye on him. "I'm not a drunk. You've mistaken *me* for my father."

"Jane," Suzanne gasped. "What a horrible thing to say." Her hand flexed.

For a second, I thought she might slap me. Ignoring her, I held up the shot glass. "Give me one more while I'm waiting for food." I hollered so Eddie could hear me in the kitchen. "I'm a paying customer."

"Not today," Eddie called from the kitchen.

I put my head on the bar and waited. Mark had talked about war being a shitstorm—the sand, the wind, the enemy. I didn't have to travel halfway around the world to learn about it. The Gs chattered until I wanted to scream. I had thought tequila would shut them up.

A few minutes later, the aromas of red beans and rice set my mouth watering. Fried chicken livers on the side. Oh my.

"I don't tolerate drunks. Will throw your ass out with the trash." Eddie placed the bowl in front of me. Handed me a spoon and napkin.

"One more, pretty please?" I held up the shot glass, fluttered my lashes, offering my best flirtation—which was a bit rusty. It had not been pressed into service since…Mark and I first married. And my son was too young to be taken in by the affectations of a southern miss.

I plunked my glass on the bar again. It *tinked* when it hit. Okay, the potency of the *Gran Patrón* washed like a warm wave over me. Bringing with it bravery and carrying my filters away. I swayed in my seat.

"Eat first." Eddie crossed his arms over his chest. He planted his feet a step wider, a bouncer's stance.

"Fine." I rolled my eyes. "Thought bartenders were supposed to be closet shrinks. You don't want to hear my problems. Don't want to serve me booze. Don't want my money." With my feet hooked on the rung of the tall barstool, I rose, hands on the bar, and leaned closer to Eddie. "But you want me to eat?"

"Look, little miss, I'm not too old to paddle your ass. Put it back on that stool. Stop being a brat…and *don't* disrespect your father again."

"You old Jasper." I sat, shaking my finger at him. "You'd—"

"Jane, enough." Suzanne's soft voice filtered past my mental haze and hot frustration. She placed her hand on my arm and squeezed. "We need to find Maggie. She hasn't answered any calls or texts. So eat. Then we go. No more alcohol."

A waitress came through the kitchen door and headed toward us. "Garlic bread. More carbs ought to soak up some of the booze. Maybe soak up some of that snotty attitude."

I spooned a mouthful of my favorite New Orleans dish into my mouth.

"What's up with Maggie?" Eddie removed my shot glass and replaced it with a glass of water.

"I've called her cell. Left a message at the camp. Even called my house," Suzanne told him. "No Maggie."

"Could she have gone to one of her shops or the spa?" I wanted to help, but I was dreading the showdown.

"I called the shop while you were in the ladies' room. They haven't seen or heard from her today. I'm worried." Suzanne pulled her keys from her purse. I guess that was a hint for me to hurry.

I slapped my hand on the bar. My spoon clattered against the bowl. "You know, the thing about Maggie…" I had a thought. Where did it go? I blinked trying to recall what I was about to say.

"What?" Suzanne snapped.

"Oh. Yeah. Suz, Maggie doesn't need our help." I waved my finger back and forth like a metronome in front of her face. "Underneath that sweet bubblegum-pink, she's the strongest one of us all."

Suzanne's face scrunched. "What?"

"Emotionally, Maggie's stronger. She loves hard and deep. Look at all she faced as a child." I swiveled on the barstool toward Suzanne. "That is untold strength."

"Well. Maybe. Maybe not—"

"What did I do when faced with a crisis?"

"You rallied for your mom. For Mrs. Dupuis. For Maggie, and for me. You made us the Belles, blood sisters—"

"I'm talkin' about my own crisis. Not some…misplaced…sense of childhood justice. I'm talkin' about when Momma died."

"Jane—"

"Stop. Interrupting. Me." I growled like a *loup-garou*—a Cajun were-wolf—or at least what I thought one sounded like. "I'm tryin' to tell ya somethin' here."

Eddie clanked the spoon against the bowl. "Jane, eat. Then talk."

I ate another bite. "I'll take that other shot now."

Eddie pushed the glass of water closer in front of me.

"Let's go, Jane." Suzanne stood. She flicked her wrist in a shooing motion, suggesting Eddie remove the food from in front of me.

"I am eating. And I'm trying to say, in my enlightened alcohol state, is that Maggie being needy fed into my need to caretake. I couldn't cure Momma, her fate was a one-way ticket to cancer hell. Helping Maggie made me feel confident. Competent. And that comforted me."

"You still are all those things."

"Nope. None of them. I came back for a reason. I need something from Maggie. From you. From my dad."

"What?"

I slid off the barstool and stumbled. "Nope. Not going to tell. You won't tell me your decision. I'm not telling you my secret."

Suzanne's face pinched in pain. "You are so f-ing frustrating. Let's go."

She didn't wait on me but strode to the door.

I was drunk enough that I could've crawled on my hands and knees. That would've kept the world from swaying off-center. I was not better than my father. He was on the road to recovery… I was on my way to hell.

Maggie startled awake. A loud rumbling, the roar of a semi bumping down an oyster-shell alley. The grinding of gears. What the heck was going on? The end of the world?

She shoved hair from the side of her face and sat up on the couch. She must have been sleeping for a while.

Outside the windows, a flock of seagulls soared across the sky. A guy in a johnboat puttered past the opening of the canal. She spied her reflection in the mirror. Wasn't sure she knew the person staring back.

Heartache kicked in when she noticed her list crumpled on the floor. Her list of all the good things about Jane and all the things that hurt made her ooze pain.

The headliner of the hurt list—Mark loved Jane more.

She'd always known it but thought she could love him enough for both of them to make their marriage work. On her honeymoon, she'd had a *knowing* about Mark having a son. After which, she'd waited and waited and waited for the doctor to tell her she was pregnant.

Year after year, try after try, she was neurotic about having a baby… and driving Mark away with her brand of crazy. She didn't dare tell Jane she'd gotten that *knowing* wrong. Jane was the one who birthed the Maucele heir.

But if sin was sin, then Jane's lie was no greater than her own. Just the consequences of it oceans apart.

Fitting the pieces of life together gave her a clear picture of the puzzle, but what would stop the pain? What would help her trust her friends again?

The roller coaster of chaos she endured growing up with the "Crazies"— how she referred to her bio-family—twined together, blending the past with the present.

As a kid, her faith in the church, faith in love, faith in God when everyone around had failed her had kept her afloat…until she met Jane.

Whatever she knew about friendship, sisterhood, and a solid family life, she'd learned because of Jane.

Maggie uncrumpled the list. What did she want? Besides the pain of Mark's loss to lessen. Family—family of choice. That meant Suzanne, Grant, Mr. Landry, Sonny Boy, and Jane.

The best place to start was at the beginning with the tried and true. Prayer and confession. After that, she would listen. Not judge. Work hard to be a good friend, a good second daughter to Mr. Landry, and an excellent second mother to Sonny Boy.

No longer would desperation drive her decisions. She could *create* the happy life she craved, even though she was no longer Mark's wife.

The only hurdle to jump—getting Jane to move home.

Suzanne entered her family room and stopped. Her heart oozed with love.

Jane slept on the couch, her head rolled to the side and her feet stretched out on an ottoman in front of her. Her son slept, too. His head in her lap, his body stretched out long on the couch.

Love squeezed Suzanne's heart. Thick dark lashes against Sonny Boy's sweet-cream skin. His Cupid's bow mouth was slightly open. His apple cheeks begged to be pinched. His adorable factor pushed way past a ten.

She resisted the urge to scoop him up and hug him to death. Well, "to death" was a bad choice of words…but hug him so tight they'd be fused together and time nor distance nor anything else would make them part.

But love was a samurai sword. It slashed her heart.

Love for her husband. Love for her nephew. Love for her friends.

The chasm between them had to be healed. Had to be.

Were other secrets lurking to tear them further apart?

She walked to the kitchen and opened the fridge. Never before had she sought food for comfort. Running or squats or the elliptical machine cured her cravings in the past. Never before had she been pregnant. Never before did she teeter on the verge of destroying her life with Grant…

Rifling through the fridge, she tried to find something to quell the jitters in her stomach. In the pantry, junk food didn't exist. She didn't keep chips, cookies, or candy around. The gnawing craving in her belly wouldn't quit. Grabbing her keys and purse, she started for the back door for a quick run to the store—there she would find satisfaction, even if only briefly.

Once in the car, she backed down the driveway. The gates opened automatically. She stopped when her cell phone rang. Digging through her purse for it, she used lightning finger speed to press the talk button. "You better be fine or you better be dead!"

"I'm happy to talk to you, too." Maggie sounded…cheerful.

"I've been worried sick all day. Was a bag of chips away from calling the police to report you missing."

"A bag of chips? Wow. That's serious. Didn't mean to scare you. Though I'm happy to learn I was missed."

"I'm in no condition for this kind of crap," Suzanne ground out the words between clenched teeth.

"What's your condition?"

Suzanne caught herself. Sucked in a deep breath and let it go. "We three—you, me, and Jane need to have a sit-down. A come-to-Jesus talk."

"Good idea." Maggie's reply came too easy. She'd expected to have to prod, beg, and if necessary, use guilt and shame to get Maggie to submit.

"Really?"

"Tomorrow afternoon. Three p.m. I'm going to work in the salon in the morning. Let me know where you want to meet."

"Ah. Sure."

"Suzanne." Maggie's calm tone floored her. It rang with sanity. "All will be okay. Whatever it is. It'll all work out, just like it's supposed to."

"You've been reading my self-help books?"

Maggie chuckled softly, like she used to do…before Mark died.

"Maggie, don't mean to cut you off, but Grant's calling. He never calls during the day—unless it's an emergency. I've got to jump." She disconnected with Maggie and answered the incoming call. "Hello." She tried for a smooth, sexy greeting.

"How's my angel?" Grant asked. "Love you."

"Everything okay?" Worry cut through her mind. Uneasiness rose into her throat. She couldn't handle another problem today.

"I have a surprise for you."

There was no way he could know about the baby…unless the doctor contacted him. She covered her belly with her hand.

"I need you, Maggie, and Jane at the house tomorrow at three."

What was he up to?

"I'll…I'll see what I can do. What's going on?"

"You know I'm putty when you're around so it's a good thing I'm here. You can't wheedle this news out of me. Got a surprise arriving—one you can share with the girls. No hints or clues, so don't even ask."

Suzanne sucked on her bottom lip. She loved this man. The sound of his voice warmed her core, her blood, her feminine parts. In her sexiest voice, she whispered, "I have ways to make you talk."

Grant's deep chuckle made her body tingle. She loved him so much.

"Woman, that song you like, "I've Got You Under My Skin," is the story of my life. I'll call you tomorrow when your gift is scheduled to arrive. Headed home day after that. How's the visit with Jane?" Grant laughed. "Can't wait to see the dog. I can just picture the four of you in…"

"In?" Suzanne prompted.

"Never mind. I'll call you at midnight. We'll talk dirty to each other. Miss you like crazy."

A tingling wave rolled over her. Suzanne smiled, thinking about what she'd wear to make her feel sexy for their private chat.

A crying baby in the background stopped her thoughts. "Where are you?"

"About to enter a restaurant for dinner with a client."

"Must be family friendly place… I mean, because of the crying."

"Actually, I didn't pick it. Hadn't given the kid thing a thought. A crying baby would ruin dinner."

She pressed her hand more firmly on her belly.

Husband? Or baby?

What the hell was she going to do?

Chapter 27 - Suzanne

Suzanne stretched in bed. Sunlight peeked through a small crack in an opening between the silk drapes in her bedroom. It had to be early, before seven a.m., since no hammering and banging and back-up bells broke the morning quiet. A slice of paradise to be savored.

Stretching her arms wide, she ran one hand over the space beside her in bed where Grant slept. The spot was cool to the touch, not warm from his body. His presence had been only a dream. Yet, still a good one, after a night of sexy whispered innuendos and double entendres that heated her up and made her miss him more.

Rap. Rap. Rap.

The loud knocking drew her attention away from intimate thoughts. She recognized the sound. Made with a small fist. She smiled. Sometimes life gave joy and crap in the same six-pack.

The door squeaked open. Hand holding fast to the doorknob, Sonny Boy slid inside. Light from the hall backlit his short silhouette. She swore she caught the shine of a halo over his head.

"Auntie Suzanne?" Sonny Boy's voice reached her as a loud whisper. "You awake?"

"I'm awake, little nephew."

"Okay. Latisha said you have to come to breakfast."

Feet scampered across the room. He jumped to grab the covers like Tarzan grabbing for a vine. Suzanne sat up, held tight to the bedding as he climbed up. Sonny Boy knelt beside her. Bright-eyed, he looked ready for a new adventure in his cute khaki shorts with pockets on the sides—to hold special finds—and a light blue, cotton shirt. Beside her, he seemed taller than when she'd first met him. Had he sprouted like sugarcane growing in the fields?

"Auntie Suzanne, what's a nephew?"

The question surprised her. If Jane wasn't going to tell the boy, she certainly would. "Let's see if we can work this puzzle out."

She grabbed two pillows and plopped one on either side of her legs. "This is your daddy, and this one is your mommy. Now, go get that small pillow off my chair."

Sonny Boy stretched out on his stomach, scooted to the end of the bed, then lowered himself, feet first to the floor. He ran for the embroidered silk pillow. When he returned, he tossed it at her, then began his climb back up the bed.

She placed the small pillow so it straddled her lap. "This pillow is you. You're the child, the son of the mommy and the daddy."

He twisted his mouth to one side, trying take in the information.

Squelching a giggle, she continued. "So in our pillow story, I'm connected to the daddy. I'm the sister to the daddy. That makes me your aunt. That makes you my nephew." She opened her arms, and he fell into her for a hug. She rubbed the top of his head, then kissed the spot where she'd rubbed.

"I am Aunt Maggie's nephew, too?"

Oh boy—pun intended. Maggie was his stepmother. But was she still? Did legal nuances matter? All he needed to know now was he had a family that included Maggie. Someday, when he was old enough, he'd learn the ins and outs about all of his family connections. He was lucky to have Maggie.

"You're her nephew, too."

"What did I tell you, Sonny Boy?" Latisha stood in the doorway and scolded. "I sent you in here to wake her up. Get her to the table. Your momma's waiting. She's not looking so hot."

"Go. Git. Gone." Suzanne shooed Sonny Boy. "I'll be there in a minute. Start without me."

Sonny Boy ran to the door where Latisha waited with hands on hips. He scampered past her and took off down the hall shouting, "Choo-choo. Choo-choo."

"Latisha, wait. I need tea this morning. I'm moving away from caffeine. Would you please make me some?"

"Sure. If you don't hurry, breakfast, I made your favorite—grits and eggs, bacon, fruit, and toast—will be cold. I'll put water on for tea right now."

Suzanne dressed quickly in shorts and a tank top. She walked barefoot toward the kitchen, texting Grant with hearts and a kissy face to start his day out right.

"So what do you want to do today?" Suzanne overheard Jane ask Sonny Boy. She followed their voices to the dining room.

"Dunno."

"How about we work on some reading for an hour, then go swimming? We can change our pasty white coloring to something with a little tan? Maybe Auntie Suzanne will join us? Then, Momma's going to need a nap right after lunch. You're going with Grandpops."

"Grand-*pops*. Grand-*pops*. Grand-*pops*." Sonny Boy giggled.

"The pool sounds fun." Suzanne moved to Sonny Boy's side and kissed his chipmunk cheeks. He held his fork in his fist like a spike as he chewed pancakes.

"How are you feeling today, Jane?"

Jane swallowed two Tylenol, grimaced, and lifted a cup of coffee in salute.

Suzanne cast a discerning eye over her. Clear complexion–porcelain pink, but with a slight pallor underneath. Dark fringed lashes framing deep-set brown eyes, but with dark under-eye circles. She mustn't have slept well and had to have a boat-sized headache, if not a full-fledged hangover. Compliments of tequila.

Suzanne dropped into the chair next to her nephew. Latisha arrived with a cup of tea in one hand and a breakfast plate in the other. She set down the tea, then slid the plate in front of Suzanne. "Thank you, Latisha."

Suzanne's attention centered on Sonny Boy making faces as he chewed another mouthful of pancakes. Suzanne took a bite of bacon. The smokiness of it, the smell of cheese in the grits, and the runniness of the egg's yellow yolk caused her stomach to lurch, as though she'd plunged a hundred feet. Her fork clattered against the china plate. She pushed away and raced from the table.

"What's wrong with Auntie Suzanne?"

I waited outside the hall restroom. "Suzanne? Are you okay? I brought a glass of water."

"Door's open," Suzanne squeaked.

Turning the knob, I opened the door. Suzanne sat on a rug on the floor. Her back was against a wall, her knees bent, arms wrapped around her legs. She rested her head on top of her knees. She looked pale through her tan.

Hunkering down beside her, I stroked her hair, gathered it together into a ponytail.

"Was it like this for you?" Suzanne asked.

"Yes. Pretty much."

"What did you do?"

"Bought stock in soda crackers. Nibbled constantly. Kept a fresh bottle of water in the bathroom at all times."

"Ohhh," Suzanne groaned.

"It'll get better. I promise."

We sat together. The voices of Latisha and Sonny Boy joking drifted to us. My little man never failed to make me smile. Well, him being lost made the smile turn upside down. However, no harm had come, in the end.

"You lie." Suzanne narrowed her eyes at me.

"I've never regretted being a single mom, not for a single second. Motherhood has been so much more rewarding than marriage. Though, I guess I haven't given marriage a fair shot. I envy those women who manage both well—like you. Grant's kids may be stepchildren, but they're still your children, too, because of him." I put my arm around Suzanne, hoping to comfort her.

It had only taken a few days for me to realize family and friends made juggling responsibility for Christopher much easier. Although single parenthood wasn't my ideal recommendation, joy and love were abundant between me and my son. And my definition of family included the two women I'd considered my sisters for years.

"I let that damn man get me this way," Suzanne hissed. "If I'm forced to leave him because of this… And I can't even get drunk!"

"Take it from me, drinking isn't what it's cracked up to be. It makes you tired and grouchy and not fit for human consumption. Can make you lose your lunch. And with a kid around, you can't let any of it show."

"All my fitness training will pay off, right? My body won't get totally disfigured by what's happening to it?"

"Disfigured? It's going to change with the baby growing, and it will change again after the baby is born. I wouldn't call any of it disfigurement."

"Jane"—Suzanne gripped my hand—"you have to stay. I can't do this."

"We'll talk about it." I dodged the topic. I would tell her and Maggie together. "Do you need more time in here, or is it safe to leave?"

"Some sun might help me. Maggie's coming at three this afternoon."

"You talked to Maggie? When?"

"Last night while you cuddled on the couch with your boy. Then Grant called. Says he has a surprise for me, for us. And he's coming home tomorrow."

I laughed. "Guess a surprise will be waiting for him. But slow down a second. Maggie's mad at me still, remember?"

"She was in an odd mood. Said everything would work out just fine."

Had Maggie had a change of heart? Or was that mock tranquility before the hurricane?

"I certainly welcome a truce. What's the mystery about the present?"

"We have to wait to find out."

"You're a lucky girl, Suzanne."

"I used to think so . . . now, not so sure anymore."

Maggie found an empty spot and parked in front of Suzanne's house. Construction trucks still lined the street. She waved at Mr. Landry and Sonny Boy when they pulled away from the curb. Mr. Landry waved back. Sonny Boy threw kisses.

She pressed her hands to her chest. It beat with love for him. Who knew she could love a child so painfully much?

Walking up the sidewalk to the house, she checked her watch. She managed to arrive thirty minutes early. She pushed the doorbell, then fanned herself with the proof for the new brochure for the spa. She and Suzanne needed to review it, sign off on it, before it went to the printers. Unless part of what Suzanne planned was to have Jane take over the business duties. That would suit Maggie just fine.

The fanning proved useless. Humidity plastered the gauzy cotton against her body.

"Hello, Miss Maggie," Latisha greeted her at the door. "Don't you look pretty? You could sit in a garden and make all the dahlias jealous."

"Thank you. What a sweet thing to say. How're you doing today?"

"I've got a new drink for you to try. Made by puréeing fresh fruit. I'll bring you a glass." Latisha walked her to the family room, motioned for her to have a seat, then headed toward the kitchen.

Six photo albums, neatly stacked on the coffee table, encapsulated each year between their thirteenth and eighteenth birthdays. She grinned. Her life was chronicled between those pages. Memories of swimming parties, pizza parties, and dance parties. Boat rides, football games, and Mardi Gras.

Beside the six was a large, white leather album. It had been Mark's—his wedding album with Jane. She remembered discovering him going through it on his front porch after it arrived in the mail. His sad expression had pinched her heart.

When he asked her to marry him, he'd passed the album to Suzanne. She'd wondered about his reason, though was glad it didn't have a place in their home. Blind jealousy had bitten her back then. Now she was glad Suzanne had kept it. A link for her with Jane—and shared treasured memories of Mark's and Jane's families—they were her family, too.

"Maggie. You're here." Suzanne's face lit with a welcoming smile.

She rushed to hug Suzanne.

"I'm glad to know you're okay." Jane took a step closer.

"I'm sorry I worried you." Maggie held her arms open to Jane, who closed the distance between them.

"Oh, Maggie. Maggie. I'm sorry."

"It's good. We'll all be okay. I know it." As Maggie spoke, a *knowing* filled her. This involved all of them. She grinned. Maybe she had finally matured?

Beep. Beep. A car horn blasted outside. Then blasted again. *Beep. Beep.*

"What in the world?"

Maggie followed Suzanne to the front door. Jane arrived last.

A tall man with trimmed silver hair in a chauffeur's uniform, complete with a patent-leather brimmed hat, stood at attention and pointed to a shiny convertible, then walked back to stand beside the car.

"What the?" Suzanne muttered.

"A convertible with a driver?" Jane cocked her heard.

"He's going to have heatstroke in those clothes with this humidity." Maggie opened the door wider. "And that's not *any* convertible." She started out the door. "It's a LeBaron." She squealed.

Jane and Suzanne covered their ears. Latisha came running, shouting, "What? What? What?"

"Mrs. Saulnier?" The uniformed man took off his driver's cap and held it under his arm.

"That's me."

Maggie jerked on Jane's arm. "It's just like Baron."

A cell phone rang. The driver pulled it from his pocket. "Yes, sir. She's here with her friends." The driver held out the phone out to her.

Suzanne pointed at herself. "For me?"

The man nodded.

"Hello? Grant? I'll put you on speaker."

"Hey, girls!" Grant sounded pleased with himself. "Like your present? I've heard the stories—Suzanne told me how important Jane's convertible had been, so I thought, maybe this car would make more happy memories for you. It's Baron II. Completely refurbished... Except this isn't intended to be a male magnet. No picking up guys." He laughed.

"Thank you!" Maggie and Jane hollered.

"Suzanne, love you. Talk to you later." And Grant was gone.

The driver held out the keys to Suzanne. Another car approached. It stopped. The driver smiled just before climbing in it and driving away.

"Wow. Wow. What do you think?" Maggie asked.

Suzanne's face was ghostly pale. She trembled as if freezing in the heat. Her eyes rounded. "How could he do this? What do I think? I think…this is totally, completely, utterly impractical for a baby!"

Chapter 28

I rushed to Suzanne's side.

"A baby…I thought…" Maggie sputtered.

"A baby." Suzanne swayed on her feet. Maggie and I kept her from crumbling into a heap.

Moist air wrapped around us like shrink-wrap. The sun stamped its heat on us. The punctuating clatter of nail guns echoed from across the street. All of it ruining paradise.

Latisha ushered us toward the house like she was directing a plane on a runway. We helped Suzanne up the sidewalk to the front door.

"What's happened to her?" Latisha held the door open.

"Not sure." Maggie's brow creased with concern.

"Maybe she got too hot," I offered, but if I had to bet money, I'd say her worlds collided. The past slammed into the present because of the car and Grant's call, and all her thoughts were about the future…her and her baby.

I'd never seen Suzanne look pale before. *Fragile.*

I was worried, worried, worried. Like one more drop of water would overflow the whole bucket. Upset the balance of her life.

"She didn't eat breakfast," Latisha said. "And I made her favorites. Y'all drink too much or something last night?" Latisha lifted an accusing eyebrow at me. She pulled pillows off the chaise in the front parlor to make room for Suzanne to sit.

"We absolutely did not have any alcohol last night. Of any kind," I stated. I wasn't going to tell her I got wasted at Eddie's. That it was during the afternoon.

"Well then, did y'all eat something funny?" Latisha whispered.

"I am not dead. I can hear you," Suzanne spoke up.

"I'll get some water." Latisha left them for the kitchen.

Suzanne sat back on the chaise. Maggie slid a round tufted ottoman next to it and took a seat. She grasped Suzanne's wrist, checking her pulse while I stood feeling useless.

"Maggie? What? You're a hairdresser, not a nurse." Suzanne tried to pull back. Her cheeks bloomed with a slight flush of color.

Maggie held firm. "I've had lots of first aid classes. I'm the only one of us three with a Red Cross Lifeguard certificate. *And* I took a Child and Infant CPR class."

"Really?" I asked. Kudos to Maggie. That made me believe Sonny Boy would be safer in her care, and I also got her sarcastic jab at me.

"Yes, because…because," Maggie stuttered. "Because if something happened to a child at the spa, then I wanted to know how to handle it."

"How many children come to the spa?" She opened the door for questioning, and I was walking through it.

"Stop." Suzanne pulled her wrist from Maggie's grasp and clutched the glass of water Latisha offered. After a sip, Suzanne glared first at Maggie, then at me. "I got a bit warm. A combination of sun, humidity, and *maybe* lack of food."

"If you think you can eat, even a cracker, you need to do that. I think we need to contact your doctor." My suggestion was not without merit.

Suzanne scowled at me. Maggie nodded in agreement.

"No. Doctor." Suzanne heaved a sigh.

"A baby, Suz. A baby. Think about the baby." Maggie started to reach for Suzanne but then laced her fingers together in her lap.

"I'm hungry. Latisha, would you warm me some of the grits? But no egg. No eggs for breakfast again until I ask for them."

"Done." Latasha scooted from the room.

Suzanne could practice avoidance behavior all she wanted, but she was up against a mom with a boy—I had my ways of getting people to comply. "You will eat. You will rest. You will nap."

"Let me worry down a few crackers and then let's go somewhere to talk.

"I have the perfect place." Maggie rose. "It's a surprise, so don't ask."

A little while later, after Suzanne finished eating, she continued her world-class scowl while we loaded up in Baron II. I adjusted the mirrors—I refused to allow Suzanne to drive. She sat shotgun. Maggie sat in the middle of the backseat. Just like when we were in high school. The girls were back together again—my cup runneth over with joy.

And the Gs were only whispering for the first time in…years.

I allowed myself to rush headfirst into a feeling of happiness. *Giddy.* Optimism.

We headed toward St. Charles Avenue in the car. My body wanted to move to the music on the radio—New Orleans Funk. "I have missed my city." I wanted to soak up the sights, smells, sounds.

"PK. It's changed," Maggie said. "Go over to Canal, please."

"I never understood hell until Katrina." Suzanne's pain echoed in her voice. "What was a single mom to do when she needed diapers and formula and the stores all closed? Chaos. Looting. Killings. The National Guard patrolled, but crime still went up." Suzanne took a breath. "Grant has worked hard to help with the rebirth of New Orleans."

I swallowed past the lump in my throat. I wanted to talk about happy things. About Sonny Boy having a family, about the comfort that gave to me, about making the most of life. Suzanne needed to talk about her crossroad—a teeter-totter of choices. A husband on one side. A baby on the other. A promise of unhappiness if she couldn't have both. What did Maggie need to discuss?

"Turn right," Maggie commanded. In the rearview mirror, I noticed she pointed, and I followed her instructions, winding my way through narrow one-way streets to a boutique hotel in the French Quarter with parking. "I had no idea this was here."

"Pull into an empty spot," Maggie directed.

A half dozen contractor vehicles occupied other spaces. Two guys were unloading boxes from one truck.

"Goody!" Maggie clapped. "More tile."

"Exactly, where are we?"

Suzanne unbuckled her seat belt and opened the car door. "Come"—she crooked her finger at me—"see your future."

"Future?" I trailed along, terrified of what lay ahead.

Suzanne opened the door. The door to the lobby of the boutique hotel, but it represented so much more—a new beginning. "This way, Jane."

A thread of hope twined together with optimism. She and Maggie hadn't fully plotted this plan, but sometimes going with the flow produced the best results. Fingers crossed. But the question looming in the air like a storm cloud above their heads—Would Jane say yes?

Waving at the woman at the boutique hotel's registration desk, Suzanne continued down the hall with Jane jammed between her and Maggie. Their steps kept time with the beat of smooth jazz filtering throughout the lobby. A swell of pride rose in her chest when she spied the frosted glass door with the name of their business in beautiful French script.

"Welcome to Avignon Spa." She opened the door. Jane stepped across the threshold. Maggie followed.

"This is your future, Jane." Maggie opened her arms and lifted her hands, encouraging Jane to take in her surroundings—polished teak reception desk, teak shelves that would soon be lined with bath and skin products, green tiles—the color of green sea glass—and white leather club chairs. Bamboo plants had been ordered and would create a serene and relaxing atmosphere. Soft music would soothe frayed nerves. Nerves, like the attack she was having now, uncertain about what to say. How to convince her friend to stay?

Jane pivoted in a tight circle. Her eyes cut from side to side. "Exactly how is this *my* future?"

"Let's go into the relaxation room." Suzanne motioned for Maggie to show the way.

"Why don't we talk here?" Maggie asked.

"Because." Suzanne pinned Maggie with a stare. "Jane needs to see what our business has to offer."

"As you wish." Maggie went through a door separating the spa's lobby from the rest of the place. "Rooms for massage. Rooms for facials. Rooms for body scrubs." Maggie bobbed her head from side to side as though the amenities were obvious as they continued down the hall. "Those are unisex. Then there's the steam room. Sauna—one for men and one for women."

"A spa for men and women," Jane said. "Nice."

Suzanne continued the tour. "This room is almost finished. Tile is done. There will be a waterfall flowing into an authentic large Japanese soaking tub. A cooling pool in the next room—unisex, too. And a food and juice bar. Some of the décor was purchased on trips Grant and I made—like the big wall clock in the relaxation room came from our Paris trip."

Jane smiled and nodded. "This is first class. Your clients are going to love it."

"Our clients," Maggie corrected.

"I meant yours and Suzanne's."

"What Maggie is saying—"

"Suzanne, I can speak for myself. Jane, we want you to be our business partner. Equal partner in the spa. We want you to run it."

Surprise flashed on Jane's face. It changed to uncertainty, then to confusion.

"But…" Jane waved her hands as though trying to gather information from the air. "What?"

"Hiring, firing, scheduling, advertising. You would be the CEO of Avignon Spa."

"I have a job," Jane said hesitantly.

Suzanne eyed her. Jane's brain was working, gears turning, questions forming.

"As Suzanne said, let's go to the relaxation room."

Once there, Suzanne sat on one end of the u-shaped couch. Maggie sat on the other—strategically they'd put Jane in the middle.

"We need you here, Jane. I need you," Suzanne said.

"I need you," Maggie chimed in. "Your dad needs you, too."

"And we believe you need us." Suzanne cocked her head.

"I don't have any money to invest."

"Not true. You have the money Mark left you." Maggie nodded.

"But...but...I want that for you and for Sonny Boy's college fund."

"You're not alone any longer, Jane. We're family. We're going to help."

"I...I...there's so much you don't know. Don't understand. Don't have a clue." Jane's words came out strangled and broken.

"Now's the time for honesty." Maggie bowed her head and pressed her palms together in prayer. Was she praying for strength, guidance, or perseverance?

"I'll go first." Suzanne stood and faced her friends. "I'm pregnant. I've considered my options. Having the baby or *not*."

Maggie gasped. "You can't. I won't let you...*not*."

"It's not your decision to make." Suzanne's words came out harsh, like sandpaper on a wound. Maggie flinched.

Suzanne paced a few steps, then turned and retraced her steps. "But I've made up my mind. I want this baby. And I'll need both of you to help me get through this—it means a whole different life for me. A different place to live. A different schedule. A different body."

Jane rose and walked toward her, her arms open. Suzanne fell into her hug. "I don't know what I'm going to do without Grant." She sucked in a short breath. A sob escaped. She was really going to do it—give up her husband for her baby—but the idea of that loss broke her heart.

Until the moment she voiced the words, she truly hadn't made a final decision about the baby. And now that she had, a sliver of hope emerged. Shining bright like a sliver moon in a dark night sky.

Maggie came and wrapped her arms around her and Jane.

"I need to sit," Suzanne said. "I'm going to be a mother." The shock of it dazed her. "I'm going to be a mother."

"It's the best job in the world," Jane said.

Maggie sniffed. Dabbed at her eyes and turned away.

"Maggie"—Suzanne offered her hand—"we're going to have this baby together."

Jane hefted out a deep sigh. "Maggie's gonna be busy in the future… with two."

The Gs screamed at me, shattering the serenity of the relaxation room. *Tell them. Tell them. Tell. Them.*

They screamed so loud I wanted to cover my ears with my hands and crumble to the floor. The truth was burning a hot hole through me.

I grabbed Maggie's and Suzanne's wrists. Somewhere, long ago in a relationship book, I'd read couples should hold hands when they fought—the physical connection kept the emotional connection from spiraling out of control. My relationship with Maggie and Suzanne was as deep and meaningful as any I'd ever had.

A wad of truth shot from my gut to my throat. "I *have* to tell y'all."

Maggie put her hand on my shoulder. "Jane, you're worrying me. Tell us what?"

Suzanne's free hand went to her stomach. "Yes?"

"Sonny Boy. Insurance money. Can..can…cancer…" I blurted out the truth in the order of importance, nearly choking on the last word.

Maggie gasped. "Sonny Boy needs the insurance money because he has cancer? That poor baby. Poor baby. I'm so sorry." She pulled me closer to hug me. Her trembling vibrated into me. "How can we help? What can do?"

I shook my head faster than a drummer on speed beating a bass. My mouth refused to open. Words trapped.

"Maggie, I think you have mixed it up." Suzanne tugged and guided me to the couch. "Sit."

I did. A shudder ripped through me. I let go of my friends. Wrapped my arms around my stomach and rocked back and forth.

The truth ran in my head like a TV news feed announcing doom and destruction. Just saying the word I shared had slammed my confidence the way a hammer crushes a glass ball, made the fragility of life real, and slammed a pain through me so hard I feared my heart was truly gushing.

I had avoided speaking the word *cancer* aloud to anyone since getting the diagnosis.

Suzanne and Maggie both knelt at my feet. Each grasped my hands. Tears welled in Suzanne's eyes. I rocked to keep from flying apart.

My boy. My boy. My boy. How could I leave him?

"I don't know what you mean by insurance money…" Suzanne's words came out slow and measured. "But I'm guessing it's money Mark left you."

I bobbed my head up and down.

"He left me and Maggie money, too. But the…" Suzanne's voice dropped to a whisper. "The cancer part…it's you?"

I swallowed hard. Opened my mouth to speak. I struggled to say a word, then slowly nodded. Tears spilled from my eyes.

"Oh, Jane." Suzanne pulled me in for a hug.

I drew a ragged breath and looked at Maggie, her face twisted in suffering—strained and severe. She fully understood my raw, unavoidable, and fatal truth.

I sobbed more.

They let me cry, loving me, supporting me, aching for me.

A carousel of emotions spun through me.

I had wasted so much time.

Wasted friendship.

Wasted love.

Wasted my relationship with my father.

In time, I would be only a memory.

I was going to die.

Chapter 29 – Jane, Maggie, Suzanne

I cried.

Curled up on the couch in the relaxation room, I cried for Momma and all the time I'd lost with my father. I cried for Mark, so loving and so loved, yet so unsettled in life. I cried because I'd cheated him out of a relationship with his son. I cried because I'd denied my precious son a chance to know his father.

I cried over my betrayal, for not telling anyone the truth.

I cried to release the fear, guilt, shame—the cancer of my soul.

I cried until I had no more tears.

Until my ragged breath evened out.

Until exhaustion claimed me.

Then, unable to stay awake, I drifted off to sleep—half praying I wouldn't wake.

Maggie curled her feet beside her on the big u-shaped couch when Suzanne covered Jane, who slept fitfully. It was as though Jane had run out of steam and just stopped. Occasionally, she mumbled nonsensically. Was she talking to her mom or Mark?

"She doesn't look well…but I never got a *knowing*." Maggie's heart tick-tocked like a metronome between fear for Jane's future and aching angst. "That she might be sick."

"I've never seen her cry so much or so hard. Not even when her momma died," Suzanne whispered back.

"Her hurt is tangled with mine," Maggie confessed. "I understand she didn't want to hurt me, but to not trust that we could work through it… that crushed me. She was my Google-for-answers. Look where her decisions have landed us now. But she needs us. She's sick, Suz. Sick. That trumps any anger or hurt I feel." She silently called upon angels to pull sickness from Jane's body. "We must help her."

"I always knew you could forgive her."

Maggie's heart squeezed tighter. "Of course." But she was used to leaning on Jane…and now Jane needed her. Was she up to the task?

"Can you *fully* accept Sonny Boy? Jane, not you, had Mark's baby."

Suzanne's words burned a brand on her heart. Maggie's skittering pulse shot up. Her faith was her backbone. She wasn't having a crisis of faith or conscience. "*Because* she had Mark's child, I will forgive her. She's given us a living reminder of him."

"Jane was right about you."

"About me?"

"She once said you were far stronger than either of us knew."

"Only with support of my friends." Love lifted some sadness. She and Suzanne and Jane were sisters. Sisters disagree. Sisters fight. And sisters always love.

"Cancer…Maggie…how will we deal with that? I never felt so helpless. This is not so dissimilar to learning about Mark's death. I'm overwhelmed. I want my family. I want Grant and his children. I want you and Jane and Sonny Boy. Even Mr. Landry. I want Halloween, Thanksgiving, and Christmas together. Mardi Gras and Easter. Christ, I'll go to church again if that will make everything better."

Maggie allowed a slight grin to lift the corners of her mouth. Suz couldn't help her irreverence, but her commitments were always one-ton strong.

"Maggie, I'm scared. Has Jane let things go for too long? And what about Sonny Boy? He deserves the full island experience. Just like we had growing up."

"He will. We'll make sure of it. And someday the camp will be his. Mark would want that."

"Mauceles have held it for several generations. Sonny Boy is the next one. Can you imagine teaching his kids to swim there?" Suzanne's wobbly words held optimism, her eyes and mouth curled with sadness.

Maggie choked back building sorrow.

She would be strong.

Suzanne curled into herself. Like a slippery fish loose in a boat, her emotions flip-flopped, enough to rock the boat and pitch her into the water. Wet would be bad enough, but the currents could carry her far from safety.

She didn't have Jane's modicum of sensitivity, nor did she have Maggie's gift of *knowing*, but she'd bet her life that Jane had the same type of cancer that took her mother. They were going to lose Jane. It was just a matter of when.

God. Goddammit. How can you do this to Jane? What about to Maggie and me? Not to mention an innocent— Sonny Boy. You're going to wreck his world. Why?

It made no sense.

Now when Jane was facing death, how could she have a child? Could this be an example of one door closing and another door opening? Would Jane live see the birth of her child? Was this the sign she needed to validate having the baby?

She wanted to be a mother. But her dream was a child having a mother and a father. How could she walk away from Grant? Her knight in shining armor. The love of her life. Her man was smart and all heart. Generous. Thoughtful. Loving. She would never ever find that combination in another.

A swell of nausea rolled up. The result of heartache or morning sickness, she couldn't tell. It tossed her stomach—that awful seasick feeling. When the pit in her stomach rose to the back of her throat, she made a beeline for her purse.

"Are you okay?" Maggie asked. She remained curled on the couch while Jane slept.

"Saltine crackers."

"Let me get you some water." Maggie went behind the bar and reappeared with a cold bottle.

"Boy or girl"—Suzanne rubbed her stomach—"you are loved." She sunk back onto the couch.

"I am blessed." Maggie handed over the bottle. "Sonny Boy and your little one." Maggie's soft smile widened. Her face glowed. She was a true Madonna.

Suzanne closed her eyes, relaxing into a daydream…

A view from the camp, the dark waters of the Rigolets, seagulls hovering on a wind current, and gliding pelicans searching for food. The putter of a fishing boat chugging its way to Lake Saint Catherine, headed toward Lake Pontchartrain drifted to her.

The dream slid into another… she riding shotgun in Baron, Jane at the wheel, Maggie in the middle of the backseat with the wind catching their hair when they crossed the lake on the causeway, and the radio blaring… what song?

She listened closely.

Ahh, the Pointer Sisters belting out "We Are Family."

She and Maggie and Jane had all they needed to rebuild and be better than ever—just like their city. Love was the bricks. Hope, the mortar. Joy, the spotlight on their happiness.

But…

Would were they strong enough to keep Jane from dying?

Chapter 30

Waking up was like lifting out of a fog. Uncurling from a fetal position, I blinked and pushed away the blanket covering me. My swollen eyes wouldn't open all the way. My legs tingled—pinpricks of pain. My shoulders tightened. My body ached. Had I been in the ring with a prizefighter?

I spied Suzanne. She had never left my side. I glanced at the big Paris clock. I'd only dozed for a few minutes. Still, my dearest friends had waited in silent vigil and given me time to catch my breath.

Maggie handed me a towel and a bottle of water. Then she, too, sat next to me.

Tell them. Tell them. Tell. Them.

I had to speak the words or choke on them. Truth clogged my brain, and I had to share about everything. I touched Maggie's hand. "Hear my confession." My words came out slow and hoarse. "Please." I wanted absolution from my sins. My hands trembled.

Maggie patted my hand, a caring motherly friend offering support. Then she made the sign of the cross and folded her hands, prayer-like, in her lap. "I'll listen."

"Forgive me for I have sinned…I loved Boston," I rasped. "A relief after Momma. It gave me a sense of home, minus the mental torture and emotional pain. But Mark grew distant, depressed. Hated his job. Didn't want to go back to school. Didn't know what he wanted to do… He joined the Army."

"Didn't talk to you about it first?" Maggie asked.

I shook my head. "I was terrified for him…and for me. How *could* he leave me? He was my rock."

"Just like a man." Suzanne grunted.

"Suz, shush," Maggie said. "Go on, Jane."

"After Army basic training, he went to Afghanistan. I was afraid to pray…after praying for Momma, she still died. Praying for Mark might jinx things. Thankfully, Mark walked through the door. He came home alive. But he wasn't the same. And after all that time apart, I wasn't either." Her shoulders sagged.

"He left the military. Hated Boston more than he had before. Hated cold weather. Wanted sand, not snow. He hated everything. Someone told him they didn't trust Southerners because all the politeness and friendliness was disingenuous. 'No one could be that nice.' It pissed him off."

"Someone actually said that to him?" Maggie croaked.

"Yes, at the grocery store. Watching him fight living in Boston was like reliving Momma's fight all over again. He'd fought in Afghanistan—he didn't need to fight to live here. Mark was miserable. I couldn't save Momma, but I *could* save Mark."

"My brother always was a bayou boy."

"Suzanne, be quiet," Maggie chastised. "That's all well and good, Jane, but *why* did you sleep with Mark after you divorced him?"

Maggie's directness grabbed me by the throat, stopped my breath. "Because I loved him, wanted him, needed him."

I didn't intend my words to be cruel to Maggie, but I continued on the path of truth. "He gave me no warning when he showed up that weekend. Called from the airport. I was so homesick. And there came *home* wrapped up as Mark. He looked hot. Tan, toned, and a dimpled smile. I swear, I didn't know things were serious between the two of you. But," I paused. Maggie deserved to know how humanly flawed I was. The ugliness of my soul. "I did know you were dating."

Maggie's chin quivered. Her brows crinkled. Her shoulders rose and fell. Her anguish silent, except for those telltale signs.

There was no way I could confess that after a crazy, hot weekend in bed, Mark had proposed. His offer of remarriage came with a hitch—I had to return to New Orleans. Then a quiet marriage ceremony with no fanfare. It would be as though we'd never been divorced at all.

Those words I would take to my grave.

He didn't understand, a wild weekend of making love did not a marriage make.

I had wanted to move home. But…too many memories and too many ghosts. Mark and I were too different. Not like the difference between champagne and beer, but more like boiling water and ice cream—not able to coexist in the same space. The place where we made sense was in bed. Mark didn't see it that way…and he left burning mad.

"Maggie, we had a weekend. That's all. The boy I married had grown into a man who needed a special kind of woman. *You* were her."

"How do I *really* know Sonny Boy is his?" Maggie jumped up and paced. "How? I am here for you, Jane. I'm angry you kept secrets from us. Angrier you're sick."

"Maggie"—Suzanne went to her—"sit down, please. I am certain the boy is my nephew. He has the same birthmark as his father."

"If you want a DNA test, we'll get one." I'd do anything to lessen Maggie's pain.

"*You're* going to need one. Not for me." Maggie jerked away from Suzanne. She continued pacing.

"What's that mean?" Suzanne asked.

"Your father"—she pointed at Suzanne—"is trying to take the camp from me. He's got a lawyer. Property's been passed down via the Maucele family for generations. The lawyer says since Mark didn't leave a will…the only one who can rightfully inherit would be an heir. Your father doesn't know about Christopher Marcus…so as the only living Maucele, he's trying to claim the property. He can't have it."

I had never before witnessed Maggie burn with steely determination.

"He. *Can't.* Have. It. It's not his. It should be mine…but now it belongs to Mark's son."

"What?" I couldn't take in what she was telling me.

Suzanne sighed. "Louisiana property law. I should've thought about that."

"I can't deal with that right now." My head swam. The current about to carry me under. "Tell me what to do. I don't have it in me to fight a legal battle. Maggie, one of the reasons I contacted Mark the day he died—"

"You spoke to Mark?" Shock shook Maggie's voice.

"Yes," I sputtered. "Because I knew I was sick. I've been through this once. I needed you to be the mother I cannot be and Mark needed to be a father." My biggest fear turned out to be exactly what I needed most.

Maggie sank to the floor. Her mouth gaped. Her eyes round with surprise. "You talked to him the day he died?"

I nodded.

"Did he tell you…"—her face crinkled with pain—"we talked about a divorce?"

I stared at Maggie.

I didn't think any news could have shocked me more.

Maggie's fist went to her mouth. "He's dead," she wailed. "I wanted to die, too."

"No. Maggie." Suzanne wrapped an arm around her shoulder. "We all loved Mark. You, probably more than us, but we each cared deeply in our own way. He had a demon. A restlessness that ran deep."

"It's *you* who doesn't understand." Maggie shook her fists as though she wanted to shake Suzanne. "The insurance people paid me a visit after the funeral. They'd read the police report. Had Mark's death certificate. They interviewed me, suggesting, but never came out and said it."

The hair on the back of my neck stood up. A chill ran down my arms.

"What?" Terror flashed in Suzanne's eyes. "I have a copy of the death certificate. There's nothing unusual about it. What do you know?"

Maggie wiped her tears. "They hinted that Mark tried to kill himself." Maggie spoke barely above a whisper.

"No!" I shouted. "Assholes. Who were they? I'm going to talk with them."

"Whoa. Take a pause." Suzanne flapped her hands as though that would lower the tension. "Let's deal with one issue at a time. Let's just be calm. The insurance assholes paid us. We know even without Maggie's gift of *knowing*—Mark wouldn't commit suicide."

"Never would he commit suicide, yeah?" I nodded. "He'd just learned he had a son. He had Maggie. He had everything to live for."

We stood in the middle of the relaxation room and hugged. It was the first honest hug I'd given my friends in years. The first hug I felt as though I truly deserved from them.

Cancer would not deter me.

I still had a to-do list to tend to.

Everything for Sonny Boy's future.

Chapter 31 - Suzanne

The next morning, Suzanne opened the plantation shutters in her family room. "Wakey, wakey. The day waits for no woman."

Nothing like sunshine to start a new day. Yes, the sun *had* shined yesterday, but the day had ended as gloomy and fraught with tension like a hurricane chugged on its way. And there had already been enough tears shed to flood New Orleans.

When neither Jane nor Maggie stirred, she said, "The sun rose over the West Bank today." Then she flipped the shutters open and closed, flashing sunlight like sending Morse code into the room.

Maggie groaned and pulled a pillow over her face. Jane chucked a pillow at her.

"Hey there. Watch it. Don't hurt the pregnant one." Last night, her friends had tried to settle the world's problems and failed to make it to their beds. When Jane refused to speak more about her cancer and condition—preferring denial for a few days more—they talked about Sonny Boy's future, sometimes laughing, sometimes crying, sometime giggling.

Suzanne, sleeping for two, had abandoned Maggie and Jane at midnight to fend for themselves.

This morning, no blood on the floor or furniture. A good thing. Hope for the day had risen with the sun.

"Right. Pregnant," Jane moaned. "Maggie, she's going to be impossible for months."

"And Janey, you're going to be here to help me keep her in check—help me stay sane." Maggie yawned.

"Ladies, Grant comes home today. You two have to help me pack."

"But—" Maggie and Jane groaned in unison.

Their chorus made her chuckle. "We have to pick up Sonny Boy, too."

Her happiness splintered with the reminder of the airport and delivering Grant her news. She chickened out during their call last night. Instead of the truth, she'd told her wonderful husband she was bone weary after wrangling Maggie and Jane. Well, it wasn't a total lie. He'd told her how much he loved her. Couldn't wait to show her. And if it didn't break some secret girlfriend code, he looked forward to a ride in Baron II.

He couldn't have been more wonderful, and she couldn't have felt any worse.

Keeping the pregnancy from him had prolonged her fantasy about their future. Prolonged her agony about the truth.

Soon her life would change forever. Would she remain a Cinderella, or would her glass slipper shatter?

"Let's go." Suzanne opened the shutters full tilt.

"She's gone from cheerleader to drill sergeant." Jane's feet touched the floor, her body melted off the couch. "I'm up."

"Come help me pack." Suzanne pointed down the hall.

A while later, Suzanne rode shotgun in the front seat with Jane behind the wheel of Baron II. Maggie sat in the backseat, keeping Sonny Boy company. They pulled into the airport parking lot and found a spot.

"How do we explain about Sonny Boy?" Maggie led the way, holding Sonny Boy's hand, toward baggage claim.

"I've given that some thought. What if we point Grant out, send Sonny Boy to make his own introduction, and watch what happens?" Jane's grin quirked to one side. Suzanne swatted at her.

"No way," Maggie said.

"Who's Grant?" Sonny Boy asked over his shoulder at his mother, and Maggie made sure he never let go of her hand.

"That would be *your* Uncle Grant. He's married to this one here." Jane pointed to Suzanne.

"It would certainly disarm my husband." Suzanne considered the merit of Jane's plan.

"I'm outnumbered again." Maggie shook her head. "We don't have a leash or a rope. Christopher has to be attached on this end before I'll let him walk about free on the other."

Jane laughed. "You *do* learn quickly."

"I've got my eyes *trained* on this little guy now." Maggie chuckled.

They entered baggage claim where other passengers were snatching up their luggage and bolting for the door—tourists crazy ready for a Bourbon Street experience. Suzanne halted and the rest of her group followed. She crouched down and grasped Sonny Boy's shoulders, making direct eye contact. "I want you to look over there." She pointed to Grant in his dark gray suit. "See that man with the gray suitcase?"

"Yep."

"What do you say?" Jane prompted.

"I mean, yes, ma'am."

"I want you to run to him, throw your arms around his legs, just like you did to Aunt Maggie and me when we first met. Will you do that?"

"Yes." He nodded, excitement dancing in his eyes.

"Then bark like a dog. Bark loud. Call him Uncle Grant. *And then* tell him you're Sonny Boy."

"Okay."

"The best response to Auntie Suzanne is 'yes, ma'am.' You sure you've got all that?" Jane crouched on the other side of her son.

"Yes, Momma."

"Tell me what you're going to do."

"I'm gonna run over and bark at that man—Uncle Grant."

Suzanne, Maggie, and Jane giggled. "That'll work."

They stood off to the side, close enough see and hear all that was about to take place. Sonny Boy took off running.

Bam!

He grabbed Grant by the legs, causing him to drop his phone.

"Ah…what…who?" Grant fumbled to pick up his phone with Sonny Boy attached to his leg.

"Woof! Woof! Woof!"

Grant's eyes darted from side to side as though trying to piece together what was happening. He released his hold on his suitcase and peeled the boy's arms from his legs. "Hey, little fella, you lost?" He hunkered down in front of the kid.

"Woof!"

Grant frowned. "How about, one woof is yes, and two woofs are no? Are you lost?"

"Woof! Woof!"

"Do you know where your parents are?"

Sonny Boy cocked his head to one side and didn't respond.

"Do you have a name?"

"Woof!"

"You're clearly a bright little guy." Grant chuckled, but his brow furrowed. "Tell me your name."

"It's me, Uncle Grant. Sonny Boy."

Grant stiffened. Suzanne couldn't tell if it was from shock or surprise.

"How do you know my name is Grant?"

Sonny Boy pointed.

Suzanne felt the laser beam of the boy's point heating the middle of her chest. "Busted." She stepped forward. With a stomach full of butterflies fighting for freedom, she crossed the space to her husband, not remembering a time when he looked more distinguished with his air of confidence than he did right then. "Hi, darlin'. I see you've met Jane's dog, I mean boy. Her son."

Grant's eyes widened. "You're joking?"

"Look at this face." She pointed to the apple of her cheek. "Does it say 'I'm joking'? " She let him fold her into his arms. She pressed the full length of her body close to his and kissed him hard. He was heaven in male form. Hormones or not, the man made her hot. Hot. Hot.

Sonny Boy wrapped his arms around both their legs.

"Hmm. That's what I call a homecoming," Grant said.

"Woof!"

"Hey, Grant! Welcome back. How's our favorite husband?" Jane asked.

Suzanne threw her a keep-your-mitts-off-my-man look.

"Don't give me attitude, Suz. Maggie's a widow. I'm divorced. You're the only one with a husband. At the moment, he's our favorite." Jane shook her finger at Suzanne, then reached for her son's hand. "Little guy, let's go before your aunt and uncle stumble on top of you."

"You *have* a son?" Grant looked down at Sonny Boy as though studying him for secret tells. "It's true? Sonny Boy isn't a dog?"

"Absolutely." Jane beamed.

"You mean, this child is *the* one?"

Suz studied her husband. It was rare he was caught unaware of facts or figures or information at any meeting. This little peek at his vulnerability made him that much more endearing.

But how much was he going to hate her exploding news and expanding waistline?

"The very same. Wouldn't come to the phone that day you overheard me talking."

"Shit, I mean, crap. Christ, I don't know what I mean. Can I pick him up?"

Suzanne laughed. "Honey, he's not a toy and he won't bite—or at least I don't think so. He's also housebroken." Her shoulders shook while she tried to conceal her giggles. "You won't bite Uncle Grant, will you?" she asked her nephew.

"Woof! Woof!"

Jane rolled her eyes, then Maggie chimed in, "Now see what you've started, Auntie Suzanne."

"Auntie?" Grant asked, his voice hitched up a notch as he picked up Sonny Boy. "Wait. He called me Uncle Grant. He's my nephew?"

"Your nephew by marriage. Come on. Let's go home. We have a lot to talk about." Suzanne linked her arm through her husband's. They didn't need a public display. The news that she had to share required privacy, a family moment. She pulled his suitcase while he carried Sonny Boy, gazing at the child as though the boy were a modern marvel.

Maggie and Jane fell in behind her, walking toward the terminal exit.

"He doesn't stand a chance," Maggie said.

"Is that a *knowing*?" Suzanne asked. Grant didn't stand a chance at resisting Sonny Boy?

"Not a *knowing* like my others, but he's got *love* written all over his aura."

"But that isn't the question, is it?" Suzanne trudged forward.

Before the afternoon was over, she'd have her answers.

An hour later, back at home, Suzanne paced in their large bedroom. It had shrunk to the size of a prison cell after she confessed about her condition. Two packed bags sat on the floor in the corner. Ready for flight while Maggie and Jane and Sonny Boy waited by the pool. Waited for word of her future.

Grant sat on the love seat. Still. Solemn. Silent.

She retraced her steps. "As I said, I'm pregnant, and I know that's a violation of our agreement."

His eyes followed her but revealed nothing of his feelings. If he didn't speak soon, it wouldn't be only morning sickness that had her running for the bathroom.

"Say something, please." She sank to the floor at his feet. She took his hands in hers, and a recollection about Maggie's explanation about pain over Mark's death skittered through her. "Irrational panic," Maggie had said. She now understood that feeling.

Grant remained silent.

Panic lifted through her like an elevator shooting to the top floor. She loved him. Wanted him. Wanted to be a mother to his child. Their child. She'd stoop to the indignity of pleading, even on her knees, if it would help Grant understand the importance of them being a family for their child.

"You…already packed…your bags? You're…leaving me?" Grant's words tumbled out stilted. Had understanding finally spread through all parts of his brain?

Her gut clenched. Her throat tightened as though pliers were clamping tighter. She couldn't force words from her lips.

"What you must think of me after these years of marriage." Grant pulled his hands from hers. She felt him go away from her the same as if he'd left the room. She shivered against the chill of a breeze blowing in the chasm growing between them.

"Suzanne, please get up." Grant's strangled voice ripped through her. The butterfly revolt in her stomach had her racing to the bathroom.

She hovered over the toilet. Coughed. Scrunched her eyes closed. Swallowed back fear and then collapsed onto the cold marble floor and cried.

A few breaths later, Grant scooped her up. His warm, strong arms carried her. Her body melted, limp like a rag doll, as he took her to their bed. Laid her gently down. Stretched out on the bed beside her. His fingers smoothed away dampness on her face.

His eyes held her captive with bonds of tenderness.

But hurt lurked there. Maybe a spark of fear, too.

And she'd been the one to put that there. All her fault.

"Listen to me, Suzanne Maucele Saulnier." He pulled her closer and kissed her temple. "I'm not a *loup garou*. I'm not going anywhere. And neither are you. We're in this together."

Suzanne looked deeper into his eyes, seeking hope, reassurance of the truth of his words.

"I won't lie and say I'm not surprised about the pregnancy…more than a little shocked even. However, I'm older and wiser than when we married. I will love this baby. I'll be a *good* father. I'll continue to be a *great* husband… but you'll never know how wonderful it can be if you don't give us a chance. We're partners. What's mine is yours"—he chuckled—"and you know the saying, what's yours is yours. I will always be yours."

Suzanne sucked in a breath, surprise lifted her, and she struggled up on her elbows. "You mean that?" She panted. Fought to catch her breath. Trembling, she sank back onto the bed.

"If it will make you happy, we'll have a prenup-burning ceremony. That paper was my attorney covering his ass. I hadn't thought about the document…probably since you inked your signature on it."

"Total truth?" She'd worried for nothing? For nothing? He…he loved her that much? Warmth began to spread slowly through her, heating up all the cold dark spots where fear had rooted.

Grant chuckled. His expression befuddled over her doubts. "You're my wife. I love you."

She scooted close to him, wrapped her arms around his neck, and planted a deep kiss on his sensuous mouth, one to sear his soul and tattoo his words on his lips. "I don't want you to feel trapped by my decision to have this baby. You'll be seventy when this baby goes to college." But he was brawny and healthy and bold…age was only a number for him.

"I've made up my mind, too. I want you and I want the baby—a package deal. Would it make you feel better to have a parenting contract?"

Leaning back, she pulled him over on top of her. Breathless from the kiss, she slackened her grip and sighed. "No contract needed. Just love."

"Suzanne, I've traveled the world. Mostly alone. You came into my life and the sunrise looked brighter. The moon over water shined more enchantingly. Simple things. Woman, never will you have to live without my love."

She reached for his belt buckle and began to unbuckle it. "Grant, my darling husband, you are my sun and my moon. We are going to be so happy together with the new addition to our family." The urge to have his hands on her and their bodies merging pressed her forward.

"Babe, we have a nephew now. And a little one on the way. Life is good. But you have to stop what you're doing…" She felt his hands clasp over hers, stilling her action.

"I have a surprise of my own," he said. "One I believe will make you, Maggie, and Jane happy. I want to share this news now…and also let your friends know that any escape from me you planned has crashed and burned."

"A surprise?"

Chapter 32

Trees blocked the afternoon sun and cast a canopy of shadow over the pool deck. A gentle breezed caressed my skin. I tried to nap on a poolside chaise—Maggie and my son slept as though on a bed of clouds—when I closed my eyes, it set the Gs chattering.

Tell them. Tell them. Tell them.

Now that Suzanne was sharing her secret with Grant, I had to share my final one.

That daunting decision made my blood pressure rise, setting off tremors in my heart like a Richter-scale-eight earthquake. If I'd been handed a pen to write my name, it would've come out as squiggles and dots.

Movement from inside the house caught my attention. A sigh of partial relief washed over me. Together, Grant and Suzanne waved in the window, motioning us inside. Their smiles and laced fingers answered my question about their future. Sunny. And my Sonny Boy would soon have a cousin.

That shored up my confidence a bit.

"Maggie"—I rose and shook her foot—"let's go inside."

"Didn't hear any shouting, door slamming, or gunfire…so maybe they worked things out." Maggie yawned.

"Look." I pointed when she opened her eyes. "Body language reveals so much."

"Do we get them to come out here, or do we wake Sonny Boy and take him inside?" Maggie's expression softened. She watched my boy stretched out on the chair, his arms flung wide and mouth slightly open, sleeping hard.

"He's managed to sleep through the construction noise across the street… Would you ask Grant and Suzanne to come out here? Better than waking this one"—I tickled his cheek, and he swatted the air where my hand had been—"and having a grumpy kid to deal with."

Maggie rose and headed toward the door. "I'll bring some sweet tea for us, too."

A few minutes later, Grant carried a tray with four glasses of tea, a bowl of snacks, and a stack of napkins.

"Let's sit at the table." I pointed at the far end of the pool deck to the table and chairs.

While we ladies sat, Grant, acting as butler, placed napkins in front of each of us and then a filled glass of tea. He placed the tray of snacks in the center, scooted his chair close to Suzanne, and draped his arm over her shoulder, a protective and unifying gesture. Steady energy vibrated from them. They were solid in their stand to face the future.

If I had a list of worries, I could now check Suzanne and Grant off that list.

I reached for my drink. The Gs started shouting.

Now. Now. Now.

"Cheers." Suzanne lifted her glass. "Grant and I are making our first official announcement to the two of you. We're having a baby!"

"Wonderful." I clutched my hands to my chest at the heartfelt news, jumped up, and circled the table to wrap them in a hug from behind, planting kisses on the tops of their heads. Joy filled me. Joy was a necessary ingredient in the prescription I would need to see me through my journey.

When I returned to my seat, Maggie lifted her glass. "I'm so happy for you." Her voice wavered. "I know Mark is smiling in Heaven over this news. Congratulations." Her eyes glistened. We clinked glasses and sipped. Suzanne and Grant glowed.

Maggie's words struck me. Mark was in Heaven. Of course, he was. And Momma was there, too. Three of us would have more power than me alone. Together we would watch over the ones we loved. I giggled at the idea of being a helicopter parent…from the other side. I could dash and dart weightlessly. Effortlessly. Tickle my boy in his sleep. No, I had no proof of Heaven or life after death, but I had an ocean of faith…and believed I *could* be forgiven for my past transgressions.

"Thank you for sharing this moment with Suzanne and me." Grant leaned forward and leaned his arms on the edge of the table. "There is more good news to tell you."

"Twins?" Maggie's eyes widened. "You're going to have twins. No"—she shook her head—"that's not right. They're going to be like twins. Makes no sense. But I just got a flash of two boys—related by blood—playing together and one of them was yours." She pointed at Suzanne and Grant.

"The other boy?" I whispered. Was Maggie having a *knowing* that truly foretold the future?

"Too fuzzy for me to see. The other boy is older. His back was to me."

"Suzanne wants a gender reveal party. I guess we'll get confirmation of Maggie's *knowing* then." Grant's smile was endearing. "While that will be exciting, my news requires a prompt answer from you, Jane, and then I make a phone call to put it all into motion."

"Me?" Tingles shot up my spine. My track record in decision-making bumped in the negative numbers, way in the red of any bottom line. And if Grant was involved in a project, whatever it was, it had to be big. He did nothing in small measures.

"Jane, we want you to move back to New Orleans. I figured work had to be the only anchor keeping you in Boston. I can purchase controlling interest in the magazine where you work and secure them two additional contracts to produce magazines for our local market. The operation will be moved to New Orleans. If you're willing to take the helm."

"Grant, Maggie and I offered Jane partnership in the spa. But…" Suzanne placed her hand on Grant's arm as though to restrain his enthusiasm. "Jane has other news," she said quietly.

I scrunched my eyes closed. Had I heard him right? Grant was rich and powerful, but always just Grant to me. He would go to all this time and trouble…for me?

Opening one eye first, then the other, I found Maggie and Suzanne leaning forward toward me just like Grant, they were like petals of a flower with me as the one messing up perfection.

"Jane, please say something." Suzanne tapped the top of my hand.

The Gs screeched. "*Tell them. Tell them. Tell them.*"

I covered the top of my head with my hands. How did I keep my brain from exploding? How did I shut the Gs up? Shut them down?

Tell. Tell. Tell.

I swallowed hard. My eyes flooded with tears. I blinked. Blinked again.

I opened my mouth to speak. Snapped it shut.

I couldn't say the words.

They were a death sentence for me.

Now. Now. Now.

Before my last ounce of strength ebbed, I placed my hands in my lap. Sat up straight. Glanced at my son, he remained fast asleep. I turned back to my family around the table. The family of my heart. As much as I hated bringing gloom, grief, and guilt to the table, the door had opened and I had to walk through. Deliver my news.

Time slowed.

The back-up beeper from a work truck blared in perfect rhythm with some universal pulse.

Grant stretched his arm across the table, wiggled his fingers, an offer of support.

"I had hoped…" I swallowed hard and lifted my chin. "For a *perfect* way to tell you *my* news. It's not right to rob you of the splendor of this moment, be the downer after your joyous announcement."

Expectant eyes stared at me. I gazed at each of my friends. "We always joked that Mark was the optimistic one. Even on his headstone it says, 'Good things come in threes.' You thought I was pessimistic. I consider myself a realist. I am *again* dealing in threes. Triple-negative."

"What? You said *again*. Explain." Suzanne frowned.

"I can't accept Grant's offer because I can't handle the job."

Maggie snorted. "You're Jane. Of course, you will." She waved away the sentiment of my words.

"You two know"—I reached my hands out to Maggie and Suzanne. They grasped mine, giving me support. It flowed warm, welcoming, wise through me—"the pain, the sadness, the grief I endured when Momma was sick and dying. Well… about eighteen months after Sonny Boy was born, I was diagnosed with breast cancer. Later, I'll fill you in on the anatomy and medical jargon, but it was an aggressive form. Survival rate goes up after five years…"

"And Sonny Boy is going to be five." The hopefulness in Maggie's voice was a blossom of love popping open in my chest.

"He will be soon. But my five-year mark would happen when he passes six and a half, headed for seven. What I learned, what caused me to call Mark, what causes me to reach out to you, is the current testing. My triple-negative breast cancer is back."

"We'll fight this." Suzanne slapped her hands on the table and stood, a warrior of a woman. "You'll take treatment. You'll get better. You'll run the spa business. No doubts about it."

"Awww, Suz, I love you." Tears slid down my face. I shook my head. Each day forward from today was a gift. I couldn't count on many tomorrows.

Maggie grabbed both of my hands in hers. "This is…this is…*shitty*. What can we do?" If her tone had been a sword against cancer, mine would've been gone. So fierce was the look in her eye and the grit in her words. She squeezed my hands and murmured, "I love you. I love you."

Grant rose. Mopped his face. Then he came around the table to me. Pulling back my chair as though I weighed as much as a pillow, he gently tugged me from my seat and wrapped me in a bear hug—he always hugged like he truly meant it. I always loved that about him. He might not be my husband, but he was still the best husband around.

When he released me, I gathered my thoughts and leaned on the table facing my family, my palms flat against the cool stone tabletop. "Maggie, you *need* to be strong. Sonny Boy *needs* a mother. I *need* you to be that woman. Suzanne and Grant have two children with a third on the way… They'll help you, but you're Top Dog, Wonder Woman, and it's superhero time. My dad will have an active part in Sonny Boy's life, too. It will be three of you for Sunday dinners. But it will take all of you together—"

"Jane," Suzanne wailed.

I fanned my face to stay the tears. "Together, you will make Mark real for Christopher Marcus." The whimper in my voice set off another round of tears.

My friends stared. Their surprise and disbelief resonated with me. But now that I'd started down the path of truth, I had to finish. "I know…y'all…will keep…my memory…alive."

Silence followed.

Silence flowed.

"How long do we have?" Maggie demanded. "Why did you wait so long? Aggressive is never good. I can't accept this." She shook her head, and shook her head, and shook her head. "No." She got up and stormed toward the house.

"Maggie, please wait." I started after her, but Grant and Suzanne held me back with a group hug. Sonny Boy began to stir.

"Shhh, Jane." Suzanne put her finger to her lips. "Don't upset our boy. Let's go in the house. Maggie will settle down. She's always the emotional one. I'm so glad the truth is known. Now we can begin to deal with the future."

The truth will set you free? That's what they say.

So I have to grab bits of joy as I'm forced to walk through hell before I'm truly free, yeah?

Grant carried my son from the pool into the house, jostling him like a sack of potatoes. I listened intently to Christopher Marcus's laughter. A tinkling sound like rainwater dancing over rocks in a stream, like "Twinkle, Twinkle, Little Star" on the piano in high C. And yet, all boy.

He set Christopher on his feet, and my son ran to the refrigerator. "Tea, please." Grant followed him and complied.

More than ever, I wanted to hold my boy close. I wanted his voice, his touch, his scent to permeate my being. I wanted to never let him go. However, it was the one thing I must do.

But had my plan for Maggie to be his mother turned out to be fool's gold?

"She's not here." Suzanne returned from the garage. "Baron II is gone as well."

My stomach dropped to my knees. "We have to find her." Had my secret been too much on the heels of Mark's death?

"Ladies, I'll get Mr. Landry on the phone—have him come have dinner with this little dude and me. We'll order in. You go." He shooed us toward the garage.

Intuition flashed. I could see Maggie in my mind's eye. "I'm driving." I pulled the keys from Suzanne's hand. "I know where she is."

Suzanne sighed. "This is a lot to take in. Drive. I'm worn out. Wake me if I fall asleep. I suddenly feel quite tired."

"Pregnancy."

I put the car in gear and backed, heading toward the island.

Suzanne dozed. I wished for her to feel the wonder and love of pregnancy and then motherhood. I prayed I'd live to see my nephew born. Everything in me believed Maggie when she said Suzanne and Grant would have a boy.

When I arrived at the bridge and crossed over to the island, Suzanne woke. She smiled and leaned her head back, clearly in a pleasant hormone haze of impending motherhood.

I found the road I sought and turned.

"Where are you going?" Suzanne asked. "I know you haven't forgotten how to get to the camp."

"I want to see things from a different vantage point."

"Look." Suzanne leaned forward in her seat as we rolled down the alley. "They're rebuilding at the Dupuis place. That old woman can't be..." Suzanne's mouth gaped.

A silver-haired woman rested in a lawn chair underneath the shade of a picnic-table umbrella with one knee crossed over the other. Her hair was secured in a twist. She wore a casual blue and white seersucker dress and bounced her foot as if keeping time to music. In contrast to the pilings and concrete pillars going up, she glowed, regal and elegant.

"Mrs. Dupuis? Can't be." Suzanne continued to stare as the car inched closer.

That's when I spied Maggie on the other side of the woman. "I knew she'd be here." I stopped the car and shut off the engine. "That woman can be none other than Mrs. Dupuis." Surprise dunked me like a paddle wheel, spinning me into the water and then pulling me up. The past had risen again.

Suzanne and I stepped out of the car. "Mrs. Dupuis?" I asked, just in case I was wrong.

Maggie stood. Back straight. A challenge I couldn't decipher. Her eyes were red-rimmed. A wariness rimmed them, too. She twisted a tattered tissue in her hands. Tiny bits floating off in the gentle breeze.

The older woman looked up. "Yes. I'm Mrs. Dupuis."

"I'm Jane, and this is Suzanne."

"Yes, I remember. We've been waiting for you. Maggie and I."

A prickle ran down my spine. Maggie and she had been waiting?

Maggie nodded.

Energy rippled through me. Brought me understanding. Maggie was healing. Her grief lifting…enough for her to have a knowing.

"You're rebuilding?" Suzanne stepped closer to the woman. I stepped closer, too.

"Want to bring my family together again. Enjoy what's left of my life"

"I would've thought…" Suzanne mumbled.

"What's that, dear?"

Suzanne cleared her throat. "I would have thought that after Mr. Dupuis died here, this is the last place you'd want to be."

Mrs. Dupuis cocked her head to one side. "Honey, this property came from my family. I'm not going to let that old jasper ruin what's left of my life. "But you know…" She crooked her finger, inviting us closer. "Die? Die! He didn't die that night." Her eyes grew wide, and just a bit crazy.

"He disappeared into the swamp *hoping* I'd go to jail for murder." She winked at us. "But joke was on *him*. With no body and *no* witnesses—no case. When the police finally found him, they prosecuted him for battery, domestic violence, attempted murder. He was in jail all these years."

"Oh." The surprise of finding her and then discovering the truth of the past had me swirling. I squatted and placed my hands on the uneven shells for support. Mrs. Dupuis came home. Was reuniting her family. Making the most of her life…her story could've been written just for me.

"No witnesses was a *good* thing for *me* at his trial. No way to muddy the waters…if you catch my wave. The man wasn't much into managing details. He never changed his life insurance beneficiary. So now I have the money to rebuild my home."

The lie we'd told *had* protected her.

"I think we need to go." Maggie moved toward me. "Mrs. Dupuis, thank you for the talk. I know I'll be seeing more of you." Maggie helped me stand.

"Don't be strangers, girls," Mrs. Dupuis called out as we walked to Suzanne's car.

"Jane, let's go to *our* camp." Maggie's choice of words settled on me. The camp was the place that felt most like home.

I blinked back the wetness in my eyes. I'd missed a lot in all my years away. Ignored my problems. Refused to see them. I'd caused so much hurt. But I'd done some good, too.

My cell phone dinged with a text message when I pulled the car onto the concrete pad by the Maucele camp.

I checked the message after shutting off the car. It came from Beth. So much had happened so quickly, I hadn't had time to talk with her. She wasn't going to take the news of my condition lightly. But I hoped she'd forgive my delay in sharing the truth.

Pops and I will be there for Sonny Boy's birthday. Thanks for the invite. So excited to see you both and meet your southern family.

This time, I knew the perfect time to reveal the truth to her and Mr. Finley. After Sonny Boy's birthday party, which I decided would take place on an afternoon riverboat cruise.

I followed Maggie to the dock. She sat and dangled her feet. I could imagine her there with Sonny Boy, teaching him how to catch fish and set a trap for crabs. I sat beside her. She draped her arm over my shoulder and leaned her head against mine. Suzanne came from behind us. She sat next to me, too.

Once again, I was sandwiched between my old friends.

Silence lingered between us. A new calm found me.

"Jane," Maggie started. "I know that I haven't proven myself to be the… most responsible of caregivers for Christopher since you arrived. I'm somewhat confused and overwhelmed and deeply touched that you would even consider entrusting him to me. But I can't wrap my head around what you said. All I hear is 'aggressive' and 'cancer' blaring in my ears."

"Shh. There's time." I didn't want to talk about the future. I needed to enjoy the moment with my oldest, bestest friends. "We'll get it all sorted out."

"Don't be strong for us," Suzanne said. "You've taught us how to be strong. Let us be that for you." A tear slipped from the corner of her eye.

I wrapped my arm around her shoulder. My friends and I began to sway to the music.

The music of the seagulls.

The music of the tides.

The music of life.

Theirs and mine made three-strand twine.

Together we could weather anything.

Chapter 33

Nine months later...

I tried to pucker my lips. My sight was fuzzy in the dimly lit room.

"Momma, I love you. Forever and ever." Christopher Marcus leaned over me, kissed my forehead, each of my cheeks, and my lips. He squeezed my shoulder. My life was complete.

We had all prepared him the best we could for what was to come.

The wide smile I gave him only existed in my hopes. I managed to tap my finger on my chest over my heart. "Love you, too."

"Let's let her rest," Suzanne said. He scampered from the room.

Pulling the sheet up slowly over my shoulder took all my effort. I fought against wincing. Thankfully, documents distracted Suz, and she didn't see my scrunched face.

My hospital bed sat beside the window in the guest room at her house. It afforded me a view of the side garden and part of the pool—so I could watch my son play when Maggie brought him for the weekend. They were outside now, laughing and giggling. Grant had joined the fun.

"Grant. Good man. Christopher…dives…a pro," I told Suzanne.

"He's a good big brother to his little cousin. He's so cute when he gives Alexander a bottle. It means so much that the boys will have a solid family bond. My Alexander is blessed."

"Zander…handful. Chris teach him tricks." My chuckle turned into a cough.

"I'll take it." A worried expression flashed before Suzanne caught herself. Everyone only smiled when they came to see me. She glanced at the baby monitor and glowed with adoration for the sleeping child in the other room.

Christopher Marcus. He had been the real glue that reunited all of us. My little guy was growing up. His fifth birthday had passed, and now he was headed for six. Confident. So loved. Funny as hell.

Which was the proof I needed to know I'd made the right decision to have him live with Maggie.

After his party, when Beth and Mr. Finley returned to Salem last June, they packed up our stuff and had it shipped to Maggie's. Then I'd been less sick, and we had a good time going through the boxes—it was like having two Christmases last year.

In the fall, Christopher went to school, played T-ball, and learned judo. To him, it was an adventure. I laughed remembering our negotiations about music. He and I finally agreed he'd take lessons for at least a year when he turned seven, after which he could decide if he would continue or not. My secret mission—to have him play trumpet in a marching band. A band that had a spot in a Mardi Gras parade. Mark would want Christopher immersed in our culture.

Then Fate did the dance that only it can do. Three months ago, my treatment took a nosedive…sinking like a riverboat after striking a submerged stump in the Mississippi.

I'd gotten too sick. Tired too easily. Too little energy to do much. Suzanne and Grant were incredibly gracious and moved me—now the resident invalid—into their home. A generous gesture since their lives changed with the arrival of Alexander Marcus, who was now nearly a month old.

I wanted Christopher Marcus with me, but we all agreed that him living with Maggie would be a good plan. Allow for a transitional time.

I didn't want him by my side during the day in, day out of my decline—I had to spare him that. I wanted him all smiles when he was with me.

He video-chatted with me daily, sometimes twice, when he came home from school excited over a happening at school. We chatted nearly every night during the week so I could tuck him in bed virtually. And he came every weekend to visit me.

Of course, Maggie stayed, too. We were a family.

As I predicted, she was perfect. She hovered the right amount. Gave me time alone with Sonny Boy and herded him out when she sensed I needed sleep. She loved him. And she'd forgiven me.

My father came for dinner every Sunday. Always a brave face. Always strong. No hints of scratches, nicks, or dents in his sobriety. I was right to believe in his recovery. He would be a rock for Suzanne, Maggie, and his grandson.

Sometimes he stopped by after work to visit. He brought me beignets or pralines. They were sweet to look at even though I had no interest in food these days.

Sometimes he took Sonny Boy to church with him…but I had agreed to allow Maggie to raise him Catholic, with the caveat that she had to teach him about spiritual things, too.

I found joyful moments in each day. Highlights. I cherished each one. I had started a joy journal for Maggie to give to Sonny Boy someday, but lately Suzanne had to write the entries…I had grown too weak.

And I had a new secret. One I hadn't shared. Mark had taken to visiting me. The first time, I thought I was dreaming. His company made all pain and worry slip away. He comforted me, my dear old friend. He came more often now.

"The judge finalized the adoption. Maggie is waiting for you to tell Sonny Boy. I hear from the attorney that my father is requesting visitation with Christopher Marcus." Suzanne rose, straightened my blanket, and pulled it up around my neck.

I had no energy for a fight. "Can't deal…with him. Maggie and you." Even if they said yes to her father's demands, it wouldn't be long before he would disappear on his own. Family commitment wasn't high on his list of the right things to do in life.

Suzanne rubbed her hand over the silk scarf covering my head. "While the baby is down for his morning nap, let's go over the checklist. I have it right here." She picked up a clipboard from the table beside the bed. "Insurance money set up as an education fund for Christopher—check. Money in trust for his needs—check. Yes, we'll find him an appropriate car when he turns sixteen."

I nodded.

"Final deed to the camp, in his name jointly with Maggie's, is in the safe deposit box—check and check. Adoption done. We've accomplished all you requested."

"Good," I whispered, my body heavy against the bed. My arms and legs were leaden. "Love him. Not spoil him."

I had restored my friendships. Rebuilt them to last a lifetime. Didn't matter that I wouldn't be physically near any longer…after all, I hadn't lived nearby for many years. Despite their hurt and anger at me, Suzanne and Maggie had always counted me as friend, family, and loved me even greater than that.

"How about a sip of water?" Suzanne brought a straw to my lips.

I closed my eyes and shook my head.

Jane, are you ready to fly with the wind in your hair? I brought my motorcycle to take you home. Climb on.

Now Mark?

Yeah, it's time.

Epilogue

*F**ive years later…*

 "See." I nudged Mark in the side. Momma nodded at me and smiled a proud-grandma smile. The day was cool and the sun shone brightly on this February Sunday during carnival. The day all "saints go marching in" in New Orleans.

"That's our boy." Mark fist-bumped me. "But I have to find a way to communicate to Maggie that it's okay for the boy to play football."

"Like father, like son." My chest felt too small for the pride swelling within me.

We sat on the top row of risers installed by a Canal Street hotel to watch Krewe of Mid-City roll. Mark wore a lion costume and flicked his tail like a pom-pom. Momma dressed as a 1920's flapper. I wore a purple, green, and gold jester costume.

It was too bad no one could see us.

A few revelers in the stands around us sensed our presence. One lady rubbed near my face as if trying to rub away steam on a bathroom mirror to get a peek at a reflection. I slid away.

I still hadn't fully acclimated to being on the spiritual side of life.

The woman scratched her head, closed her eyes, mentally shooting out tentacles as though trying to connect with me.

No way. Not today. Today was about my boy.

I clapped in time to the rhythm of the music. Christopher Marcus Landry-Maucele played trumpet in a kids' marching band. He was tall for ten, like his daddy. Broad-shouldered, too. Maggie had made sure his uniform fit him well and got him got him cushy boot insoles for marching the nearly five-mile-long parade route. He would get a ride from time to time on the band trailer bringing up the rear.

On the street below, on the opposite side of Canal Street, Maggie, Suzanne, Grant, and my dad cheered as the band neared. Zander, on Grant's shoulders, tossed beads at the kids in the band.

Christopher reached with one hand and snagged a purple strand from his cousin, draped it around his neck, missed a note, but not a step, and continued playing.

Then he looked up in the stands. Directly. At. Me.

He smiled.

I gasped. Grabbed Mark's arm. "He can see us!" Joy burst forth. My tears were pearls of pure happiness.

Mark shook his head. "Darlin', that's a stretch. He may sense us, strongly sense us, but you have to accept, he won't see us until it's his time. He's meant for *that* world."

Sonny Boy lifted his trumpet in salute, same as the rest of the brass line. My heart beat as loud and full as the drummer banging the bass drum.

Grant got Sonny Boy hooked on the trumpet, taking him to venues and concerts to meet famous horn players. He taught him about Satchmo. He made music exciting for my boy.

Maggie taught him about fishing and crabbing. My boy loved fried soft-shell crab po'boys. He learned about the power of the tides and the swells of the full moon. Maggie also taught him about compassion.

I was sad that she only occasionally accepted a date, and she never brought a man home to meet Sonny Boy. I hoped in time she might find a man for her and Christopher Marcus to love…but I knew which man still had Maggie's heart.

Suzanne taught my son proper manners, even made him write thank-you notes. Sent him to a different camp every summer, though last year, the space camp was a bust.

My dad took him to LSU football games and occasionally to see the Saints play. And every Sunday—rain, shine, or hurricane—Dad had brunch with Maggie and Christopher Marcus after church, where my boy made a joyful noise.

And together the three as a family visited my grave on my birthday and Mother's Day, and visited Momma's, too. They went to the mausoleum on Mark's birthday and Father's Day, sat on the bench in front of Mark's headstone on the wall, and Maggie told the story of how she, Suzanne, and I had been reunited there…all because of our love for Mark.

"That's my daddy," Sonny Boy would say. After a few minutes, he would tug on Maggie's hand to leave and tell her, "My daddy wouldn't want us to be sad. He'd want us to live in the sunshine."

I would nod. My face wet with tears. Tears of joy. Tears of love.

There were no secrets now.

No pain now.

No gloom, grief, or guilt that love hadn't cured.

The End

Acknowledgements

*I*f ever the phrase "it takes a village" represented a button of truth, *Unspoken Words* pushed that button many times. I'm proud to share with you the story-behind-the-story of this book through introducing you to those involved in bringing this book to publication.

When I lived in Kansas, I attended an Oklahoma writing conference hosted by Oklahoma Writers Federation, Inc. (OWFI) at the insistence of Mary Lane Kamberg. I consider her to be my first true writing mentor. Thank you, Mary Lane, for being supportive and helpful and teaching me so much about writing.

At OWFI, I met New York Times Best Selling Author Jodi Thomas, who invited all to attend the inaugural Writer's Academy at West Texas A&M. I was one of twelve in Jodi's first class. She has remained a great inspiration to me, and I cherish her words, "Triumph comes through perseverance." Unspoken Words was born from a homework assignment she gave during the second year I attended the Academy.

From Jodi's inaugural class, I am still in contact with several of the other writers, and I regularly meet via Zoom with two of them. It's a blessing to spend time with author Gina Popp and author Jan Morrill (Vanek). They are encouraging and provide honest feedback about my writing. Their input continues to help me grow as a writer; they help make my stories shine.

As the story of Unspoken Words began to unfold to me, I had research to do. I was aware of Louisiana law being different from every other state, with its Louisiana Civil Code. So, I went to my "source," my husband, and asked if he had a contact who would consider talking with me about probate and wills in Louisiana. He reached out to attorney Andrew D. Egan, and Andrew—who practices law in Georgia, not Louisiana—and provided attorney Joshua P. Monteleone's contact information. Thank you, Andrew. I appreciate your generosity.

My excitement overcame my trepidation—many men tune-out when I say I write women's fiction—and I called Joshua. He was so helpful in listening about the storyline and my questions about how laws in Louisiana are applied in my story's specific scenario. He provided answers to each question, making sure I understood the potential ramifications of the story conflict I was setting up. Joshua, I can't tell you what your time and patience has meant to me. I am very grateful. (And I hope your wife will enjoy the book.)

As you will learn when reading *Unspoken Words*, the story reflects aspects of religion, more specifically Catholicism. I grew up within the Lutheran faith with formal liturgy, and while the two denominations are similar, they're dissimilar, too. I turned to my well-respected friend, Maurice Baalman, for further insights about the Catholic faith. Over the years of working on *Unspoken Words*, I have had the pleasure of learning nuances and receiving caring and respectful replies to my questions from him. Maurice, I most humbly thank you for walking me through the field of questions. I hope there will be other opportunities to talk again.

There are many iterations of this story. There have been many working titles. There have been many people who have read bits and pieces of the story. However, the one person who first read it, front to back, was editor Cheryl Walz. We met at a writing conference in Georgia. She's a poet at heart. Taught English for a number of years. She works diligently to bring out the best in my words, she's careful about "voice," and asks questions. Cheryl, I am eternally grateful for your support and guidance with this book.

While writing *Unspoken Words*, my husband and I moved from Kansas to Georgia. Then during COVID, I volunteered to help with a regional dog club, which resulted in me spending a lot of time in South Carolina. Joining Lowcountry RWA became a logical next step. This nonprofit writing group seeks to educate and support writers of different experience levels, and as such, launched an anthology. I was fortunate to be part of that project.

ACKNOWLEDGEMENTS

Every book project has multiple parts for production: beta readers, editors, formatters, cover artists are just a few. Each step is a specialty. Through this project, I was impressed by the formatter, Suzanna L. Chriscoe of Elefont Books Cover Design & Author Services. She took multiple stories and merge them into a single book with consistency despite the hodge-podge presented to her.

After that, she and I worked together on a project for a writing client of mine, which segued into us working together on my projects. I was thrilled when she agreed to create the cover for *Unspoken Words*. I'd found a photograph from a New Orleans photographer that captured the vibe I wanted to convey. It fits perfectly with this story. Suzanna's background and experience brought all the pieces together to make it work. Thank you, Suzanna. I trust and respect your opinions and expertise.

I offer a big "thank you" to photographer Alex Demyan for his artistic talent and graciously granting me the opportunity to use his photo, "Streetcar Named Desire," for the cover of *Unspoken Words*. I hope on my next trip to New Orleans we'll get to meet.

I offer a special note of thanks to Teresa E. Russ. Our book relationship has spanned ten years. She's been a supportive and guiding voice for me, always encouraging me. She's the owner of Poised Pen Productions, which she started soon after we met for the first time at a donut shop in Ocala, Florida. Teresa, I can't thank you enough for all you've done. Your constructive criticism, continuing support, and constant enthusiasm has been invaluable. Thank you.

And a heartfelt hug and big kiss to my husband, Don. What a journey it's been! I look forward to what is ahead. And, when I told you my plans for *Unspoken Words*, you replied with, "Finally!" Your love, support, and enthusiasm made me so happy!

About the Author

*L*inda Joyce believes stories are as integral to her life as breathing. She shares the joys and agonies of characters and often wishes their stories would continue far beyond "The End." She lives in metro-Atlanta with her very patient husband and their three fur babies—Jake, Maxence, and Sugar. Linda's addicted to Cajun and Japanese food. She's a fan of smooth jazz. She will deny traditional jazz music hurts her ears—that could get her banished from her hometown, New Orleans. Her current life's adventure includes learning enough Kanji to be able to read a Japanese newspaper.

Connect with Linda

- Website: http://www.linda-joyce.com
- Facebook: https://www.facebook.com/LindaJoyceAuthor
- Instagram: http://instagram.com/lindajoycewrites
- Pinterest: http://pinterest.com/LindaJoyceWorld/boards
- Goodreads: http://www.goodreads.com/author/show/6950241.Linda_Joyce
- Amazon author page: http://www.amazon.com/Linda-Joyce/e/B00BODDROS/
- Newsletter: https://www.linda-joyce.com/sign-up-for-letters-from-linda/
- BookBub: https://www.bookbub.com/authors/linda-joyce

Discussion Questions for UNSPOKEN WORDS

About the book

- What type of reader would most enjoy this book?
- Was the book thought-provoking?
- Did the book change any of your opinions?
- Did you learn something new from the characters' perspective? If so, what?
- What emotions, if any, did the book bring forth for you? Did you laugh, cry, or cringe?
- How did this book relate to your own life? Did it awaken any memories or create any connections for you?
- Did you highlight any parts from the book?
- Do you have a favorite quote or quotes? If so, share which and why?
- What was the main message of the book?
- How did the book make you think or feel about a certain issue?
- How relatable are the messages of the book to your own life, or today's society?

About the characters

- Who was your favorite character and why?
- Which character was the most complex or interesting and why?
- How did the characters change or grow in the story?
- How did secondary characters influence the story?
- Which character did you relate to the most and why?

- Which character did you dislike or disagree with the most and why? Did that change over the story?
- Which character would you have given advice to and why?
- What do you think happens to the characters after the novel concludes?
- About the author and the story
- How did the author create conflict and tension in the book?
- What was the main conflict or problem in the story and how was it resolved?
- How did the author keep you interested or surprised throughout the story?
- What was the most memorable or shocking scene or twist in the story?
- What was the most satisfying or disappointing part of the story?
- Was the ending satisfying or did you want more?
- What was your favorite scenes from the book?

About the author

- Why do you think the author wrote this book and what was their purpose or goal?
- How much do you think the author's personal views or biases influenced the book and how do you feel about that?
- How does this book compare to other books by the same author or in the same genre?
- If you could ask the author one question about this book, what would it be?
- Did you find the author's writing style easy to read or hard to read?
- How long did it take you to get into the book?
- How did the author use language, tone, structure, imagery, dialogue, etc. to tell the story and create an effect on the reader?
- Did the author use any literary devices, techniques, or styles to enhance their writing, and to what effect?
- What did you like or dislike about the author's writing style and why?
- How would you describe the author's writing style in a few words?